ML Miller

979-8-9917880-0-7 (PRINT)

979-8-9917880-3-8 (eBook)

Cover Design: ML Miller

Editing: EJL Editing

Proofreading: Brandee Paschall Books LLC

Formatting: EJL Editing

To those who turn pages
for an escape—welcome to mine.

"He'll make a final sweep past the Prost grandstand!

...He won in Abu Dhabi, and he wins the Formula 1 season opener! Beckham Wright is your Australian Grand Prix winner!"

Furio Team Radio:

"You've done it, Beck! Brilliant drive!"

"Hope you're thirsty, Coop."

CHAPTER 1

HIGH TIME

SOPHIE

BECK'S CHEST RISES AND falls, warm against my cheek. I stare up at the contours of his face. God took time creating that face, those eyes, his mouth, his mind. Abu Dhabi wasn't a fluke. He won again, and yes, Coop cried again. I held it together, barely, until the last two turns. Once I saw the first tears fall from his race engineer's eyes, I was a goner. Ella's arms were squeezed around me, and we held a collective breath until he crossed the finish line.

Abu Dhabi was the first time Beck stood on the top step of the podium. Coop stood on stage with him, the happiest of all happy tears wetting his face. I was a wreck—James, Elizabeth—we all were. And I thought I'd cried my fill that day until Ana asked me to stand by her side for her wedding. She and Ren will be married in Monaco come July.

I run my fingertips over his chest. Like I've done a hundred times, and I'm still not bored of it. I certainly didn't know what I was getting myself into last summer break, not the half of it, really. But that's what happens when you're in free fall. You take chances far quicker than you normally would. And probably not often, but sometimes, those moments of spontaneous chance can bloom into the most beautiful thing in your life. Like the man whose bare chest my cheek rests against. He was my *I've got nothing to lose* and us together? Well, it's the *perfect formula*.

After instructing me to lie low for the final race, Beck went and pulled the grand gesture of the century by parading me into the Abu Dhabi paddock on the morning every camera lens was pointed at him. There was a flood of press following that day, a social media storm. A clip of us went absolutely viral. But the season was over, and he and I became even more inseparable. We practically went into hibernation during the offseason. Dad ran off with Evelyn for most of the holidays. In fact, the only time I left Beck's side for longer than his workouts with his trainer, Charlie, was when Ella and I took a three-day trip across the pond. *In the Know* wanted to have us on in person at their podcast studio in New York City. I owed them answers after my guest segment, and Ella was dying to go.

I've never actually learned another person the way I've learned Beck. We're completely in sync with one another, and at this point, we've developed our own unspoken language. I know all of his nods, the tiny ones he does with his chin when I'm not by his side. The slightest tilt of his head adds a layer of urgency when he's got to get his hands on me. I know all of his stares, especially the ones pointed at me. When his gaze shifts into that soft but fiery focus, I know he's undressing me with his eyes. But what's more, he can read me too. He knows how I go when all I need is to be tucked up under his chin; he knows how my eyes beg when I long for his lips on me. Even our social batteries have the same lifespan. We're different from Ella, Carmen, Tommy and Oliver's ever-ready batteries. Don't get me wrong, we love a party, but we have our limits. And when we hit that wall, we enjoy rotting in bed. And by rotting in bed, I mean naked, most likely on top of each other.

Our time underground is over, the season's kicked off, and it's started out swimmingly. I've got to get used to spending time away from him—and fast. We tried it during preseason testing. But it only worked for a day because it aligned with spring fashion week. And only because Ana and I were invited to sit front row at the Dior show in Paris. Absolutely epic, but I ended up flying to Bahrain the next morning to be with him. I can't do that this week. Ella and I fly home from Melbourne, and the grid is off to Brazil.

I slowly lift my cheek off his chest and peek at the clock. My head does a little spin—the party started at the race win and extended well beyond Furio's afterparty celebration. I've got to check on Ella, if she made it back to our room or if I need to go find her at some nightclub. Day club?

I wiggle out of bed and throw a robe over my nightwear. I take a key off the desk and quietly sneak out of Beck's room. I tiptoe two doors down to the room Ella and I shared until last night.

To my surprise, Ella's awake. She walks toward me through the chaos of clothes on the floor, combing her blonde locks with her fingers and blinking the way she does when she's passed out in her contacts.

"Oi! I didn't think you'd be up!"

She smiles and quickly darts into the bathroom. I zigzag through the mess in the hall and round the corner into our room.

"What the *fu*—!" I shriek, hand flying to my mouth.

Tommy Young's bare tattooed chest stops me dead in my tracks. Ella giggles in the bathroom. My eyes dart from *him* to the bathroom wall and back.

"You—*you* slept in here?" I stutter.

Tommy smiles.

"Wait, you didn't—"

"Do me a favor and don't lift up the covers," he says.

And my jaw drops. "That's my side of the bed!" I squeal, now glaring at him.

He crosses his arms over his naked torso and does a little shrug. "You left her to fend for herself. Couldn't let her sleep in here alone…"

I cover my eyes, walk in further, then plop down at the foot of the bed—on Ella's side, that is. I lie back on the comforter and keep my palms against my eye sockets. Tommy's laughing—and I'm dying inside, now eternally grateful I won't be spending another night in this bed. I drag my fingers down my cheeks and stare up at the ceiling. Ella emerges from the bathroom, glasses perched on her nose.

"Surprise!" she giggles.

I glare at her then turn onto my stomach. She pulls the covers up to meet the pillows and crawls onto the bed, sitting cross-legged next to Tommy.

"Yes—very much surprised, thank you." I watch them exchange a smirk before Tommy's gaze falls.

He runs his finger across the underside of her toes. "You've got a freckle on the bottom of your foot."

Ella cocks an eyebrow, eyeing him over the rim of her glasses. "You got a thing for feet, Young?"

Her chest is flushed. Tommy's bottom lip is extra pink at the minute. His dark hair is tossed around, surely from bedhead and not from…

"Hold please! Were you"—I gesture between them—"about to do it again?!"

He snorts a laugh. "As I said, don't lift up the covers."

"Tommy!" I groan, dropping my face into my hands. "What about Emma?"

"Did you speak to her yesterday?"

I snap my head back up. "She was at the race?"

He nods. "Not sure why. She's been radio silent with me for a month. She was in the Holt garage yesterday."

Ella begins chewing on her fingernail.

"With Ian's girlfriend?" I offer.

"Who knows," he says, waving his hand and changing the topic. "Where's our winner?"

"Sleeping." I push up off the bed and stand.

"You two headed home soon?" He looks between Ella and me.

"In a few hours. Beck is taking us to the airport." I set my hands on my hips. "That means when I get back, you better be clothed or gone!"

"Copy that." He shudders, looking around. "The state of this room is giving me anxiety."

Ella rolls her eyes.

"I've got to shower anyway. Getting breakfast with Edgeman, MACH's new sponsor." He nudges Ella. "Can't show up hungover and smelling like sex."

Now I'm rolling my eyes.

"Did you see the rep they had in our garage? *Fucking* dime."

I shake my head, hands still at my hips. "Maybe you'll get lucky with *her* in Brazil!"

I turn on my heel.

"I'll let you know at Easter!" he yells after me.

I let our door slam and charge back to Beck's room, now fully awake. Not because I found a surprise man in bed with Ella—*that's not uncommon.* But because the man this time happens to be a fellow Formula 1 driver and my boyfriend's best mate. I reenter Beck's room less gently than when I'd left. His feet stir at the end of the bed beneath the covers.

"Where'd you run off to?" he asks, bringing a hand behind his head.

"Had to make sure Ella was alive. You'll never guess who I found *naked* in bed with her!" I say, still flustered.

He lifts an eyebrow then throws his head back laughing.

"This isn't funny!" I stomp.

"Baby, it was high time," he says, amused. "Surprised it took this long."

I suppose he's right. Ella is Ella, and Tommy is, well, Tommy.

"What about Emma? Last I knew, they were still talking."

His head shifts side to side. "They're on and off. Been like that for a while."

His other arm slips out from the bedcovers. He yawns, stretching back, biceps flexing as both arms now rest behind his head. God, I love the way he looks in the morning. My head tilts to the side.

"This winning—" I say quizzically. "Is this going to be a regular thing now?"

He smiles all coy.

"I'm going to have to practice my cute cry face."

"You don't need practice," he throws back the covers, exposing his carved chest and stomach. "Now get that sweet ass over here."

My fingers find the tie on my dressing gown, and I watch him watch me release the knot and let it fall open.

"Is there something I can do for the leader of the championship?"

"*Current* leader," he says humbly.

I shrug the robe off my shoulders, letting it slip off my body. "Is there something I can do for the *current* leader of the world drivers' championship?"

A wicked grin appears. "I want you to come on my face."

I gulp, nearly shiver. "I asked what I could do for *you*."

"We'll get to me. But now"—he pauses, wetting his lips—"nothing would please me more than burying my face in your *p*—"

"Beck!" I shriek.

His eyes go hot, igniting a fire deep in my belly. One by one, I push the straps of the baby blue silk chemise from my shoulders. The silk slides down, brushing my nipples as it tumbles to the floor and pools around my feet. I hook my thumbs into the sides of my thong. He sucks his bottom lip between his teeth, watching me peel it off.

I cover what I can, crawl onto the foot of the bed and make my way up to him. His hands run up my outer thighs and find a grip on my bum. I sit astride his waist using my forearm to cover my chest. He reaches for my wrist, guides my arm away like I knew he would. I lean forward, lose sight of my fingers in his hair and get lost in his eyes. It's not lost time at all really, the vast amount of time I've stared into them. *It's not time I want back.*

"I love this," I say, running the pad of my thumb along his jawline over the coarse stubble he's let grow in. It's darker than his chunky brown hair I adore running my fingers through; it makes the dimples he gets when he smiles a certain way that much more dimply.

"Good," he says, staring up at me. "It will stay."

It's true, I love the way it looks, but even more, I love the way it feels against my skin when he moves his mouth over my body.

He tucks a chunk of hair behind my ear, and his eyes flick for half a second to the two-carat diamond that's sat in my earlobe. The diamond earrings he gave me for my birthday last month that I most definitely forgot to take out last night.

His gaze falls to my lips. "I fucking love you, Sophie."

He hooks his hands around the back of my legs and yanks me forward. I squeak as his forearms wrap around my legs, holding me in place over his face. It's his breath I feel first, before his warm tongue slides against me. My mouth falls open, my fingers find a hold in his hair. *My word.* He dives even deeper, tightening his grip around my legs so I can't pull away even if I wanted to. I reach for the headboard, and without my consent, my hips start to rock back and forth as I watch this boy of mine devour me. Even that is enough to get me off—*he's mine*. And I'll love him for as long as he'll have me.

CHAPTER 2

AN ITCH

ROOMIE TRIO

Ella:

Headed back to the homeland!

Sophie:

Ella forgot to mention she took Tommy to bed last night.

Carmen:

EXCUSE ME?!

Carmen:

Thomas Young????

Carmen:

Dicked down DOWN UNDER???

Sophie comes over the partition of our seats on the A380. "Please enlighten me as to how *he* ended up in our bed."

"Pretty straightforward." I shrug. "Youse left us at the lobby bar—we were deep in, giggling, and one thing led to another."

She blinks, presses her eyes closed all dramatic.

"Don't look at me like that, Soph!" I swat her away. "With all the sex you're having? I had an itch that desperately needed to be scratched!"

Her eyes go wide, wildly looking around at the passengers still boarding. Not sure why she's being so weird, because it's not that weird at all—*I did make out with him that one time last summer, remember?*

She pulls in close, voice low, "Weren't you just with Henry before we left?!"

"*Yes*—but I didn't sleep with him," I say defensively. "Well, not that night at least."

"I think Tommy's still on and off with Emma!" she whispers.

"From what I *recall*, last night he was groaning '*Ella*'—not Emma. And I can assure you the only name he was praising this morning was mine."

"My word," she says, putting her hand to her mouth.

I reach over to smack her arm. "I'm only joking. We only had a go at it last night. And on the Emma front, that sounds like a him problem, not a me problem."

"And? How was he then?" She asks reluctantly because she knows I'll tell her regardless.

"Shockingly good. I thought he'd be a typical male—I mean, this is Tommy we're talking about, but he's a giver!"

She takes a deep breath, exhales through her nose. It's all a bit hazy, to be honest, but it was good. I remember that much. The kind of good that made me question why we hadn't done that before? But maybe that was the tequila talking. Everything feels good when tequila's in the bloodstream. Except the morning after, of course. But goddamn, he was easy to look at this morning sans clothes.

"He's proper fit, that one."

"Offseason workouts." She nods.

"Would have liked to have round two this morning before this long haul, but thanks to your early bird check-in, I missed that workout op."

"My apologies." She presses her lips together to hide her smile.

I lift an eyebrow. "Thought Beck would surely have you busy on your back."

Her cheeks go red, and she looks away. Don't know why she gets all shy about it—talking about sex. She happily listens to my sexcapades. Well, maybe not always happily. She'll never divulge sober; I can usually pry a few things out of her if she's hit the bottle hard enough.

A smile touches her lips. "Perhaps I was busy when I arrived back."

"Do tell!"

She puts her nose in the air and shakes her head.

It was worth a shot. "Still can't believe he won. That was mad fun."

"I know," she says, her eyes going sad. "I wish I could be there this week."

She's struggling. They're addicts for each other, those two. But this will be the first big stint of them spending separate time. Pulling them apart at the departures curb was like separating aero-grade magnets. Kept snapping back to each other when one would try to let go.

"Duty calls! Can't be in two places at once."

"Unfortunately," she sighs. "I am excited to see the final samples for Beurre!"

"You going to make me wear the thong again?"

"Lord knows I'm not wearing it!" she states. "Wait, we decided no thong!"

"Right, just that cheeky bottom that may as well be." I snort. "And you'll get to see your dad!"

"Home at last!" Her face lights up. "I'm glad he's finally having some fun with his money."

"I'm sure Evelyn's also enjoying the fruits of his labor," I say, though I probably shouldn't have. Evelyn's got money, but not like George Collins has money.

She looks away, pretending to be concerned with the contents of her backpack. It's not even sailing season, and George whisked Evelyn off for a month once fashion week wrapped. That's right, they're still dating. I wouldn't even call it dating, but the terms boyfriend and girlfriend when referring to someone over the age of fifty sounds a bit ridiculous. They are proper together, and I wouldn't be surprised if the next step is taken soon. How much does a chartered yacht even cost for that stint of time?

"And what about Alston? You haven't seen your dad in a minute."

"Six months?" I shrug. "Emmett's coming as a buffer."

That's what my brother does. He eases the tension between Dad and me. Sorry—Alston and me. On the father-daughter relationship front, Soph and I couldn't be more opposites. But trust me when I say that's not me complaining.

I grab my *Neverfull*, which is curiously *always full*, and dig for my airplane pouch. Sophie's phone goes off in rapid succession. She drags her thumb across the screen sideways, all giddy.

I'm nosy, so I lean over to snoop. "Are you looking at pictures of puppies again?"

"Mia sent a new batch," she says, turning the phone in my direction.

Like little white baby seals, they are. "And how's the little one doing?"

"*Finn.*" She points to the tiny off-white pup half the size of his plump brothers and sisters. "They had the vet out and are trying to bottle-feed him. Poor little thing's just not putting on any weight."

"That's because that fat one is hogging all the milk!"

Sophie giggles. "He's called *Pirelli*! Beck named him."

I dump the contents of my pouch onto the tray table and begin an aesthetic arrangement. "When do you get to see them again?"

"Easter," she says all cheery. "They should have their eyes open by then."

I nod down at the buffet of skincare. "You ready?"

"If you insist." She rips out two cleansing wipes from the package.

I press the Octobuddy on the back of my phone against the window and open the camera because *I absolutely do insist*. And good heavens, look at this lighting! It must not go to waste! The Melbourne sun left its mark on my nose and cheeks. I fluff my hair, shift in my seat and start recording.

"Get ready with us for a twenty-two-hour travel day."

I drag my fingernails along the packaging then run a cleansing cloth over my face and under my eyes using my phone as a mirror. People love a good ASMR-style GRWM, and they happen to be forty-five times easier to edit. Sophie finishes with the toner and hands it over. I turn the label to the camera and tap my fingernails against the glass bottle. These products are from Fylter, a new American clean beauty brand we're working with, hoping to score a massive deal with them this year. I tilt my face, squeeze three serum droplets from the pipette onto my cheek and pass it to Sophie. I smile and flutter my lashes as I press the serum into my skin before grabbing the next Fylter step.

CHAPTER 3
DADDY ISSUES

ELLA

MANCHESTER IS FUCKING COLD. I didn't do myself any favors deciding to "work" from the hotel bed. I didn't make it far, closed my laptop and set a thirty-seven-minute timer. Slept through that alarm and several others. When I finally came to, I was so warm I actually thought about canceling on Dad. But I came all the way the fuck up here for him. So here I am speed walking two blocks, twenty minutes late to dinner. Could have been ten minutes late, but I had to get a proper picture of my outfit at the hotel with geotags.

Emmett and Dad are already seated. I see they've ordered for me. A dark red waits across from them at the table. My brother jumps up. He's wearing an olive jumper and an itchy cream scarf that I'm buried against when he picks me up in a bear hug and squeezes the life out of me. Let's be honest, he's the one who ordered my wine; Dad doesn't know what I like. I almost take my seat, but Dad pushes up from the table for an awkward one-arm hug.

"Sorry, took a nap and overslept," I say, taking my seat.

Emmett picks up his drink. "You at the Edwardian?"

I nod.

"You know you can stay at the house," Dad says.

Never. I pick up the menu and pretend I'm engrossed in reading it. "It's no trouble. I quite fancy their spa."

Like I'd make that mistake again. I stayed with Dad and Jules once two Christmases ago and learned my lesson—vowed to never come up here again without a guaranteed rezzy.

Alston was "around" until I was seven—that's when they split. And by around I mean for the mere two or three hours he was home during the time I was still awake because I was just a wee girl then. Mum and I stayed in Fulham. Emmett bounced back and forth between ours and Dad's new place. I saw Dad "regularly" for a year until he met Jules. That's when he fucked off to Manchester and made himself a new family entirely.

He's good-looking, my dad. Tall, stately. I suppose I have him to thank for my long legs, but I won't. Mum married him for his looks and money. I don't blame her. It's rare you find two of the three partner requirements. But when the looks and money don't make up for the lack of love and you bring kids into the mix, you get my type of childhood. I don't know which is worse. I didn't have a parent pass like Sophie, but instead I had a parent who was very much alive choose to not be in my life.

I take a long draw of wine when the waiter leaves with our order. I'm a witch, did you know? Not literally, and I'm mostly good, but I have my moments. Those moments I speak of often come out in the presence of Alston.

"How's the family?" I ask because it's polite, though my tone isn't without a bit of snark.

I dropped the word *other* from that question because I'm feeling nice. And because technically, it's his only family due to the fact that I don't consider what we had with him to be a family.

"Kids are a handful," he says, taking a sip of his greyhound.

I yawn, bored.

"But not anything on your level," he adds.

Not feeling nice anymore.

"Like you were around to see the worst of it," I say under my breath. I pick up my wine and smile. "Just wait until they get to uni."

Emmett attempts to squash a smile but has to pick up his drink for cover.

Jules, the much younger woman he remarried, got the husband Mum never got, and those two strawberry-blond rotten children of theirs got the dad I never did. Perhaps they won't be such menaces—they haven't had the absent-father experience. If I sound bitter, sure, I am, but I'm more bitter for Mum. Jules got the looks, the money and the love. *Alston Humphrey 2.0.* It was when he remarried that I really started acting out. But at university, I took it to a whole other level. That's when I met Sophie, and we moved into her dad's spare flat. Sophie was somehow still able to pull top marks. And I—well, I passed, didn't I? She's got the book smarts, but I've got the street smarts.

Alston clears his throat. "For Emmett, this is a continued celebration. He's just been made junior partner at the firm."

I lift my glass across the table to Emmett. "Like father, like son. Congrats, brother."

"And what's new with you?" Emmett asks.

"Loads going on at the moment—working to get an exclusive deal with Fylter, a new clean beauty brand—"

"Do you think these sorts of opportunities will last?" Alston interrupts.

"Come again?" I ask defensively, even though I absolutely heard the question.

Emmett inserts himself to cut the tension. "What's the longevity of this line of work?"

I stare at them from across the table.

"I'd feel more assured if you had a stable job," Alston says. "And perhaps dated a nice boy."

"Nice boy, *singular,* Ella," Emmett teases. "Enough with the man-eater antics."

Alston shifts uncomfortably—at the term man-eater, perhaps?

Emmett knows I keep a stacked bench at the ready. Ready when I need a plus one, arm candy for an event or feel like being wined and dined. *Dating* these boys is a stretch. *Nice* boys might also be a stretch. Nice looking? Absolutely. And these bench picks are strategic as hell. Yes, they're mostly models, but Colin—yes, that Colin from the Beurre campaign last fall—also bartends at de la Roche. Jack is a DJ. He's alright at it, not as fire as Ollie, of course, and Liam is best mates with the most exclusive club promoters in Paris. Letting them in my bed doesn't mean I let them *in* in. I keep it fun, surface level, until I'm bored, which is usually quite fast, then it's onto the next. It's quite useful keeping them and the three others in rotation.

"Why?" I ask. "So I can end up like you and Mum? Married, miserable then divorced?"

Alston huffs, annoyed, and picks up his greyhound.

"Sophie's found someone. That looks proper serious," Emmett offers.

"Besotted, those two. It's a bit nauseating at times, the way they're always petting each other."

I take another large pull from my glass.

"Speaking of nauseating, how about you and miss thing? You're pasted all over her Instagram."

"Annabelle." Emmett smiles. "Thinking about taking her to Dubai to see Mum."

And with the sheer mention of Mum, Alston picks up his drink even though he's just set it down.

"You'll have to come back for Easter and meet her."

"Could maybe swing that. Bit busy at the moment with this *creative director role.*" I accentuate the words in an attempt to gain my father's attention. "As for a '*stable job,*' you realize influencer marketing is only growing."

"That's the gig you got with Sophie, no?" Emmett asks.

I nod. "Beurre brought Sophie and me onboard for their show at Miami Swim Week."

"Love Miami," Emmett says.

"I even convinced them to put Ollie on the decks for the show. Live and everything."

"Sophie's following's gone gangbusters," Emmett says. "On this trajectory, she'll surpass you by summer."

I swallow because that comment strikes a chord and sets off a peculiar feeling in my stomach. But it's true, thanks to some little teenybopper's edit of Beck's paddock gesture in Abu Dhabi going viral on TikTok. She and Beck are on every "couple goals" board on Pinterest. The *In the Know* hosts claimed she and Beck are well on their way to becoming the next Pookie and Jett. And if you've been living under a rock, they're the viral, sickeningly perfect married couple from the States.

Alston glances at his phone, stands up and walks off to take a call. Emmett scoots his chair back and nods toward the door. I follow.

Outside, Emmett pulls a pack of Marlboro 100's from the inside pocket of his coat.

"Can he be any more of an asshole?" I huff. "And you, for that matter. I told Sophie I was excited to see you."

He snorts a laugh, puts a cigarette between his lips and extends the open pack to me. Sophie would kill me. It's *"unbecoming,"* she would say. But this dinner is fifteen times more dreadful than I imagined. I grab one from the pack, and Emmett holds the lighter for me. I take a drag. *Sweet Jesus.* I cough a bit because I don't smoke, and my virgin lungs are perfectly spotless. That's a lie. It's just been a minute, and when I say a minute, I mean more like a year.

"I'm glad to see you still have your blistering confidence." Emmett leans back against the brick. "But your daddy issues were starting to show in there."

I take another drag. "And what about your daddy issues?"

"Men don't have daddy issues."

"Following in his very footsteps to please him is the definition of daddy issues. Even more so than rebelling!" I exhale. "I'm not going to get some corporate job just to placate him. And when did he suddenly start caring about my wellbeing? Now that I'm grown, and am perfectly capable of taking care of myself?"

Emmett points his stupid finger at me as if I just proved his point. "Daddy issues."

I roll my eyes and take another drag. "Whatever. Not all girls are meant to be a daddy's girl; some are destined to be mummy's little cutthroat."

He snorts a laugh. "You've certainly achieved that."

"Does he grimace every time he has to tell someone his daughter is an *influencer*? Oh wait, I'm assuming he even refers to me as his daughter."

Emmett shrugs. "He only wants you to think long term, what your professional future looks like."

"I was just a guest at the Australian Grand Prix, for fuck's sake."

He lifts an eyebrow. "A guest of Sophie's."

"Also was a guest on one of the top podcasts in the States."

"*In the know at the water cooler*," he mumbles, air quoting, with his cigarette between his lips. "Annabelle watched. Was that not the Sophie Collins catch-up episode?"

That feeling in my stomach is back. Is he trying to tell me I am becoming irrelevant?

"I can do this work for years to come." I shrug. "And if push ever came to shove, there's always the option to sell pictures of my feet online."

Emmett bursts out laughing.

Not sure if it's the cigarette or the berating dinner conversation that's left this horrible lingering taste in my mouth. Back at the hotel, I climb into bed. Shouldn't have left my warm little post; that dinner was miss-able. I open Instagram and tap through the photos I posted. My outfit pre-dinner and a picture I snapped with Emmett outside the restaurant already has thousands of likes. Annabelle's already thrown it a heart-eye emoji comment. And the restaurant reposted it to their story. See? Relevant.

I click on my profile and check my follower count. *1.4 million.* Still. I open my follower analytics; I got a nice bump from the podcast, mostly girlies from the States, but since then, my growth has been a bit stagnant. Yes, the podcast was a follow-up episode from Sophie's original appearance, but they asked me to come too. I spoke just as much as she did, if not more.

Swiping to my Reels tab, I swallow, shocked at how noticeable it is. My videos with Sophie average double the views. It was fun having her as my project last year; I brought her into the influencer space. She was dreadful at it, but the moment she met Beck, her success took off and hasn't stopped. I never thought she'd get this big.

I'm not jealous because that would imply she has something I don't. Now, I was jealous when Sophie and Ana received exclusive invites to the Dior show, but who wouldn't be? They were photographed like mad. "*F1 WAGs awaken for Dior Paris*."

I open Sophie's page. She's just over 800k. *Fuck.* She'll surpass me well before summer. She's already flown past Carmen, but Carmen's off in Carmen's own little tennis world at Roland Garros.

It's a funny feeling. I've never felt threatened in this space before. What's more annoying is while my following means everything to me, Sophie couldn't care less. She's quiet, and only speaks up when she's properly provoked. She goes days without posting (I've even seen a week!) and has said no to so many oppies I can't keep count. She'll get excited about deals here and there, but she could leave it all tomorrow and not look back. For me, it's my *raison d'être*, my passion, my career. Working is always top of mind and has been since the minute I started gaining attention in school.

She doesn't need it though. Her trust alone has her set for life. Not to mention if she and Beck were to work out. I don't have that privilege, the privilege not to care. And I'll never rely on a man—Alston included. I needed his money for school but haven't since. And I make sure I don't. Just like Mum—I've learned from the best. That's why she works so hard. I quite literally despise the term "boss bitch," but look it up in the dictionary, and you'll find Alice Humphrey's picture. She won't give Alston the satisfaction of riding his gravy train. She started grinding the day Jules came into the picture. She's got her own money now. Even bought her own place in Boulogne-Billancourt.

I click on Sophie's tagged photos and spot my outfit from Sunday. It's a photo more of her and less of me ripped from *Thread* magazine.

Head to toe elegance: Sophie Collins with friend in the F1 paddock in Melbourne.

I nearly faint. With *friend*? I'm not even named? Fucking hell, I'm not even bloody tagged. Don't like the feeling that's in my stomach again. I tap the account that reposted it, and recognize the shop immediately: F1_LOL. I click the link in the bio to open the *Lights Out Ladies* gossip blog. It's the first post in the feed.

Sophie has surpassed Ella! Never thought I'd see the day when Ella was the irrelevant one.

I expand the comments:

Someone's uploaded the Beurre post when we were announced as co-creative directors.

Sophie scored a deal to creative direct!

Wait—I thought Beurre Swim was Ella's thing?

It was, but now Sophie has more weight.

I scroll to more comments:

Ella still has loads more followers and a boatload of brand deals in comparison.

Fair, but Sophie's more selective with the brands she works with—she doesn't get out of bed for anyone. Less deals, but the deals she does are only with prestigious brands.

She said in the ITK interview she'd be walking in the Eden Eves fall shows again!

I swallow. I know I've just said I've never felt threatened, but perhaps I spoke too soon. Did these knobs forget Sophie was only in the show last year because of me? I brought her into this space. I made her those connections. I've actually handcrafted my own competition. And right now, I'm not winning. Have you ever felt the foundation of your entire existence being rocked to the bloody core? It's a panicky *perhaps I'm not doing enough* sort of feeling. Success is not an option for me. That's why I'll do anything to keep my edge. I won't sit back while I descend into a flop era. My eyes flick to the comment box, and I stare at the random username I created last year when we discovered the page. *Don't engage* the angel on my right shoulder chirps. But the devil on my left is rubbing his hands together. Have you got them too? Little shits they are, always bickering. My fingers start typing:

Of course she's in the show again. Her dad's shagging the designer. I think it's important to remember Sophie exists because of Ella, and if Sophie wasn't dating Beck, she'd be…?

Blistering confidence. My confidence—it's a front. My self-worth is shit.

CHAPTER 4
WITHDRAWALS & NIGHTMARES

SOPHIE

Dad and Evelyn are running late for our drinks at the club. It's busy tonight, but they've saved his favorite table for us. I wait at the bar, sitting beneath the heat from the stained-glass pendant lights twisting the two-carat stone in my left earlobe, sort of in a daze. My eyes keep fixating on the shelved baccarat behind the bar because I'm exhausted and I've got the stares. The chaser I've been waiting for is placed in front of me, breaking me out of my fog. I was in the back of the Uber when I noticed it. My bag was open in my lap—I've missed two days' worth of birth control.

Inside my purse, I pop Monday and Tuesday out of the pack. It's quite confusing for my jet-lagged brain which day it even is because it's a different day in Melbourne than it is in London, and how many days can you even take at one time?

"Sophie Collins alone at the bar?"

My hands freeze as a voice from my past lingers in the air. Have I succumbed to hallucinations? *Impossible.* He lives in New York City. I let go of the loose pills and slowly turn to confirm it's only a ghost over my shoulder. But he's not a ghost. He's here, and he's standing right behind me. Like I could forget the way my name sounds falling out of his mouth. I move my bag off my lap onto the seat beside me and slip off the stool.

"Fredrick—what are you doing here?"

He moves in, quickly kissing my cheek. His dark five-o'clock shadow leaves a tingling trail on my skin. Black hair, beaming smile. He's got on a crisp white button-down with a cashmere sweater loosely tied over his shoulders.

"I've just moved back," he says, slipping a hand into the pocket of his dark gray trousers.

My brain short-circuits, and I stare into his piercing icy blue eyes. "You're living here?" I begin to comprehend. "...In London...again?"

He smiles, amused. "I accepted a CFO position at a cybersecurity firm." He turns his head, nodding to a large table on the back wall. "Here with some colleagues."

I gulp. "Lovely!"

He sets his hand on the back of the barstool I was sitting at and steps closer. He smells the same as I remember, same cologne—D&G *Light Blue*. His eyes pinch. "And you're here...alone?"

"I'm meeting my dad for drinks."

"Right." He nods. "Still dating the pilot, I presume?"

"Beck. Yes—he's in Brazil."

But even that doesn't make him take a step back. He stays close, peering down at me. And it's déjà vu—only it's not, because he never looked at me like this in public when we were a *we*.

"Funny enough, Edgeman is a major sponsor for MACH. Our logo's on the rear wing."

I blink quickly. "*E-Edgeman?*" I studder.

"That's right. We'll be around the paddock at a few of the European races."

My brain's still short-circuiting because he must be talking about a different paddock. A different MACH? I reach back for my wine because it's a good cover for putting some distance between us. I bring it and my arms across my chest.

"I look forward to meeting—*Beck*."

It sounds strange coming out of his mouth, like it's hard for him to say Beck's name. I muster a half-smile.

He nods again at his table. "We're going to head to the next spot."

I suck in a breath as he reaches out and puts his hand on my wrist. His eyes fall down my body then flick back up to mine.

"It's good to see you."

I swallow because he has the audacity to keep his hand wrapped around my wrist. I cannot possibly say *and you,* so I nod like the mute I currently am with my three remaining brain cells. He releases my wrist, and I stare at the back of his head moving away from me, exactly how I remember it from a little more than a year ago, the last time I saw him. The day he left the flat and left me and my broken, jilted heart bleeding out.

I spin back to the bar and bring the wine glass to my lips. I suck down two large gulps. My heart is a drum, and these fucking lights above me have my temples starting to sweat. I climb back up onto the stool. *Fredrick will be in the paddock?*

There are loads of footsteps. Could that be his lot leaving? I can't turn around. I peek down at myself—black turtleneck jumper, tweed skirt, tights and Prada brushed leather booties. I look alright. A bit tired, that's for certain. You want to look a certain way the first time you see your ex post breakup. *Why is that?* I lift my wine and take another hefty gulp. It gets quieter, and I listen closely for the sound of his voice and about jump when the bartender sings out Dad's name, announcing his arrival.

Dad reaches across the bar and shakes the barkeep's hand. Evelyn's in tow. I quickly glance behind me, at the now empty table. I put on a face like I haven't just been ambushed and hop off the seat.

"The sailors have returned!" Says the only man I anticipated seeing this evening.

And I rush into Dad's open arms.

At his favorite table, I order another wine, he orders an old fashioned for himself and a martini for Evelyn. They're asking about Melbourne, going on about how they watched the sunrise while watching the race and popped champagne on the boat for Beck. But I keep spinning my earring. My mind is bloody racing because Fredrick is back, and he said something about meeting Beck and being in the paddock. It sounds epic, this boat they were on, the way they are going on and on about it. And my world feels a bit like it's being tossed around in the swell they're describing, but my heart is in São Paulo, and Beck's the only person that can calm me down. Only I can't tell him why I need calming down.

"Besides the few days of chop, it was smooth sailing!" Dad smiles, looking at Evelyn.

I tip my glass back, emptying it, and uncross my legs, hoping that having both feet planted on the ground will steady the rocking. He's holding her hand on the table. Still weird seeing my dad like this with another woman. She doesn't look anything like Mum. She's blonde, with green eyes. But he's happy. And he loves her, I can tell. He hasn't told me that yet though. If he has to date someone, I'll take it being the best friend of my best friend's mother. The waiter picks up my glass and delivers a fresh five ounces.

"You've got your Paris lease until the end of this year, haven't you?"

I nod. "We extended. We weren't quite ready to leave."

"Are things any better?" Evelyn asks.

"People will lurk, hang out across the street sometimes, but nothing crazy."

We thought about moving after our whole address being leaked debacle, but we couldn't stomach leaving our charming apartment or Pierre behind.

"That's good to hear," Dad says. "I might need to reclaim the flat."

"Oh?"

"We've been talking about renovating the house." Evelyn smiles.

I blink. *We?*

"Thought maybe I'd stay in Mayfair instead of living through a reno."

"We've gotten a few bids for the work and are meeting with some interior designers."

"Bids?" I say. "This is more than an idea then."

"I reckon it's time," Dad smiles. "Evelyn's put her place on the market."

I nearly choke on my wine. Is this them telling me they're moving in together? To the flat, then into my childhood home? Where my mother lived?

"Interesting!" I manage.

I adjust in my seat, sitting up straighter. Is this all Dad's idea, or is it Evelyn's? I spin the stem of my glass between my fingers and stare into my wine. "You wouldn't touch the garden, right?"

Dad's eyes go soft. "Of course not, darling. Strictly interior! Open the first floor up a bit, take down some walls, update things."

I settle back, knowing my mother's garden will be untouched. I know it's been fifteen years, but I still think of it as her house. Would Dad actually move Evelyn in? That's where this is heading, isn't it? He can't sell it; I won't let him. All our memories are there. It's big for a townhouse, and in a highly sought after Kensington postcode. And rare as they come with a front drive, front garden and a massive one in the back. The garden where Mum was always wrist deep in the dirt.

"But enough of that," Evelyn says. "I want to hear about Beurre!"

"We get to see the final samples Thursday," I say, welcoming the change in topic.

"It's been awesome with how much they've let us do—we got to pick the patterns, the styles, a lot of the show aesthetics—Ella even pushed to have Oliver DJ so Carmen will be there too."

"That sounds like Ella," Evelyn says. "How fun you get to do these things with her."

"How does Beck feel about the show?" Dad asks.

"He's not *overly* enthusiastic," I say, taking a sip. "He'll actually be rather close. The show is the day after Montreal, the first race in the triple-header over there."

Beck doesn't like the thought of anyone's eyes but his on my body. Especially when the only fabric covering me will be a bikini. I did the photoshoot with Beurre last year and walked a runway *in clothes* twice (Evelyn's clothes). Now I'm marrying the two, and I'm proper nervous, but the opportunity is unmatched. It's Beurre's first appearance at Miami Swim Week, and it's an honor to be asked to provide creative direction. I've truly enjoyed being behind the scenes on the business side of things thus far—that's much more up my alley. Feels good to stretch the numbers and business muscles in my brain again.

"I need to catch up with James," Dad says. "He sent me a picture of the litter of pups last week!"

Evelyn's face lights up.

Last week? I pull my phone out because I get daily pictures from Mia, loads of them. *Puppies. Pregnant. Birth control. Fuck.* Monday and Tuesday are somewhere loose in the bottom of my purse. I cannot forget! I hand my phone over with the latest photos. Dad pulls his glasses from his pocket and perches them on his nose.

"How many are there?" he asks.

"Eight. Five boys, three girls." I point to the little one with the brown collar. "This is Mia's favorite. He's called *Finn*."

"They've gotten fluffier!" Evelyn says excitedly. "I grew up with an English cream! They're my favorite."

I point to the one in the red collar. "Beck picked the fattest little boy of the bunch and named him *Pirelli*."

"Did you name one?" he asks, scrolling to the next picture.

I shake my head. "It was too fun watching Mia and Louie think of names. *Honey, Jasmine* and *Penny* are the girls. Then *Rajah, Scout Junior* and *Little Bear*."

"Will they keep any?" Evelyn asks.

"James says no, but Mia's quite persuasive."

So much so, she also talked her way into getting a cellphone—an iPhone, nonetheless! Mia's original vision for her birthday present was a horse. So, James was delighted when a stray hound showed up on their property the first week of December with no name and no collar. Suddenly, Mia didn't want a horse. All she wanted was to keep the dog, Scout—that's what they named him. He's a good-looking dog. A yellow lab mix, they think. But a young, rambunctious thing, who acts like he's never been on a lead in his life. Then Scout, that naughty boy, went and got the eighty-five-year-old neighbor's English cream, Gemma, pregnant. And three weeks ago, Gemma decided the Wright's barn was the perfect place to have her pups. They were born two days before we left for Australia. On Mother's Day. A hard day for me historically, so I welcomed it. A day I usually spend with Dad, but now Dad has Evelyn, and they were already off. I was glad to spend it at the Wright's, celebrating Elizabeth and new puppy mum, Gemma. That's how over break the Wrights went from zero pets, to one dog and eight puppies.

I watch Evelyn's face continue to light up each time my dad swipes to another picture. The pups are adorable. All precious and creamy white with plump little bellies. All but the runt, Mia's favorite, James's favorite, too, I suspect. Evelyn's eyes go wide with delight when Dad says they'll have to take a drive out there to see them.

I don't want to stay at the flat tonight. Ella's not here, and it's looking like it won't be ours for much longer. It's fair. The flat was only meant to be our place during university. We've well overstayed our welcome, and Dad's footed the bill for all of it. When they drop me off after drinks, I wait for Dad's car to turn the corner, then request an Uber to Battersea.

The minute I let myself in to Beck's, I start a kettle, because he's actually got one now, then dump my purse out onto the counter. His place doesn't echo like it once did. I had the track prints professionally hung, and I've managed to keep a few of the plants we bought alive. His helmets are off the floor and sat on floating shelves in his room. He's even got a rug and telly accompanying the couch in the living room now. His trophy from the European karting championship is in the corner. Besides those bits, he's still my simple Beck.

Over break, I went on a Bake-Off kick. He was over the moon. I felt silly and inspired one night, and he went out and bought me a KitchenAid mixer and all sorts of baking bits and bobs. That's the only reason some of his cabinets have contents. It didn't end well, but that's okay. I live in Paris, where I can buy world-renowned sweets of any kind. I knew I couldn't cook, but that night I also learned I can't bake. Beck sampled everything, of course, and gave it all scores way nicer than deserved. Ella cooks for us sometimes. She makes a killer avocado toast with eggs à la Française. When my water's ready, I grab Monday and Tuesday and chase the tiny peach pills with my sleepy tea.

I have some of my own things here, but I pull on one of Beck's T-shirts and sink into his plush bed. He texted an hour ago asking how drinks went with Dad. The club was—*eventful*. I might be losing the place I call home in London, my childhood home could be ripped to the studs, and *oh!* Remember my ex? Yes, the one I was pasted next to in the tabloids last year? He's back, and he's conveniently working for a sponsor of a Formula 1 team! Tommy's team, to be exact! Bravo! *I should tell him.* Now's not the time, not during a race week, not when we're apart. Is it entirely necessary though? If it is in fact true that Fredrick will walk among the guests in the paddock...Beck will find out eventually, no? I can't think of what to do at the minute. It's a decision to make at another time when I've slept and don't have wine mixed with sleepy tea brain.

Drinks were drunk!

Dad misses you.

Beck:

I miss you.

Going to dinner with the team.

XX

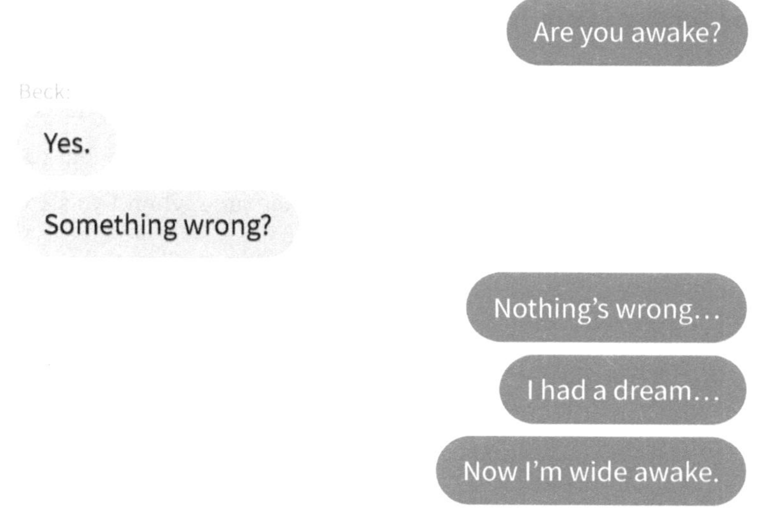

I gasp, and my eyes fly open. It's not a nightmare, quite the opposite, actually. I'm sweating. My heart's pounding, and I'm all wound up and on the edge of release. *My word.* Is it possible to orgasm in a dream? Fucking hell, I was almost there. My body's on the brink—hot, needy and wet. *Very wet.* Scratch that. This is a nightmare. Being that close only to wake up and miss the grand finale fireworks? Alone? *Torture.* I lick my lips and reach for my phone on the nightstand, shocked when I realize I've only been asleep for two hours.

He's calling. I hit accept because that's what I wanted to happen.

"Was it a bad dream?" he asks, the minute I answer.

"It was a"—I pause—"steamy dream."

"Oh?" He waits for more.

"Are you alone?" I ask self-consciously.

"Mm-hmm." He says and again waits for more. "You've got to tell me about it."

I swallow because I'm shy about these things, and I can't imagine repeating out loud the happenings of this dream—no, *nightmare*. I try to form a semi-appropriate retelling.

"We were in your kitchen, and well... you sort of put me up on the counter."

"And this dream—did it leave you hot and bothered?"

He's smiling. I can tell from his voice.

"Hot and—" I pause again.

He blows out a breath. "You're soaking wet, aren't you?"

"Mm-hmm."

"*Fuckkkk,*" he groans. "I'd be lapping that up."

I sink my teeth into my bottom lip because that's quite literally where the dream abruptly ended.

"You at yours?"

My heart jumps. I never told him I had come here earlier.

"No—I'm in your bed."

"Even better," he says. "I want to make you feel good..."

"How?"

"You've never done this before, have you?" he says, amused.

I gulp. "Done what?"

"My, my." He clicks his tongue. "Put me on speaker so you've got both hands."

I pull the phone away from my ear and hit the speaker icon, then lay it down beside me.

"What have you got on?" His voice is heavier now.

"Panties, one of your shirts. Wet panties," I clarify.

"Take them off."

The sharpness in his tone sends a shiver down my legs. I pull my hands under the covers.

"Are you—?"

"*So fucking hard*. Take them off, Sophie," he demands. "I'm right here with you."

My word. Didn't realize he was playing along. I slide my panties down and kick them off into the abyss under the covers. I flinch as I bring my finger through the mess between my legs.

"Are they off?"

"Yes," I whisper.

"Good girl," he praises.

"I don't know how to do this," I whine. "I just want you."

"I know, baby, but this will have to do. I'll talk you through it."

It's a bit ridiculous; I can't make it a week without his hands on me? I'm a hopeless addict. Fucking withdrawals, that's what this is. My body's buzzing like it's got a charge running through it at the minute. And the way his voice is coming through the phone is only amplifying the charge.

"Now, close your eyes, Sophie."

CHAPTER 5

ME? DRIVE?

It's HARDLY LIGHT OUT, but it's the second time I've heard my phone vibrating. I instantly sit up the moment I see Elizabeth's name on the screen.

"Sophie," she says shakily.

"What is it?"

"It's Finn—he died." She sniffles. "Sometime overnight."

"No!" I gasp. My heart shatters.

"We woke up Mia so she could say goodbye before we buried him."

"Is she alright?"

"No." Her voice cracks. "Now I wish we hadn't woken her. We didn't know what to do, if she would be more upset with us burying him without her, or—"

"I'm coming," I say frantically. I throw the covers back and lunge out of bed.

When I hang up with Elizabeth, I dial Beck on speaker and toss my phone on the bathroom counter. I quickly brush out the ends of my hair. The ringing stops as we connect.

"Guessing you heard?" Beck sighs.

"I'm sorry. What time is it there?"

"It's alright," he yawns. "Mia called me sobbing. Mum said they're keeping them home from school."

"I'm going out to your parents."

"How are you getting there?"

I pause mid-knotting my hair in a bun on top of my head. Didn't think that far ahead. *Uber? Taxi?*

"Take the car, Sophie. There's another set of keys in the kitchen drawer by the sink."

"Me? Drive?" Nerves pile onto the sickness already sloshing around in my stomach.

"The Range Rover."

"Obviously the Range Rover!" I snap.

Beck snorts a laugh. I didn't mean to yell. I'm just panicking over the thought of driving, is all.

"It's easy to drive, and there are loads of cameras. You can do it, Sophie."

"This is horrible," I say before biting the inside of my lip to try to hold back the tears.

"When you get in the car, call me back if you need help."

We spent so much time out there over break, I know the route like the back of my hand. Beck provides a few final words of encouragement before we hang up. I splash water on my face and moisturize before brushing my teeth.

I'm naked under his T-shirt. I'll leave him the treat of finding my panties in the bed as he requested. I throw on a pair of track pants and a jumper and head for the kitchen. There are two sets of keys in the drawer. Both with distinct logos. I roll my eyes and grab the Range Rover keys.

I take the lift to the garage floor and pass the double spot where Beck's new Ferrari 812 sits. I start to panic again after I've climbed up into the driver's seat of the SUV. I can't do this. I never sit on this side of the car! Let alone operate the thing! I tap my phone screen on. Don't have service down here to call him even if I wanted. *Push brake to start* are the instructions illuminated on the dash. Like I can reach the bloody pedal? I look around for the seat adjustment and move the seat forward. I raise it until I can see well over the steering wheel and into the rearview mirror without craning my neck. I take a deep breath, hold the brake and push the start button. I should give myself some grace—because why would I be comfortable driving? My boyfriend is a professional racing driver, and when he's not driving me, *we have a driver,* and when we don't, I'm on a train or a plane or the jet. I've never had my own car. *Who has their own car?* I can count the number of times I've driven Dad's car on one hand. *Dad.* Should I ring him? Make him drive me to the Wrights? I don't have service, and it's a workday. I take another breath. *Get it together.* I'm twenty-fucking-five, and I *can* drive a car. I put my foot on the brake and shift into reverse, using every camera angle on the center console to guide me.

An hour and twenty-five minutes later (should have been an hour), I pull into the Wrights' drive. It's dreary out—the sky is gray and spitting mist. Literally had to pull the car over to figure out how to turn the wipers on three minutes in. Too many options, far too many buttons. I could have called Beck, but that's embarrassing, and I figured it out, *eventually.* I put the car in park and stretch my cramped fingers. He called while I was on the M25, but I was far too scared to take a hand off the wheel and accept the call. I check his messages.

Beck:

No need to answer, wanted to check on you.

You're doing great

I'm following your dot

Another message comes through:

Proud of you <3

I did it!

Means the world you went out there

Give everyone a kiss for me

<3

I turn the car off and open the door. It's quiet. There is no Mia or Louie in the red doorway or waiting on the stoop like usual. And Scout, the free ranger, didn't chase the car down the drive and isn't running in circles like his normal excitable self. In fact, I don't see Scout anywhere. I hurry up the steps, grab the door handle and push inside. I've always loved the way their house smells, like home even when they're not cooking a feast. It's quiet inside too. I find James in the kitchen, he spins around from the sink, eyes more glassy than normal.

"Thank you for coming." He swallows.

"I drove Beck's car," I say, still astonished by my own feat but feel the need to clarify. "Not the Ferrari."

James smiles. "Did you do okay then?"

"I did alright," I say, stretching my fingers that are still sweaty from my death grip on the steering wheel.

"Good for you!" he says, pulling me in for a hug. "Next time, you can bring the 812," he says, patting my back.

When he lets go of me, he blinks quickly. "Rough morning out here." He blows out a breath. "Told Mia only yesterday she could keep the little one."

My heart sinks. *I knew it.* "Are they in the barn?"

He nods.

I open the patio door and head across the damp grass. The stable lights are on, and the door is slightly ajar under the red sign that I helped Mia paint *Scout's House* on. The door creaks as I sneak in. Scout's tail slaps against the floor, he lifts his head but doesn't get up. Louie does. He jumps up from the blanket pallet in the middle of the floor and runs over to me. Elizabeth gives me a warm smile as she continues petting Gemma's head. Mia's forehead is on her knees. She's squeezing her arms around her legs as the now seven darling puppies squirm around in front of her. They've grown quite a lot. Even with the space heaters whirring, I can hear their little noises as they climb over each other, trying to nurse. I bite down on my lip again to hold back the tears. I put my hand on Louie's back and make my way over.

"Thank you," Elizabeth mouths to me.

I drop down to my knees next to Beck's little sister and wrap my arms around her.

"Mia, I'm so sorry."

"He's the one I wanted to keep," she cries.

"Do you think Gemma knows?" Louie asks, standing next to me, playing with my hair scrunchie.

It's rather obvious. Her eyes are sad, and her head hasn't come up off the floor. Most of the pups have tiny slits where their eyes are starting to open. I wonder if little Finn got to see a glimpse of the world before—Tears pool in my eyes. I blink quickly. I've got to be strong.

"I think she knows," I tell him. "But I also think she's very happy to have you sitting with her."

"She hasn't seen Finn's grave," Louie says.

I hate that word.

"She will," Elizabeth says, squeezing her son's hand. "And the beautiful flowers you picked for him."

Mia's head finally lifts from her knees. "I picked flowers—Louie picked weeds!"

I've never seen Mia cry. She's like Ella, tough as nails. But today her eyes are sodden, and her face is red, full of tears.

"I wish Beck were here," Louie says, sitting down next to me.

"Me too," I say quickly because my voice catches. My eyes fill up again. "He'd be right here with us."

"I've never known anyone that's died," Mia chokes. She looks up at me. "When your mum died—how did you not stay sad forever?"

Elizabeth scoots next to us and puts her arm around me and her daughter.

"I know right now it feels like you'll be sad forever," I say. "But Finn wouldn't want you to be sad. You know why?"

"Why?" she cries.

"Because seven other puppies need you, Mia. All of his brothers and sisters need you. And Finn can only rest easy when he knows you'll be okay to take care of them."

CHAPTER 6
ASK ME ANYTHING

ELLA

PARIS IS WHERE MOST of our PR packages are sent—boatloads of them. Drives Pierre nuts when we take up the building's parcel closet. Which happens when we're away for a bit like we just were. Sophie always gets overwhelmed when we gather the packages on the floor to sort through them and unbox the gifted goods. She looks pleased at the minute, unloading a box from La Mer, same as she did when she unboxed the bits from Guerlain.

"You drove the *Autobiography* to Surrey?" Carmen asks her, still in disbelief.

"Didn't put a scratch on it!" she says proudly. "About took off the side mirror getting it back into the garage, but that's neither here nor there."

I reach for the next parcel and start to open it, stopping when I realize it's got Sophie's name on it. Her pile's not as big as mine, of course not—but it's grown. Instead of an unboxing video, I'll film a haul later; we've got girlie catch-up to do with Carmen.

"This one's yours, love," I say, tossing the package to her on the couch.

"You think Mia will keep a different puppy?" Carmen asks, her eyes sad.

"At this point, I think James would let her keep all of them."

I move on to the next box. Fairly basic packaging—personalized card with a nice note on top of wine-colored leggings, a sports bra and a cropped tee. I have a similar set from a different brand, also gifted. Everyone did the jewel tones—sort of overdone at this point, but it's a cute set I'll wear and post to throw the brand a bone. I swear I haven't had to buy workout clothes for years.

"And what's this about us getting the boot?" Carmen whines.

"See!" Sophie cries. "It was literally one thing after another! And those were both *after* running into him!"

I refold the leggings and butt in to ask the important questions.

"And...?" I inquire. "How'd he look?"

Sophie gives me eyes.

"That good?" I say, egging her on.

She rolls them now. "He looked like he's always looked—not that I'm looking anymore."

"So hot as fuck?" I smile. "Got it."

She contemplates my chosen unit of measurement for a moment. She used to get so mad when I'd chant that TikTok sound—you know, the one where you're looking for a man in finance, with a trust fund, who's 6'5". Fredrick's even got the blue eyes!

"You think you'll actually run into him at a race?" Carmen asks.

"I hope to God not! But they're a main sponsor—and I swear he said European races, the first would be Spain..."

Carmen shakes her head and shifts her focus to me. "And Alston berating you! Bloody hell!—both of your visits sound horrible!"

"Call me a masochist, but I'm going back for Easter—not for Alston, but to meet Emmett's new girlfriend," I say, grabbing another package.

"Well, if you need an escape, nip on down to Ollie's."

"Party with the Goddards?" I lift a brow, ripping the package open.

She nods, all excited. "How about some good news, then?"

"*Please*," Sophie begs.

"It was touch and go, but Ollie survived Music Week, and he's locking down a sick hotel for us to stay at in Miami."

Sophie claps. "And we will claim your front-row spot for the show!"

***

Four nights later, I go out for dinner with Adrien. He's the newest addition to my Paris bench, and he's a looker, this one. Body like a god, dirty blond hair, green eyes and brilliant in bed. He's a newly signed model I actually met through Ollie on a wild night out. He's got his hands all over me at dinner, which I don't mind. The first two buttons of his shirt have been undone since he picked me up, which has me seriously contemplating going home with him after. We go live on Instagram for a bit at the table because he's thirsty—newly signed model thirsty—and because we look like an absolute smoke show together.

When we leave the brasserie, post heavy moment against the wall outside, I ask him to take me home because I'm craving something a bit different. The craving first came during our meeting with Beurre this morning. It was a four-hour marathon—got to try on the samples, review the schedule, the seating chart and see a virtual walk-through of the show space. So when Adrien drops me at ours, I don't go inside. I take a stroll to our nearest Franprix and do something I haven't done in years.

I open our front door and hold my purse tight under my arm. It's noisy. Three garment bags from an AquaDuo delivery now hang on the doorframe in the entry. We're attending their store event on Saturday. I step into the living room, where the girls are sat next to each other on the couch, eyes beaming and glued to the computer in Sophie's lap. Empty wine glasses sit on the table in front of them, and popcorn's strewn about the herringbone.

"Did he win again?" I ask.

"He was phenomenal!" Carmen sings, then motions to the floor. "Hence the mess."

Sophie's eyes flick up from the screen for half a second. "Back so soon?"

"And alone?" Carmen adds.

I ignore the inquiries, sit on the arm of the sofa and peek at the laptop. It's the post-race press conference. Beck's on the couch between Leo and that hot one Elijah. *No Tommy.*

Elijah's got the microphone, talking into it, looking absolutely beat and rather annoyed. "...we can't just be waiting around for Beck to make a mistake because he's not making many of those these days."

"Beck, you've now won both races this season. You're undoubtedly the biggest threat on the grid, and for the first time in seven years, Furio's leading the constructor's championship. What is the team saying?"

Beck smiles and flips his microphone up. "I mean—they've invested so much in me, it's time I started showing them I was worth it."

And that's when Sophie turns to mush, going full goo-goo eyes at the screen.

"Moving to you, Leo. You secured your third championship last year. This is, however, the first podium appearance for either Valor car this season, with Valor sitting third in the constructor's championship. Does this car feel like the championship-winning car it was last year?"

"At the moment, no. We are struggling on the straights, with the balance—we are struggling with everything, really."

"Don't see Luca in there, did he do alright?" I ask.

Sophie taps the speaker button, turning the volume down.

"He got eighth and left immediately! Skipped interviews to get to the airport and get home."

"Is it go-time, then?"

"Still on baby watch, but Pippa's due date was five days ago!"

Carmen shakes her head. "Can you imagine if he missed—"

Sophie smacks her arm. "Bad vibes, Carmen! She'd better have him this week while he's home!"

I wonder how Tommy fared. I don't ask though. He wasn't happy with his performance at his home race. Though I think he'd forgotten just how unhappy he was once he was in bed with me.

"George called too." Carmen frowns.

Sophie looks up at me. "The reno is a go. Since we'll be home for Easter, we can bring some of our things back. My dad will take care of the rest."

Carmen claps her hands. "He's letting us take the telly!"

I push up off the couch and head for my room. "The end of an era."

That series of words fell out of my mouth rather unconsciously. Probably since I've been thinking nonstop about how possibly, what if, it's the end of *my* era? My era of being the it-girl, the sought after one, the one who's always been the centerpiece of photographs.

I push up my window and swing my leg out over the windowsill. I crawl up between the dormers and sit on the softly slanted part of the roof. My room might be the smallest, but it's also the only one where you can escape out onto the roof like this. I unzip my Le Bisou Perle and take out my Franprix goods. One pack—a pack I won't even finish—and a tiny lighter.

I rip the plastic off the outside of the pack and slide out a cigarette. I cup my hand to light it and shut my eyes, taking that first satisfying drag. And for a moment, all the commotion in my head quiets. *Damn you, Emmett.* I pull it from my lips and exhale, trying to suppress the cough that's tickling my throat. I shimmy out the loose brick on the side of the dormer and stick the pack and lighter behind it.

Sucks we've got to leave, but we've been squatting at the flat in since uni. I suppose it's time we hand it back over—we're hardly there much these days. Leaving this apartment would be harder because of this spot. I lie back and stare up at the night sky. It's my one place where I can escape the noise if you will. Not truly because you can hear plenty noise from the street, but up here on the roof, I've got my own little safe space—that's just mine.

I must be mental going back to Manchester, but Mum's in Dubai with her latest high-priority client. And Emmett already told Annabelle she'd get to meet me. And thank fuck the Edwardian had a room available. Meeting a fangirl like Annabelle might help get me out of this self-doubting headspace I'm sat in at the minute. Since that dinner, I haven't thought of much else, to be honest. It kept churning up during the Beurre meeting, when more than any time before, the team sought out Sophie's opinion on things. Fylter loved the GRWM long-haul flight edition. They reached out, commented and everything. But did they love it like they did because Sophie was in it? Would they have loved it as much if it were only me?

I roll onto my stomach and open my Instagram. I tap through my story until I reach the video and question prompt I posted before dinner.

Heading to dinner with a cute boy. Ask me anything in case I'm bored later.

Well, I'm bored and it's later, so I open the responses and take another drag. I scroll past a few predictable requests, different iterations of *show me your boobs*, before my eyes catch on a question.

"Can you link the dress Sophie wore for Melbourne quali?"

Skip.

"Who are you on a date with?"

There's an easy one. And another excuse to post a photo of myself. I reply with a shot of me and Adrien at the table. Tag him because I know he'll repost it, and he should—we both look ridiculously good.

Then my gold mine is delivered.

"I want to try Fylter! What should I order first?"

I set my cigarette down and push it out of the frame before I start a video reply.

"Depends on whether you're looking for skincare or makeup. On the makeup front, try Fylter's honey gloss and crème blush. Absolutely stunning colors. I've hit the pan on two of their blushes already. And if you want skincare, I've linked my videos where I review the entire line with both my morning and night routines."

I exchange the phone for my cigarette, returning to my back and view of the sky. When I get through this cigarette, I think I'll have one more.

CHAPTER 7
WE GET TO CAMP?

SOPHIE

LUCA MADE IT TO Milan—and just in time. Two hours after his arrival, he and Pippa went to the hospital, and Luca Giovanni Lombardo was born. *Baby Luca*—itty-bitty and perfect with a full head of black hair. Beck flew back to headquarters with Charlie, half to prep on the sim and half to celebrate. The team had a massive party waiting for the win in Brazil.

I was itching to skip the AquaDuo pop-up when Beck left HQ a day early, but I was good. I fulfilled my duties. I've pulled back a bit from things. I only entertain the big events—our Beurre collab, of course, a brand trip we're taking with Fylter in May and anything RIMI related. Stuart's okay with it too. He doesn't hound me about little things anymore.

I push my bag and empty suitcase for moving day through Beck's front door. I kick off my shoes when he turns the corner—barefoot, bare-chested, with gray sweatpants hanging off his waist. His hair is a mess, like he's just woken up. *My word.* I ditch my things and jump into his arms, kissing him like I haven't kissed him in a year, although it hasn't even been a fortnight. He holds me against him, carrying me backward until he falls back onto the couch, and I'm astride his lap.

"I missed you," he says, staring at me with those all-consuming eyes.

I run my fingers through his hair. I often question if he's real or if he's a figure from a dream, and I've just not woken up. It's been a long time now for it all to be a dream—can it be I'm truly living in such a pinch-me reality?

"Two for two." I smile.

He gives a small, humble shrug. "Got lucky."

"Did Coop cry again?"

"Not sure—I did get him good on the podium down the back of his shirt."

Payback for the absolute dousing Coop gave him in Melbourne.

"I'm sorry I wasn't there."

He reaches up, runs his thumb over my collarbone. "As much as I'd like to keep you at all times—I want you to have your own things."

I fall into his chest, tucking my head up under his chin and breathing in my favorite smell in the whole world. His scent isn't loud or overbearing. It's warm and soft and muted, like cologne you sprayed on a jumper the day before.

His arms close around me, and he nods at the door. "Moving your things tomorrow?"

"I'm a bit sad about it."

He tilts his head, trying to find my eyes.

"Well, I've got your answer—move your stuff in here."

I push off his chest, straightening back up. "*What?*"

He looks amused. "When you're in London, you're over here anyway." His eyes dart around the room. "And look at the touch you've put on this place. You made it lose its echo."

"I have my drawer."

"Drawers," he corrects me, running the fabric of my dress through his fingers.

"I can't move in here, Beck…" I say nervously.

His eyes pinch. "Why's that now?"

Of the million thoughts flying through my mind, I somehow land on a semi-solid one.

"We haven't been together even a year…"

Not to mention I've never lived with a man! Am I even allowed to live with a man?! Despite Dad's absolute adoration for Beck, I can't say he'd be keen on that. And well—I live in Paris!

"I know." He smiles, tucking my hair behind my ear. "But you should think about it. I won't have this place for much longer."

That much is true. He's had an agent scouting for places in Monaco. Ana and Ren made the move, and she hasn't stepped foot back in England since. I've got loads more I need to tell him, but his gaze falls down my body, and his hands start to wander well past the fabric of my dress.

"Where's Tommy?" I ask because I know where this is heading.

"The gym." His eyes flick up but get stuck on my lips. "We'll head out when he gets back."

I swallow. "When's that?"

The corners of his mouth perk up. "He just left."

He pushes my cardigan off my shoulders, and I let it fall to the floor behind me. Then he reaches for the bottom of my dress and takes it over my head.

He sucks in a bit of air. "My God, I fancy this."

It's new. A matching lacy periwinkle set. And my tights are sheer enough to see as much.

He wraps his hands under my legs and stands from the couch, sets me up on the counter.

"Is this not how your dream started?" he whispers against my lips.

I nod. "But I was completely naked."

His fingertips brush my stomach and hook into the top of my tights. "You know how hard it was having you on the phone and not being able to taste you?"

I lean to the side as he pulls the top of my tights and panties from under my left bum cheek then to the other side. The marble is bitter cold, chills race over my skin as he pulls the tights off my feet. His lips part as he pushes my legs open.

"What happened next?" he asks, amused.

I touch behind my ear. "You started kissing me here, then..." I slide my hand down until I reach my collarbone.

I told you how his stubble feels against my skin. His fingers have found their favorite spot between my legs as his lips move down the path I'd laid out. I grab for him, feeling the way I've already made him go through the front of his sweats.

"Now what?" he asks, breath hot against my skin.

I feel bold, brave, way braver than usual and loads braver than I was on the phone. I've got my answer, but it comes out more as a command.

"Eat me," I whisper.

He pulls back in shock, eyes wild, staring at me like he's intoxicated. He grabs for my ankles. I lie back onto the marble, and he sets my heels at the edge of the counter. And I know it sounds cliché, but what happens when he brings his mouth between my legs is a dream come true.

Happiness has returned to the Wrights. When we pull up, Louie's in the drive, pushing the puppies around in an old pram. Gemma and Scout are tearing through the yard, chasing after each other.

Tommy makes it three steps out of the car and goes to mush when Mia plops a puppy in his arms. *Little Bear*. She hasn't picked a new favorite, but Beck is pleased because the rest of the family is quite taken with Pirelli. We've been here twenty minutes and haven't made it inside. We needed a proper puppy fix first.

"Alright, Louie!" Elizabeth calls. "Put the puppies back! They need their Easter dinner too!"

I give Rajah and Jasmine a kiss on the head because I doubled up and have both against my chest.

Inside, the kitchen is in a charming disarray. The dining room is dolled up—table draped in gingham, doily place settings, bunny salt and pepper shakers and the most darling napkin rings I've ever seen. James is finishing the icing on a massive three-layer carrot cake.

Beck falls into an armchair in the family room and nods at the telly.

"*Bridgerton*?" he says, unimpressed. "Again?"

James shakes his head. *Obviously not his choice.*

Beck nods toward Elizabeth. "You didn't get your fix over break?"

We did, in fact, binge-watch every episode. But that was only after we gave *Squid Game* a try—and that was quite literally horrifying. Gripping plot, but terribly gruesome. Beck and James were hooked, so we were forced to finish season one. That's when Elizabeth and I switched to something lighter and the boys dipped out five minutes into the pilot.

"It's called a rewatch, son! And your Dad's banned me from watching more Bake-Off for fear he'll become obese," Elizabeth says, pausing the telly.

"Sort of matches the Easter vibes!" Tommy says.

"Thank you, Tommy!" she says, grabbing his hand. "I've made up the pullout bed in the study for you."

He sets his hand on top of hers adoringly.

"Sophie, you'll be upstairs, and, Beck, you've got the couch."

"The couch?" he deadpans.

"Unless you want to snuggle with Tommy!"

Elizabeth hurries into the kitchen and returns holding a pink basket with a white ruffle liner. James is behind her, licking the remaining icing from the spatula.

"Happy Easter, my dear!" She kisses my cheeks and sets the basket overflowing with pastel packaged sweets in my hands.

Beck and Tommy exchange a look. "What are we? Chopped liver?"

We're sat for Easter dinner. Beck and I on one side of the table, with an open seat beside me. Tommy's across from us, sitting between Mia and Louie while James and Elizabeth sit at either head. The conversation has moved to Ana and Ren's wedding. Over summer break, the boys will stand with Ren and two others. I'll stand with Ren's sister and two of Ana's crazy cousins—her words, not mine.

Beck nudges me. "You going to show me your dress?"

I shake my head playfully.

"She showed me!" Mia boasts.

True. I tried everything to cheer her up that morning I drove out here. Ana picked for us—stunning baby blue satin gowns with a fitted corset.

"You think they're endgame?" Mia asks.

"Ren and Ana? They're the definition of endgame," I validate.

Beck cocks an eyebrow at her. "*Endgame?*"

"Taylor Swift," Mia says, annoyed. "Get some cultural ed, big bro."

I'm glad to see her usual sass has returned.

"Your dad finally home?" James asks, diverting the conversation.

I nod. "And they are—full steam ahead."

"That's such a shame I didn't meet Evelyn at the show last year," Elizabeth says. "We've got to have them both out, James!"

Rounds with James at Wentworth are about the only time Dad and Evelyn have separate time these days. And no, work doesn't count because every time I ring him during the workday, he's on the other line with her!

"You think they're *endgame*?" Tommy asks me, mocking Mia.

I shift uncomfortably in my seat. "I suppose time will tell."

He elbows Mia. "When are you going to come cheer for me then?"

"We're coming to Silverstone!" Louie shouts, mouth full.

Elizabeth eyes me. "He loves the RV park."

"You ever slept in an RV, Sophie?" Tommy asks with a shit-eating grin on his face.

My eyes flick around the table. "We get to camp there? I've never been camping before!"

Mia chokes a laugh. James and Elizabeth exchange a smile.

Beck pats my thigh beneath the tablecloth. "We aren't camping, love...we sleep in motorhomes."

"Like million-quid motorhomes," Tommy adds.

I frown. "That's got to half count as camping!"

"It doesn't," Mia says bluntly.

James is highly entertained. "You'll 'camp'"—he air quotes—"before then in Austin."

Beck's hand remains in my lap. "Soph won't be at COTA," he says, fingertips sliding under my dress. Our eyes meet. "You've got your brand trip then, no?"

"Mm-hmm," I mutter, squeezing my thighs together. I glance around the table. "St. Barths."

Elizabeth lifts her wine. "Worthy trip, dear!"

Tommy nods at James. "You see the competition we've got on the rear wing of the car?"

"Who? Edgeman?" James asks.

I drop my fork because my heart's jumped to my throat.

Tommy nods, and my heart pounds in my ears.

"Small fish in the grand scheme," James says. "Give 'em a year or so to fatten up, and they'll be prime for us to gobble up."

I adjust in my seat while the conversation flows on around us, thankfully changing topics again. But I'm still over here praying Edgeman stays a teeny, tiny, unappetizing fish because I'd simply die if James came across Fredrick professionally. Beck's fingers slowly ascend and move back and forth across my upper thigh.

My eyes drift over and snag on his.

"You going to finish?" he asks, eyes hungry, a wicked grin on his face.

I stare, stunned by his table-side naughtiness.

"Your plate." He winks.

Oh. *Jesus.* I shake my head.

He leans in, much closer than needed, and stabs my remaining carrots with his fork. All while taking the opportunity to hook one of his fingers onto the side of my panties. He leans back into his seat with his fork full, finger still engaged. One *feast* has already been had, and we're nearly finished with another. I bring my hand to my lips and give him eyes.

"You didn't get your fill before?" I whisper, nodding to my lap.

"I'll never get my fill," he says, crunching into the carrot.

"No phone at the table, Mia!" Elizabeth snaps.

Across and two seats to my right, Mia rolls her eyes.

"What do you even use that for?" Tommy teases her.

Mia scoffs. "Texting my friends, of course."

"Texting boys at the dinner table?" Tommy accuses.

"Ew!" she squeals.

"You don't like boys yet?"

She scrunches her nose.

"Only a matter of time," Beck adds. "Wasn't it one of your little friends at school who was caught holding hands with a boy the other week?"

She shivers, disgusted. "Boys text me, but I don't text them back."

Elizabeth and James exchange a worried look.

Beck nudges my arm. "You teach her that?"

I raise my palm defensively. "I didn't teach her anything!"

Mia looks over, confused.

"The night I met Sophie, I got her number from Ella," Beck explains.

"The pretty blonde one?" Mia asks.

I glance at Tommy. He's got his tongue in his cheek.

Beck nods. "Well, I texted her, and she went and left me on read."

James's jaw drops.

"I didn't think I would ever see him again!" I say, still on the defensive.

Beck shakes his head. "Had me up all night wondering if Ella slipped me the wrong number on purpose."

"See, Mia? Better start replying," Tommy says, wiggling his finger at us. "Start of a great love story here..."

Elizabeth rests her face in her palm. "Tommy, do not encourage her."

"And where's your girlfriend?" Mia asks him with a load of sass.

"Don't have one anymore."

"Why's that?" she presses.

Tommy clears his throat.

Mouthful of potatoes, Louie looks up at Tommy. "Nobody likes you?"

Tommy's mouth twists, and he looks down at his plate. "Guess not."

***

I volunteered to finish the washing-up for James. I hand Tommy the last plate and flip the faucet off. Beck's wiping down the counter.

"I heard a disgusting rumor from Alek," Tommy says while towel drying the plate.

My heart drops.

"About Emma," he adds.

"What is it?"

"Sleeping with the enemy." He sets the plate down and leans against the counter. "Word on the street says she's been dating Bergmann since February. Maybe even before then."

My word. Now the Holt garage makes sense. "I'm sorry, Tommy."

He crosses his arms over his chest. "I told you she'd been distant."

I take the towel from him and dry my hands. "Have you tried to talk to her?"

"And say what?" He scoffs. "Hear you're fucking Imre now?"

I gulp.

"It's true what they say about her, you know. Proper jersey chaser, that one. It's sort of eating me up—like I've just got to know, you know?"

Beck walks over, pulls me against him. "If you must know—I mean, all the details and shit—Sophie knows where to find them."

A few moments later, Tommy returns to the kitchen. He sets his laptop in front of me, and I take a seat at the stool under the counter. I haven't been back to the page in months. Of course, there are times when I wonder what's been said on it, but I proudly haven't peeked. I bring up the *Lights Out Ladies* gossip page, it's as active as ever and, yes—the Imre and Emma gossip is pasted all over it. There are photos too. Loads of them. I open one of the posts; it has over two hundred comments.

HOLY SHIT! Emma Trautmann holding hands on a date with Imre Bergmann! Tommy who?!

The photos are clear as day—all the evidence you need—from unfortunately more than one occasion. I scan the comments as they stand behind me.

Are we shocked? Told you she's a jersey chaser. She moved through football, rugby, and now she's moving through the F1 grid.

"Christ!" Tommy says over my shoulder.

I spin around, and he drags his hands down his face.

"Mate, you can be mad she went for your archnemesis, but you can't be mad she's talking to other guys," Beck says to him. "You did just hook up with Ella…"

True. I spin back, close the post and scroll down the page. When the familiar stained-glass pendants that hang over the main bar at Storey House appear…illuminating my face…*and his*, my heart nosedives to my stomach.

"When was this?" Beck says from behind me.

Tommy comes back to look over my shoulder.

Fuck. I stare at the heading, fingers frozen on the trackpad.

While Beck's away, Sophie will play?

I clear my throat. "Last week…at the club," I manage.

"That's him, isn't it?" Beck asks.

I keep staring because he knows it's him, and I'm without words. I don't recall us standing *that* close. Surely the angle of the picture is making it look worse than it truly was. Tommy retreats. I close the page and push the laptop away.

Beck walks off. He swings open the patio door and leaves it ajar. I push my stool back and follow him outside. I step down onto the stone and close the patio door behind me. He's got his back to me, his hands in his pockets.

"Baby?" I say meekly.

I approach him slowly. His back is still turned, so I creep my hands around his waist. I take it as a good sign when he doesn't pull away, so I rest the side of my nose below his shoulder blades and wait. A few beats pass before he speaks.

"We don't lie to each other, Sophie," he says calmly.

And it's a lance straight through the heart. I should have told him. I thought about it, but I was waiting for the right time, remember?

"What were you doing with him?"

"I wasn't *with* him. I was waiting for Dad at the club when we met for drinks that night, and he was—there." I pause.

He turns to face me, and our eyes meet. It's written all over his face—quite weird to have his cross and annoyed look pointed at me.

"I'm sorry. I should have said I ran into him." I pause again to gauge his reaction.

He breathes out his nose. "What did he say then?"

Even his tone is irritated now.

"He's moved back...just started a new job. He was there with colleagues."

"You didn't feel like you could tell me?"

"No, I did." I say, putting my hands on his chest and stepping into him. "I didn't want to bring it up or cause an issue before a race."

"Not communicating causes issues," he says plainly.

"I know. I'm sorry. You were gone—I didn't want to tell you over the phone—and when you did get home..." I drag my fingers down his stomach, attempting to lighten the mood. "Well, we were busy with *other things* that don't include talking."

I look up at him and smile. He doesn't.

"I'm going to be gone a lot, Sophie."

"I know—"

He stares down at me. "You loved him."

The way he states it as fact and not a question at all catches me off guard.

"Back then? Maybe, but not anymore." I shake my head and move my hands back up to his chest. "And hardly the way I love you."

His face softens a bit. His hands finally leave his pockets, run up my neck and cradle my face.

"Reckon we're even now, no?" He smirks.

My brow furrows because, surely, he isn't referring to his pictures with his ex-girlfriend Sabrina last year in Portugal. When I realize that is, in fact, exactly what he's referring to, I play push him away, but he's solid as a rock and doesn't flinch, so I end up stumbling two steps backward.

"Hardly! Your picture was voluntary!" I fuss. "I didn't know my photo was being taken."

"There are always going to be eyes on you." He pulls me back against his chest. "He not know we're together?"

"Of course he does. He asked about—you." The words catch in my throat. I hesitate. *Break the full news now. Why wait?* I take a breath. "The position he took—believe it or not—he's to be the CFO of that MACH sponsor, Edgeman."

Beck lifts an eyebrow.

"He'll be at some of the races…"

He huffs a laugh. "Isn't that convenient?"

I stare at him confused because *convenient* is not a word I would use to describe any part of this situation.

"The world is small," he says, shaking his head, "but I don't think it's that small."

"What are you saying?"

"He still loves you."

He lifts his finger and runs it down the length of my nose. "How could he not?"

Again, I'm caught without words, shocked. Does he actually think Fredrick sought out that job to be near me? That he moved back for…? No—*no, no, no.* It's got to be sheer dumb luck our paths ever crossed again.

"Well," Beck sighs, "I look forward to meeting him."

Sort of sinister because if I'm not mistaken, that was the exact bit Fredrick said. Tommy taps on the window and waves a PlayStation controller at Beck from the family room.

Back inside, Tommy flashes me an apologetic smile. I know Beck's still annoyed with me because he's not saying much of anything. Not to me, anyway. When he eases down into the corner of the sofa, he swings his legs up onto the cushions and pulls me into his lap. Feel a bit better he still wants me close. I take my usual spot between his legs and lie back onto his stomach. He brings his arms around me and holds the controller on my chest. I can only watch so much *Grand Turismo* before my eyes get heavy. I nod off a few times but come to every time Tommy yells an expletive or Beck rapid fires on the controller.

I don't know how many races have passed, but I finally get brave and look up at him. "Will you take me upstairs?"

He doesn't look down or respond but pauses the game. He sets the controller aside, and I sit up.

"Be right back," he says to Tommy.

Tommy smiles at me. "Goodnight, pretty girl."

"Happy Easter, Tommy."

I walk ahead of him up the stairs. And I want to cry because his hands don't touch me once, and he can never not touch me when I walk in front of him, especially up the stairs.

He sits on the foot of the bed in his old room—*my room* when we stay the night out here—while I finish up in the bathroom. He doesn't say anything, and I have to peek out once to make sure he's still there.

I flip the light off in the bathroom, and he stands up, pulls the covers back, and I slide into bed. When he pulls the covers over me, I grab his hand, and he finally locks eyes with me. He's angry. I understand it. I look down at his hand and hold it with both of mine.

"I'm sorry I didn't tell you sooner."

"I know." He swallows. He leans down and kisses me quickly before leaving.

We never sleep together at his parents. He respects their wishes, and so do I, but I sure wish he were with me tonight. Nothing inappropriate either. We keep it PG-*ish* in the house. The front drive is a different story. Out front, in the back of his car, has seen all maturity ratings. Don't judge—sometimes we're out here for days on end, and desperation gets the best of us. I sort of feel like texting him now for a driveway rendezvous but text the girls back instead.

ROOMIE TRIO

Ella:

What time are we being evicted tomorrow?

Let's meet at 11.

Also that FUCKING gossip page has struck once again

Someone snagged a picture of me and F at Storey House

Ella:

Hold please.

I wait about ten seconds, if that.

Ella:

When I wake up on my own the next morning, I lose all hope that this row would resolve overnight. Beck always wakes up first, and he always comes and crawls into bed with me to get me up.

I tiptoe downstairs in my pajamas. His place on the couch is empty.

"Beck's out lifting," James says from the kitchen.

"Oh!" I say, startled.

I spin around, James is standing over the sink with a plate of carrot cake in hand.

"I should be out there with him." He shrugs. "But this cake was staring at me."

I smile and turn on my heel. *Lifting and getting his anger out, perhaps?* I walk through the foyer and pass by the study. Tommy's still out cold. I pass the stairs, heading for the utility room. I can hear the music before I turn the doorknob. I quickly step out onto the landing and close the door. One of the garage bays is half converted to a gym. The music's blaring. Beck bench presses a weight-stacked bar. I swallow because he's a specimen to behold, and he's mine. *Mine as long as I stop fucking it up.* No shirt, black sweatpants, his delicious muscles flexing with each rep. The bar clangs as he racks the weight. I step down onto the garage floor. He heaves himself up, and I curl my toes half due to the fact the floor is cold but half because he pulls his hat on backward and that makes me go mad inside. He sees me now, and his eyes burn into me.

He moves to the stereo and turns the music down. The muscles on his back appear even more pronounced with a layer of shiny sweat.

"Good morning," he says, turning around.

"You didn't wake me," I say nervously. "I would have come down here with you."

He makes his way over to me, and towers over my face. I try to read if he's still angry, but his eyes soften. He reaches down for my left leg and lifts it to his hip. I reach my hands around the back of his neck as he grabs my right leg and lifts me around his waist. He stares at my lips and starts walking until my back meets the wall. His breath is heavy, I squeeze my legs tighter around him and he brushes the tip of his nose against mine.

"Let's get out of here," he whispers.

CHAPTER 8
CHOCOLATE BUNNY

ELLA

MOVING OUT WASN'T SO bad, hardly lifted a finger, to be honest. George had hired hands and packers waiting for us. What we couldn't fit in suitcases, he's shipping to Paris. Shipping as in he's paying for it to be delivered within the next few days because why not? The expedited delivery is only quadruple the price. And yes, that includes the telly Carmen was going on about. It's one of those big, expensive ones that looks like a piece of framed art. I did lift a finger for the surprise pair of drawers that showed up when my bed was moved. Not sure if they were Henry's or Jack's, and how can that even be? They left the flat one night in just their trousers?

Soph and I came to Beck's after and have since been pillaging her Easter basket. Tommy's on the couch, halfway through a carrot-shaped bag of orange jellybeans. And no, it's not awkward because we aren't like that—we're friends, and we happened to have hooked up. Sophie giggles as she puts another tiny, speckled chocolate egg to Beck's lips. She's been giggling for ten minutes, perched up on the counter while he's between her legs, practically nose to nose with her. Thought they were fighting?

"You two are sick," I announce, though they don't notice.

"The sickest," Tommy agrees.

"And our fuckboy has a broken heart." I give him sad eyes and plop down next to him.

Not that I believe he actually has a heart. He's got a head. And I'm not talking about the one that's sat atop his neck. I'm talking about the one between his legs.

"Fuckboy?" he asks, annoyed. "Why do you call me that?"

"Not only did you bring up your ex whilst still naked in my bed, you then proceeded to talk about some fit sponsor you want to bang."

Tommy huffs a laugh. "Like you weren't texting three different guys that night at the bar."

"Like you don't have a little black book of blondes waiting for you on a rainy day!"

He rolls his easy little golden eyes at me.

"Since your heart's still broken, guess that means you didn't get lucky with her in Brazil?"

"I don't have a broken heart, okay?" he says, though his face says otherwise. "I'm just annoyed it had to be Imre. Not some footballer but my fucking archnemesis."

For half a second, I feel for him, but then it hits me like a rogue wave, and I suddenly realize the window of opportunity that's been opened. Holy. Fuck. It's my business mindset—always on, always churning. What's another iron in the fire? We could *both* benefit from his predicament.

I toss my hair over my shoulder and bat my eyelashes. I'm a witch, remember? I have many tricks. A good witch. "I reckon you could always stir up some rumors of your own."

"Like what?" he says unenthusiastically.

I put the cauldron on the fire and crack my knuckles, ready to stir.

"Next race—" I say, holding his gaze with my softest baby blues, the look I know pushes men to their knees, "show up with *me*."

Tommy lifts an eyebrow. Beck looks over his shoulder.

"You can appear unbothered by the new...*coupling*, and I—well, I can shut my dad up about dating." I shrug as if that's truly my aim.

"Wait—" Sophie stops feeding Beck. "You mean pretend to be together?"

Tommy's slowly nodding his head, as if it's something to consider. "It's not the worst idea I've ever heard."

I could jump, but I keep my cool. Forget maintaining relevancy, this is aiming for the bloody stratosphere. Me? A WAG? *It's brilliant.*

"You will never pull that off!" Sophie giggles.

"How's that?" I fire back defensively. "The lovebirds' best mates fall for one another? It's such an easy sell! Besides, I saw how it all works in Melbourne."

Tommy's lit up now, nibbling at the bait. "Youse can hang out in the paddock, stay with each other. But you'll obviously watch from our garage."

"And what about your parents? You're going to lie to them?" Sophie asks him.

"They won't be at any races until after break."

He's playing ball. I'll keep control of the spoon for now in this brew I'm stirring up.

"I'll tell Mum, Carmen, Oliver—but that's it! No one else outside of this room can know." I lock eyes with Sophie. "You can't tell Ana!"

Her brow furrows. "And what about your bench?"

"I'll have to do some reshuffling of the seats."

"You can't have an active bench and a boyfriend!"

"Fine!" I snap. "I'll alert the bench that they've been put on temporary leave."

I do have drinks on the books with Colin when we return to Paris, but that can be sorted.

"Hold up." Tommy lifts his hand. "How many bros are on this bench?"

"Six in rotation at the minute," I proudly provide.

His eyes go wide.

"But that covers two countries, depending on my location! Two here, four in Paris, but that's beside the point."

He shakes his head, eyes still wide.

"I go to a lot of events, okay?"

He sniffs. "Do you even like these guys?"

"I like them alright, but they're just—friends."

"With benefits?"

I smirk. "A girl's gotta eat, Tommy."

Beck throws his head back, laughing. Tommy's head shakes once again. Not sure why, I have needs, and God forbid a man provide one useful thing every now and then.

Tommy rubs his temples like I'm forcing him to use his brain. "How will this work then?"

I actually jump to my feet now. The deal is being sealed!

"When's the next race?" I ask, trying to keep my voice calm.

"No soft launch?" Beck interjects.

"Fuck a soft launch." Tommy flicks his hand. "We've got Jeddah next week, then Barcelona."

I look to Sophie for confirmation. The brew in the cauldron is near bubbling.

"I'll be at Barcelona," she says, awfully quiet, unsure of this scheme.

"We'll go hard in Barcelona then!" Brew is at a full boil. I move my hands to my hips. "Now, in the meantime…" I ponder a beat, but it hits me quite fast. "Take off your shirt."

"Woah, girl!" Beck says.

"Why?" Tommy snorts.

"Trust me!"

He eyes me suspiciously but nonetheless, lifts his shirt off over his head. Taking instruction is something he'll need to get used to—and fast. I march to the counter and pluck the massive foil-wrapped chocolate bunny centerpiece from Sophie's basket.

"That's mine!" she cries.

"I'll get you another one." Beck pulls her back against him.

I peel open the foil and retake my seat next to a shirtless Tommy. I scoot closer, come up under his arm and lean back against him. I flip my phone to selfie mode, the perfect amount of his fit chest and telling markings behind me. Fragments of the cuff tattoo on his bicep, and the cupid and compass on his chest frame around me. I bite down on the bunny ear and snap a photo.

Genius. I sit up and sink my teeth into the chocolate.

"See? Perfect!" I say, mouth full.

"You can't see my face!" Tommy scowls.

"*Exactly.* It's just enough to get people talking. It will take no time at all for someone to recognize that chest."

Sophie runs over for a look. "You're putting that on Instagram?!"

"Not *in feed*—that would be terribly thirsty. It's proper story crumbs. Now put your shirt back on."

"Why?" Tommy smirks. "Too distracting?"

I slap his bare stomach and throw his shirt at his head. He grabs the chocolate bunny from me and bites off the other ear. I throw some cheeky text over the photo and add it to my story.

"You know, to pull this off"—Beck pulls Sophie back against him and rests his chin on top of her head—"you'll have to act like you actually get on with each other."

"*Easy*. Do you know who my mother is? I've watched her craft the most believable PR relationships for years."

Head witch, Alice Humphrey, crafts impeccable brews, that one.

Tommy pokes my ribs. "You have to be nice to me. Follow me around and shit."

I roll my eyes. "I'll be nice—when it's convenient for me."

And you best believe I'll make it convenient every chance I get. As annoying as it will be, acting like some lovestruck fool, these are unparalleled attention opportunities.

"And if you're interviewed about him?" Sophie asks.

"I know his record." I shrug. "Four seasons, all raced with MACH. Four podiums, zero wins."

"Ouch!" Beck says.

Tommy looks floored.

"What?!" I say with attitude, a bit offended by his shock at my knowledge. "I do my research."

He's meant to be a prodigy—racing's in his family. He won the Formula 3 championship, came second to Beck in Formula 2, and is still waiting for his breakthrough in Formula 1.

"Birthday is December third," I continue.

"How do you know that?" he asks as if I just recited his password.

"The internet, you twat! What's my birthday then?"

He narrows his eyes as if in deep thought, then confidently blurts out, "*July*!"

"August." I blink, unimpressed. "Second. Let's see about a softball then, something more up your alley." I puff my chest out and meet his eyes. "What's my cup size?"

Beck snorts.

Tommy's eyes flip from my face to my chest and back in rapid succession. "Your *boobs*?"

I nod encouragingly.

He licks his lips, brings his hands out in front of him and starts gripping the air, like he's cupping some invisible floating tits.

I swat his wrist.

"What? I'm trying to remember!" He flips his finger under the bottom hem of my baby tee and nods his chin at me. "Lemme see them again."

"Fuck off!" I smack his hand away. "They weren't memorable?"

"Oh, baby girl—they were memorable," he says, running his tongue over his teeth.

"I guess when you've seen a hundred pairs..." I say, exasperated. Hundred pairs, hell, a thousand pairs, and I'm confident mine qualify top three! Just look at them!

He winks. "Send me a picture later for the wank bank."

"The what?" Sophie lifts an eyebrow.

Beck snorts another laugh.

"Ah! Innocence is *such* bliss." I push up off the couch.

"This should be a riot," Beck laughs.

I walk into the bathroom and close the door. Sometimes I surprise myself with my own genius. I snap a screenshot of my Instagram story and open the *Lights Out Ladies* gossip page. In my profile settings, I click the pencil next to the username field and think for a moment.

Paddock_Insider, that will do. Hit save to lock in my adjustment, and on the main feed, I upload the screenshot of my story:

Well, well, well...what do we have here?

CHAPTER 9
FORK, KNIFE & SPOON

SOPHIE

I'VE ALWAYS BEEN GOOD at yoga—the moves, anyway. The mind-body connection and being content thing, not so much. Especially when I've got something heavy on my mind like is it even remotely possible that a baby could be growing in my stomach? My period's always been predictable, so why is it choosing to be elusive this month? I know the added panic isn't helping. How many times do we girls convince ourselves we've fallen pregnant? When I was nauseous all day yesterday, I brushed it off. The cream I used in my tea must have been bad. Now, I'm not so sure. I did switch contraceptive brands, and there were those two days I took late. My bridesmaid's dress is quite fitted. It would never hide the belly I would have in a few months' time. Not to mention I'm to walk in a Beurre bikini at the start of June—and we definitely didn't cater to any form of maternity style. We've been on a Lagree kick, which is hard as hell, so I was relieved when Carmen signed us up for good old-fashioned yoga this morning. I made the decision on the mat—mid camatkarasana—buy a test after class and shut my mind up once and for all.

On the footpath, two steps behind Carmen and Ella, I add the test to my online cart. I can't go into a store and buy it; someone might see, as

I've been reminded that eyes are always on me. It's far too early to take one, but I checkout for delivery anyway. I pick up the pace and fall in line beside Carmen.

"Do you think it wise to involve yourself in a love triangle?" Carmen asks.

"It's not a love triangle!" Ella scoffs. "It's a revenge plot. Having me on his arm will help him get over Emma," she says, all sure of herself. "And for once, maybe Alston will be pleased with me."

"Since when do you care what your dad thinks?" Carmen asks, taking the words straight out of my mouth.

"You're sure you want to offer yourself up as this season's sacrificial lamb?" I add.

Ella flicks her hand. "I can handle it."

That I believe. I was a fish out of water, and my relationship was real.

"Are you going to bed him again?" Carmen asks mockingly.

"That was one time—I was hungry, and he gave me my fill," she says, elbowing her. "No bedroom benefits of a real girlfriend."

"And when you get hungry again?" Carmen teases.

"I'll feed myself," she snaps.

I link arms with Carmen, who is as much a skeptic of this plan working as I am.

"All I'm saying is—two fire signs fake dating?" She snorts a laugh. "It's destined for disaster!"

I can't help but smile. Ella hates when Carmen starts talking astrology.

"You're a knife, he's a knife," she continues.

"Come again?" Ella says, stopping in the middle of the walk.

Reasonable reaction. I haven't heard cutlery terms used in her astrological explanations before.

"Everyone is either a knife, a fork or a spoon," Carmen explains. "Me, for example, I'm the comfort in our group, the nurturing one, the spoon! You—you're the knife."

Two knives? *Does sound dangerous.*

Ella narrows her eyes. "And what TikTok rabbit hole of bullshit did you pull that from?"

CHAPTER 10
OUR BOYFRIENDS ARE FIGHTING

ELLA

I CANCELED DRINKS WITH Colin and put the rest of the bench on hold. Yes, it took a load of calls and one house call. Adrien was the house call, but I made him come to me to pick up the few things he left in my room the last time we had our clothes off. I told each of them I was trying the exclusive dating thing out. Henry gave me a look over FaceTime like I'd just fed him the biggest load of bullshit because I quite literally had. Colin asked if hell had frozen over, to which I said hell is most definitely still on fire, and I'd be back on the scene in no time. I gave Adrien a wee pat on the cheek when he tried to kiss me because as far as the world knows—or will know—I am exclusively dating Tommy Young.

There's a delivery boy holding the door open for me as I come back inside. He heads to Pierre's desk with a small brown bag. I hop up the first two steps and stop when I hear him speak. The delivery is bound for our apartment. I spin around and traipse back down the stairs because I'm feeling nice.

"*Bonjour!* 403?" I smile at him.

He stares and nods slowly, dumbfounded by my beauty, most likely.

"I'll save you the trip up." I wink.

I snatch the bag and head for the stairs. When I turn on the first landing, Mr. Delivery's still staring. My backside's exquisite. I continue up, now out of sight, and inspect the bag. It's got Sophie's name on the receipt; whatever's inside came from the pharmacy. I walk up one more landing then carefully bend back the arms of the staple securing the bag. I take a peek inside and freeze.

A pregnancy test stares back at me.

Usually, the sight of a pregnancy test brings on that awful anxious energy, especially if you're the one needing it. It's not anxiety I'm feeling at the minute, the longer I stare at it, the more hurt I feel. Don't get me wrong, this is a her problem, but a her problem her best friend would very much appreciate being briefed on, nonetheless. I've had my share of scares, Carmen as well, but Sophie hasn't mentioned anything. I wonder if she's confided in Ana? Those two have gotten incredibly close. Ana's put her in her bloody wedding, for God's sake. *My* best friend. How dare she not tell me something like this! I've always been her first call, but she's got Ana now, and she has Beck. Maybe she doesn't need me like she once did.

I start to close the bag, but stop, peering down the stairs to make sure no one is coming. The angel on my shoulder jolts awake, rubbing her eyes. I reach inside the bag, pull out the test and take a picture of it on top of the receipt. A door slams shut. I drop the test back inside and quickly bend the staple ends, securing the bag closed once again. My heart's already racing, but I take off up the stairs. When I push inside, Sophie's practically in the doorway.

"All good with Adrien?" she asks all doe-eyed and happy.

"Yeah—" I pant, catching my breath. "I mean, heartbroken of course...this was just delivered!" I say, holding the bag out to her. "Saved you a trip up the stairs."

Since I can't go out for drinks with anyone, I might as well support my fake boyfriend. Carmen pops the cork on a bottle of red. I bring three glasses down from the cupboard.

"None for me," Sophie says.

I stop and study her.

"No wine?" Carmen asks, oblivious.

"Why, love?" I gently interrogate.

"I think I'll make a tea instead." Sophie jumps up from the couch. "The wine will make me fall asleep!"

I watch her fill the kettle. It's been hours, and she still hasn't said anything. I wonder if she's taken the test. Carmen hands me a Carmen-sized pour. A mix of bevvies for qualifying then!

Jeddah is a night race, a floodlit track with loads of squiggles. Thanks to George, our telly from the flat arrived and has since been installed. Much better setup than watching on a laptop.

Sophie and Carmen are laser focused on the qualifying broadcast. I'm focused-ish, but I'm also using the time for a wee bit of research in preparation for Barcelona. I switch profiles to my finsta and navigate to Emma's Instagram. She now has three in-feed pictures with Imre. The latest is from his hometown, Berlin. I click through her story, quite basic if you ask me. I click back to rewatch her attempt an aesthetic lip gloss application bit—she's got the *#ad* in the corner and everything.

"Does Emma have a deal with BASE?"

Sophie's eyes remain on the broadcast. "Who's that?" she asks, distracted.

"Fylter's main competitor in the clean beauty space."

"Are they now?"

"Yes." *And you should know that.*

Her eyes finally leave the screen. "Stuart said Fylter's picking their ambassadors soon! I do love their stuff."

And at the sheer mention of the ambassadorship coming from her lips, the devil on my shoulder is busy calling our banners. I swallow. The Fylter deal is *mine*. I want to be the face, the exclusive. I deserve it. Knowing more than the most basic data on the competitive landscape shows my seriousness for this business. And my deservedness.

The quickest fifteen have made it to round two of qualifying—the usual suspects. I fling Emma's grid way back to the early Tommy days. She posted him a lot. And then I see my face. A group picture taken last year at the angels and demons party. Tommy's arm is around her waist, his other arm around my neck. The three of us are standing front and center in the photo, all dressed in white. The only time I ever met her. We got on alright, didn't end the night as besties or anything.

Carmen glances down at my phone. "Are people still asking about your picture?"

"All going perfectly according to plan." I smile, bringing the wine to my lips.

My covert post on the site went absolutely *bananas*. It wasn't five minutes before someone commented:

"I spy Tommy Young's chest! I know every tat!"

Story replies flooded my DMs. I've strategically declined to answer a single thing about the status of Tommy's and my *whatever-ship*. I'm waiting to give a big, bold dramatic answer—the hard launch that he wanted. I pull up the gossip site and open the post to check the latest:

"This is starting to look like a nothingburger...Ella isn't at the race."

I pull my phone in closer and type a quick reply:

Neither is Sophie, hardly any of the WAGs are there.

In the main feed, I'm in another post. This one's a picture of us moving.

"Mayfair move out! Why are the girls abandoning Sophie's flat?"

I skim the speculation in the comments, people making up all sorts of things, and add my own comment:

It's not 'Sophie's flat' her dad owns it.

Carmen gasps. I flick my eyes up to the screen.

> **"And a big brush with the wall on the exit of the final turn! Tommy Young narrowly escaping an incident at turn 27!"**

His lap clocks in, Tommy's name moves up to eighth.
"Will Beck have enough time to go again?" Carmen asks.

"Yes, he's on an outlap." Sophie sips the last of her tea then goes back to subconsciously spinning the diamond bracelet around her wrist.

My phone buzzes. Someone's replied to my comment:

"Paddock insider? Prove it."

Tisk tisk, *don't tempt me, people*. Fine. Baby crumb. I check the girls' status, still locked in on the broadcast, so my fingers start flying:

Barcelona is set to be an eventful affair! All signs point to Ella Humphrey making her paddock debut with Tommy at the Spanish Grand Prix. In addition, you might spot a familiar face in the C-suite of MACH's newest sponsor. A blast from a certain WAG's not-so-distant past.

Why, you ask, am I acting like an animal? I'm not sure I have a straight answer at the minute. I set my phone down. Two minutes are left in Q2, and Tommy's fallen to the drop zone in P12.

"Let's go onboard with Beckham Wright as he's set to start a flying lap. We've got loads of traffic on track in these final moments of the session. The track is gripping up more and more every lap, and we have loads of late runners waiting for the last running window. Beck's sitting P10, but on a fresh set of rubber for his final flying lap.

And we've got a yellow flag! Sector one!"

"Who?" Carmen squeals.

"It's Tommy!" Sophie says, grabbing my wrist.

The broadcast hovers over the track. His car is crawling—the left end of his front wing is in pieces. A white car is across the track in the wall.

"My word! That's Imre!" she says, her fingers pressing to her lips.

"No way!"

Tommy splits, abandoning parts of wing on the track. Beck steers through the debris and trails behind him. Sophie's hands come over her face. The yellow flag's gone red.

A Furio team radio message displays on the broadcast.

"Abort."

WRI: "F***** hell! What is it?"

"Debris on track turn 5 and 6."

WRI: "Are we through?"

"Negative."

WRI: *"****!!!!!!"*

Carmen groans. "Beck is out then?"

"And it's confirmed! Ian's lap did clock in just before the flag, so that lap will stand. And it was enough for P10! That late yellow flag brings heavy consequences for our back-to-back race winner. Beckham Wright finds himself out in Q2 in Jeddah! Missing out on the top ten shootout for the first time this season!"

"They both are," Sophie confirms. "Tommy's out, as well as Alek, Imre, and Antione." She blows out a breath. "At least Luca made it through."

"Let's replay—we've got Tommy on a cooldown lap, Imre on a flier. And something goes awry as he reaches the high-speed section after turn 3...yes...Imre botches turn 4, loses the racing line into the blind corners at turn 5 where Tommy was. Could have been much worse; he just clips Tommy's end plate before putting it into the wall."

Imre's walking away from the scene unharmed while his car's being removed from the barrier. Marshals are scanning the track, picking up any remaining debris. The broadcast flips to the pitlane, where the remaining contenders wait in their garages. Then the cameras focus on the eliminated drivers—up and out of their cars. Tommy takes off his helmet and waits for an approaching Beck, but as he reaches out to put his hand on Beck's shoulder, Beck shoves it away. Sophie's eyes go wide, and she closes her lips.

"Oh! And a moment there between best mates! Beck's obviously frustrated with that result."

"Our boyfriends are fighting!" I shriek.

"You sure you don't want any?" Carmen says, tipping her glass to Sophie.

The cameras relentlessly follow them.

"Let's see if we can hear from our surprise Q2 exits."

"Beck, can you describe that moment between you and Tommy?"

Beck doesn't stop, but the man with the microphone keeps up with him.

"It's frustrating—" he sighs. "I'm trying to fight for a championship, and you see it. It's always something with those two."

"Do you feel confident you can make up ground tomorrow?"

"Starting P11?" he says, exasperated. "I mean there's always a chance for a safety car around here—I'll do my best."

He walks off, and the cameras catch Tommy.

"Tommy, can you tell us what you said to Beck when he sort of brushed you off there—"

"It's all good, mate. I get it." Tommy shrugs. "He's not ready to hear anything."

"What happened out there with Imre? We saw the wheel banging that happened between the two of you in Melbourne, the scraps you had multiple times last year—"

"This circuit's tight. We're used to issues with traffic during quali. But I couldn't have been further off the racing line. Knowing Imre, he was driving with his eyes closed? But I'm sure he'll say I was impeding or some shit."

"Well, good luck out there tomorrow."

After the girls have gone to bed, I open my window and climb out onto the roof. You've got to be careful coming out here when you've had a drink, and when Carmen's played sommelier, you're in for it. Countless times I've dropped my phone, and it's nearly slipped over the edge. I hold on to it with a death grip and secure my secret fix behind the loose brick.

Alright?

Tommy:

I'm good.

Front wing got clipped by that fucking halfwit.

You and Beck okay?

He was heated

All good now, baby girl

<3

You watch?

Oui

<3

Ready for hard launch?

I was born ready

CHAPTER 11
MONZA WITH WALLS

SOPHIE

I KNOW YOU'RE WONDERING—THE test was negative. I'm not overly convinced, however, because after I took it, I read that the most accurate results are taken right when you wake up. I took mine in the late afternoon. Having slept on it, I'm tempted to order another and take it tomorrow morning. I've got to know before next weekend. It's Beck's birthday.

The birthday plans? A family party at his parents' house. The puppies are standing, taking a few wobbly steps before they fall over. Pirelli was the first to walk. *That's my boy* was Beck's response in the group chat. I want to make his birthday special, but I also know he wouldn't want anything big or remotely over the top. Thus, Elizabeth and I landed on a family puppy party with loads of pudding. My birthday was a perfect low-key weekend. Beck told me to pack a bag and drove me out to a little cottage he rented near Tintagel Castle. Loads of snuggling and snogging and—*yes*. Like I said, low-key until he pulled out the flawless two-carat diamond earrings. He's got good taste.

The family party includes Tommy. He'll be at HQ anyway, and I want to drag Ella there because it's been a minute since their little plan came about, and perhaps they're due for a warm-up before their debut in Spain.

Another reason I need to figure things out and why I am adding another test to my cart.

Everything between the boys is sorted, but of course the cameras weren't around for Beck's apology to Tommy. He finally rang me last night, hours after qualifying, still upset and still sure his weekend was blown. But he's Beckham Wright, and tonight he's picking cars off one by one. At the start, he passed Ian for tenth into turn one. Then three cars ahead of him took themselves out in the chaos of the sector one corners. Not even half a lap in, he was up from eleventh to seventh when the red flags waved. Since the safety car ended, it's been carnage for the remaining 44 of 50 high-speed laps under the floodlights. *Monza with walls* they keep calling it, and these walls are *tight*—like Singapore claustrophobic tight. It doesn't faze Beck; he continues to push the car to the absolute limit, overtaking at every opportunity. What's truly mad was seeing the Furio team order to swap the cars come through. Luca couldn't close the gap to the Makellos ahead, after the gap continued to increase, the call was made to let Beck pass and attack further up the grid.

"Another day at the office for Beckham Wright! An unbelievable comeback! He started eleventh, and he will complete the podium!

...The pendulum has swung in Valor's favor! With a one-two here in Jeddah, they take over the lead of the constructor's championship! And Leo's finally taking a bite out of Beck's championship lead.

It's third place for Furio's second seat, and maybe it's time to drop that label when referring to Beck—a changing of the guard may be underway at Furio HQ!"

Beckham Wright - *Furio*	65
Leo VanBelle - *Valor Racing*	50
Elijah Kaplan - *Valor Racing*	42
Geoffrey Hahn - *Makellos*	38
Ren Enatsu - *Makellos*	37
Tommy Young - *MACH*	18
Eduardo Almada - *Avanti Racing*	13
Luca Lombardo - *Furio*	12
Aleksandr Kholodov - *MACH*	9
Imre Bergmann - *HOLT Motorsport*	8
Qian Liu - *Avanti Racing*	6
Ian Matisse - *HOLT Motorsport*	3
Wit Nowak - *Noorden*	2
Antoine Auclair -*Trueno GP*	0
Gordon Whitlock -*Noorden*	0
Sanjay Patel - *Trueno GP*	0
Mateo Barrera - *ETHER*	0
Amir Bishara - *Force5*	0
Julien Baker – *Force5*	0
Cameron Christiansen - *ETHER*	0

It's a bit overwhelming seeing his name at the top of the standings. He finished sixth in the championship last year, and even with today's disappointment, he's still got a healthy lead. What's even crazier is seeing Luca's name so low after clinching third in last year's championship behind only the Valors.

Beck:

Can you do me a favor?

Yes?

I've got a shoot next week for a piece in Dish.

Will you come?

Dish magazine. They're notorious for their bare-chested athlete covers and spreads. The magazine every housewife stops their trolley for in the Sainsbury checkout.

I will be there.

Someone's got to keep your clothes on.

Clothes on. Check.

"Three races, three podiums."

Something like that…

Wish it were three races, three wins.

Quite the stellar record, love

<3

Also, change of plans for my birthday

Told Mum and Dad we won't be coming out

My brow furrows as he types another message.

Pippa and Luca have requested our presence at the baptism

A smile takes over my frown.

Lake Como.

Pack your bags xx

CHAPTER 12

JOHN SUMMIT

ELLA

CELESTE IS TECHNICALLY THE boss, but we all know who keeps the lights on around here.

"Tommy Young?" she asks again in disbelief.

I fan out my fingers. Surely there's time for a mani today. "That's right," I say coolly.

Her eyes pinch, she licks her lips. "And we don't expect that to garner any negative attention?"

I huff. "Any negative attention it would receive is well worth it."

Celeste is my rep at the agency. My *Stuart*, if you will—far more superior though, of course. She's the best of the best but has always had a play-it-safe attitude. As you can imagine, I often push her limits. I've worked with her for years, which also means she knows me—not certain she's buying my falling in love since our last one-on-one. Across the desk, she crosses her arms. Make that definitely not buying it.

"Have we heard any more from Fylter then?" I say, moving to more pressing matters.

"*Very interested*—still taking their time picking their ambassadors."

"Is there a timeline for the announcement?" I ask, attempting to hide the desperation in my voice.

"Not yet. You'll know when I know."

I find that insanely annoying. *Just pick me.* What are they waiting for?

"Have they had any feedback?" I pry.

"You continue to impress them. Your videos are a guaranteed success across the board for views, reach, engagement—it hasn't gone unnoticed."

That's right. That's what I offer. And that's why brands pay top dollar. As I said, Sophie goes days without posting—I go hours. If I'm not posting, I'm not showing up for work. And the term *showing up for work* is a complete misrepresentation of my work ethic. I go above and beyond. When I'm gifted an outfit, at the very least I'll post it in a story. The attention that story receives? *They're hooked.* An offer rolls in shortly thereafter. When I link the items in my outfit—a skirt, for example—it's guaranteed to sell out. Every size, every color. And when I post links for similar styles, those sell out too. The days of massive marketing teams are over. Hand your product to an influencer like me, and I will reach one hundredfold what your whole team could.

Celeste slides an iPad across the desk.

"The contract I need you to look at is time-sensitive. *Le Laboratoire* has brought forth an oppy to host a class with an instructor for the grand opening of the new studio. I mentioned it to Stuart, I don't know if you want to do this with Sophie or—"

"No! I can do it!" I interject. "She's quite busy, and well, I've been cheating on yoga with Lagree prepping for Miami."

I flip through the contract. It's not a lie; she's headed to London for Beck's shoot with *Dish Magazine,* and when that wraps, it's wheels up to Italy for the royal baptism.

"Well, then"—Celeste starts typing—"they want to start with one session, and if it fills up with plenty of demand, there's an opportunity to add a second."

Come on, Celeste.

I set down the iPad and scoot it back to her. "Add a second and see if they want a third."

I hit the street and ring Carmen to meet me for nails. Ollie's home for once, taking a break from the DJ globetrotting. I miss him terribly. Is it weird I consider Carmen's boyfriend one of my best friends? He's been briefed on the revenge dating scheme but was no doubt three sheets to the wind when Carmen laid it all out in front of him. I'm no expert in the world of motorsport, but I did grow up with an annoyingly fanatic older brother. I know this much: MACH is known to be a top-tier team, and their performance this season is looking quite midfield. Recall Tommy's aforementioned record I brilliantly recited from his previous three seasons. His record so far this year? Well, that's a him problem, not a me problem. He finished eighth at his home race and eighth again in Jeddah, while Alek, his teammate, snagged the final point in tenth. The best finish MACH's had this season was Tommy's fifth place in Brazil. It's giving—*we can do better.* Don't roll your eyes—I'm no halfwit who thinks I can affect the outcome of a race. I'm just saying, maybe with me on his arm, Tommy's confidence will get a boost.

This nail salon isn't the most aesthetic, but it's the best Russian manicure I've ever found. If there's one thing I gatekeep from my followers, it's the name of this place. Don't ask, I won't tell you either. I would gladly blast this establishment's name, but I don't for selfish reasons, for the fear I'd never again be able to walk in without an appointment whenever I please. I pull my hand back to scroll on my phone. The comments and questions are still showing up everywhere—on my posts, on story replies, in my DMs. *Are you hooking up with Tommy Young? Where's Tommy? Are you and Tommy just friends?* It's been rather hard keeping my mouth shut and not giving so much as another crumb. Has this felt like a hurry up and wait scenario to you? Well how the fuck do you think I feel! Only a few days more before I can finally show up and show out on media day.

Even with my back to the door, I know they've arrived from the sudden giggle-filled clumsy commotion.

"Oi!" Ollie calls. He comes behind me and plants a kiss on the top of my head. I watch him saunter by, high as a kite—eyes half open, walking like the ground is coated in honey.

"What have you been doing?" I roll my eyes.

He winks at me then falls back into a pedicure chair.

Carmen pulls the seat out next to me. "Can I get what she's having, please?"

"A Russian," I clarify. "Testing what I want to get for the paddock."

"You going to do orange?"

"Absolutely not!" I study her, lower my voice. "Are you stoned?"

Carmen giggles and looks over at Ollie. "Not like he is."

I scoot my phone down the bench with the link pulled up. "I'm hosting two sessions for *Le Laboratoire* this week." I nod down at the screen. "Sign up before I mass blast it."

I've got the perfect butter-yellow set from alo I'll save for the opening. Ollie rolls up his trousers then melts back into the chair. He roughs up his fluffy blond hair then drags a hand down his face.

"Well then, Ollie, tell me about Music Week."

"It was sick." He half grins, eyes heavy. "Went to SPACE for twelve hours on the last day."

Space the nightclub, not outer space. Although if you ask him, whatever he ingested most likely did get him in touch with outer space.

"Was hungover for about three days after."

I toss him an unimpressed look. He lowers his feet into the bubbly foot bath.

"You could probably use a yoga class or two," I say, eyebrow up. "Dry you out a bit."

"Sign me up, babe," he sighs. "A steam room, a hyperbaric chamber, an IV drip, a fuckin' juice cleanse—sign me up for all of it."

It is a bit of a medical miracle he's alive. Imagine Beck and Tommy's schedule, but replace the racing and racetracks with endless nightclubs, appearances and back-to-back all-nighters, all fueled by alcohol and whatever other substances are around.

"How was it then, professionally?" I ask, sounding a bit more parental than I meant to.

"Great networking. Met loads of people."

"Have you managed to get me John Summit's number yet?"

Carmen swats my wrist. "Ella, you've got a boyfriend now."

Ollie snorts. "How's that?"

"Keep up, babe!" Carmen scolds, raising her eyebrows. "We talked about this."

His eyes pinch and slowly his head starts to nod. "*Righhhhht.* Ella locked down the Aussie."

I wink at him. What's that the girlies say? *"I'd climb John Summit?"* Think I saw it on a hat once. I wouldn't wear the hat, but I would indeed take a climb.

"Boyfriend or not, he's a hall pass! Keep working."

Ollie salutes me, then closes his eyes.

"And when we're in Miami, we can nip off to the clubs one night," I say, holding up a finger. "And only after our work is done. I'm depending on you to not go full-on shit show before then."

Carmen laughs.

Fucking hell. I sound like an anal bitch on a power trip—but someone's got to keep him in line. He cannot fuck around with the Beurre op, and Carmen's quite literally the most chilled girlfriend that's ever existed.

He closes his eyes again, a cheeky grin spreading across his face. "I will be on my best behavior, Mum."

Ollie pays because he's a doll like that. When we hit the footpath, he takes the middle spot and slings his arms over our shoulders. "What's next, loves?" he asks, looking from me to Carmen then back at me. "Shall we crash out in Pierre Hermé?"

Fuck. I love him.

CHAPTER 13
YOU AND ME, KID

SOPHIE

HAVE YOU EVER CRIED in the Burberry on New Bond? No? Well, have you ever held a newborn onesie in the Burberry on New Bond while menstruating? That's right, my period finally showed up. On set with *Dish Magazine*. Annoying timing, but I've never been more relieved to see it. Every test I took was negative—three in total. Stressing myself to a pulp about it obviously wasn't helping, but nonetheless, I am not with child.

There were no shots of Beck completely shirtless, by the way. There was a bit of skin for one side shot where he pulled up the edge of his shirt. That cut muscle that traces down his hip and leads beyond his waistband and jeans—*mm-hmm, that one*—it was heavily in focus. My favorite photos, however, were the close-up headshots, not really even headshots because he had his helmet on. They were more like *eyeshots*. Let me tell you about his eyes when he flips up the visor on his helmet—*my word*. There's something magical about them, the way they twinkle? The way they smile? I adore his entire face, but well, you remember what his eyes do to me.

They say don't go to the grocer's hungry. I say don't go baby gift shopping whilst on your period. The Burberry shopping assistant thinks I'm mad. It started when I set the newborn check sneakers in the palm of my hand, she rushed over with the tiny check cuff socks, and I bloody cried. Had to get both. Then I picked up the tiny check cotton jumpsuit, the white check trim playsuit and the check alpaca wool silk blend cardigan in case baby Luca gets cold. I couldn't pass by the baby calico check label joggers and matching jumper, so I grabbed those too for when he's a bit bigger. Also picked up one of their cotton hoodies for Beck, and because I know I'll end up naked in it at some point this weekend. Now, it's all being gift-packaged in perfect mocha boxes with ribbon.

I decide to walk to the flat after because the weather isn't particularly dreadful, and I'm right here anyway. Dad is supposedly there, overseeing some work being done. I use my key and let myself in. It's loud, with multiple conversations and tools running. The place is unrecognizable and reeks of paint. Sheets of tarp cover every inch of the floor, plastic covers the windows. I round the corner and Dad's standing with his hands on his hips, watching an electrician on a ladder fiddle with a light on the ceiling. A painter is walking on some mad-looking stilts, rolling a wall in the living room with a fresh coat of white.

"*Ahem*," I say, trying to announce my presence carefully. I don't want to be the cause of a fall.

"Darling!" Dad says, turning to me. He moves his glasses to his head and pulls me and all my bags against him.

"You do some damage on New Bond?"

"Just Burberry." I shrug, slowly scanning the room. Rather astonishing, seeing the flat empty like this. The place I spent all of university, all the years at my first (and only) big girl job, the place I called home up until last year when we moved part time to Paris.

"When's the move-in then?" I ask, attempting to shake the weird feeling I was starting to get.

"Hopefully next week." He smiles. "As soon as the painting's finished, I've got a professional cleaning crew coming to really scrub the place."

Scrub? *Rude.*

"Right—got to get out all our germs," I say sarcastically.

He lifts a brow. "I know who your roommates are. Ella's bathroom will take them a day, at least!"

I try to squash my smile. *Touché.* I mean, Carmen's been with Ollie for forever, and her makeshift bedroom? That's a lot of sex in what's meant to be a proper dining room. Don't get me started on what germs live in Ella's old lair. Maybe it's the current stage of my cycle, but I'm a bit sad. Sort of feel like I'm being pushed out of the nest, like another of the few remaining strings tethering Dad and me together has been cut. Sort of scary, now that I think of it—only my cellphone remains under his name, and only one of my credit cards still routes back to him. I'm almost properly grown-up!

I adore Northern Italy—I mean, all of Italy is brilliant but spending Beck's birthday in an Italian villa on the lake? Took a flurry of last-minute planning on my part, how we could celebrate, and he will be over the moon with what I've planned for him tomorrow.

Today, however, is the baptism of Luca Giovanni Lombardo, and it may as well be a historic event. The dress code alone is gala-worthy. Tuxedos, gowns, fascinators—and it's a madhouse of paparazzi outside. Beck holds our gift box under one arm and me in the other, weaving through the gathered crowd outside what must be a million-year-old stone duomo.

Massive wooden doors are parted for us at the top of the steps. Inside, the pews are already filling in. Beck checks his phone, pockets it, then leads me to an interior door. Beyond it, you can hear a pin drop. My heels click on the stone floor as we proceed down a dim hallway. Beck slows before an open door and peers inside. That's when I see Pippa. Dressed to the nines, her eyes are closed as she rocks a tiny cocoon in her arms.

"Brother!" Luca's voice booms.

Pippa's eyes fly open, and her smile illuminates the room. She rises from the chair and floats over to me in a silk floral masterpiece that's got to be Dolce & Gabbana. Ella would know. Behind her, a long intricate baptismal gown lies on the table.

Luca and Beck aggressively embrace—the way boys do.

"My word! You look gorgeous!" I say, kissing her cheeks.

"It's lovely to see you," she says, voice low. "I'm so glad you could make it."

She tilts the cocoon away from her chest and proudly states, "This is Luca."

And in her arms, she's holding what might be the most beautiful baby I've ever seen. Have you ever seen a 1000 percent Italian baby? Perfect olive skin and a load of jet-black hair, he has. Beck's arm comes around me, and his face lights up.

"Do you want to hold him?" Pippa says.

"I can hold him?" I squeak.

I take a seat in the chair she was sat at, and she lowers baby Luca into my arms. I've never held a baby this tiny, this new. He squirms a little, and his hand pokes out of the swaddle. His eyelids open softly, and his glassy eyes match his hair, dark and lovely like Luca's.

"Hello there," I whisper. I slowly move my index finger against his hand, and he weakly hooks three of his fingers around it. *And it absolutely breaks me.* My bottom lip starts to quiver.

I look up at Pippa through teary eyes. "He's so handsome!"

"You're in trouble, Beck!" Luca says, slapping him on the back.

"Oh dear, I am," Beck says, stepping toward me. "My turn."

Pippa helps with the transfer, and I all but die at the sight of Beck standing there rocking his arms while Baby Luca stares up at him.

"Hello, little man." Beck smiles. "I drive alongside your daddy."

"Well ahead of him lately, Beck," Pippa chimes. "You've been driving like a madman!"

Beck can't take his eyes off the baby. "And who do you think I've learned all that from?"

Luca's beaming.

Baby Luca starts to fuss, and Beck begins swaying to soothe him. "Hush now! He'll teach you too."

I didn't know it was possible to love him more than I already do, but I fall a bit harder in that moment—*a lot.*

"I think I need one of these." His gaze flicks up for half a second, then turns back down to the baby.

And my ovaries convulse.

"When can he watch from the garage then?" Beck asks.

Pippa laughs. "I'm not sure we'll get to a race until after break."

"How are you doing?" I ask her.

"Managing," she sighs. "I'm just glad he made it back! It was perfect timing. We got some time together before he left for Jeddah. I was a mess, and that was only one race."

Luca and Beck start talking shop.

She looks over at baby Luca still in Beck's arms, and her eyes go sad. "I'm going to be a wreck after Barcelona," she says, voice lowered.

I swallow. The tripleheader following the off week after the Spanish Grand Prix—no breaks, back-to-back weeks in Montreal, Austin then Mexico City.

"My mum is staying with me until he gets back."

"Can I do anything for you?" I ask.

She turns to me and grabs hold of my wrist. "Be there for Luca for me? While I can't?"

"Of course." I nod.

"I've never seen him struggle like this."

I continue nodding because her face is truly panicked.

"Did you see what Sophie brought you, little man?" Beck says, breaking us out of the moment.

"You didn't have to do that!" She pats my wrist.

"Oh, I did!"

He leans down closer to baby Luca's face and whispers, "She bought out the whole Burberry collection for you."

Every pew is full. There's overflow on the back wall and probably beyond the doors. Pippa and Luca saved us seats in the reserved section up front. Loads of people came from the factory, friends and what must be every member of both their families. I flinch when organ chords suddenly drown out the soft whispers. I love organs. I love how you can feel every note in the deepest part of your stomach. And the acoustics in the massive duomo make it that much more overwhelmingly powerful and beautiful. Chills. Like the first time I heard the overture for Phantom of the Opera live. It's even putting chills around my eyeballs.

When we rise for the procession, Beck pulls me close. And, *my word*, Pippa and Luca look phenomenal together. Baby Luca's in his long white gown, and Luca is absolutely beaming, looking happier than I've seen him look all year.

The whole mass is in Italian, every word, every hymn. Baby Luca stayed quiet as a mouse the whole service—until he was taken to the baptismal font. There's soft laughter in the congregation as he starts to fuss, and when they pour the oil and water on his little head, he cries out. His little screams ring and echo throughout the ancient duomo. *And I'm a goner*. Face is fully wet. Beck brings the back of my hand, which has been in his the whole time, to his lips. Even his eyes look a bit misty.

———

The next morning, Beck pulls his hat on backward, which instantly makes my nether regions feel some type of way. He stares out at the lake from the window in our room. I flip the light off in the bathroom and join him.

"You ready?" I ask.

He spins to face me, pokes his finger through the cutout of my black Prada mini, brushing my cleavage. "What's this little number?" he asks playfully.

"We are going to be late!" I try to grab his finger, but he's annoyingly quick and pulls it back before I have the chance.

I swing my backpack holding our change of clothes over my shoulders.

As soon as the lift doors open, I make him close his eyes. Rather obvious if he has them open because we have to walk down to the dock, and I want to keep the surprise a surprise for as long as possible. I leave his side and open the door, and his right eye peeps open.

"Beckham Wright! You keep those eyes closed!"

I grab his arm and lead him outside, guiding him down the path and checking his eyelids every few seconds. When we get to the stone steps leading down to the villa's private dock, I stop him. It's not quite warm enough to swim, so this will have to do.

"Alright—open."

He's already smiling, but when his eyelids flip open, his whole face lights up. A glistening mahogany Riva Aquarama bobs alongside the dock. He likes boats, he *loves* the water.

"Happy birthday, baby."

"You did all this?" he asks. He hooks his arm around my neck, pulling me into him. I squeal as he bends me backward and lays it on me good, smothering me in kisses. He straightens me back on my feet, and my cheeks are hot because we have an audience, but he doesn't care. He never has.

"Benvenuti!" the captain says, helping me into the boat.

He shakes Beck's hand. "I am Giuseppe. It's an honor to 'ave you on board, Mr. Wright!"

Beck swats the air with his hand like he's nothing special.

"Miss Sophie 'as request the boat, so it's yours for the 'ole day. I take you anywhere you want to go—but she want us back before sunset," he explains.

I give him an approving nod because he remembered my request exactly.

"What happens then?" Beck eyes me, amused.

"The next surprise." I squeeze his fingers.

Setting aside, there's something undoubtedly romantic about these wooden boats. Put this boat on deep blue water surrounded by carved mountains, picturesque villages, with an Italian flag flapping in the breeze—well that's just next level.

I wrap my cardigan around me and scoop my legs up, snuggling further into him. "I like this boat."

"I'll get us a boat," he says. "Something bigger, perhaps? So we can sleep on it?"

"Bigger?" Big dreams this one.

"Or keep it small, so we can cruise around." He shrugs. "We'll always have our place for sleeping."

Our place. Monaco—his next move. He always talks about it as if it's *our* next move, which I love, but it also makes me nervous. Not a bad nervous, more a *holy shit is this it? Am I about to be a grown up?* kind of nervous. You can't keep him out of the water, and there, he'll live at the water's edge.

He nods his chin at me. "You got a wetsuit?"

"You've got one?"

"No—" He smiles. "We'll have to go get fitted."

He's the master at making plans for us. From the moment I met him, he's made plans for us—big, small, risky, adventurous—and I've never been inclined to say no.

"Is your birthday what you hoped it would be?"

"No, it's better." He kisses my hand. "Yesterday—now today."

"Luca was cute in pictures, but my word, he's gorgeous. I can't believe we got to hold him."

"That was pretty epic."

"You think Luca's alright?"

"How do you mean?"

"This season he seems to be struggling a bit, no?"

"The Melbourne DNF was a wash—that was the car—but yeah, he's been on the back foot a bit since."

"And you're winning…"

His mouth twists. "I felt really good in the car right away, with the setup and he struggled a bit during testing—I mean, he's got a lot on his plate at the minute. He'll be alright."

Guiseppe slows the boat before a tiny colorful village—*Nesso*. Postcard beauty. We stand and move to the edge of the boat. Guiseppe stands and keeps two fingers on the top of the wheel. He points to a stone bridge arching over the water, connecting two sides of the village.

"*Orrido di Nesso*, behind dis bridge you can see the gorge falls," Guiseppe explains. "Very popular swimming spot!"

"Can you jump from the bridge?" Beck asks.

He nods. "Oh yes. Very popular in summer. Now the water's about sixteen degrees."

I look up at Beck—the wheels in his brain are turning. *Absolutely not.*

"Legend says jumping from Ponte della Civera bring you years of good luck!" Guiseppe explains, animatedly gesturing with his hands.

"Summer…*hmmm*," Beck looks at the nonexistent timepiece on his wrist. "Close enough!"

"We 'aven't 'ad a Furio win at Monza in years…" Guiseppe shrugs and flashes him an encouraging smile.

"Ooof—you got me there." Beck snorts a laugh, then turns to me. "You heard the man. We've got to jump."

"No—*you've* got to jump," I correct him.

He slowly shakes his head and grabs my hand. "It's you and me, kid."

Fuck. I can't tell him no on his birthday.

Giuseppe pulls the boat alongside the stone steps leading out of the lake. Beck climbs out of the boat and sucks in a breath in the knee-deep water.

"Too cold?" I ask.

He shakes his head and holds his arms out for me. "Nope!" he exclaims, lying through his teeth.

He lifts me out and plops me three stairs higher onto completely dry stone. *Calculated.* The stone under my bare feet isn't close to warm, so I can only imagine what this water will feel like. It can't be worse than that cold plunge he made me try over break. I lasted for about five seconds, and that wasn't even head under. I can do this, *right?*

The falls are rushing in the carved gorge behind us at the crest of the bridge. Beck pats the stone on the raised edge.

"Let's get you up there first."

I reluctantly lift my foot up as he helps me climb up onto the side of the bridge.

"Careful now!" he says, holding my hand as I slowly rise from my crouched position to stand. "Alright, don't go anywhere." His fingers leave mine.

I grip my toes on the stone and give my feet a wider base. He hoists himself up and stands up next to me with probably the biggest smile I've ever seen on his face. He looks down at the water, then at me.

"You're my best friend in the whole world," he says, retaking my hand.

My heart's pounding—can't fully appreciate what he just said because I'm anticipating the imminent plunge. I give him a shaky smile. Guiseppe waves from the boat, and Beck starts counting back from three.

"One!" he yells.

I push off the stone, and we free-fall. I barely get out a scream before crashing into the water. I lose his hand and gasp, coming up for air because my body's being pierced by a million needles—frozen needles. I frantically flap my limbs in the water, my dress weighing me down.

"Come here, baby!" Beck holds out his hands.

He grabs my waist but holds me an arm's length away.

"Tell me you love me." He smiles like the absolute devil he is.

I shake my head, and my teeth chatter.

"Tell me!"

"I jumped off a bridge for you!" I scream, huffing and puffing, breathlessly kicking my feet.

But he's not satisfied, and my body's now numb.

"You—are the—only! Person I would—do that for!" I spit out.

"Tell me then!"

I shake my head harder.

He playfully digs his fingers into my ribs, and I squeal.

"Let's hear it!"

"I love you, okay?!" I yell it louder than intended. I use all my might to grab onto his shoulders, then all my weight to dunk his head back under the water.

He surfaces, his smile wide, and wraps my legs around his warm trunk. I koala-grip around the remaining parts of his body. He holds us both afloat and stares all over my face as my teeth chatter.

"You are so pretty it hurts," he whispers from lips that I swear are slowly turning purple.

I squeeze tighter around him and push my lips against his.

Guiseppe's got towels waiting when he collects us from the water. It's a rush to my system getting out of the cold and into the warm air—I suppose that's the obsession with the cryotherapy buzz these days. I guess it wasn't so bad; maybe I'll try to cold plunge for ten seconds next time. I duck down into the cabin, body wrapped in a towel, and wink, closing the door in Beck's face. Not that I don't want him in here, but because I know what would happen if we were behind a closed door, and that's entirely inappropriate with only Giuseppe aboard.

I spin my hair up on top of my head and pull the Burberry hoodie on, which covers me down to mid-thigh. Beck's back on the bench seat, sans shirt, his bottom half wrapped in a towel. Giuseppe fires up the boat, excited to show us the next destination. Beck pulls me onto his lap, and I snuggle up under his chin as we take off.

"You're the best, you know that?" he says.

I nod. "You know that whole page of desserts on the menu at the villa?"

I touch the tip of my nose with his. He finds my eyes, interested.

"It's all being brought to our balcony while we watch the sunset."

He licks his lips. "My girl."

CHAPTER 14
MILKMAID DRESS

ELLA

TOMMY CUT HIS HAIR. Which was...*a choice*. Not drastically but noticeably—a *choice* nonetheless, given our forthcoming debut. Thank God it looks alright. Saw him last night when Soph and I arrived. It's still his black waves up top, but the sides now have more of a fade.

It's Beck's trainer's preference that he and Sophie sleep in separate rooms. Perfect for our situation because we can sleep together and most importantly—get ready together. A sacred female ritual.

"You think Tommy did that for her?" I ask in nothing but my knickers.

"Did what?"

"The fresh chop," I say matter-of-factly.

"Perhaps?" Sophie shrugs. "It suits him quite well."

I step into my dress and turn in the mirror to grab the zipper.

"Woah—" she says, staring at my reflection.

I puff out my chest and run my hands down my waist. Utter perfection. It's a white milkmaid-style dress that snatches my waist to the gods and makes the girls look phenomenal. I've got Tommy's heart to avenge and followers to gain.

"That's a debut dress!" Sophie says approvingly.

"Thought it would turn heads."

"What bag are you wearing?"

"Mini Lady Dior—classic." I loop the paddock lanyard around the handle and tie it back on itself. I can't have it hanging on my chest and taking away from the dress.

"You nervous? About seeing F?" I ask, digging for Fylter's Honey Gloss in my bag.

"You think he'll actually be here?"

"He said European races, no? I'm afraid we're in Europe."

She chews on her lip and starts fiddling with her hands in her lap.

I stick my phone onto the mirror. I overlined my lips a wee bit today—you know that trick? I hit record and apply the gloss for a juicy top layer.

We pack up and head to the lift to meet the boys in the lobby.

"Goddamn, Ella," Tommy says, blinking like mad eyeing me.

It might not sound like a proper greeting to you—it is, however, the exact reaction I was aiming for. Sophie's already up under Beck's arm. He's smiling down at her like she's the light from the bloody sun.

I step beside Tommy and wrap my hand around his arm because *we're dating*, and there are eyes everywhere in this hotel lobby. "You think she's here?"

"She's here," he says quickly. "Posted all over her fucking story."

I frown, and we make for the door. He's still watching her stories? *Rookie move.* I've got to teach the man how to make a proper finsta. We look a lot alike, she and I. She's pretty, but I'm prettier. Shoulder-length hair, blonde (of course), which makes my near waist-length locks that much more impressive.

Sophie gives me an encouraging nod before she climbs into the back seat of a black SUV. *Like I need encouragement.* Our car is white, and Sam, Tommy's trainer, is up front with the driver. Met Sam in Melbourne, funny guy. I imagine you have to be chilled with a sense of humor to spend such ungodly amounts of time with Tommy. We climb into the back seat and pull away. I catch Tommy's eye flicking over at me a few times while Sam is going on with the driver about the weather. Lovely today, not so lovely outlook for the full weekend.

Tommy looks down at himself, then back at me. "Do I look cute enough?"

He holds out his arms and looks down at his orange-collared team shirt and trousers.

"It will do," I say, nose in the air. I crack a smile. "Your hair looks nice; you get that done for me?"

He gives me a cocky wink, but it's all show. He's nervous—keeps running his palms on his thighs. This is his act to mess up. I'm on my game.

I sniff a laugh. "There, there," I say, patting the back of his hand. "Calm down."

"Shut up." He rolls his eyes and lowers his voice. "We got a plan for this or what?"

I shake my head, smile growing a bit more. "Just follow my lead."

The car stops before the busy paddock entrance. *Showtime.* The Formula 1 paddock is basically a four-day red carpet extravaganza without the carpet and the dress code. Our doors are opened, I slip my sunglasses on and hop out. Every photographer is after the coveted driver arrival shot, and it's cameras galore beyond the swipe gates. I was quite literally born for this moment. I follow behind Tommy, swipe my badge and step through the gate as the green check flashes. *Cake.* He reaches for me, going for my hand I think, but I'm not a super touchy person, and we will *not* be holding hands. I whip off my sunglasses, flashing my baby blues, and toss my bouncing hair over my shoulder. I smile up at him, and his hand finds my lower back. I've been making entrances all my life. I just have that look, you know? I've always been the girl people turn and stare at. And you bet these cameras are driving my ego through the roof. We're the float in the parade that everyone's been talking about and waiting for, grabbing the attention of every eye, every lens. And most importantly, Tommy's beaming.

We continue down the footpath into the colorful row of hospitality suites, and his jaw clenches, his nostrils flare a bit. I scan the crowd ahead and spot her. Her with *him*, Emma and Imre. Tommy pulls me a little tighter against him. Photos are one thing, but seeing them together in the flesh? Hand in hand? Her eyes dart away from us, she turns and follows Imre into their suite. And that's when I believe it. Tommy does have a heart. One that's properly hurt even though he won't admit it. He breathes out through his nose as we pass the Holt suite. The glossy orange MACH suite is sat one beyond it. *Brilliant.*

"Time to seal the deal." I look up at him. "Stop and kiss me."

"Bossy little thing, aren't you?" he says, amused.

"If you didn't already know that about me, you're really in for it, Young."

"Wait, you're serious?" He lifts a brow.

"Dead! Now fucking kiss me, Tommy!"

And there, a few steps in front of the MACH suite entrance, Tommy slows. He turns to me, hands slipping around my waist. I bring my palm to his cheek as he leans in for a kiss and our lips meet. No tongue, but our mouths are slightly open so our lips can linger a second. He pulls back a bit, and my eyes open to his sticky toffee-colored eyes fixed on my lips.

"Christ, that felt good." He smiles, hands still around me, now more on my backside than my waist. "Your evil plan might work, after all."

I give him a micro-wink, keep my palm on his face and wipe the gloss smudged on his bottom lip with my thumb.

"Voilà." I pat his cheek. "Now hands off my ass, Young."

He snorts a laugh and steps back, licking his lips. "What is that?"

"Watermelon Honey Gloss from Fylter," I recite passionately.

He's still smirking, obviously pleased. Did he actually expect anything but a flawless performance from me?

"What now?" I ask. "Do I follow you around all day? Be at your beck and call?" I flutter my eyes sarcastically.

"Yeah, right." He nods across the way. "Sophie's just there."

Tommy heads inside. And there she is, with just the man I want to see with camera in hand, *David Campbell*. Formally met him in Melbourne, but I obviously knew him before that from Sophie's viral interviews last year. He's wearing a similar bucket hat to what he had on in Australia. I saunter over, shoulders back and ready to smash my first WAG interview.

"Ella, good to see you again!" David says.

Scratch that, it's the same bucket hat.

I toss him my most charming smile. "Cheering for a different team this week, I'm afraid."

He shakes his head. "You never know with paddock gossip, but I take it the mumblings this time are true? You and Tommy?"

"Guilty," I say, fluttering my lashes like I'm proper in love. "We've always fancied each other a bit."

What is this man doing? Pick up your camera! Start recording, fool! But then he looks to Sophie and starts asking about the royal baptism. I impatiently listen to Sophie's retelling because I've heard it twice over already. And I literally have to curl my toes to keep my foot from tapping.

"What a blessing!" he says at the conclusion. He checks his watch, a bit flustered. "I've got to be out!" He looks between us. "Can I grab a quick picture?"

I nod—*obviously*. Sophie puts her arm around me.

David tilts his head. "Let's have some fun with this. Go back-to-back."

We lean against each other, cross our arms over our chests, and he clicks our photo.

"Best mates, rival WAGs," David approves, looking at the screen. "Thanks, girls!"

Sophie giggles as he departs. "The rival WAG is over in the Holt suite."

"Did you see us come in?" I ask.

"Watched the whole thing from here—*including* that kiss! You'd make a fine actress!" she whispers.

I flip my hair, arrogantly. She had her doubts, remember?

"Now I've got to go find Ana! Go to the suite and hang out with Tommy. He'll be in and out of media engagements all day."

AnA, aNa, AnA—told you. She heads off, and I walk to the MACH suite to find my boyfriend.

Sam's at a table, working through a fluffy brunch soufflé. He points to a hallway with his fork. I head that way and stop when I spot the back of a blonde pixie cut I know belongs to Holly Fields, Tommy's PR rep.

"What was that?" she asks a bit snappy, standing in the doorway of Tommy's driver's room.

I take a few silent steps backward. Didn't formally meet her in Melbourne, but I'll bet she knows my name. Follows Tommy around like Sam does as part of his entourage. Sam and Holly are Beck's Charlie and Shannon.

"She's your…?" Holly pauses for his answer.

"We're dating," he says, plain as day.

"Tommy—"

"What?" he says, rather annoyed.

There's silence, then she lets out a breath. "You've got Imre in the press conference today. We'll brief before."

"Opposite ends of the couch, please, Holls!"

I come around the corner as she turns on her heel nearly straight into me.

"Good morning, Holly!" I flash her a cheeky grin. "Love your hair."

"Hello, Ella, glad to have you with us." She gives me a half-smile and steers around me.

I don't take it personally. Can you imagine being responsible for the upkeep of Tommy's image? Wouldn't want that job. If I remember correctly, I would be the fourth girl of his she's met in four seasons. I watch her leave. She could use a good moisturizer. I should bring her one! Lord knows I've got twenty or more unopened. I wonder if she was keen on his bare chest in the background of my story. You think she has a finsta?

I step into Tommy's room, look over my shoulder, then back at him. "Is she onto us?"

"No, she's just annoying," he says, pushing off the table. "You hungry?"

"Why does she look at me like she hates me?"

He stares down at me and pokes my chest. "Cause you're pretty."

CHAPTER 15
WAG SWAPPING

SOPHIE

YES, I WANT TO find Ana, but more so, I don't want to be hanging around outside the MACH hospitality suite in case a certain someone whose name starts with an F happens to be here. Low probability he'd be around for media day, but I'm not taking any chances. Beck hasn't said anything, so I'm not going to say anything—do you suppose he remembers it's a possibility?

I make my way toward the Makellos suite when Ana comes out of nowhere and throws her arm around me.

"What on earth is going on?!" she whisper-yells. "Am I this out of the loop from all this wedding shit?"

Word travels like wildfire in this paddock. *It's rather terrifying.* I stop and drag her off to the side, out of the flow of traffic.

"Tommy and Ella? Are they dating?" Ana presses.

"They're *whatevering*." I shrug. I don't like lying to her, but I promised Ella I wouldn't tell, and telling would just be lying to someone else!

"Sophie?" a high-pitched voice chimes from behind me.

I swallow and put on my best brave face as Emma catches up to us. If Ella can put on an act like the one I just witnessed, maybe I can too?

"Emma!" I kiss her cheeks, proceeding with the act of oblivion.

"Sorry," she says, flustered. "I saw you walk off—*alone*—and followed you."

"And you're here with Imre?" Ana asks bluntly, still coming to terms with all the WAG swapping.

Emma's eyes dart around, a bit surprised.

"Suppose you're shocked to see me." She smiles. "Guess I'm living up to what the blogs say about me—but what of it? I like athletes."

Ana looks at me and shrugs. "Suppose we like them too."

That makes us all laugh a bit. Ana's one of those people who doesn't try to be funny—she just is. I put forth my best foot, pretend like I haven't researched the entirety of the Emma-Imre timeline with her ex over my shoulder and start with the obvious question.

"Tell us! When did you start seeing one another?" I ask excitedly.

"He messaged me in January, and we started talking a bit, finally met up and—" She shrugs. "He's actually a great guy!"

She looks around us at the many wandering eyes. "I know it looks bad, given his and Tommy's history...but with Tommy it was so on again off again. For months, I felt like I was just one of his many options, and I was over it!"

Ana's mouth twists.

"And point proven," Emma says, crossing her arms, cocking an eyebrow at me. "Saw him walk in with Ella today."

I press my lips together. Of course, she remembers Ella. The girl who forced shots down her throat at the angels and demons party.

"That's a newer...pairing," I say delicately. *Pairing?* Fuck, I'm awkward.

She rolls her eyes. "I always knew he had a thing for her."

I can't tell her *she's wrong*—can't tell her this is really all a ploy to get back at her for getting on with Imre—so I bite my lip because unlike my best friend, I am not cut out to be an actress.

"Well"—she shrugs—"I hope she's careful. But you won't see me interrupting an enemy making a mistake."

I blink a few times, pick my jaw up off the ground. *Enemy?*

"We're quite glad to see you again!" I say uncomfortably, but as sincerely as possible.

"Me too." She smiles, gives Ana and me a quick hug before turning back down the paddock.

We watch her for a few moments as she walks away from us.

"Well—that was...awkward," I say, gathering my thoughts.

"She sounds a bit bitter, no?"

"I would say the term 'enemy' is rather bitter."

Ana huffs, flinging her hand through the air. "And once again my seating chart is simply fucked! I've already redone it seventeen times!"

I squash a smile.

"Had Emma as Tommy's plus one at the head table! Now, I've got to squeeze her in next to Imre? And Ella? Do I swap her in beside Tommy?"

She's looking to me for an answer? There's no way those two won't have killed each other by then. Did they even decide on any sort of timeline? How long are they planning to keep up this charade?

"Let's push that question to Ren, he can get it sorted with Tommy," I say, linking arms with her. "Now, come. Apparently Patrizio is looking for me."

I steer Ana toward the Furio suite.

"What day are you coming in next week?" she asks.

"Early, I suppose. Beck wants to look at a few places."

She claps her hands excitedly. "Please tell me we're one step closer to being neighbors?!"

"Beck will be your neighbor," I correct her. "I will be a rather common guest."

She shakes her head, disappointed. "I have another fitting on Saturday in Paris, so I'll miss quali."

"Is your mum coming in?"

"No, she's come in for all the other appointments. I was going to do this one alone." She shrugs. "Make it quick."

"Why didn't you tell me! Ren's sister will be in too, no? Let's make a little bridal weekend of it!"

"Yes," she says apprehensively. "But so are both of my unhinged cousins."

"Five of us? That's perfect!" I'm already starting an itinerary in my head. "Let me make all the arrangements!"

"What about the race? It's Monaco—Beck won't mind?"

"This is your wedding, Ana. We've got to do a little something before!" I say, a bit sad for her. "We'll come back early on Sunday for the race."

"Early-early?" she confirms.

"Crack of dawn!"

"Alright!" Her face lights up. "I'm in."

Eek!! I'm honestly over the moon to plan a little hen do for her. The suite doors part, and we step up into the dining area. Patrizio, team Furio's head chef, gives me a wave from the back counter.

"I hope you're hungry," I whisper to Ana.

When he notices her on my arm, he disappears into the kitchen in his usual striped pants and reappears holding two dessert plates.

"Tezting something-a new!" he says, scooting the plates toward us. Decadent triple-layer squares are sat in the center. He spins around to grab forks.

Ana starts to fidget. I give Patrizio a look, and he gives one right back. Whatever it is, the top layer is sauced cherries, and I know for a fact he did that with me in mind.

"Plate another one and come to the terrace with us!"

His eyes dart to the kitchen before coming back to me. "I 'ave three minutes."

"Plenty of time!"

Patrizio rushes off, and I pick up my dish.

"He can have mine," Ana whispers.

My stomach twists. I knew it was sort of a problem again, her eating, with the upcoming wedding and all.

"Trust me, Ana. This is worth it." I don't know if that's any way in the realm of the right thing to say, but she picks up her plate, and the three of us head upstairs. We pass the media room, packed with reporters. Beck glances up and smiles. He's surrounded—dozens of phones and recorders litter the tabletop in front of him. We hurry past and make our way out onto the terrace.

It's a gorgeous day to dig into a gorgeous dessert before noon. Tart sauced cherries are atop some dreamy Italian cream layer before a thick butter-rich biscuit base.

"*Magnificc!*" Ana says, already going in for a second bite.

"Think Beck will like dis?" Patrizio asks, inspecting a forkful.

"Has he ever not liked something you've made? Especially something sweet?"

"*Vero.*" He smiles.

Ana finishes the final bite. *Proud of her*. She licks the last of the cream off her fork and turns to Patrizio. "Do you happen to make wedding cakes?"

CHAPTER 16
MY CARDS ARE SHOWING

SOPHIE

PLANNING THE ULTIMATE BRIDAL weekend in Paris while checking in with Ella every few hours, kept me busy all of Friday and this morning. *Not that she needs checking in on.* I booked a suite for the bridal party at the Shangri-La. I've got a more chilled day planned, first with yoga at *Le Laboratoire,* a gorgeous new studio that opened and offers private sessions, followed by a spa afternoon at Spa La Mer. Spa La Mer because La Mer is the absolute best, and Ana deserves as much. On Saturday, we'll have Ana's gown fitting, lunch and shopping, then end with a night out. It's her wedding, I'm giving her the bridal weekend every girl deserves. It's the least I can do.

Beck collects me from the dining room for qualifying, racing suit unzipped, hanging from his hips.

"You get the male strippers lined up?" He smirks.

"Buttoned-up male servants I could get behind! This is an elegant bridal weekend, not some sleazy bachelorette thing!"

"Whatever you say, love," he says, kissing the back of my hand and keeping it in his.

We step out into the paddock, and my heart stops. I knew it was a possibility, but when considering the probability, I actually thought the chances were on the low end. But there he is. Dark hair, icy eyes you can't miss, standing there with some other suits. Our eyes meet, and I yank mine back to the pavement. The others are staring because Beck is Beck, but I feel *his* eyes in particular boring into me. It's only a stone's throw across the way to the garage, but Fredrick excuses himself and steps away from the group, directly into our line of sight. It's unavoidable. Could this possibly be happening at a worse time? I think not. And why is he smiling like that?

"F-Fredrick!" I stammer as we slow to a halt. "Beck—this is Fredrick...he's with Edgeman, the new MACH sponsor."

He's also my ex-boss, ex-secret-boyfriend and the reason I was in utter shambles a year ago. Beck swallows and sizes him up before reaching for his hand with a smile.

"Great to meet you," Beck says confidently, not showing any cards.

"And you," Fredrick says, his icy blue eyes wandering from Beck to me, then back to Beck.

Their hands bob up and down as my ears ring with piercing sirens.

Beck steps back and tangles his fingers back into mine. I pull in closer, so my cheek's nearly touching his arm. *Can this be over now?*

"You're having quite the season," Fredrick says, trying his absolute hardest not to look at me.

"Doing alright," Beck says humbly.

"Well." Fredrick nods. "Good luck out there today."

"Thanks, mate." Beck steps forward and gives Fredrick a firm, and in no way gentle pat on the shoulder before pulling me past him into the garage.

Sirens are still ringing in my ears. As we turn at the end of the hall, I peek up at Beck. His jaw's set and his eyes are focused forward, concentrated. When we reach the headset display, he stops and backs me up against the wall. My breath hitches, finding his eyes. They're not *angry*, but I wouldn't call the fire burning in them the result of being overly pleased with the situation. His cards are showing a bit now.

"I don't like him," he says, deadpan, not blinking.

"Nor I," I declare.

He smiles, which makes me smile, relieved.

"I didn't imagine you would."

He breathes out of his nose, still toe-to-toe with me and the wall as he reaches up and grabs my headset from the display. His eyes fall to my mouth and he drags his thumb across my bottom lip.

"I think I'll take pole today," he says gallantly.

I nod twice before he presses his lips in the exact spot he'd taken his thumb across.

"Let's do it then." He winks, setting the headset in my hands. He spins around and continues into the garage.

CHAPTER 17
RITUALS

ELLA

TOMMY CHUGS A FEW gulps of an orange Lucozade, the one with the sporty sippy top. He just finished his warm-up with Sam, and I just finished an unreal jacket potato. I swear the food in this hospitality suite could challenge a Michelin-star restaurant. I unwrap a lolly and pop it into my mouth. Tommy nods me over, and we head out for quali. When the suite door's part, I put my hand before him and stall us there on the MACH front steps.

"You good?" Tommy asks, looking over at me.

Fredrick wasn't here for media day, and he wasn't here for practice, but he's here now, and he's shaking Beck's hand. Sophie's a ghost.

"Oh, fuck, is that the ex?" Tommy asks, scooping his arm around my neck, using me as something to lean on.

I nod and keep watching, twirling the delicious pink lemonade lolly in my mouth. "Did you meet him?"

"Maybe? Reckon I shook his hand when the sponsors came through the garage earlier. Wasn't actually paying attention, though."

I roll my eyes. "And that hot one you were going on about?"

"The one there in Melbourne? Didn't see her. Would have remembered that," he says with a shit-eating grin on his face.

The exchange ends, and Beck and Sophie disappear into the Furio garage. I pull the lolly out of my mouth.

His eyes pinch. "Where'd you get that?"

"We went out and got Beck some sweet bits last night."

He grabs my wrist, leans down and puts his whole dirty, disgusting mouth over my perfect pink lolly.

"Tommy!" I scream louder than I intended, but ultimately, as loud as he deserved.

He makes a slurping sound as he sucks on it, straightens up and licks his lips. "You're so whiny! Like we haven't swapped spit before?" He pokes my ribs. "Let's go, you."

I roll my eyes and stick the contaminated thing back in my mouth.

"He looks like the boys you date," he says, guiding me across the way.

I huff a laugh. "Looks sure, but that one's got brains."

Maybe no street smarts though. *What the hell was Fredrick thinking?*

"Has to be weird for Beck to shake hands with the only other guy she's been with."

"What?!" Tommy's eyebrows shoot up, bewildered.

Fucking hell. Guess that wasn't public fact.

I nod. "Lost her V-card to him and everything."

He's still staring at me, speechless. He shakes his head, then opens his stupid grinning mouth. "How'd she end up besties with you?"

"I ought to smack you."

"You're serious?" he asks again, still in disbelief.

I nod repeatedly.

"Christ, I'd probably put that guy through a wall."

"Oh, shut up!" I say, though I'm surprised Beck didn't do as much.

Tommy reaches up and smacks the *Onward & Upward* sign in the garage hall.

"Why do you insist on hitting that every time we come in here?"

"Just a habit."

Tommy passes me the Lucozade and grabs a spare headset for me. Sophie's got her own, you know? Her headset's got a little engraved nameplate below it. I take a swig from the sippy top, then hand it back. *Gross*, we've swapped spit again.

"There are better flavors, you know."

He shakes his head. "Only orange." He puts a headset in my hands, then blows out a breath. "Wish me luck. I'm gunna fuckin' need it."

I pull the headset around my neck and take my place next to Viktoria at the monitors in the back of the garage. She got in this morning. Russian. Sharp jaw. A stunner, but awfully quiet.

"How's Alex feeling?"

"Frustrated," she sighs. "He said he'll be lucky to make it to Q3."

I'm quite good at this WAG thing. Sitting and looking pretty is one of my many specialties. There's also loads of downtime—perfect for making content, which I've always got a backlog ready. Sitting pretty as the followers come in in droves. Our media day arrival picture's been blasted, but you know that, you saw it. Celeste is getting hammered with offers. I reposted our debut image and got a million requests for a link to the milkmaid dress. And that David—*he's not a fool after all*. I forgive him for the lack of an interview. Unbeknownst to me, he snapped Tommy's and my picture right as we were lip-locked in front of the MACH suite. Logo and everything over my head. I would have reposted that one, but it's a bit much, don't you think? Besides, it's the obvious favorite of the gossip accounts, so plenty of eyes have been on it.

Tommy zips up his racing suit and starts clicking his fingers like mad. Sam walks up, hands him a pair of earphones, which he puts in before climbing into the car. Alek's leaning against the bench, talking with his engineer in the opposite bay. The monitors before me switch to Tommy's front-facing camera. He's got his eyes closed, sitting there in the cockpit. Sam rests a hand on the monitors.

"What's he taking a wee nap?" I ask.

Sam chuckles, looking back at me. "No, he likes to visualize the lap to music."

Hmm.

"Rituals," he says, flashing his eyebrows.

"The same way he has to hit that emblem in the tunnel?"

"Exactly."

He's a creature of habit, that one, that's for sure. What do you suppose he's listening to, anyway? A few moments later, Tommy's eyes flip open, and Sam moves to the car to collect the earphones.

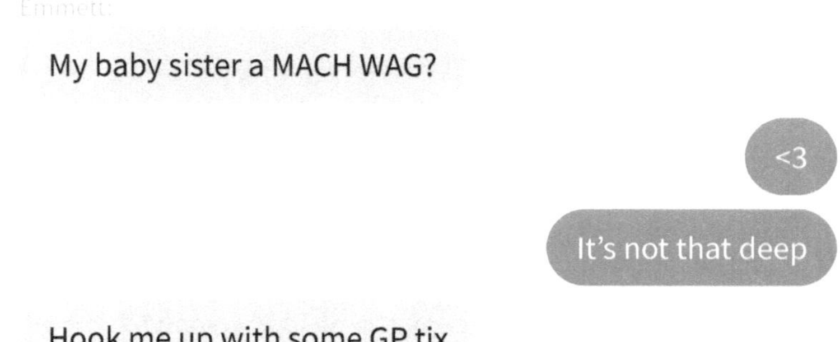

Get lost

You still cross with Dad?

I'm always cross with Alston

You still cross with me?

You're on thin ice

Do I get to meet him?

No.

Maybe.

Idk.

I suppose Annabelle keeps him up to speed on relevant information these days. Emmett even knowing the term WAG is proper assurance of that. And yes, I'm being short because I'm still a touch angry with him for ganging up on me with Alston. Those two stirred up all my bad thoughts in the first place. But maybe I should be thankful? If I weren't so riled up by the two of them, I may have never crafted this genius plan to climb my way back to the top.

On the Emma front—she's fairly easy to avoid, not that I'm avoiding her. I'd say hello if she approached me. I went to dinner with Soph and Ana on Thursday. They'd spoken to Emma that morning, and from what they'd reported, she wasn't entirely happy about seeing me with Tommy.

Suppose that's confirmation she witnessed our kiss? And if not, I'm sure she caught the photo. Not a me problem. That's a him problem.

Viktoria moves her headset over her ears. I drop my phone in my bag and pull mine on.

"All good?" Tommy's engineer asks.

"Just dandy," Tommy replies.

Tommy's waved out of his bay, his and Alek's tyres squeal as they pull out of the garage and join the other cars scrambling to join the queue in the pitlane. Sophie goes on and on about the radios and hearing Beck's voice from the car. Tommy's voice sounds a bit deeper, rougher maybe? It's alright, I suppose.

"Green light at the end of the pitlane! A gorgeous day at the Catalyuna circuit! Air temperature's twenty-six degrees, with a track temperature of forty-one. But it will be our last day of sun as the clouds are expected to roll in tomorrow morning, giving us a chance of a wet race."

It's different seeing Tommy in his element at work rather than the playboy party boy who can go shot for shot with me. He's serious and intense. I understand the hype, why girls swoon over these boys. Seeing them control a car around a corner at 240 km/h could make anyone feel some type of way.

Quali rounds fly by. It's such a high-stakes game. Emmett always enjoyed watching qualifying as much as the actual race. Both MACH boys scraped by in ninth and tenth to make it to Q3. Imre was knocked out, but so was Luca, which shocked the commentators. A load of cars are on outlaps, warming up for the final runs in the last moments of Q3. Both Valors hold the provisional front row. Alek's car is backed into the garage, in sixth.

1 VAN

2 KAP

3 ENA

4 HAH

5 WRI

6 KHO

7 ALM

8 YOU

9 MAT

10 NOW

Tommy's finishing his final flier, trying to climb from eighth position.

"And the clock has run out!

Tommy Young enters the fast sweepers at turns 13 and 14 on par to beat his personal best sector pace! But we'll have laps coming in from Elijah, Ian, Wit, Geoff and the remaining Furio."

His orange MACH flies down the main straight. His name shoots up two positions in the standings.

"And that will get him P6! Ahead of his teammate! But here comes Elijah across the line! Who takes provisional pole from Leo!

...And not for long—Geoff takes it from right out underneath him! And how about this lap from Ian Matisse!"

Fuck. Tommy and Alek drop.

"It's a mighty lap from the only Holt to make it to Q3! Ian will start ahead of both MACHs, taking sixth, but watch out for Wit Nowak!"

This is madness. I slip my fingernail between my teeth and bite down on the tip. It doesn't help. Wit's name flies up in the standings, dropping ours again. The mechanics groan, Sam puts his hands on his hips, frustrated.

"Wit Nowak has not only put a Noorden in Q3, he's put a Noorden in the top five!"

The broadcast moves to Beck dropping down the hill into turn five.

"Can Beck break into the front row?"

The floor of his car sparks as he throws it into the kerb at turn nine. Both of his sectors are purple. Tommy's car is backed into the bay before me. Eighth place is better than a Q2 exit. There's something to celebrate. Viktoria's looking pleased with Alek's P9.

"Something has lit a fire in Beck today! And it's a mega lap! By six hundredths of a second, Beckham Wright puts the car on pole for the first time this season!"

The final shift happens in the standings.

"And there's the starting grid for the Spanish Grand Prix. Furio takes pole and Makellos is split by the Valors!"

1 WRI

2 HAH

3 KAP

4 VAN

5 ENA

6 NOW

7 MAT

8 YOU

9 KHO

10 ALM

CHAPTER 18

WHOLE HEART

BECK SAID HE WAS going to take pole—and things he did? *That.* Ella's waiting for me at the end of the tunnel.

"I think I know the source of that *fire* the commentators were going on about," she says, taking my arm, heading for the media pen. "I believe it shook Beck's hand right before quali."

"You saw?"

"I saw the handshake," she says, waiting for more.

"Thankfully, that's about all it was."

Luca's handed a microphone at the far-right corner of the media pen. I'm absolutely gutted for him. I steer us in that direction because I want to hear his interview and because the two Holt racing suits to our left mean Emma could be close by.

"Luca, not the best qualifying result today—a Q2 exit, starting eleventh on the grid tomorrow...why do you think that is, given your teammate is starting from pole?"

"Yes, rough quali," he says, rubbing the back of his neck. "Still struggling with the new setup of the car. Beck 'as understand the car in a way that I 'aven't yet."

Ella pokes me. "Emma keeps looking at us. Should we say hello?"

"No! Be nice!" I swat her hand and scan the crowd. Emma's directly across the media pen from us, her eyes flicking from Imre to us.

"Nice? I am nice! I didn't do anything wrong! She's the one who went off and slept with the enemy!"

"And you're the one that's dating *and snogging* her ex in the middle of the paddock!" I huff. "The ex she was with for years!"

"Impeccable timing, that kiss," Ella says, pleased with herself.

Emma continues to flick her gaze over at us. Luca moves to the next station.

"Did she say something else to you?" Ella prods.

I'm not trying to start drama, and I will not be bringing up the enemy comment until we are safely out of the country.

"No—she just said to be careful."

"Is that a threat?"

"Not like that! She means be careful with Tommy."

She swats her hand through the air. "I eat boys like Tommy for brekkie."

The MACH duo enters the media tent, and Tommy's immediately grabbed for an interview.

"Who the fuck is that?" Ella asks, staring down the busty, red-lipped, red-haired reporter that's got her hand on Tommy's arm.

"I've forgotten her name. She's from that broadcast in the States."

"She touch everyone like that?"

I lift a brow. "You jealous?"

She watches on, blinking, disgusted as they share a flirtatious giggle. My eyes dart around. It's becoming quite busy. *Get me out of this minefield.* Emma, Fredrick—who knows what other threats are looming. "We can leave soon, you know—the boys will be in debriefs for hours."

Ella nods over my shoulder. "You tell yours. I'll tell mine."

I'm bombarded from behind. Beck's arms scoop around me as his lips press into my temple. He smacks Ella's waiting high five. He's wearing a full smile, my favorite kind, where even his eyes are smiling. He brings his sweaty head against mine and his lips to my ear. "Maybe your ex should shake my hand more often."

I push him away and change the subject. "I had a bad thought," I say quietly.

"Tell me, love." He hooks his finger into the front of my shorts and pulls me against him.

"I'm worried about Luca," I whisper.

He takes a long exhale, walks me a few steps away from all the cameras waiting to get their time with him.

"I can't imagine—I mean, fucking hell; he just became a father and...Pippa can't be here."

"You reckon that's it?"

"In this sport, your whole head and your whole heart have to be in it every second." He shrugs. "And maybe his whole head is here, but half of his heart isn't."

I pause the chewing I've begun on my bottom lip. "They wouldn't fire him, right?"

"Everyone's got performance clauses in their contracts. If you aren't performing, actions are taken."

"What can we do?"

He puts his arm around my shoulder and leads me back to the crowd at the media pen. "We could always crash his room tonight? Show up with your face mask supplies?"

"Are you mocking me?"

He smirks down at me, his smile wry. "*Never.*"

"I seem to remember my little spa service helping you!"

He brings the back of my hand to his lips. "Of course it did."

CHAPTER 19
STRAIGHTJACKET INSPIRED

ELLA

I SAVED THE VINTAGE Gaultier dress for today—for *lights out and away we go*. Tommy likes it. He liked it even better when I told him it's both bondage and straightjacket inspired. The dress photographs rather well, I look forward to seeing David's shots of our morning arrival. It's a sold-out show—over three hundred thousand fans. That's thousands of gasps that were had when Beck lost the lead into turn one. He got a poor launch and dropped to third. Fredrick's here again, not in the garage though. They're up in the fancy suites above the main straight grandstand. I'm sure Beck is bloody fuming. They had a massive error during his first pitstop too.

Tommy started on softs and was able to overtake Ian fairly fast for seventh. *Hasn't accomplished much since.* Shortly after, he pitted for mediums, and the first rain hit. Hardly rain, more of a sprinkle. A few cars wiggled, but they all stayed out on slicks. It's rolling in again though. The wind has picked up, and the clouds are much darker than before.

Lap 57/66

1 HAH

2 VAN

3 ENA

4 KAP

5 WRI

6 NOW

7 YOU

8 KHO

9 LOM

10 MAT

Static fills my headset.

"We're predicting the next wave of brief rain to hit around lap sixty-two," Tommy's engineer reports.

"I'd say sooner, mate," Tommy replies almost immediately.

The cameras hover over the main straight, following our back-to-back orange cars chasing a pink one.

"The MACHs are right on pace with each other. Both are super talented drivers, but they just don't have the equipment underneath them to even challenge the likes of the top three teams…and they've still got a Noorden out ahead of them!"

"...And you see again the car struggle on the straights even with the DRS! Tommy's a brilliant driver, the likes of which we saw at his podium finish at Zandvoort last year, but MACH has not given him the equipment to deliver this season thus far."

"...Valor was quick to deliver upgrades, which have massively improved their performance over what we saw at the start of the season. I know MACHs working on the car, hoping to bring major updates before the break...Alek's contract remains in place, but it does make you question if Tommy Young's eye will be wandering elsewhere for an open seat for next season."

Leave MACH? I watch for a reaction from Sam, but he just folds his arms and watches on. The rain begins spewing. Tommy's onboard screen in front of me starts to get hazy, and the mechanics nervously shift about. With eight laps remaining, the whole grid slows.

CHAPTER 20
TIME TO HUNT

SOPHIE

BECK IS LIVID. I haven't heard him over the radio like this since his DRS failed at Monza last year. He was already upset after he lost pole, but then his car fell off the jack during his pitstop, and instead of a pit time of two seconds, it took *twelve*. I knot my fingers together. *Let's add a drizzle to the mix.*

"Hold steady, Beck. Get it to the pitlane," Coop encourages.

"Beck has not been pleased with the Furio tyre strategy today. They've got him on a chewed-through set of softs. He has absolutely no grip to begin with, if he can make it through the last handful of corners…"

And on cue, his back end slides, and he loses control of the car.

"And he's off the road! Wit Nowak passes the championship leader, but Beck rejoins the track, dropping to sixth! That's the benefit of fresher rubber, but they'll all be called in to get off the slicks."

I exchange a nervous look with Charlie. The mechanics are already anticipating a double-stack pit.

"Get me on wets, Coop!" Beck yells over the radio.

"Sticking with Plan C. Pit for inters, and we can hold our position," Coop replies.

Hold sixth? Beck will be fuming.

"No!" Beck yells back. "I'm not dawdling on inters! Get me on fucking wets!"

Knew that was coming.

"If it dries up, our pace—"

"You see this drying?" Beck yells, interrupting him.

It's not torrential rain. It's already letting up a bit, but the track is soaked. There's spray off the cars. The visibility's not the *worst* I've witnessed in his onboard. There's commotion at the pit wall. Coop's arguing with the tyre strategist at the end of the engineering island.

"And our race leader is off the road! And he may have picked up a load of floor damage!"

Coop frantically grabs the mic on his headset. "Box, Beck, box for wets."

The yellow flag message flashes but returns to green. Geoff gets back on track, but after Leo, Ren and Elijah pass. All four exit for the pitlane. Ren and the Valors swap for inters, but Geoff's car crawls into the pit box.

"And Furio dives to the pitlane! They've swapped and have full wets waiting for Beck! And there's a new race leader as Makellos retires Geoffrey Hahn's car."

1 VAN

2 ENA

3 KAP

4 NOW

5 WRI

6 YOU

7 KHO

8 LOM

9 MAT

10 BER

Beck pulls in, and 2.3 seconds later, squeals off on full wet tyres. Luca's car immediately fills the pit box. The mechanics fit him with the same compound.

"You reckon that's the right call? Full wets? It's been noticed! Trueno readies wets for Sanjay and Antoine. Will any other teams copy the Furio call to pass up the inters?"

The front four are holding their positions, running in the tracks of one another.

"Time to *hunt*," Beck says, pleased with the ammunition he requested.

The pitlane receives the rest of the grid. It's a mix of inters and wets. MACH sticks to inters, and Holt goes full wet. Ren loses traction while attempting to make a move on Leo, and he pulls back, holding second.

"Beck is driving angry! But he's got the rubber to make moves now in the mirrors of the Noorden! Wit Nowak does not have the confidence to defend—to veer from the tracks of the front runners! But Beck leaves the racing line, takes the outside and passes on the soaked tarmac into fourth!"

The garage goes mad. He's not the only one—Luca's done the same, overtaking Alek for seventh. The Holts are charging, Sanjay too.

Lap 64/66

"Fancy another hunt, Coop?" Beck calls over the radio.

"That Valor looks awfully tasty!" Coop yells.

Tommy's holding it together on inters. He nearly dropped it making a move on Wit but secured the overtake for fifth. Alek has fallen victim to both Holts.

1 VAN

2 ENA

3 KAP

4 WRI

5 YOU

6 NOW

7 LOM

8 MAT

9 BER

10 KHO

"The full wet gamble is proving dominant! Beck's now stalking the Valor of Elijah Kaplan! Luca makes the move on Wit Nowak, and so does Ian Matisse! And Beck sends it! Clawing his way back to the podium!"

My word. The knots in my stomach loosen. He's an absolute dream. Out-strategizing his own race strategists.

"You got two more in you?" Coop asks as Beck flies down the main straight, starting the final lap.

"I'll see what I can do."

Leo is a master, even on inters, and Ren will also be a challenge to pass, but Beck is closing the gap quickly. Luca and Ian battle into turn one. The mechanics gasp as they go wheel to wheel, but Luca ultimately concedes. *Damn.* He falls back to seventh. It's a wild last lap. Alek falls victim to Sanjay on the wets. Wit to Imre. Luca's on Ian's tail, looking to make a move and retake sixth. And Beck is putting maddening pressure on Ren.

Leo exits turn fourteen, followed by Ren, with Beck on his heels. In succession, they fly down the main straight and my hand flies over my mouth.

"And that's a Valor win in Barcelona! Ren holds firm on the inters and takes second! And Beckham Wright! With more laps drying out the track, he'd have never had the pace! But he called the shots. He wanted to hunt, and hunt he did! He started pole, suffered a

massive drop, but fought his way back to complete the podium! Beckham Wright takes third!"

Charlie pulls my headset off, and we rush through the garage, aiming for the podium celebration area.

Coop guides us to the front of the Furio crowd, and we wait behind the fence. Ana's across the way, smiling like mad surrounded by a charged team Makellos. No one bothered to grab umbrellas. Not even Shannon. And truly, no one actually cares. A podium finish after the race was so touch and go feels nearly as good as a win. The team is rowdy, shaking one another by the shoulders. Leo and Ren park up, and Beck pulls in behind the third-place flag. He lifts himself from the car, flips his visor up, and *my word*. I told you God took time on him.

CHAPTER 21
PUT A LABEL ON IT

THAT REDHEAD SO-CALLED REPORTER is proper annoying. She's a bit touchy with everyone, but you can tell Tommy's her favorite. Her hair is not even red—it's that fake purply red. Suppose it matches her fake boobs, which are so fake it's actually offensive. She's speaking to Alek now but not petting him nearly the way she does Tommy. I'm standing under an umbrella that Viktoria's holding. I'd offer to hold it, but I prefer two hands for my phone. It's hardly raining anymore, but it's catching the random drops.

Alice Humphrey:

Saw you on the race broadcast!

Good for you for helping your friend, darling.

How did I look?

Exquisite!

I see you raided my wardrobe.

Tommy appears happy enough. He's animated in his interview, gripping the microphone with his little symbol-tattooed fingers. He looks rather good sweaty, all athletic and shit—but gross, *never mind*. Sam's beside us with an orange Lucozade on hand for him. Fifth place for Tommy. Not brilliant but not terrible, considering Alek fell apart and ended eleventh, just outside the points.

"Cheers, mate." Tommy nods, finishing an interview. He moves closer and waits for Qian to finish at the next station. He looks over at me and winks before his eyes drop. A moment later, my phone vibrates.

Pet names are stupid. I hate it when he calls me that. That's a lie—I don't actually mind it—but I stand by all other pet names being stupid.

Hot.

Should I say hi to Emma?

Who?

Lol

Same time next week, then, Humphrey?

Monaco?

Oui, oui

I was hoping this wasn't a one and done. *Monaco*—with all its glitz and glam.

You can stay at mine.

Need a date for our team dinner Thursday on the CEO's yacht…

I look good on a yacht.

"What are you smiling at?" Sophie says, crashing in.

"Making plans for Monaco."

"Beck was awesome out there!" Viktoria says to her. They exchange a hug.

"I'm glad he pulled through; he was *not* happy!"

Sophie settles in beside me. She's damp, having had to stand in the rain and champagne spray under the podium. I did it with her in Melbourne for Beck's win. It was mad fun. Maybe I'll get another opportunity to do as much if Tommy can pull off a podium. Chances of that are looking rather slim at the minute.

Sophie peeks at Viktoria. She's busy watching Alek with the same swoony eyes that Sophie gets.

"You going to be okay?" she asks.

"Since you're ditching me and playing host for Ana all weekend?"

She blinks at me. "Ella, I'm sorry. None of the other girls have planned anything for her! She doesn't have an Ella or Carmen."

"I'll be fine!" I shrug. "I'm staying with him."

"At his place?"

"Yeah? Why not?"

My eyes snag on the showstopper rapidly approaching. I clear my throat, grit my teeth and try to whisper-yell, "Incoming! Incoming!"

Her eyes dart over her shoulder. Fredrick stops and motions for her.

CHAPTER 22
HIGH RISK HIGH REWARD

I STEP TO THE side of the footpath with my heart in my throat, stopping out of earshot from the media pen crowd.

"Did you enjoy the race?" I ask Fredrick nervously.

"*Sophh*," he says, drawing out my name a bit.

"Don't do that," I warn.

"Do what?" He smirks, his icy eyes pinching.

"Say my name like that," I reply firmly.

He catches my arm, but I pull it away, shocked he has the audacity. *Is he drunk?*

His eyes flick over my face. "I miss you."

"Don't do this," I say as sternly as possible.

He pulls back, but only a tad. I blink and look away, but he's still staring.

"It's hard to see you with him—you must feel it still."

I swallow. "What are you saying?"

He looks around and lifts his hand. "You don't want this." He takes a step closer and rests his hand against the signage behind me, boxing me in. I recoil and catch Luca's gaze in my periphery at the edge of the media pen.

I glance up at him. "What do you know about what I want?"

He smiles a bit. "I know that *we* could have everything we ever wanted, everything we used to talk about," he says plain as day, as if the last eighteen months were a wash.

"*We?*" I scoff. "There was never a *we* that existed anywhere but in private."

He lifts his other hand, then stops and pockets it, resisting the urge to touch me. It was aiming for my face. I know it.

"I was trying to protect us, and you know that," he says softly. "I loved you that much—I walked away."

I shake my head. *You don't leave someone you love like that.* I huff a laugh. "What happened to you being happy for me?"

"I was, but—I'm back now." He smiles.

The three years he and I spent in the shadows, avoiding the inevitable, flash play in my mind. And despite what anyone said, I always defended his wanting to keep us a secret. But when it all came crashing down, he ran when he could have stayed. It's bubbling up inside me now. There's no use trying to suppress it, so I let it tear out of me.

"It's too late for that...you should have been a man when it mattered."

His lips part. I watch it wash over him, and it's *freeing*—like the closure I never got and have held in all this time.

He wets his lips, takes a breath, then gives me a condescending look. "You're smarter than this. You truly want to be some professional athlete's wife that gets cheated on?"

My heart is a jackhammer. I push off the wall, and he steps back.

"You don't know him!" I yell, far louder than expected.

Luca's on the move, out of the pen, storming over in his red racing suit.

"You might be his right now, but you're not going to be his forever!" Fredrick fires back.

The nerve!

"Sophie!" Luca calls, holding up his phone, jogging over to join us.

He and Fredrick exchange a look, and Fredrick steps back another two paces. They're about the same age, he and Luca—and that makes me feel strange.

Luca steps beside me and points down at his blank phone screen. "Pippa needs to talk."

"Right!" I say, grabbing it, thankful for an escape, any escape.

I force a smile and nod farewell to Fredrick, attempting to downplay the whole interaction, though Luca's not dumb.

I let out a massive breath as he leads me away and realize my hands are not only gripping his phone for dear life but also trembling. Pippa is *not*, in fact, on the phone at all. Luca pockets it and puts his arm around my shoulder.

"You look like you may 'ave need a rescue," he says out of the corner of his mouth.

"Yes, thank you—I very much did," I mutter, embarrassed.

"You don't 'ave to thank me. He was on the grid walk. Beck told me who that is."

"Oh! I—yeah—I think he must have had a bit to drink."

Pippa requested that I be there for Luca, and here he is, *being there for me*. Rescuing *me*.

Beck walks out of the media center and immediately spots us. He's already angry with himself with the third-place finish after starting pole, and now he looks proper confused. Luca drops his arm from my shoulder; I again attempt a smile.

"That Fredrick was cornering 'er," Luca leaks.

No. Please.

"WHAT?!" Beck's eyes run wild. The normal fire they burn for me is now rage-fueled.

I shake my head and put my hands on his chest. "No, it's all fine!"

"Did he fucking touch you?!" he yells, eyes darting madly around the paddock.

People turn and stare, startled.

"No!" I latch onto his arms above his elbows.

"Where is he, then? Is he still here?" he asks, his voice still raised.

"He's left!" I lie, trying to defuse the situation before it becomes a *situation.* I push into him with all my might, trying to turn him, but he's a brick wall, and he's still looking about furiously.

"Come with me! I've got you something!" I grab his fingers, trying to coerce him into the suite.

His eyes catch mine. "For the first time in my life, I don't feel like eating."

My eyes go sad. He huffs, shakes his head and reluctantly turns toward the suite. Did meeting Fredrick make him feel like a boy? Because it shouldn't. I said what I said. Beck's a bigger man than Fredrick could ever be. I do have something sweet for him—I always do—but I want something else.

I hastily take the stairs to the first floor, and he follows. I close the door of his driver's room and flip the lock.

"The fuck did he say?" he asks, voice still booming.

His blood is hot. Mine is too, but that's the way our blood always runs when we're in here alone with the door locked. But now? After seeing his reaction? The usual pull I feel toward him is on another level entirely. I stand before him, undo the Velcro and unzip the top of his racing suit. The veins in his neck are bulging, his skin is dewy. It's risky, but you know what they say about high-risk. *And it always is.* I slip my hands inside around his torso.

"Only things he didn't mean," I finally answer. "You don't need to worry about him."

I push up on my tiptoes and kiss down the side of his neck. He's salty, his skin raging with heat.

His hands come around me. "I don't need to put my fist through his face?"

"No, baby," I breathe against his neck. I slip my hand down the front of his racing suit.

"Right now, I need you inside me," I plead, with my breath, with my hands, with every nerve ending running through me.

He swallows heavily. "I'm not done out there."

My heels resettle on the floor. I stare up at him through my eyelashes. Stare at the masterpiece of a man in front of me. "It can be quick."

There's a twitch against my hand. The fury in his eyes slowly cools and softens to the fiery burn I recognize.

It doesn't take much convincing—none, actually. In a matter of moments, I've kicked off my panties, he's out of his suit and fireproofs, sat up on the massage table, and I'm on my knees, straddling his waist. He's gripping my hips, slowly guiding me down onto him. My mouth falls open, the muscles deep inside me already pulsing from the fullness of him.

"*Fucking hell,* Sophie," he groans.

I rest a palm on the wall behind him and wrap my other hand around the back of his head. He pushes the skirt of my dress up to the crook of my thighs, staring at where we're now joined. *He loves having me in a dress.* Our lips brush repeatedly as I rock my hips.

His hands run up my back and take an overhand grip on my shoulders. He buries his head between my breasts. *He's got leverage now*, and he uses it to pull me down faster, deeper onto him. I latch my fingers into his hair and lose all control of the noises I was trying to hold in. Noises definitely not safe for the workplace. His hand flies over my mouth, my cries now muffled against it. His thighs tense, and he holds me in place, deep down on him as he pours into me. My chest is heaving, his breath hot in my cleavage.

He tilts his head up, and I rest my forehead against his, still breathless.

"You're mine," he commands, framing my face with his hands.

And I think I might come again.

"And you're mine," I pant, pressing my lips against his.

His head rests back against the wall, then falls to the side. He stares to the floor and sighs. "I've got to put all that back on now."

CHAPTER 23
THE BELLE OF BRITAIN

ELLA

SOPHIE'S DONE IT. A million followers. And she hardly noticed, didn't make any deal of it. I met with Celeste this morning and saw the preparations for her celebration at the agency. Stuart's got a whole thing set up for her. I'm going mad with this Fylter deal hanging over my head—because no, they still haven't made their pick. The fact they didn't have Celeste's phone ringing off the hook with a deal offer is bonkers. Did they not see my pictures in the paddock breaking the internet all weekend? I've been checking like mad for my WAG rating to get posted. I'm on pins and needles. Sophie's took a minute last year. My patience is running thin. I finish my cigarette, *my second*, then climb back through my window.

I trudge down the stairs, two cases in tow. The wheels on the rollers slam onto the marble in the lobby. Carmen and Pierre glance up from behind his desk.

Carmen frowns, eyeing my luggage. "You're not staying for Soph's party?"

"Can't, unfortunately. Have a thing with Tommy tonight," I say, knowing full well it's in the best interest of my mental health to skip, regardless.

I wheel my bags over. They're both actively engaged with something behind his desk. "What's that?"

"It's the *Dish* spread!" Carmen squeals, holding up the magazine.

"Look at our Sophie!" Pierre sings. "She looks to die for!"

Sophie? I snatch the magazine from Pierre and flip the pages back. It's a six-page Beckham Wright spread.

Britain's Racing Royalty. Three races, three-peat podium.

Defending champion, Leo Van Belle, stunned by the Brit in Furio's second seat, saying this year's championship 'could be anyone's.'

I flip forward. Sophie's picture is on page four, that's where I start reading.

Besides bagging podiums, Beckham Wright has bagged the Belle of Britain

It's a double threat when you add Beck's partner to the mix. London native Sophie Collins has taken the fashion world by storm. After a career shift from the world of finance, she's landed deals with luxury travel brand RIMI and walked runways for the Eden Eves label. When she's not parading on runways, she's a distinguished guest in the crowd, as she was this spring with fellow F1 WAG Ana Wong at Dior's show in Paris. Her influence will take her back to the runway with Beurre at Miami Swim Week, where she will debut a line she had a hand in creative directing. What's next for Britain's sweethearts? The pair are eyeing a move to Monaco. When Beck was asked about his relationship, the ladies present all but melted: "You ask any driver, and they'll tell you it—Formula 1—can be a lonely sport. But with Sophie by my side, I feel unstoppable." Wright explained. "She's got the world in the palm of her hand, and she chooses to hang out in a smelly garage most weekends. If that's not love, I'm not sure what is."

I swallow. "Our little rockstar."

I flip the magazine closed and toss it onto the counter in front of Pierre. My Uber's outside, flashing lights and all.

"Well, I'm off to Monaco!"

"You want to take this copy?" Carmen asks, extending the magazine in her hands. "I picked up three!"

"No. I'll catch it online on the train." I lean in and kiss her cheek, blow Pierre a kiss too.

I flop down into the back seat of my Uber. I'm sweating, though it's not even warm. *The Belle of Britain?* And that's when I feel it—the Fylter deal slipping through my fingers. Why would they pick me when they can sign the belle of *fucking* Britain?

The car pulls from the curb, and I open the gossip page. Remember when I said I'd do anything to keep my edge? I suppose that means I'll do anything—*to anyone.* The devil on my shoulder is furiously clapping his hands, while the angel on my other has fully flown the coop.

There's already a post of the magazine on the page. And it has hundreds of comments. My fingers are flying, typing my own:

Belle of Britain? Career shift? People are pretty quick to forget she was fired for sleeping with her boss.

I open the new post prompt and chaotically swipe through my recent photos—the picture flies by. I stop and scroll back. My angel reappears, screeching warnings, but the devil pounces and throws a hand over her mouth. I've lost it, all control of my emotions and my actions. I upload the picture of the pregnancy test, with her name fully legible on the receipt, and type a header:

Has the Belle of Britain fallen victim to the Furio baby fever?!

CHAPTER 24

MIND THE GAP

I STAYED OFF MY phone for the whole train ride. That's a lie. I listened to three podcast episodes of *In the Know*. Don't ask me what was said though, because I was half listening while half questioning if I had really just done the thing I very much just did. I'm not a good witch. I'm a wicked witch. I threw a nuke and slammed the vault door shut behind me.

Tommy opens his front door, his gaze immediately falling to my bags. He leans out of the doorway and looks down the hall. "Where are the girls?"

"What are you talking about? I'm alone," I huff, annoyed.

"You moving in? All these are yours?" he asks, bewildered.

"Shut up and help me," I say, pushing a bag his way.

He grabs the handle and holds the door open. "You need two full-size suitcases for four days?"

"I needed three," I snap, pushing past him.

"You got in alright then? I gave the front desk your name."

I nod. *Holy shit,* his place is immaculate.

Tommy holds out his hands. "Well, this is it."

179

He waves me over to the kitchen, passing the crystal-clear view of the port out the massive living room windows.

"Saw that Chianti you like," he says, leaning down and opening a wine fridge. "Bought a few bottles."

My lips part—I'm bewildered, to be honest. I take a breath and turn the bitch dial down a few notches. It's not any Chianti in his hand, it's the one I die for. The *Isole e Olena Chianti Classico*. I stare at him a moment. He's got a memory, this one. I only ordered it that one time at our group dinner in Italy after I bitched him out for taking the waiter's wine suggestion over mine.

He reshelves it, shuts the door and moves to the refrigerator. There's an entire shelf of orange Lucozade. Perfectly spaced, labels all aligned, like every other item inside. His housekeeper must be anal as all get out.

"What's with the orange? There are other colors, you know..."

"Rituals, Ella."

I lift a brow. "And tell me, what would happen if the team started stocking another color in the suite?"

"I'd probably crash out, okay?" he says, grimacing at the thought.

I cross my arms. "You know, you should really have worked a deal with them. Get you a steady supply and a sponsorship?"

"You should take that idea to Holly," he says with a shit-eating smirk. "She'd take a suggestion from you pretty well, no?"

I roll my eyes.

He opens a drawer and sets a gold key on the counter. "Hold on to my spare, so you can be in and out without me if you need."

I follow him back through the living room; the pillows on his couch even have that perfect dent after you've properly fluffed and karate chopped them.

"Did the maid just leave?" I ask, following him into the hall.

"Don't have one. I keep it tidy."

He pushes open the first door. "This is the bedroom. There's a bathroom in there too."

"Is there only one bedroom?" I ask, peering into yet again another spotless space.

"There are two, but the other is my sim room."

I eye the man-child tour guide. "You have a room dedicated to playing video games?"

He shakes his head, probably regretting his decision to have me stay here, but may I remind you it was *his* idea, not mine. There's a hall bath and a room beside it with his racing rig, a couch and a load of helmets hung on the wall in three rows, perfectly offset.

He nods at the couch along the wall. "I'll sleep in here. You can take my bed."

"Don't be silly. You're the one that's got to perform, I'll bunk up in here."

"You sure?" he asks, rather shocked.

"Positive," I say with a flutter of my lashes.

"*Right...*" he says, tone suspicious. "Let me grab your bags."

He leaves, and I push the curtains aside to take a look at the view. Is Sophie truly moving here? She hasn't said anything to me or Carmen. She must be planning it all out with Ana.

When Tommy's back with my bags, I lay them flat but don't unzip them—he might have a panic attack.

"Did Beck buy a place?" I ask.

"Not yet. I went and saw a spot with him yesterday down the street."

"You think he's all in with Sophie?"

"Oh yeah." He sniffs. "He's got it bad."

"That's got to be a lot of pressure dating her."

"What do you mean?"

"Her dad's got more money than God." I shrug. "She's used to a certain lifestyle…"

"Beck's well on his way…it was a big place, a three-bedroom."

"Why does he like her so much?" I blurt out. And as soon as I say it, I regret wording it that way.

Tommy gives me a funny look.

"I mean—what does he say about her?" I follow up quickly.

"Just look at him. He worships the ground she walks on. He'd marry her tomorrow if he knew she'd say yes."

I swallow, force a smile, then 180 the subject. "Tell me then, what's on our agenda, Young?"

He lifts his arms, tattoos peeking out, and rests his hands over his head on the door frame. "If we want our photo taken, thought we'd take the car out for a bit."

My eyes light up.

"Then come back, freshen up for dinner—head down to the port."

"To the yacht?" I ask, practically salivating.

He waggles his eyebrows. "Sound good? I'll call down and have the car waiting out front."

God bless the principality of Monaco. I change into a darling sundress and the Dway slides from Dior. His building has proper security, but that isn't stopping the mass of people outside from pointing their phones at us. Tommy opens the passenger door of his charcoal McLaren 720s Spider. And if you don't have a brother or you're not a car guru, it's a fucking sick convertible.

He lowers into the driver's seat and fires up the engine. *Instant dopamine hit.*

"How many girls have you taken for a ride?" I ask, running my finger over the carbon fiber interior details.

"A ride-ride or a ride in the car?" He smirks.

I smack his arm. "The car, you sleaze!"

"You'd be the first in this car." He winks. "Wait—I suppose there was one other."

I roll my eyes.

"If it were my mum, it doesn't count though, right?"

I find myself smiling at that.

"It's new." He shrugs, then spins the wheel, pulling out from the covered valet drive.

The cockpit is doused with sun, his left hand joins his right on the wheel and a two-tone Rolex Daytona flashes on his wrist. I believe it's the same one John Mayer wears.

"Is that new as well?" I nod my chin at the beauty.

"Ella Humphrey's my girlfriend," he says, looking over, brow arched. "Had to pull out all the stops."

We creep down the crowded streets. All eyes on the footpath are drawn to us and our delightfully noisy chariot. I keep my hands in my lap, channeling my most graceful and chic self.

"Favorite watering hole right there," Tommy says, pointing to a discreet café. He nods across the street to his favorite corner store.

I twist my hair up into a claw clip. "Who can I expect at dinner?"

"Alek, Vik, Sam, our CEO, team principal and our race engineers."

"No Holly?" I ask with a bit too much excitement.

He smiles, amused. "She didn't make the cut."

"Ronan, the CEO, is an old friend of my dad's. That's why it sucks when we're underperforming. I hate to be negative. I don't want to hurt the relationship, but when MACH's not being spoken about as a top team—*it's difficult.*"

"It would be hard to leave, then?" I ask, not sure if Sam or anyone fills him in with what's said on the broadcasts, but I assume Holly does.

"I've considered it, but yes, it would be quite hard," he sighs. "We'll see. We've got a massive upgrade package coming. It's just taking a while."

He clicks through his Spotify and lands on Rüfüs du Sol.

"Is this what you listen to? When you put on headphones and take your little nap in the car?"

"Nap!" He throws his head back. "No, the *nap* songs are upbeat. Ones that really block out the world and get me in the zone."

The rituals. I reckon smoking on the roof has become a bit of a ritual for me lately—not a good one, obviously.

"Loads of swimming spots off this road. I'll have to take you cliff jumping sometime."

Probably a good thing we don't have cliffs in Paris, or I might be eyeing one for the day I lose the Fylter deal to Sophie. I rest my head back and close my eyes. *Innerbloom* is usually a *never skip* song, but in this moment, it's a touch too deep. I need to snap out of this—whatever *this* is.

"We're out of town, no?" I say, straightening back up. "I can let my hair down?"

"You do you, baby girl." He winks, his golden eyes practically glowing.

We're able to keep a proper speed now, the car's drenched in sunshine, twisting around the bends in the road, hugging onto the side of the cliff. I swear the water looks even more spectacular when you're viewing it from a top-down supercar. Highly recommend.

I snatch his phone to change the song, after the drop, obviously. I'm not a bloody terrorist! *This should do the trick.* I spin the volume knob higher for Tate McRae's *Sports Car*. Tommy shakes his head. I slip my feet out of my sandals and take the clip out of my hair. I fluff it out, let the breeze swim through it, then shift in my seat to put my feet up on top of the door.

He runs the tip of his tongue across his teeth, eyeing me. "Legs for *fucking days*."

I stretch my arms in the air, body practically diagonal across the passenger seat. I wiggle my toes in the breeze, and his eyes continue to flick between me and the road. Sun-warmed skin, the top down, a vibey song. It's dopamine to the nth degree. Next time I'm going dark—on the verge of doing something absolutely reckless—I'll chase this feeling.

"You're staring at my feet again, Young," I tease.

"Cause they're leaving prints on my €350,000 car."

"You love it," I say before jacking up the volume even higher.

For a second, he acts like he doesn't know the words until Tate hits the chorus, and he can no longer help it. The words appear on his lips before he throws his head back and starts to shimmy along with me.

***

My hair was an absolute mess, took me forever to untangle it. All worth it, of course, for the story I posted during my joyride in the passenger seat.

I pin-curled my hair for dinner. Made a proper mess of the bathroom counter. A complete contrast to what's happening in the bathroom cabinets, where everything's in orderly rows and the bottle sizes descend from left to right. When I threw my cold storage skincare in the fridge earlier, I came back to find it out of my tote, organized in an acrylic tray.

He would quite literally die if he saw my bathroom. Our drawers and cabinets? With all the product we're sent? *Tragic.*

I give my curls a final brush and spray when Tommy appears outside the door. "Wow, Ella."

I watch him in the mirror as his eyes track down my body.

"A proper gown for a proper evening!" I turn in the mirror to give myself a look at the cowl-back emerald silk slip dress that hugs my body in all the right places.

I spin to face him and suck in a bit of air. *Alright, Young.* Two can play. He's buttoned up in a crisp white shirt, black trousers and matching tuxedo jacket. Could literally stand in for James Bond or any other sexy secret agent. He reaches up and rests his hands above his head on the doorframe like he did earlier.

"I've never seen you like this!" he slips. "I mean on your Instagram, but not in real life."

I lift an eyebrow. "You stalk my Instagram?"

"No!" he says quickly, all defensive. "I mean...you just come up on my feed a lot."

I grab his jacket and pull him into the bathroom. "We've got work to do."

He stumbles in and freezes, eyes set on the counter. The counter covered with endless palettes and brushes, skincare, every hair product and tool imaginable, with other random bits and bobs I threw into my vanity case. His lips part, panic washes over his face. I try not to laugh.

"Ella"—he swallows—"this bathroom is destroyed."

I lift his chin up. "Don't you worry—there'll be no trace of me when I leave." I step beside him and size us up together in the mirror. Getting proper content is a me problem that I'm hereby making an us problem, whether he likes it or not. "I didn't have time to film a *'get ready with me,'* so an outfit check will have to do," I exhale. "And yes, you're in it."

"The fuck is that?"

I grab my phone and clutch from the counter and push past him. "You stalk my Instagram, you should know!"

He follows me out to the living room, grabs my hand and gives me a spin. "Look at you!"

"I know, I know," I say, waltzing out of the spin and heading for the windows. I squish the suction cups of my Octobuddy against the glass slider.

"Follow my lead! We've just got to say what we're wearing. Easy peasy."

I back away. The lighting is perfect with the last of the sunset glow beaming through. I grab his arm and adjust our position.

"Am I cute enough to be in this?" he says, staring at his own reflection.

"Fishing for compliments again, are we?"

He snorts a laugh. "Let's make a deal—I'll follow your lead if you can go one night without your phone."

My neck jerks like someone's just slapped me. "That's absurd!"

"One night," he says, standing firm, crossing his arms. "You can do it."

I blink and stutter something illegible.

"If there's an emergency," he adds, "mine's in proper working order."

More blinks. "Fine!" I snap. "But we're posting this first!"

The nerve on this one!

"Stand here." I grab his arms, make final adjustments before I return to start the recording.

"Outfit check before reporting for duty to our yacht dinner in Monaco." I wink.

I back up and run my hand down my hip. "Dress is Maison Sous," I do a quick turn to showcase the back. I move my hair over my shoulder for a proper view, then kick my foot up behind me. "Shoes are Gianvito Rossi, bag is Cult Gaia and earrings are Chaumet."

I turn to Tommy, who's absolutely beaming at me, and give him a little nod. "Your turn, boyfriend."

"Right," he says, turning to the recording. "Jacket *is...*" his eyes go blank, then shift back to me. He flicks his hand, exasperated. "Fuck! I don't know what it is!"

"Tommy!" I scold. "Get down here!" I grab him by the collar and yank him sideways to peek at the label.

I look back at the screen and shove him back upright. "*Armani.*"

"*aRmAnI,*" he repeats, undoubtedly mocking me, before the halfwit goes blank again, clueless.

"Trousers? Shirt?" I encourage.

"Right!" he chuckles. "I've also got trousers and a shirt on!"

I turn back to the screen and shake my head. Reckon a bit of comedy won't hurt. I go to retrieve my phone and stop the recording.

"Is that going to work?" he asks like he's properly invested now.

I replay it, try to squash my smile. "It's quite funny, actually."

Tommy holds out his hand, motions with his fingers, which I ignore. I take my time posting the reel to Instagram, then reluctantly hand my phone over. The second it's out of my reach, I shift uncomfortably. I watch his every move as if he's just taken my first-born child. He walks into the kitchen and drops it in a drawer, with a diabolically pleased grin across his face. He pushes the drawer closed and rubs his palms together. "Let's go, baby girl!"

Phantom phone. Have you experienced it? *It's shit.* My hand feels overly bare. And since it is, in fact, sans phone, I swear I'm feeling notification vibrations in my clutch and yet my phone is in his drawer, not rattling against my Fylter Honey Gloss. Tommy's got his hands in his pockets, head craned back, staring up at the stars.

"You're going to fall in if you don't watch where you're walking."

"Nah," he says, overconfident. "Too many yachts crammed in here at the moment."

Fact. Every billionaire is parked up in the port playground having fancy drinks, fancy meetings and fancy dinners, all tastefully mood lit by soft neons and candles.

It's not the biggest boat, definitely not the smallest either, but certainly the only one with MACH orange details. A crew member waits at the bottom of the ramp with a basket for our shoes. Tommy crouches down and reaches for my foot before I've even got a chance to remove them myself. I swear this one's got a thing for feet. I hold his shoulder a bit annoyed because the shoes are a third of the ensemble, but nothing is keeping me off this boat. Three decks are visible from the stern, and the whole thing's got a shine on it like it's just been waxed twice over. Another crew member arrives; we exchange our shoes for the champagne she's holding on a silver tray.

We walk barefoot through a white parlor on the lower deck. He's looking even more Bond-esque aboard the vessel.

He takes a swig of champagne. "You ever been on a boat this big?"

"How big is it?"

He tosses me a cheeky wink. "You know how big it is."

I can't even roll my eyes; walked myself straight into that one.

"Think it's just over fifty meters," he says, pleased with himself. I follow him up a narrow staircase to the second level, which might be more pristine than the first.

"I've been thinking of ideas for my birthday, and those ideas include a weekend on a boat like this."

His ears perk up. "Am I invited?"

"That depends, Young," I say, deciding to challenge him. "When is my birthday?"

"*Augustttt...?*" He lingers.

"Look at you!" I laugh. "You can be taught! Well, sort of."

We step outside onto a massive open-air deck, where a string trio is sat in the corner, playing soft classical music. The lights are low, and a sprawling dinner table set for fifteen is littered with candles. The aesthetics, the vibe—*exquisite*. There's a photographer taking pictures, but when I tell you I need my phone—*I need my phone*. Tommy parades me around for proper introductions. A few wives are here, including the CEO's, whose hands look like the only hard labor they've endured is keeping afloat the ten carats of canary diamonds spread across her fingers. She absolutely lights up when she spots Tommy and floats over in a chiffon gown with a pashmina over her shoulders. She greets me all excited, then holds Tommy close and tells me I picked the perfect man. *How well do you know him, Miss Amelia?* Tommy eats it up. It's a bit odd the way adults fawn over him. Beck's mum treats him like one of her own. When he visits MACH HQ, he stays at the Wright's even when Beck's not around. We take our seats across from Alek and Viktoria. Sam's beside me. The crew doesn't make a peep as they refill champagne, take and set plates. The crew must be forty strong, with a new face appearing every few seconds. I decide then that being waited on hand and foot at sea will make a proper twenty-fifth.

When all glasses have been topped off, Tommy scoots back and rises from his seat. He lifts his champagne, and the murmurs at the table go quiet, and I go a bit nervous because I haven't any idea how this will go.

"A toast to the team—may we have another strong race around Monaco together," he says with a nod, then looks down at me, dead in the eye. "And a toast to the ladies and my beautiful girlfriend, who make us look and feel like a million bucks."

I miss the "cheers" because the blood is pounding in my ears, but I go through the motions, clinking my glass with others around the table. My sexy secret agent fake boyfriend retakes his seat. Don't know why I ever questioned his acting skills. Mine are still superior, but I'll give him top marks for that. The conversation picks back up. Our mains are brought out and set before us in unison. In perfect harmony, the dome plate covers are lifted, and the crew disappears.

He pokes my leg under the table, nods down at my fingers twisting in my lap. Twisting something mad because they're not used to being free and without a phone to hold. "Doing okay there, Humphrey?"

"Don't even miss it!" I lie, grabbing for my fork. You know what it's like to post something before you get on a plane, a plane that turns out to have shit Wi-Fi, so it's hours until you get to see any reactions? Feels a bit like that. Can't believe he talked me into leaving it behind. It's probably sparked a bloody fire in that drawer from incessant notifications piling up.

When dessert is had, Amelia convinces a tipsy Ronan to leave the table for dancing. Alek and Viktoria follow soon after. I hate the phrase "Money doesn't buy you happiness" because Amelia and Ronan look awfully fucking happy waltzing on the deck of their yacht. Mum deserves a life like this—dripping in diamonds, married to a CEO, hosting fancy dinner parties. I try only a single spoonful of the berry pavlova—because, well, *Beurre*—and retire my spoon.

I find Tommy's eyes and bat my lashes. "I quite like dancing."

His eyes narrow as he steals the berries off my plate and spoons them into his mouth before he pushes back from the table.

"Don't hurt yourself out there," Sam teases him.

Tommy tosses his napkin in Sam's face and takes my hand. I can feel all eyes on deck follow us. We look positively magnificent. But you know as much, you saw our outfit check. He leads me from the table, then stops and just sort of stands there, looking down at me.

I lift an eyebrow. "Go on, then. Put your hands on me."

He swallows, steps forward and pulls me against him. With his hand on my lower back, his feet start to move, and it's a funny little dance we do. It's the sort that sets off a funny little dance in my chest—one I don't recognize and choose to ignore. I stare at the buttons on my secret agent's shirt for a moment as our bodies slowly sway together, and the tips of his fingers slightly move against my skin.

I glance around me; Vik has her cheek on Alek's chest, which absolutely will not be happening here. I peek up at my secret agent, who's peering down at me. I tilt my head back a bit, soften my gaze and let him properly sink into the depths of my *what Ella wants, Ella gets* stare.

"Is that your trick?" he asks. "That thing you do with your eyes?"

"Whatever are you talking about?" I say, tilting my head, softening them again, acting as if I'm baffled, when I taught myself this trick in lower fourth.

"That." He nods his chin at me. "They're quite blue."

"So glad you know your colors, Young."

He rolls those golden-toffee eyes of his, and his hand shifts a bit lower down my back.

"You did it the first time I met you. At Ollie's set."

My breath catches in my throat. The memory on this man—I can't even picture what I said to him, let alone how my eyes went. Did I really pull that on him then?

"And what did you think when you met me?"

"Honestly?" he says.

I nod.

He checks around us, then his eyes come back to me, and he pulls in a little closer. "I saw you and thought…I would do unspeakable things to get that girl naked."

"*Nice*," I mutter, unamused.

"But," he continues, pulling back, "when we got to hanging, chatting later at the club, you were actually a really cool girl. Fun as hell."

"You didn't make a move."

"Got nervous." He shrugs. "Thought you were too cool for me, to be honest."

He smiles. "That is, until you fell into my arms a few days later on that boat, and we made out. Couldn't help myself then."

My eyes catch on his lips, on that little smirk that's turning up one corner of his mouth. His fingers shift against my backside.

"Are you wearing underwear?"

I throw him a wink. "Afraid this is a no knickers type of dress."

He sucks in a breath and quickly looks at anything but me, which makes me giggle.

"You want to get out of here?" he says, stopping our little dance.

"Can we?" I drop my hands to my sides. "I miss my phone terribly!"

After we've said our thank yous and goodbyes, his hand slips around my waist, accidentally beneath the fabric of the low-cut back of my dress. I exit beside him, and instead of fixing it, he leaves his fingers there against my skin. *Was that intentional?* Whatever the case, I step ahead of him at the top of the narrow stairs.

The same shoe-bin lady is waiting on the lower deck at the ramp. I slide into my pumps, and Tommy slips back into his Louboutins. Then my feet leave the ground as he hoists me over his shoulder and steps up onto the ramp.

"Tommy!" I squeal, nearly kicking out of my Gianvito Rossis.

"Shall we take a dip?" he says, walking down the ramp. The shoe-bin lady is laughing like mad.

"Don't even think about it!" I slap his back.

He slaps my ass in return, my ass that is up in the air over his shoulder. "Come on! You look so good wet!"

"Young! I will cut you!" I scream.

He steps off the ramp and lowers me to my feet. I flatten my dress and rearrange my hair. He thinks he's hilarious. I slap his hand away when it drifts back to my ass. "Mind the gap, Young!"

I take his arm, *on my terms*, and start the walk. He tips his head back, looking up at the stars again. I play my own window-shopping game as we pass by each boat, picking which yacht I want as my own.

"How was it then? Cutting the cord with your phone?"

"Oh—um, strange but nice, I suppose."

"Don't lie," he takes a break from the stars to look down at me. "I saw you tweaking over there at the start."

"That's only because I swear I could feel it going off!"

Still can't believe I let him talk me into leaving it and missing out on all those photo ops on the boat. I must get a yacht in order and on the books for my birthday. He said he brought his phone, though it never left his inner jacket pocket.

"Have you heard from Emma?" I inquire, wanting an update on one half of our mission.

"I haven't," he says. "I did notice she unfollowed me."

"*Tart.*" I give him sorry eyes. "Did you reciprocate?"

"Of course," he scoffs, then gets a little smile on his face. "I can only imagine how irate she was when I walked in with you last week." He looks back up to his stars. "She always thought I had a thing for you."

Not fazed by that—everyone's got at least a little thing for me.

"You think our arrangement is working then? Is it helping, having me here?"

He slings his arm around my neck. "You're pretty fun to have around, Humphrey."

"And your dad?" He looks down at me. "He pleased you've left your bench in the dust and are going steady with someone?"

"*Delighted,*" I lie.

Alston hasn't said a word, probably hasn't even noticed. However, I can assure you my engagement numbers are *fucking ecstatic.* Can't wait for a look at the analytics on the video we posted. *You think Emma has seen it?*

"Have you and Imre always been at odds?"

"We've scraped before, but he fucked my race in Spa last year, then a week later, he hit me again in Monza."

"You think she truly fancies him? What if she's using him to make *you* jealous?"

He shrugs. "She likes anything in a jersey."

"Is getting her back your end goal?"

He tosses his head around. "Don't know about that—we've been on and off for years."

"Why?"

"I don't know, Ella," he sighs. "She's fit, has the Australian thing going for her, but it's getting a bit old, and she's a bit crazy."

"How do you mean?"

He shakes his head. "She's just got some mad ways about her."

CHAPTER 25
BABY TRAPPING

SOPHIE

I WAS HAVING A lovely week, I was. Stuart surprised me with a celebration at the office. I thought I was walking into a regular chat. *One million followers*. There was a cake with lots of piped frosting zeros and loads of photos. Carmen came. Ella couldn't make it. I brought a massive slice home for Pierre. It was also the morning that Beck's feature in *Dish Magazine* hit the stands. I bought a ton of copies because he looks to die for. And do you know what he did? Before the shoot started that morning, the photographer wanted us to step in front of the camera for test shots. Unbeknownst to me, Beck went and approved one of the photos of us to be used in his feature. Have you ever opened a magazine and *bam!* Right there on a glossy page is your picture? I panicked for a second, but then I read the write-up beneath it and melted a bit.

It was also a big day on the gossip site, or so I would learn. Another surprise photo. Remember that scare I had? There's a picture of one of the tests I ordered, and it's undeniable. My name is perfectly printed on the bloody receipt. The photo got to Beck before I even knew about it. He had questions, lots of them, understandably. But it's one of those times where there's so much going on at the minute, there's not actually time to hash anything out ad nauseam. Beck's in Monaco—*it's race week*. And I'm busy playing host for Ana's bridal weekend. I usually hate being apart when these sorts of things happen, but I'm glad of it this go around. Glad to be far away from the hundreds of wandering eyes in the paddock. I made sure it was okay with Beck for me to be away for the first part of the weekend. He said it was fine as long as I promised to be there to kiss him before the race. But that was before the *news*.

It's been rather impossible to relax, despite having planned the most relaxing, decadent two days. Hosting while running a bit of damage control will drive a girl to drink—which I fully plan on partaking in this evening.

My phone rings, I push off the Victorian sofa in the tiny bridal atelier in the eighth and turn into a corner stuffed with tulle dresses. I accept the call and bring my hand over my mouth to hush my voice.

"Stuart!" I whisper into the phone. "I'm not pregnant, and I never was!"

"Is it photoshopped?" he asks.

I quickly peek over my shoulder. "Not exactly..."

Stuart chuckles. "Well, when that day comes, you'll be set for life. You should have seen the number of brands putting feelers out."

Lord.

"That's lovely. Now, I've got to go."

I return to my place on the sofa between Ana's cousins, Lili and Mira, and Ren's sister, Reina. Reina's quiet like Ren and just as sweet. The cousins are a rowdy pair, a bit of a handful and getting on Ana's last nerve. They're on their second bottle of champagne at her fitting after nearly drinking the spa dry yesterday.

"Alright," Ana's tiny voice says from behind the drapery. "Here it is—"

The designer pulls back the curtain, and Ana turns away from the mirror to face us.

My hand flies to my mouth.

"Is it too—?" she asks nervously.

"It's perfect!" I squeal, pushing back up off the sofa. Reina follows.

Ana grits her teeth. "Are you sure?"

It's *quite literally perfect.* A super intricate, embellished trumpet silhouette gown.

"Ren will love it," Reina says quietly.

Her eyes are buckets, mine too. The designer steps back, admiring her work, while the seamstress fusses at the back of the dress. "We're going to have to take it in again," she gripes in a heavy French accent.

Ana tries on the removeable illusion sleeves, then steps down from the little stage and waves me back to the dressing room. The seamstress finishes pinning—pinning, while sighing, shaking her head and blowing air—then undoes the intricate snaps before she exits.

"She's quite rude," Ana whispers.

"She's French," I say, coming over her shoulder in the mirror. "But worth it—you look like an absolute fairytale."

She runs her hands down her stomach then turns in the mirror, her eyes falling to the gaping back of the dress.

I swallow. "You're not doing it again, are you?"

"Not like before," she answers sheepishly.

"Ana," I press. "You *must eat.*"

"I swear, it's not like the past; I just get nervous for these." She spins to me and grabs my hands. "Are you okay?"

I pause. *No, I'm not okay.*

"I'm a bit in shock, I suppose—that the picture got out and is this widespread… And how dare someone leak that on Monaco weekend! It was weeks ago!"

She squeezes my fingers. "But Beck knew you had a scare?"

"It wasn't a *scare*—I was being stupid."

She's still waiting for me to answer the question.

I take a big breath. "No—I didn't tell him."

"Sophie!" she says, eyes wide.

"I wasn't going to tell him about a nonexistent problem until it was *existent*—which it never came to be!"

"Was he upset?"

"He was angry that Shannon was the deliverer of said message." I huff, "*Fucking hell!* I thought a discrete delivery would be safer than being seen buying a test myself! What is the world coming to when you can't even trust a delivery boy? It's mad!"

Ana smiles and spins back around. I help her step out of the dress and hang it up for her. It's quite heavy, especially for her tiny frame. I plop down on a little stool in the corner, pulling my phone from my bag and opening the post on *Lights Out Ladies*.

"Listen to this comment!" I say, getting her attention.

"Paddock_Insider: her inheritance may be in question now that her dad is on the verge of remarrying—who wouldn't attempt to baby trap Beckham Wright?"

Ana's mouth forms an O.

"Can you believe that? I had to look up what baby trapping meant!"

She shakes her head. *"Paddock insider?* What, do we have a mole amongst us?"

I continue, *"She's got to be pregnant; she hasn't been seen in the paddock at Monaco all week. And I wouldn't be surprised. They are always packing on the PDA."*

Ana snorts a laugh.

I look up at her, surprised. "Are we inappropriate?"

"He's *quite* handsy with you—but it's cute!" she coos.

I roll my eyes as I swipe out of the page and stand up.

She buttons her oversized cardigan, then peeks at me. "You are careful, though?"

"Of course we're careful—*ish*."

She giggles and steps into her Chanel flats.

My phone vibrates. Elizabeth's name pops up on the lock screen. A flood of panic rushes through me. She must have gotten word—she's being promoted to *Gran!*

Elizabeth Wright:

Evelyn i.s LOVELYYY

Woah girl!

Sorry we've been sat on the. patio for hours

They're golfing, we're rosé-ing

She's about convinced you dad to take home a puppy!!!

NO. WAY.

Little Bear's taken quite a liking to her!!

I think for a second, then type it out and hit send. I dropped the ball in telling Beck myself. I won't do that with her.

> If you hear anything or if my dad asks or is acting weird or suddenly drops from a heart attack

> I'm NOT pregnant.

> I'll explain later.

> WHAT????!!!!!

It's a bit shocking that she hasn't seen *The Scoop* headline. Did you see it?

"Rumors are swirling: is championship leader Beckham Wright hiding partner's pregnancy?"

I slouch. If any of this extra noise gets into his head, I swear I will go full-on Sophie rampage.

> Would it be better if I didn't come tomorrow?

Beck:

> You're coming

> Period.

> You still want a kiss before the race?

No.

I want 100.

I jump as another cork pops out in the studio, followed by a ruckus from Lili and Mira. Ana rolls her eyes and grabs her bag.

"You think they'll make it out tonight?"

"I hope not," she says, displeased.

CHAPTER 26
POUTY LIPS

ELLA

I'VE GOTTEN QUITE CLOSE with Amelia Drake, the CEO's wife. She's a bit taken with me. Followed me on Instagram and has been buddied up at my side yesterday and today. She's fascinated by influencing and wants the lowdown on every deal. I told her about Fylter, and I'm bringing her a few of their bits tomorrow. They've got next-level money, the Drakes. She showed me a picture of the yacht *with a helipad* that she wants next. When I asked if they had a helicopter, she didn't say no, she said *not yet*. Even though Mum's totally written off men and any future possibility of love, I asked Amelia about any single eligibles in her circle.

"Tommy, we need P5 or better," his race engineer says. "Get it done."

This will be his final flier. Quali has been a bit messy—Q1 was red flagged after Mateo put it into the wall at Portier. Both MACHs made it to Q2, but another red flag came when Eduardo put it into the wall after botching the Nouvelle chicane. Alek nearly scraped by into Q3 but was eliminated by none other than Imre's final run.

Tommy slides the car through Sainte Devote, only a hair's distance from the wall. The same wall he'd smacked into during first practice yesterday, ending his practice early.

His onboard is a blur of walls and signage as he twists and turns the car through the narrow streets. When he shoots out of the tunnel, I don't know how he's not bloody blind for an entire minute. He comes across the line, and his name knocks up two places in the standings.

"That's P7, Tommy," his engineer delivers.

"Fuck!" he yells. "Sorry, guys."

1 WRI

2 VAN

3 KAP

4 MAT

5 ENA

6 LOM

7 YOU

8 NOW

9 PAT

10 BER

Surprisingly, my phone didn't set fire to Tommy's drawer because our outfit check went *viral*. As of this morning, it's hit eight million views. In short order, a screenshot of my joyride story in the 720s landed on the gossip page along with snaps of us coming and going from his building. I feel a bit sick with how nuts the post went—as in the one I did when I was in that really dark place. The one with the picture. *That one.*

By the time I cooled off, it was too late to delete it. If I had to pick the most double-edged sword in the modern world, it would have to be the invention of the screenshot. Lovely feature. My screenshot library contains thousands of images, but the fact that any accident or mistake you later regret can be captured in an instant by anyone as evidence—well, that can be more of a curse than a blessing, no? A picture lives forever, and my picture had already been screenshotted and rescreenshotted. The damage was done. Then *The Scoop* picked it up. That's when the angel on my shoulder reappeared. She's since had her finger out, scolding the shoulder-slumped devil while he hides his face behind his shit wing. It's this fucking Fylter deal hanging over my head that's driving me mad.

I follow Viktoria to the media pen. The MACH duo is beat and put out with P7 and P11. Though Tommy looks alright when he's a bit pouty and sullen. But that red-haired airhead reporter must have also noticed his pouty lips. I grimace as she puts her hand on his shoulder to console him and open the group chat.

ROOMIE TRIO

Ella:

> You doing alright, Soph?

Soph:

Bridal things keeping us busy

Soph:

Might get hairy tonight. I got a table at Maison Sacré!

Well, well. There was a time when I was the only one who could get us a table there.

Soph:

Is you know who around this week?

Ella:

F?

Ella:

I did see him today.

Carmen:

When did you take that test????

Carmen:

And why wasn't I holding it when you peed on it????

Soph:

After Easter. I was being silly. I was hardly late and playing mind games with myself.

Soph:

Is there any talk about it in the paddock?

Ella:

Not that I've heard

Ella:

If so, it hasn't thrown Beck!

Ella:

P1!

Soph:

<3

An individual message from Sophie pops up.

Soph:

> Can you do me a favor and watch the clip I made for Beurre?

> I just emailed it to you!

> What clip?

Soph:

> They asked me to record a quick promo to run before the show

Soph:

> Probably thought it was an easy ask, but I had to film it three times over

I clench my jaw.

Soph:

> Did you make one too?

> Right! I'll watch it.

I open my email. No way I missed a request from Beurre, but I check anyway. There's been nothing since our last correspondence about lighting for the show. I open Sophie's video attachment and hit play.

"Be sure to tune in next week on the livestream for the Beurre show in Miami, where we'll be debuting the latest collection."

She's bright and dewy and beautiful in the sun on our teeny balcony. My nails dig into the base of my palm—I didn't realize I was clenching my fist.

CHAPTER 27
EGGPLANT

SOPHIE

ANA'S ARMS ARE DRAPED over mine and Reina's shoulders, making all three of our faces nearly touch. We're in that gushy drunk mode where you're all feelings and professing your love for one another.

"You're such a good *frienddd*," Ana slurs.

"She's such a good friend!" Reina nods, eyes hazy.

"No, you're such a good friend! I couldn't have done last year without you, Ana!"

She leans her head against mine. "We're going to be neighbors soon," she tells Reina.

I lightly shake my head, but it's disturbed by a hiccup.

Lili walks over to where we're sitting on the couch and stares down at us. "You going to make out now?"

"Shut it!" Ana shouts back. The pearl strap of her white beaded dress falls from her shoulder. I slide it back.

Mira is behind Lili, making out with a *second* mystery man she's tried to bring back to our table twice already. Both times Ana stood up and denied entry. There's a girlies-only force field in our little section of the strobe-lit nightclub. My phone vibrates between my thighs—my holding ground because it doesn't fit in my opal starfish Judith Leiber.

It's him. He's screenshotted my story—a picture of me and Ana dolled up at the hotel before we left for our big night out.

Beck:

Is this a joke?

You're stunning.

It's a lilac mini dress I'm wearing, with cap sleeves and my diamond bracelet and earrings.

You should see what's underneath

Your favorite

The blue?

Yessssss

Fucking hell

Let me see

"Is that Beck?" Ana asks.

I smile stupidly, and it's a dead giveaway.

"Ah!" she squeaks.

"You think Mr. Wright is Mr. Right?" Reina asks.

And I'm honestly shocked no one's made that play on words before.

Ana gives an enormous, exaggerated nod of her head, answering for me.

"Will you come to the loo?" I whisper in her ear.

She eyes me suspiciously but hops up.

We step out of our bubble and push through the bodies in the crowded nightclub. Twenty girls are crammed into the noisy bathroom with the intended occupancy of maybe ten. I pull Ana into a stall and flip the lock.

"What are we doing?" she giggles.

I hand her my phone and slip the sleeves of my dress off my shoulders.

"Take my picture!"

Her eyes bulge. "What!"

"It's for Beck," I whisper.

The bathroom door opens, letting in another rowdy bunch of girls. I lean against the back of the stall door and split my fingers where my nipples show through the sheer lace of the baby blue bralette cups.

"Oh my God, this is sexy!" Ana says, now completely into it.

I fold over laughing and bring the straps of my dress back up.

"Alright, one more!" Lifting the bottom of my dress, I slide my hand down the front of the matching sheer lace panties.

"Sophie Collins!" Ana shouts, eyes wide, but snaps the picture nonetheless.

And they're actually not half bad. Or maybe I'm drunker than I realize? But I honestly don't care at the minute. It's his favorite set of mine, and I miss him terribly.

I send the first shot. Triple-check, eyes squinted, that it's his text conversation that's open on the receiving end.

"Do you send Ren pictures?"

"No!" she squeals. "I'm not sexy!"

"Ana!" I scoff. "You are—*sex!!*"

She chews her bottom lip, and I lift an eyebrow.

"I simply cannot do that!" she says frantically.

My phone lights up, making her eyes light up. "He wrote back?!"

I step beside her so she can read his reply.

Beck:

Fuckkkkk

Ana giggles, puts her hand over her mouth. I message him back.

For P1 <3

What are you doing?

Was relaxing…

Now thinking of all the ways I want to wreck you

Ana squeals and stomps her feet. A very Beckham Wright message.

Tomorrow please?

And the next day.

And the next.

Now send more.

I send off the next picture, the one I know will make him go mental. No telling what he'll send back. A pair of peep-toe heels knocks on the stall door.

"You ready?" I ask.

"Wait!" she whispers, all panicky. "I want to send one!"

"Ren will drop dead!" I say, taking her phone before she changes her mind. "Now show me what you've got under that!"

She nervously lifts her dress in one hand; there's not much she's got under it in terms of undergarments. She takes the other hand and covers her bare nipple. *Ah! She's a babe!*

"Wifey material!" I shout, proud as ever.

She snatches her phone back and smiles down at her picture. "Now what do I write?"

I ponder for a second. "*Nothing.* Just send it out of the blue!"

She mashes her lips together, closes one eye and nervously sends it off to Ren.

"Alright, let's get back before they burn the place down." I turn to the door and flip the lock.

"He replied!" she shouts.

"What's he said?" I nearly scream.

Her face scrunches, eyes pinch.

"He sent a—" She looks up at me. "He sent an eggplant?"

I double over, laughing again. "That's a good thing, Ana!"

I grab her arm. "Come on, then. Reina's probably traumatized."

CHAPTER 28

FACE CARD

ELLA

WISH I HAD MY cigarettes right about now. I refill my glass before I start the novel. Three-quarters through a bottle of Chianti should do it. It's usually at this point in the bottle that my brain's nice and warm like melty cheese in a perfectly grilled toastie. Can you tell I'm hungry? I take a swig and lean back against the counter in Tommy's kitchen. Finally, my *official rating's* been posted.

It's a three-photo collage. The angel costume party picture of the three of us is in the center, though someone's drawn a red X over Emma's face. *And no,* it wasn't me. Beside it, are me and Tommy in his McLaren. And the third—our kiss in the Barcelona paddock.

Official: MACH WAG Ella Humphrey 9/10

Apologies, there's been quite pressing tea in the kettle as of late—but here it is! Just in time for the Monaco Grand Prix! A pillar of the ultimate single-girl community has fallen! Ella Humphrey goes exclusive with MACH pilot Tommy Young. An established influencer joins the WAGs in the paddock! The outfits? No notes, crushes every time. Ella hasn't seemed to get an interview yet, but I can't wait around. And TBH—she doesn't need one. We know who she is. She's always running her mouth on socials, she'd have smashed an interview. The pair finally put the 'they're just friends' notion to rest when they shared a kiss in the paddock in Barcelona—thank you, David Campbell, for capturing a still of the moment! By all accounts, Tommy looks smitten. He even joined her in a hilarious outfit check before the team dinner in Monaco Thursday. The same clip where she referred to Tommy as her boyfriend—a word I've never heard from the lips of one Ella Humphrey.⊠ What interests me is the timeline on this one. Was girl code broken? Tommy was photographed with on-again-off-again girlfriend (and known jersey chaser) Emma Trautmann just before Christmas and again in early January. In February, the first sightings of Emma and Imre emerged. Did Tommy/Ella happen before Imre/Emma? Was one the result of another? Regardless, I'm giving Ella a 9/10 simply for bringing WAG drama to the paddock. And the first user to get me footage of an Ella/Emma exchange gets a prize. Ella's Tommy's typical type—the fourth blonde bombshell we've seen on his arm. Emma's a babe, but Ella's face card never declines.

Our new couple was speculated to be hooking up during last year's summer break. Those rumors turned out to be fake news—as it was actually the beginning of Beck and Sophie's relationship. If you aren't familiar with Ella's past—she's always single, but always on a date. She leveled up from her uni days, where she was once a serial dater of diplomat's sons, and moved on to date a slew of men, all of whom look like they've stepped out of a Tom Ford catalog. And now, she's sunk her claws into MACH driver Tommy Young.

I gulp. *Damn.* Quite glowing, if you ask me. The first comments start to appear, a random username:

The plot thickens! Emma and Tommy have unfollowed each other. Emma has also unfollowed Ella and deleted all the old photos of her and Tommy from her page! Ella still follows as of now.

A comment appears from *Boxbox#6*:

Hot damn! Can we get a body count for Ella?

Another appears from a random username:

Body count for Emma too, while we're at it.

I upvote the latter, then nibble my fingernail. The comments are flying in.

Are we sure Tommy isn't just one of her many? She's always dated no less than five guys at once!

Hilarious that Emma's obvi on Base Beauty's PR list, and Ella reps Fylter so hard.

I think we've done it; people are buying *us*. Surely this will only help, not hinder, the Fylter deal...? *Fuck.* I huff and slam my phone face- down on the counter a bit hard because I'm a bit tipsy. I drag my fingers down my face.

"You alright?" Tommy asks, coming into the kitchen. "You look about as stressed as I do."

I boost myself up onto the edge of the counter and pick up my wine.

"Do I look that bad?" I ask, taking another glug.

"You never look bad," he says, still wearing his pouty lips from qualifying.

He comes toward me, lifts the wine bottle and wipes the red ring it's created on his perfect counter from my imperfect pour and walks to the sink.

Where exactly did he get that dishrag? And how could he possibly know there was a crescent stain under the bottle?

I can smell him from here—warm and fresh out of the shower. Several droplets have soaked through the T-shirt hugging his shoulders. He shuts off the faucet and turns around.

"Are you not sleeping well in there?" he asks, leaning back against the sink. "You can sleep in my bed, you know."

I huff.

"We could cuddle," he says with a flick of his eyebrows.

I narrow my eyes at him. "You wish."

"Fine, no cuddles." He shrugs, but then a shit-eating grin spreads over his face. "We could always fuck? Could help us both."

I cough, nearly choking on my own spit, and let out another little huff. "I can do it better myself," I quip, before downing another gulp.

With a suspicious expression, he pushes off the counter, and my heart skips several beats as he makes his way over to me.

He lifts a brow. "You're telling me some little toy can make your legs shake as much as I did?"

I flush and lift my wine, but he grabs it from me and takes a long pull. My mouth opens, then closes before it opens again. For maybe the first time in my life, I'm a bit tongue-tied. *Were my legs shaking in Melbourne?* It was a tequila night, God only knows what happened. Is it possible it was *that good*? Maybe that's exactly what I need—it's been a minute, having the bench on hold and all. Perhaps a body-quaking orgasm could get me out of my head and off this secret path of destruction I've been plowing. I swallow, half giving the idea the proper time of day.

He returns the glass to the counter and sets his hand on my knee. My breath quickens. He's onto me now from my lack of a quick comeback or, *fuck*, any comeback at all.

His head cocks to the side. "You don't remember?"

"I remember!" I snap, desperately trying to regain control of the conversation. *"Bits..."*

I shift a hair as he steps closer. Something ignites in my brain—that chemical that releases when I feel wanted by a man, which is 99 percent of the time, but the man in front of me just happens to be throwing me a bit.

I fight with my eyes and lose when they flick down to his lips—a bit less pouty now, still soft and puffy and completely kissable.

Fuck.

I will my eyes back up and those warm, still-melting-in-the-pot toffee eyes are fixated on me. Don't know why his eyes do funny things to my insides—like that funny dance I felt on the boat the other night. I don't even like toffee. I swallow. His gaze shifts to the wine. He picks up my glass again, downs the last gulp and places the empty beside me. I wait for his eyes to come back to me—and they do.

That's a lie, by the way. I love toffee.

"Perhaps once more wouldn't hurt..." I mutter.

"Right." He half nods, eyes pinching. "Get it out of our systems."

I blink. "Okay then, *Thomas.*"

He crinkles his nose. "No one calls me Thomas. Not my parents, not anyone."

I reach out and grab the fabric of his shirt, parting my legs and pulling him even closer.

"I'm not anyone," I say softly.

My gaze falls to his hand on my knee but only for a beat before we're back to staring. I set my hand on top of his and guide it from my knee, up my thigh and under my dress. His lips part. I push his hand against the warmth in the crook of my thighs, and that's where I leave it.

"*Fuck*, Ella," he whispers before his mouth comes at me. His hand wraps around the nape of my neck. Our lips collide, and the back of my head meets the cabinet door. He's got the deliciously bitter taste of wine on his tongue—*my wine.* His fingers slip inside my knickers, and my hands venture under his shirt, over his tight stomach. He pulls away, reaches between his shoulder blades and peels his shirt off over his head. *Fuck, he's fit.* I attempt to catch my breath, but he tosses his shirt to the floor and immediately moves back in. My hand dives down the front of his trousers, wrapping around the base of his length. *He's nearly ready.* The clasps at the back of my dress come undone with ease. *Experienced with clothing removal, this one.* He takes down the zipper, and my breasts fall free, bare in his hands.

"*My God*," he whispers against my lips.

I arch my back a bit, pushing my chest harder into his hands. "Now do you remember them?"

His lips curl into a smile. "I never forgot." *He's fully hard now.* He lifts me off the counter onto his waist and heads for his bedroom.

It's rough and rash, hot and heavy. Arms and legs all tangled up in one another. But he's right, and I hate that he's right. It's a leg-shaking, all-senses consuming release that clears my mind and makes me forget for a moment why I've been so caught up in my head.

It's dark, but the curtains are open, casting a bit of moonlight onto the bed. Tommy's on his back, and I'm propped up in the nook of his arm, level with his torso. His hand's on his chest, and I'm staring at the *VI* tattooed on his ring finger—his racing number. He's got a random collection of tattoos, but as random as they are, they're very tidy. No shading, all clean simple black lines.

"Quite the assortment of stars," I say, pointing along the outside of his pinkie.

"Everybody likes stars." He smiles.

I pick up his hand and push each of his fingers down one by one, revealing the lucky charm symbols he's got between them.

"I fancy these ones," I say, inspecting each—a clover, a horseshoe, a spade, a heart.

There's a compass on his pec muscle and directly across his chest is a cupid. I nod at the numbers that run vertically behind his ear.

"What do the numbers mean?"

"They're coordinates."

"To a treasure?"

"No," he laughs. "To my family's farm outside Melbourne."

Farm boy. My eyes trail down his shoulder, past the tribal-esque band that circles above his bicep. I lift up his hand to peep at the one he's got on the back of his arm above his elbow.

My eyes pinch. "Is this...?"

"The Deathly Hallows." He grins, all proud.

"Alright, man-child!" I mock, hiding the fact that I often identify as a witch.

"*Man-child?* Name one person who wouldn't claim Harry Potter as a literary masterpiece of our generation."

"Did you actually read them? Watching the movies doesn't count!"

"All of them!" he says defensively. "Cover to cover."

I give him a condescending *hm!* and a pat on the arm. "Didn't know you could read."

He rolls his eyes, still smiling though. "You're such a brat."

I like how easily I can get him going. It makes me giggle.

"You going to get any more?"

He wiggles the fingers of his hand that's on my backside. "I want to do my other hand. Need more lucky symbols."

"More luck? Have you ever had a bad wreck?"

"Not really. Nothing like Beck's last year." His eyes flash, and he jerks over to his bedside table and raps his knuckles against it.

"You're quite superstitious, aren't you?"

He settles back against the pillows. "A bit OCD, too, if you haven't noticed."

"Not at all!" I say sarcastically.

He shifts and stretches his back.

"What's the verdict then? You feel better?" I ask.

He winks. "And what had you looking all stressed?"

"Just work stuff," I say, eyes returning to the markings on his chest. "Getting this Fylter deal is driving me plain mad. I want it. *Bad*."

"You'll get it. If they've got any brains at all." He puts his hand on my wrist. "Will you stay in here tonight?"

My eyes flick up to his—caught off guard would be an understatement.

"That won't be necessary," I say, pulling my wrist away, resting it back against my chest. "Don't want you breaking any of your pre-race rituals."

"Fuck the rituals. They aren't exactly working, are they?" He turns onto his side, facing me so we're practically nose to nose. His eyes wander around my face, and I curse the funny feeling that's back in my stomach at the minute.

"You're going to be great tomorrow," I whisper.

He closes his eyes and sighs heavily, taking his time to reopen them. "The car's a tractor, Ella."

I smile at the discouraged farm boy in front of me. "And you're going to run the wheels off that tractor."

CHAPTER 29
PARTY FAVORS?

ELLA

I TWIST AROUND to try and crack my back. "*Getting it out of our systems*" has left me a bit sore, but a good sore? I'd made a plan to escape back to my couch in the sim room as soon as he fell asleep—*but I fell asleep*. I slept so hard I woke up to his alarm and him breathing in my face. He was funny this morning. All business, all jittery for the race. I hope he slept half as hard as I did because Monaco is fucking madness at the minute.

Speaking of madness, the gossip site has a new set of photos to feast on. Don't look at me! I didn't post them! It seems someone had eyes on the final night of the bridal bash. There's a picture of Sophie and Ana's feet stuffed into a single stall in the loo. Rotten luck. It's quite hard to come by toilets where the doors don't reach the floor. There's another picture where two of the other bridesmaids are partaking in an unmistakable round of key bumps with a couple of lads. I'm not judging—I'm no saint or stranger to that shit, but this behavior for the betrothed and one Belle of Britain? *Yikes.*

The race starts in an hour, and she's just arrived at the paddock—must have been a big night. Her eyes are low on the ground in front of her, hidden by sunglasses. I lower mine to get a look at her ensemble—this is a new outfit, and yes, I do know all of her clothes. Carmen's too. Has she become a Miu Miu beneficiary in the last three days?!

"Soph!"

Her head pops up, and she races toward me. She moves her sunglasses to her head and looks around nervously. Come downs are shit. They always get me paranoid too.

I give her head-to-toe Miu Miu ensemble another look. "Is this the new...?"

"Lovely, isn't it? A courier sent some things to the hotel for me!"

A darling mini, sunglasses, and slides that I swear I only saw on pre-order. Her VIP lanyard's fastened to their leather basket bag that's on her arm. *Fucking hell.*

Her eyes dart around. "For obvious reasons, I'll be avoiding your camp like the plague."

"Oh—*Fredrick?*" I say, a bit baffled because he is not the glaring issue I had top of mind. "Don't worry, the sponsors are watching from the boat today."

She blows out a sigh, relieved. "Has it been alright then? Staying with Tommy?"

"Great! I've taken over the place." I swat my hand and quickly change the subject. "And you? Are you really about to call this place home?"

"No." She smiles. "Beck is looking for a place, but...that line was a bit misleading."

I nod. "A wild night then? Last night?"

She shrugs. "Drank a bit. The traffic getting in was horrible."

"No other party favors?"

Sophie gulps and looks at me all doe-eyed. "W-what do you mean?"

She doesn't know.

"Oh, dear." I put my arm around her shoulder and get out my phone. "I was on the gossip site this morning—my score finally came out, and it was great! But anyway—there were some pictures..."

I pull up the site manually as if I don't have it bloody bookmarked and offer my phone.

"Blow at the bridal bash? Must be how they stay so thin." Her mouth falls open. She quickly zooms in on a picture.

"Fucking hell! Those are her cousins! I didn't know they did *co—"*

"What's happening in that picture in the toilets?"

"Not that!" she cries defensively.

"Two sets of legs in the same stall?" I say gently. "You know what that looks like..."

"We were taking pictures!"

I lift a brow. "In the loo?"

She huffs. "Naughty pictures." Her eyes flick around; I can practically see her heart beating out of her chest. "Last week I was pregnant, and this week I'm doing coke?"

My stomach turns. I take my phone back. "It's alright, Soph. This hasn't been picked up by *The Scoop*, I checked."

It falls out of my mouth, complete word vomit. *What the fuck is wrong with me?*

"Not yet!" she shouts, and her voice catches.

My heart's running mad now. This is my best friend. I'm a good witch—I don't enjoy seeing her like this. A wicked witch would revel in watching her squirm. How is her little body holding the weight of it all? Part of which was brought on by no one other than myself.

Her lip starts to quiver. "I've got to go find Beck."

Yes. *Please*, before I quite literally vomit. I give her a quick squeeze. "By some miracle, maybe I'll see you under the podium."

CHAPTER 30

PDA

SOPHIE

THE MOMENT I WALKED into hospitality, Beck didn't buy my glassy eyes and forced shaky smile for half a second. He took my hand, shut the door of his driver's room and set me up on the desk. He smiled the whole time, braced, and caught each of my tears. It sort of hit me all at once, I suppose. Everyone was staring the minute I stepped out of the car. But I think it was the way Shannon looked at me from the front steps of the suite. I saw her eyes flick down to my stomach. I was in such shock, I sort of shook my head? I guess to let her know that I'm not—*ugh*. She took a rather deep breath, relieved. A bit humiliating.

Beck sat there with me for five whole minutes in probably the busiest hours I've ever seen around the paddock. When I got the tears out, he ducked and found my eyes. And with the biggest twinkly smile, asked, *"Did you want to be pregnant?"* He might have even looked a bit disappointed when I said, *"No, thank you.* I'm glad to not be knocked up at the minute." I told him I also wasn't doing drugs last night if anyone's asked. He was proper confused by that one—had no idea what I was going on about. Not sure if it's on Shannon's radar yet. It wasn't even on mine! Mira tried to bring one of those guys back to the suite. I'm sure it was that lot supplying the *favors*. Ana said absolutely not, and she, Reina and I locked ourselves in one of the rooms and fell asleep watching *The Devil Wears Prada*.

I'm always in awe of Beck, but it's days like today that I truly can't comprehend his abilities. He can handle *anything*. Including a breakdown from his girlfriend just before he's to race in the streets of Monaco from pole. And now, here he is, still leading the Monaco Grand Prix *seventy* laps in.

"Eight more, Beck. Head down!" Coop cheers him on.

"Copy," Beck huffs, breathing heavy.

Beck passes another two back markers as he rounds turn six—the famous ultra low-speed hairpin. Only five points separate Beck and Leo in the championship after Barcelona, and if he can hold on to first, he'll extend his lead by twelve, for one hundred and five points to Leo's nine-ty-three.

I'm not saying the race is *boring*—the whole experience is truly brilliant, unparalleled really. But in terms of actual racing action on track? There's simply not room to pass! There's only been two overtakes—the first of which was unsuccessful when Ren took off his front wing on lap one, trying to pass Ian for fourth position. That incident took care of one of the two required pitstops at this circuit and ended both Ren and Ian's race. It did bump up Luca to fourth and Tommy to fifth.

The only other overtake, this one successful, happened when Tommy passed Luca through the exit of turn eight into the tunnel. That was hard to watch when you adore both pilots—I was equal parts gutted for Luca and ecstatic for Tommy.

I have to take a few breaks from Beck's onboard. I can only watch so many laps of him snaking through the streets before I get dizzy. It's beyond impressive—he's managed to keep a cool head and his car out of the wall for *seventy-eight* laps.

"Leo tried an early move but was stuck staring at the gearbox of Beck's Furio lap after lap. Beck pulled away and has maintained a gap of more than five seconds!

...And for the first time in his career, Beckham Wright will stand on the podium's highest step, holding the largest trophy in Monaco!"

Blessing in disguise?

How's that?!

Proper reason to kick Lili and Mira from the bridal party, no?

Baby Luca's even cuter with the fat little cheeks he's growing. Luca hangs up our FaceTime with Pippa and the baby. It was P5 for him. *His best finish this season*. The celebrations at the Furio afterparty are winding down. Beck's been eyeing me from across the room for the entirety of the FaceTime. His eyes are a bit weighty from the refreshments that have been flowing since the podium ceremony. He maneuvered through hordes of cameras, countless champagne dousings and hundreds of handshakes. And now he's staring at me with those hungry, heavy eyes I adore, while he half listens to the woman beside him, talking his ear off.

He signals to me with a small nod of his chin, and I walk through the crowd. He lifts his phone to his ear and covers the other with his hand. I come up under his arm, and he quickly hangs up the call and drops his phone into his inner jacket pocket. He tucks me under his chin and kisses the top of my head.

I stare up at him, and his eyes twinkle.

"I've got to show you something."

Outside, a mass of fans is held at bay, the back hinged back seat door of a Rolls Cullinan is opened by an attendant. I hurry inside. The windows are heavily tinted, and a privacy screen separates the front seats from us. The moment the door shuts, Beck has me on my back, his lips trailing down my neck, then across my sternum. His stubble titillates my skin, sending velvety warm pulses between my legs. The car starts moving. It's got one of those night-sky ceilings with the little glowing lights, have you sat in one before? A sharp left turn is made; I giggle as his weight shifts on top of me. His hands slide under my dress and up my body. His mouth finds mine, and my fingers find his hair. I moan as he takes my nipple between his fingertips. With all my might, I push my hips up into him, and he responds by sinking two fingers inside me.

"*Fuckkk*, baby," he groans into my mouth.

He's always shocked by how ready I am for him, as if I have control over how my body reacts? You try keeping your panties dry when the bedroom eyes of Beckham Wright have been locked on you for an hour straight. He works his fingers while relentlessly sucking on my neck. And *my word*, I wonder for a moment if we're about to make a mess in the backseat of this £300,000 car.

My eyes flip open, my awareness coming back to me. "We've stopped!" I breathe heavily.

But it's too late. The back seat door opens, and a flood of flashes pours in. Beck's head flips up. I tip mine back and catch a glimpse of the sea of phones outside the door just before it closes again. *Oh. Shit.*

Beck looks down at me and busts out laughing. He sits up, pulling me up with him. *No wonder the world suspects I'm pregnant.* He takes his palm down his face, amused. Heart racing, I smooth out my dress and hair.

Beck takes a deep breath and adjusts the front of his pants. "Alright, stay here!" he says, putting a hand to the door.

My eyes flick down to his waist. "You cannot get out of the car like that!"

His eyes go all smiley as he further adjusts himself. He turns his head away from me and rubs his brow. After another few deep breaths, he opens the door to his right. The volume outside the car picks up. Moments later, my door opens, *again,* and his hand reaches in. A concierge is at Beck's side, apologizing profusely for the earlier intrusion. I keep my eyes on the ground as we make our way past the mob and into the lobby of a residential tower.

Beck nods at a suited gentleman behind a desk and leads me straight to the lifts. Inside, the buttons read as numbers until they turn into *PH* prefixed labels. He hits fifteen.

"Is this a place you're looking at?" I ask.

He rests against the lift wall and pulls me against his chest.

"That depends—" he says, eyes all sparkly. "Could you see yourself living here?"

I give him a demure one-shoulder shrug.

It's a large building; there are six units on the fifteenth floor. Beck stops and unlocks the door of 1503. He reaches in and flips a light on.

"Go on, then," he says with a nod.

My footsteps echo. I fidget with my fingers as I walk toward a wall of glass overlooking Port Hercules. It's unfurnished—a beautiful, massive blank canvas.

"Leo lives in one of the penthouses, Tommy is down the street."

He comes behind me, bringing his head over my shoulder, and takes my hand.

"Ren and Ana," he says, guiding my finger, pointing it to a tower below, "are just there."

"Lovely neighbors."

"There's a whole floor with a pool deck, a sauna, a gym."

"And our boat?" I tease.

He taps the glass with the tip of my finger, pointing to the packed port. "It can be right out there."

"It's awfully dreamy," I say softly. The sea beyond the port is littered with glowing yachts that didn't secure a coveted dock spot. The view is quite literally mesmerizing.

"I promise that what happened downstairs—the crowds—it's not like that on a normal weekend." His fingers interlace with mine. "I bought it—for us."

I blink. What he said sort of hangs in the air, and for a moment, I question my hearing and comprehension abilities.

"You *what?*"

"I bought it for us, Sophie."

It seems my hearing is just fine. A million thoughts take flight at once, chaotically colliding together within the confines of my brain so not a single one can be properly processed.

I spin around and study his face—*he's serious.*

"I—I live in Paris," I manage.

He smiles, then brings the tip of his nose to mine. "*For now.*"

He lifts my hands over my head and presses them against the glass before all of his weight presses against me. His lips find my neck, and the temperature skyrockets back to what it was in the car. I want him *bad*. I rush to wrap my leg around him because his body pressed against mine, pressed against this glass, is somehow not close enough.

CHAPTER 31

ACROSS THE POND

I ADJUST EACH TUBE of lip gloss so they're perfectly spaced in front of us and the camera. Fylter sent each of us a brand-new PR box. Behind the gloss, I've laid out their highlighters, every shade of liquid eyeshadow, blush and bronzer sticks. I think even Tommy would approve of this alignment job.

"And last but not least, the holy grail Honey Gloss." I grab the rosy pink-colored tube, untwist the cap and begin applying. Sophie picks up the dark red.

"I've been loving this shade—it's the sugared watermelon." I shove the applicator back into the tube. "Tommy also happens to love the flavor."

Sophie's eyes go a bit wide.

I nudge her, amused. "Does Beck have a favorite?"

She kicks my stool.

"*I—*" Sophie says, flicking her eyes to me then back to the camera, "prefer the cherry velvet."

She begins applying the gloss. Carmen grabs an eyeshadow and samples it on the back of her hand. I give an outro, noting that Fylter's new extended line-up is dropping in July, then give a final wink before stopping the recording.

I blow out a breath, arch my back and groan.

"What happened?"

Tommy. *Tommy happened.*

"Must have slept funny. Did I tell you that asshole made me sleep on a couch?"

It's half true. I slept there Thursday and Friday. After quali and the race—well, those sleeps were in his bed. Nothing happened after the race, though. We were dead tired. We split the last bottle of Chianti—his almost podium was something to celebrate—talked and giggled until we passed out. I mean, his hands did roam a bit. I wanted something comfy, so I stole one of his T-shirts to wear over my knickers, and he couldn't resist copping a feel.

Which reminds me—I absolutely forgot to take his spare off my keyring. Suppose that's a him problem not a me problem. Did you see the photo carousel he posted on Instagram? He didn't clear any of the photos with me. Thankfully, it's rare that I take a bad picture. I'm in three of the six photos—not the first, though. *Rude.* There's one of us walking in on race day, another of us in the *720s* and the last—at the dinner table on the yacht. After the Drakes' boat and George and Evelyn's charter ventures, I absolutely must do it up for the big *two-five* with a proper yacht party. I mentioned as much to Celeste—maybe I can get a deal, something sponsored. Mum's also putting feelers out.

"I'll book us for yoga tonight!" Carmen says. "That'll help stretch you out!"

I fold my lips in—I've been stretched properly I assure you.

"I'm in!" Sophie adds. She flips her phone to Carmen.

"God, they're cute." Carmen gushes.

"Ridiculously cute! Look at how they chase after Gemma like little ducks!" She scrolls through more puppy pictures.

"Have they all got homes yet?"

"Five are accounted for. Most of them are going to church friends. But the Wrights are keeping Pirelli."

"That one's got such a sweet face," Carmen says. "Ollie wants one, like, bad! But he's gone too much!"

"Speaking of *face*, did you see Ella's rating?" Sophie asks, and I freeze.

"It was quite flattering!" Carmen confirms.

Sophie pokes my arm playfully. "You remember mine?"

I nod, a sudden wave of nausea hitting. She said it with a smile, but I remember how freaked out she was in the moment. Her rating wasn't *flattering* in any form of word.

"I also enjoyed the thought piece on the updates in the Monaco real estate market!" Carmen laughs, scrolling her phone.

Sophie's eyes roll.

"*Room for a nursery?*" Carmen reads out loud.

Sophie's hands go to her hips. "Suppose they didn't see I moved on from baby and prefer blow."

I swallow heavily.

"Obviously not," Carmen giggles, then continues: "*The Monaco Grand Prix winner celebrated with team Furio before engaging in an intimate back-seat moment with Sophie as seen in bystander videos. The destination? A luxury tower he was previously spotted at mid-week. A three-bedroom, ocean-view unit in said tower has since disappeared from the market. It is now known to have been purchased by Sir Beckham Wright.*"

I chug my water bottle, needing something in my stomach that's not food because well—*Beurre*. That on the verge of puking bit is back. It's true what they say, you know. Secrets make you sick.

"What were you doing in the back of that car?" Carmen asks, with a quirk of her eyebrows.

"He was snockered and—well, you know how he gets," Sophie says, all shy.

"A little tumble in the backseat?" Carmen teases, riling her up.

"No!" she snips. "Clothes were fully on!"

They continue banging on, and my stomach continues turning. I stare into the veins of the marble counter and chatter my teeth on the tip of my nail, the pace nearly matching the drumming of my racing heart.

"Are you going to move in?"

"Of course not! He's not even moving until break."

Carmen smiles, satisfied. "Ollie's always asking me too."

"And you say?"

"I say *hell no*. Put a ring on it first, why don't you!"

There's a giggle from Sophie.

"Besides," Carmen continues, "living with you lot is too much fun."

I never question myself, but in this instance, what I did was so evil I'm starting to question whether I actually did it. Was that truly me? Or is it possible some orb took control of my brain and started twisting wires and pulling levers when I uploaded that picture?

"Ella?" Sophie asks.

I suck in a breath, looking up to find both of them staring, not sure if I missed something.

"You alright?" Carmen asks.

My eyes dart between them.

"Of course!" I grab my water bottle, chug the last sip and crush it tightly. I slide off the stool. "Onto the next, then?"

I set up the vlog equipment in Sophie's room because mine's a proper mess, and I might have gone up to the roof for a *ritual*, and I didn't want to risk them smelling anything. Carmen jumps onto Sophie's bed. She'll spectate and keep me accountable because there's no fucking way everything I pulled is going to fit. The forecast at the circuit is looking to be quite England-like, requiring space for suitable looks for multiple climates. I start the recording and step in front of the camera.

"Pack with us for a two-week, three-leg soiree across the pond!"

Sophie unzips her case and flips it open.

"I'll be *attempting* to cram all my things into my ivory RIMOWA Essential Lite Check-In and my Classic Cabin. Soph's got her full-size RIMI and carry-on, and we've also got about twenty packing cubes."

"You going to say where you're off to?" Carmen says, flipping onto her stomach, behind the camera.

I narrow my eyes at her.

"Soph, remind me of our itinerary?"

She looks up, a bit nervous. She still gets like that in front of the camera.

"First stop will be Montreal with the boys, then we fly out for Miami Swim." Her eyes flick over for my approval before she continues. "And from there, we're off to the Fylter Beauty brand trip in St. Barth's!"

Nailed it. Two whole weeks of back-to-back fun with my best friend. Carmen and Ollie will join up with us in Miami. Finally, it's time to see all our effort come to life at the Beurre show. On the Fylter front, I've done the work and driven myself mad. If Fylter doesn't pick me, there's nothing more I can do. And if they pick her—well, I suppose it's not the end of the world.

CHAPTER 32

BABY DOT

ELLA

TOMMY ROLLS UP THE window he's been hanging out of, taking pictures, signing hats and T-shirts. I flip my phone to the selfie camera and turn my face to the side. It's gray and soggy out, a messy but chic high pony kind of day.

"Am I cute enough to be in your little picture?" Tommy asks, interrupting my photoshoot. He recaps the marker.

I lower my phone. "You were cute enough to be in all your fan's pictures."

"Yeah, but you're you."

Thomas Young! Would you look at him! He's learning.

I purse my lips and eye his outfit. "I suppose you'll do."

He's wearing a white team polo—much better than the usual orange that clashes with just about everything.

I unbuckle my seatbelt and scoot to the middle seat. I hold up my phone again, and he invades my selfie. It must be the white shirt making his golden toffee eyes appear extra warm and melty today. Did I mention I'm also in a white baby tee? He probably copied me. But enough about his eyes, with my hair pulled back from my face, I must say *my eyes* are looking like those blue glass cat's eye marbles.

I upload our selfie to my story while mindlessly chewing on the tip of my nail. Sam starts drumming on the dashboard in the front seat. We've slowed to a crawl in the queue of cars en route to the track. I tap back to watch my story from last night. Soph and I had ordered an entire cart of room service and had us a little feast in bed. Tommy uncaps the marker and pulls my hand from my mouth. He pushes my jacket sleeve down my wrist, and the tip of the marker hits the back of my hand. I continue scrolling, and he continues his little art project. I'm deep into posts from Miami Swim thus far, when I notice him staring at me. I turn to him, and his eyes flick down to my wrist, then back up.

"You should get it for real!" He smiles, proud of his work.

I've now got a small galaxy on the back of my hand. Wee stars and stardust, neat as a pin.

"Wait," he says, pulling my hand up close to his face. He marks a few final delicate details, then nods.

It almost looks like a tattoo—like his simple fine-line stamps.

"You're not going to sign it?" I glance up at him. "An original piece needs an autograph, Tommy."

Can't have people assume I'm childish enough to scribble on the back of my hand, though it's a masterful scribble. Loves stars, this one.

He pulls my hand back once more and adds a delicate *T-E-Y*. He pops the cap back on the marker.

"There you go, baby girl."

In the car park, Tommy takes my hand and helps me out of the back-seat. My feet are on the ground, but he doesn't let go of my hand. I remind myself that his hands are on me in case we encounter Emma's wandering eyes—no other reason. Sam hands him a folded-up umbrella before we set off.

It's nippy, starting to sprinkle. I suppose it's not so bad, holding hands. Beside Sam, we step onto the footbridge that crosses the water into the paddock. David Campbell's standing three-quarters of the way across, waiting for us. His usual bucket hat sits atop his head.

"Tommy! Ella!" he says, pulling his hood up over his hat and zipping his jacket up to his chin. A proper cameraman is with him today.

"Saw your outfit check last week." He smiles. "Would you mind giving me a quick outfit rundown for my channel?"

Tommy's gaze shifts to me, and I'm bloody beaming.

"We can do that right quick!" Tommy says. He drops my hand, pops open the umbrella, pulls me to his side beneath it and leaves his arm around me. He smashes his lips together, softly shaking his head because he knows I'm living for this moment. Sam bails, stepping behind the cameraman. I pull my sleeve down, trying to hide my star-adorned hand.

David steps beside us and gives the cameraman a thumbs-up.

"It's a soggy one for media day in Montreal, but I've got Tommy and Ella here, ready to give us a quick outfit check! What are we wearing today, Ella?"

I put my hand on my chest. "I've got on a simple white tee with Fendi's cropped silk windbreaker, high-waisted Frame trousers, drawstring pocket bag from Loewe, and the Hermès Oasis sandal."

They both look up from my feet, and I look up at Tommy.

"And I've got on our MACH team kit polo. Jeans are Off-White and kicks are the mid Nike Supreme AirForce 1s."

I nearly faint with his little description. His fingers tickle my side. *This clip is sure to go viral.*

"There we have it, folks!" David says, turning toward the camera. "An outfit check from one-half of team MACH!" He turns back to us. "Good luck this weekend, Tommy."

Sam's smiling, shaking his head in disbelief. David thanks us, Tommy retakes my hand, and we continue down the bridge.

"You should have said drawstring bag with an undetectable extension charm."

I roll my eyes. He's been saying that since he first saw the bag on my shoulder this morning.

"I should have shown off my flash tattoo! A Tommy Young original."

He smiles.

"What's the E for, anyway?" I ask, not like I care or anything.

"Edward."

Thomas Edward Young. The sprinkles pick up. He drops my hand and moves his arm around my waist, pulling me closer under the umbrella. We step off the bridge and turn into the paddock. Sam takes off for the suite. I slip my now-free hand into the front pocket of his jeans.

He shoots me a look.

"My fingers are cold." I shrug.

"Well, your fingers are half an inch from my dick, Ella."

"Too close?"

"Are you trying to get me hard?"

"Undetectable extension charm?" I wink.

"It's about to be a very detectable extension if you don't quit it!"

I wiggle my fingers, and he blows out a breath. "Why do you torture me?"

"Torture? I'm your girlfriend, and my hand is cold," I tease.

He blows out another breath as I dig my hand deeper.

"You're just too fun to mess with," I whisper below his ear. I give him a quick nut tap and pull my hand out.

He flinches, stopping in his tracks.

I step out from under the umbrella and pull my hood up. I wink back at him and walk the five remaining steps into MACH hospitality.

Tommy came and found me for lunch after shooting content with Alek all morning. He's across from me at a high-top table with his usual orange Lucozade. I'm in a jolly right mood. The views on David's video of us are *piling* up. I'm swinging my leg, brushing against his leg every now and then as I read the comments. Tommy reaches over and takes the brioche bun of my sandwich. I ate the middle of the sandwich, just not the carbs because, well, *Beurre*. I also have avoided washing my hands past my fingers to not disturb the stars. Not because I like them—I just don't want to hurt his feelings.

"You all ready for your show?" he asks, finishing my bun.

"Of course!"

"Is that why you're eating like a bird?"

"Precisely," I say without looking up, still scrolling, still swinging my leg under the table.

He pushes his plate away, and my ankle is snatched.

I shriek and shift in my chair, my ankle now in his grip under the table. He brings my foot higher and sets it on the stool between his legs. Stares down at it and runs his finger over my toes.

"What are you doing?" I ask as he slides my sandal off and sets it on the stool beside him.

"Looking for the freckle."

"It's on the other foot," I giggle.

"*Damn.*"

Then with both hands in his lap, he starts massaging my foot. I curl my toes because it tickles.

I stare at him. "You said you didn't have a thing for feet."

"Don't," he replies. "I just think your toes are cute."

I scan the dining room. Is this an act? His white polo sure makes his toffee eyes warm and melty—makes me forget for a second how much my toes are tickling.

"Do I get a sneak peek? Of the bikinis?"

I shake my head. "*Highly* confidential."

"Is there a theme?" he asks, continuing to massage my foot.

"The collection is called *Butter Baby*. It's all micro and mini patterns—baby gingham, baby dot, baby flower…"

"No!" His head pulls back, all exaggerated. "Baby girl in baby dot?"

I nod.

"Baby star?" He cocks an eyebrow.

I sniff a laugh. "No baby star."

"No baby star!" he says, proper outraged. "You've got to do something about that, Miss Creative Director!"

I tap my nails on the table. "I'm afraid it's a bit late in the day for changes."

"Well, I'm sad to miss it," he says, sounding rather sincere.

I shrug a shoulder. "If you happen to find yourself in Miami on Monday…"

"Opposite direction of Texas, I'm afraid."

I wiggle my toes and avoid his eyes. "If you're good, maybe I'll send you a picture."

His smile grows. "Meant to ask you, Ren's been hounding me, I guess trying to sort out place cards and shit—you'll be my date to the wedding, right?"

My heart does a stupid little skip. I swallow.

"I mean, you're my girlfriend." He shrugs. "Would look pretty weird if you're not there."

I sniff, trying to play it cool. "Will *she* be there?"

His face pulls a bit. "Ren said she's listed as Imre's plus one. Half the grid will be there."

"I suppose I could be your date...you weren't the worst dancer."

He smiles big and stops massaging to pat the top of my foot.

"I've got to run."

I pull my foot back, and he gets up from the table and comes around to my side. He stares down at me and brings his hand to my face, runs his thumb along my jawline.

"Damn. I won't be seeing you for a minute, Humphrey."

I gulp. I think he might kiss me, but his eyes shift. He grabs my plate, then his, and departs.

It'll be more than a minute I won't see him. It'll be weeks, actually. Not sure why I'm so bothered at the thought of it. I press my lips together, trying to stifle my smile. Is this what the real thing is like? A real relationship isn't this fun. Can't be. This is only fun because it's fake.

CHAPTER 33

MY GOLDEN RETRIEVER

SOPHIE

Mist continues to fall. It's a soggy day for qualifying. Luca's sector one and two are yellow as he heads for the final chicane.

"And he kisses the wall at Champion's corner! Regains control, and it's flat out to the line…and he will not improve from P9!"

1 KAP

2 HAH

3 VAN

4 MAT

5 ENA

6 BER

7 NOW

8 WRI

9 LOM

10 YOU

"Can Leo put it on pole for the third time in Montreal? He throws the car over the kerb at the final chicane, near centimeters from the wall on the exit, and..."

The mechanics groan. VAN shoots to the top of the Q3 standings. Beck will improve; he's got to on this final lap.

"...its provisional pole for the three-time world champion!"

Luca's car is backed into the garage. Beck's sector one goes purple.

"The championship is neck and neck. Only twelve points separate him from Beck in the lead, but Leo has a stellar record at this circuit. Can Beck continue to be Leo's biggest threat on the grid for another title? One thing's for certain—Beck's performance this season is the biggest threat to Luca's future with team Furio."

I gulp, looking up from the onboard monitor. That comment gives me pause. I wonder if Pippa is watching back home. Charlie folds his arms and starts his nervous sway as Beck's sector two goes purple, and he brakes for the 180-degree hairpin.

Charlie flinches, Beck's onboard swirls, his car spinning in a complete 360 off the track. Coop's hands fly to the top of his head.

"It's Beck! He's off at the hairpin! Final run aborted!"

The yellow flag banner appears then disappears. I cover my mouth as Beck flings the car to straighten it.

"I think he may have dropped the left rear in the grass and lost it into the hairpin! These moments are rare for him this year, but it's a good reminder that these drivers are not superhuman."

I yank my headset down. He'll be livid. The pace was there. He was up on Leo's lap. It's Valor that will lock out the front row tomorrow. Charlie takes his headset down and rubs his forehead.

Beck's car is jacked up and backed into the bay before me. Water streaks down the red carbon fiber body and pools on the garage floor. He grabs the halo, hoists himself up from the car and jumps out. He lifts his helmet off and throws it to the side bench. My breath hitches as it slams against the metal. He pulls off his baklava and rips out his earbuds, working out of his gloves as he walks past us, exiting the garage. Shannon quickly follows behind him.

I walk back to the suite with Charlie. He goes for a cup of tea, and I head to Beck's driver's room. The door is open a smidge, I stop when I hear Shannon's voice.

"You've got to control your temper."

I flinch as a cabinet door slams shut.

"Things are being said, Beck."

"I don't give a shit!" he yells.

"Your name and violent in the same sentence is not something I want to read again."

"*Violent?*" Beck snorts a laugh. "Violent? Really?"

I press my fingers to my lips, heart thumping in my chest. *My Beck?* My golden retriever? *Violent?*

"Your moment on camera with Tommy in Jeddah?"

He huffs but doesn't say anything.

"Barcelona? Raising your voice in the paddock and now this?"

There are footsteps approaching. Beck flings the door open and walks out. When he spots me, his eyes instantly soften, and I nearly burst out into tears. He reaches for the back of my neck, presses his lips against my forehead, then continues down the hall.

Shannon comes out, startled when she sees me.

"Is everything alright?" I ask.

"Everything's fine!" she says quickly. "There's a load of pressure on him, I know."

"What's being said?"

"You don't need to worry," she says dismissively.

My mouth opens, closes, then opens again. "Will you tell me anyway?"

She takes a breath, hesitates a moment, then says, "There's some fringe talk about him having a violent side—completely false, of course, but I prefer to keep these little moments contained is all."

I blink a lot, trying to hide that my eyes are welling up.

"He's leading the championship. He's in the spotlight—these things happen. No need to worry, Sophie," she says, offering a smile. "Now I've got to go monitor his interviews."

I slip into his room and open the wardrobe, retrieving my phone from my bag and navigating to that awful gossip site.

I don't find much, only a screenshot of a Reddit thread:

Golden retriever? Beckham Wright's violent side is starting to show!

My name's in the comments. I tap to expand the discussion.

Remember when he shoved Tommy?

I can see him being a hothead. Sophie acts rather submissive around him.

True, but she's also half his size.

Violent? *I'll show you violence if this talk continues.* He's not violent at all! And he didn't *shove* Tommy. That's a complete exaggeration! *I hate it here.* I hate that I have to leave him tonight. I swipe out of the site and grab an umbrella. I open my text messages and scan the preview from Dad.

Thought I'd share the news! I've got a new flatmate!

My word. I suppose Evelyn's place has sold. I open our text thread, and there's a picture—Little Bear's fluffy face in the backseat of Dad's car.

CHAPTER 34
NOT MY STYLE

ELLA

TOMMY'S POUTY LIPS ARE back for post-quali interviews. He'll start P10 tomorrow, Alek P11. I must say, the tortured toffee eye pouty lip combination is a bit cute. No, *gross*—endearing, maybe? Never mind. However he looks or doesn't look, I know he's disappointed and on the verge of fed-up. That's why I rushed back to the suite and shoved an orange Lucozade in my bag for him. You know, in case he gets thirsty and wants his favorite for interviews. But then Sam went and handed him a MACH branded water bottle, so I'm still carrying this stupid orange drink around.

They've been complaining about the setup of the car all weekend—too much downforce, losing too much speed on the straights. The steady drizzle's not helping at all with traction. In the garage, the tension among the strategists and engineers was about boiling over. You know who's not here? Well, Emma, for one, but maybe even more satisfying, is the fact that the handsy red-headed twat reporter is missing in action—and she'd be eating Tommy's pouty lips right up. Maybe she got fired! That would be lovely! His eyes flick over toward me, and he nods a little. Poor thing's knackered. I've heard him recite the same remarks to fourteen differ-ent reporters. *Oh!* He's on the move. Time to play girlfriend.

He unzips the top half of his racing suit, struggles out of the sleeves and lets it hang around his waist.

"*Chriiiist,*" he sighs. He puts his arm around me, and we set off for the suite. "Will it ever get any better?"

"The car is proper fucked," I say bluntly.

He huffs a teeny laugh and shakes his head.

"The weather could clear up, perhaps?" I look up at him, giving him my prettiest eyes and a flutter. "We can put our hope in that."

He tries his hardest to stifle a smile, but I know the power of my eyes.

The team's filing into the war room for the engineering meeting. Tommy passes the door and heads for his driver's room. We've got to leave anyway, Soph and I. He closes the door, and I open the cabinet to collect the rest of my things.

"You been carrying that around?" he says at my back.

I turn to face him, and his gaze moves from me down to the Lu-cozade sticking out of my purse.

"Oh, that!" I grab it and hand it over. "Meant to give it to you before interviews."

He half smiles, pops the top and sucks down a huge gulp. He sits back on the massage table.

I gather the random bits and bobs I had to take out of my purse in order to fit that bloody bottle.

"You know those days when you question everything?"

I turn back to him. His shoulders are slumped, his eyes on the floor.

"Is today one of those days?" I ask, gently closing the cabinet.

He nods, but his eyes don't move off the floor. "Like, do I only have this seat because of my family's relationship with the boss? And fuck, maybe the car's not the problem, and I'm just a terrible driver?"

"Don't be ridiculous," I say, flicking my hand. "You have the seat because you earned it. You're a phenomenal driver, and you're getting every bit out of that car as humanly possible!"

Still nothing.

"It's the car, Tommy! Look at Alek! Your situation's not like Beck and Luca—where one's winning races, and the other's floundering."

I step toward him, duck and try to meet his eyes. "The upgrades they promised are still coming, no?"

"Yeah." He blinks. "But they're delayed—now they're saying not until Silverstone."

He grabs a towel beside him and slowly drags it down his face, then tosses it to the floor.

It feels odd. I'm not a touchy person, and I'm most definitely not a consoler. I'm not saying I'm one of those kids that was never hugged, but I'd fall into the lower percentiles for having received physical affection. We weren't much of a show your feelings type of house, more of an *always-wear-your-tough-face* sort of house. Can't think of a time I've cried in the last five years besides the night Ollie brought back these insane edibles from Amsterdam. Carmen and I got so stoned our laughter turned into laugh-crying, then laugh-sobbing, with a bit of laugh-hyperventilating. But any and all forms of laugh-crying don't count.

Carmen does the consoling at ours—consoling Sophie, that is. My style of consoling a down friend involves planning a lost night—those are my specialty. A night lost in the chaos of a club, dressed to impress, with bottomless beverages and maybe something Ollie procured. But the hopelessness on Tommy's face at the minute is affecting me to the point that I'm pushing past my limits. Since when am I willingly allowing his problems to become my problems? Before I've fully decided I'm okay with it, I take another step toward him and rest my palm against his cheek.

"Everyone has these sorts of days, Tommy."

His eyes flash up, and much to my surprise, he puts his hand on top of mine and holds it there against his face. His eyes close, and with his other hand he reaches for me, pulling me so close between his legs that his forehead rests on my dress. I run my fingers through his hair. The angel on my shoulder straightens her halo, finally looking pleased with one of my actions. I'm quite literally holding him and not minding it at all. I don't want to stop. I don't want to leave him. My heart's doing that funny flutter again. I actually feel *needed*—needed by him when not a soul is watching us. My fingers carry on, running through his hair again and again. Besides our steady breathing, it's perfectly silent. Not too silent, I hope. I might simply die if he can hear—or worse, feel—the way my heart is going at the minute.

CHAPTER 35
PITTER PATTER

ELLA

"THE LENGTHS HE GOES to for you!" Sophie squeals. "Still can't get over that outfit check."

"He didn't do that for *me*—David asked for it!"

"Mm-hmm, *right*," she says, a bit snarkier than I'd like.

She's sat at the station next to me, trying to play it cool, but her legs are bouncing, even though the makeup artist reminds her to stop every two minutes. She's having second thoughts, nearly had a breakdown yesterday at rehearsal when she had to walk in her first look in front of the rehearsal group and a bunch of empty chairs. I mean—the runway *is* built over the length of a pool. Lose your line of sight, and you might be going for a swim. She decided right then she simply would not be walking without the matching tiny mesh sarongs for both passes. The sarongs we're meant to wear for our first pass only. The Beurre reps made an exception for her—didn't want to risk her entirely backing out. Plus, we're sort of in charge of part of this whole deal, being collaborators and all.

Montreal's outfit check went more bonkers than Monaco's. Even Holly got a kick out of it and reposted it on MACH's team account. I've watched it a dozen times, smile every time the wee stars on my hand pop out of my sleeve. The stars are long gone now, and no, I'm not thinking of making them permanent.

Sophie's doused with setting spray. As the mist settles, she smiles down at her phone.

"Is Beck doing any better?"

"I think so. They're headed to Texas," she sighs. "They go out early and play at Coop's ranch."

"Play?"

"Cowboys?" she shrugs. "They shoot guns and build fires and drive trucks around?"

I blink quickly. She looks as confused as I am.

My phone buzzes—it's not him, it's mum. She said she's joined the livestream. Annabelle got the livestream link from Sophie's promo that Beurre ran. Said she and Emmett would join, to which I told her *For the love of God, only watch if my brother is in the other room*. And no, I was never asked to make a promo for Beurre, and that's okay—I posted enough about it on my own. Perhaps they didn't want to ask me to do more.

"Mum says the livestream's working!"

"I'm not sure Dad's figured it out, though he'll probably be covering his eyes the whole time," she giggles.

"Evelyn's techy, she'll get him squared away," I say, lifting my phone for the front-facing camera.

I got amazing backstage getting ready vlog content, now I need some selfies. I'm perfectly spray tanned, and my hair and makeup are flawless. I've got on the white baby dot bikini that flips to black with baby white dots along the edges and tiny bows where the straps meet the fabric—my first look. I open my robe a bit more so just enough of the girls are showing and snap a picture. I contemplate for a solid ten seconds about sending it to Tommy. But Ollie appears behind me in the mirror. His cheeks are pink, understandably. He's in the presence of a dozen barefoot, bare-legged girls in robes. Tommy would be drooling.

"All ready then, loves?" he asks, putting a hand on each of our shoulders.

Sophie shakes her head, proper nervous.

"We're ready to quite literally drop jaws!" I reach for her hand and give it a squeeze.

She manages a shaky smile.

"You nervous?" I ask him.

"*Nah.*" He stands up and tosses his blond hair around in the mirror. "I'm ready to make some booties shake."

I poke his ribs, and he goes for my hair, but I slap his hand away. He's come to collect our phones for Carmen. She'll be in the front row and promised to get some content for us. Ollie pockets Sophie's phone, and I take a final look at my selfie, decide not to send it and hand mine over. He kisses the top of our heads and skedaddles. He's been well behaved, that one. Though a visitor came to our suite last night and delivered a goodie bag of God only knows what. The door adjoining our rooms was open, and Carmen came and crawled into our bed.

I hardly heard the exchange because Soph and I were busy FaceTiming Tommy and Beck. Both were miffed, going off to get drinks with some of the guys to quote, *"Forget the race they just had."* We watched what we could on Sophie's phone during rehearsal. Despite Beck finishing fifth, he's lost the lead in the championship. Leo now leads by three points. And despite my world-class pep talk after quali, Tommy had a nasty aquaplane that nearly dismantled his race. He started tenth and ended eleventh, just outside the points.

The ten-minute warning is called. Robes litter the floor. Sophie and I nip around with the Beurre reps, adjusting sarongs and the tiny gold body chains we paired with some of the looks. I'm jittery—not from nerves but excitement. *I love this shit.* It was months of hard work, and we can finally see the result in motion.

The showrunner calls the five-minute warning, and we get into position. I'm fifth in the lineup. Sophie's walking second in her first look: the baby buttercup balconette. There are ten of us in total, with two looks each. All super feminine, very coquette, but sexy too—and the way Ollie can mix a song? The aesthetic and vibe we've created are next level. Final touches come around—more lip gloss, more body glow, a spot of powder.

The monitor backstage flips on. The water beside the runway's calm, and every chair at the pool's edge is full.

"Showtime, ladies!" a Beurre rep calls. Her voice drops to a whisper. "Please do not fall into the pool!"

The lights go low, and Sophie spins around and finds my eyes.

I give her a final reassuring wink.

Ollie's EDM remix of Florence + The Machine's *Say My Name* fills the air. On the monitor, the runway illuminates, and model one in baby gingham steps out. Perfectly in step with the beat, she makes it to the end of the runway, and Sophie disappears through the curtain. I watch her emerge on the monitor. She puts her hands on her tiny hips and takes off, a little barefoot, pocket-sized princess. She's got full-coverage bottoms on, so the sheer sarong barely provides a peek of one of her cheeks on one side. She slows, makes her turn at the end of the runway and manages to avoid taking a swim. *Proud stage mum moment.* On her return lap, her eyes catch on someone in the crowd. Sophie blows a kiss. I reckon she's found Carmen, and Carmen better be getting proper footage. A few moments later, Sophie's back through the curtain, and I step forward.

"They're here!" she squeals frantically as a dresser fusses her out of her first look.

"Who?!"

"The boys! They're with Carmen!"

For the first time today, my heart goes pitter-patter. Not from nerves—*I crush a runway*—but due to the fact that those toffee eyes are about to be glued on my body, and I'll make sure of it. The girls are *girling*. They've got enough body glow on them to look half a size bigger than they truly are. I loosen the knot of the sarong covering my cheeky baby dot bottoms before I step out. Almost instantly, I spot Tommy with that unmissable orange drink between his legs. His face lights up, mouth falls open, and my body comes alive. *He's never seen me in action.*

I set my eyes on the end of the runway and take off right as the beat drops and ole Flo starts bloody belting. If you've never walked a runway, walking barefoot is actually harder than wearing heels, but I make it look like cake. I parade along, my endowments up front perfectly bouncing. They're real, you know? I've often been accused of having them done, but I'm just one of the chosen ones, I suppose. Natural as they come, feel them for yourself!

Nearing the end of the stage, I shove my thumb through the knot of my sarong and whisk it off as I spin around. I know my backside looks phenomenal, I swing my arms, sarong in hand, as I walk back to the curtain. He's clapping like mad. I keep my eyes forward but shoot him a wink at the last second. He puts his fingers in his mouth and whistles. I'm always confident on a runway, but in this moment, my legs feel a mile longer, and my hair feels bouncier than ever. I didn't fall from heaven, I floated. I step through the curtain, rushing to get out of this look and into the next because that brings me closer to having his eyes back on me.

And I *want* his eyes on me.

CHAPTER 36

OUR SONG

SOPHIE

I ABOUT TRIPPED WHEN I saw him. It startled me—stole my breath. If it hadn't been for the bare feet, I probably would have plunged into the pool. This time as I walk out, I lock eyes with Beck immediately. I'm in the periwinkle baby daisy bikini. And the way he looks at me—like I'm everything and he's nothing, when it's very much the opposite—well that's Beckham Wright's magic. Everyone else in the crowd disappears. Contrary to online gossip, I don't need drugs. *I have him.* And the way his eyes burn for me—it's the best high there is. I prance down the runway, confident as ever, because this may as well be a private show for him.

It's funny how quickly these things are over when you're walking. My stomach's been in knots about this for days, and for no reason! We spent hours perfecting the collection and the details, and now the project's over. Wrapped up and tied with a little satin bow. I'm almost sad about it? I'm not ready to move on from these pieces. Evelyn's done this for years. Does she feel the same when her line is finally paraded down the runway? The highest high, but then it's done and onto the next?

I slip back into my robe and watch the monitor, the Beurre owner and lead designer receive their applause on the runway. I'm finishing the tie around my waist when my hand is grabbed by one of the showrun-ners. Ella's in her other hand.

I suck in a breath before we're pulled back out on stage to join the owner and lead designer. This wasn't on the show schedule. Every-one's out of their seats. I lift my hand and wave. Ella takes a bow. That's when Tommy's unmistakable voice yells, *"Baby girl!"* so loudly I swear I see Ella blush.

Beyond the backstage dressing area, Ella's on a mission. The room's flooded with people reuniting after the show. I let her lead, since I can't see a thing anyway, even on my tiptoes.

"There!" she says excitedly.

I shake out of her grip and take off, launching myself into Beck's arms. He takes me for a full spin before he sets me back on the ground.

"Beckham Wright, you lie to me!"

"And thank God I did! If you saw yourself up there—*fucking hell*," he says, eyes rolling to the back of his head.

Ella smacks Tommy's chest. "Crashing our show?"

He gives a little shrug and pokes her shoulder. "You said if I were around."

"You were surprised?" Beck asks.

"Shocked!" Ella says.

"Some fuckwit tracked the jet to Opa Locka and put it on Twitter," Tommy says, relieved. "We were certain you'd see it."

"The first thing I saw was that bloody drink in your lap!"

"Had to have something to hide my hard-on," he says, hooking his arm around her neck.

"There's the co-conspirators!" Beck nods.

Ollie and Carmen rush our way. She smothers me in a hug—she knew all along!

"Works over. Time to party!" Ollie says, slapping Tommy's hand.

"Can you come out for a bit?" Ella asks. "We've got a table—"

"*Baby girl,*" Tommy interrupts her, "we're here for the night!"

Beck squeezes my hand. "Someone canceled, got the last king room available."

Ella's eyes dart around.

Tommy nudges her. "I'll stay in yours?"

"Sure!" she says quickly, maybe too quickly—almost nervous?

Ollie delivered on the post-show arrangements front. We've got the best table, directly adjacent to and a single step away from the DJ stage, at one of the best nightclubs. And it's *bonkers*. It's Ibiza on uppers. Quintessential American excess on a Monday night. There are literally girls in hoops hanging upside down from the ceiling. Every time the beat drops, lasers, pyro and confetti cannons go mad.

Beck runs his hands up the back of my neck and pulls me against him. It's mesmerizing the way it all dances in his eyes—the twinkling lights, the falling confetti.

I narrow mine. "Have you been lying this whole time about Coop's?"

"No," he says, bringing his forehead to mine, his eyes all wild and dreamy. "I swear."

I crinkle my nose.

He nods over at his best friend on the couch.

"It was Tommy's idea, actually. He turned to me last night, a few drinks in, and said, 'Are we truly going to miss our girls walking in bikinis?'"

I giggle and smile up at him.

"And I said, 'Fuck no, we're not!'"

His lips find mine. I wasn't sure what headspace he'd be in after Montreal, but I'm relieved that he's smiling and maybe not thinking about the championship for a moment.

Ella squeals as Tommy pulls her down onto his lap. They clink champagne and whisper in each other's ears. The way they look at one another—it's different now, deeper. The way he looks at her—how could he not? Everyone looks at her like that. But the way she's looking at him? Ella doesn't look at boys like that.

"They're funny together," I say, nodding over at them.

Beck watches and nods in agreement. "They are, aren't they?"

Carmen's hands slide around me, squeezing my waist from behind. Ollie's gone up on stage and is now jumping around behind the controllers with the DJ. She hands me a shot glass filled to the brim with clear liquid, then raises hers to mine. I brace myself and throw it back. A path of fire trails down my throat—vodka. Straight. *Why!* Before I've opened my eyes, she grabs the glass, grabs my hand and pulls me up onto the couch with her.

Beck sinks into the opposite couch next to Ella and Tommy. I find my footing—well, I try—and dance along with Carmen as he watches, tongue in cheek, amused. Tommy hops up, and I motion to Ella, but her eyes are on him and him only, making his way up to Ollie and the DJ. She remains seated, chewing on her nail, watching. When he rushes back down, I grab him.

He holds my arm, steadying me.

"Did you make a request?" I yell so he can hear me.

"Asked him to play my and Ella's song."

I pull my head back. "You have a song?!"

He grins wildly, helping me step down from the couch.

Something's been off with Ella. One, *she's sitting down*, and two, what's with this new nail-biting habit? I plop down next to her—still chattering on the tip of her nail, watching him. He pulls a waitress in close, leans down and whispers in her ear.

"Now what is Tommy up to?" I ask.

"Probably getting her number, that slut," Ella says, grabbing a drink and downing half of it.

The waitress puts her hand on his chest and stretches her neck, whispering back in his ear like they're trading bloody secrets. Ollie jumps down from the stage. He finds Carmen still dancing on the couch, ducks his head underneath her top and runs his hands under her skirt. *Oh dear.*

Ella shakes her head and sips on her straw. "Not my circus, not my monkeys."

"Ella!" I giggle. "Those are our monkeys!"

"Are they now?" She watches on as Ollie joins Carmen up on the couch, jumping around like a madman. "Shit, you're right!"

The song transitions from EDM to Tate McRae, and Ella freezes. Tommy points over at her and winks. The waitress is gone, and Ella's face lights up like I've never seen.

"Is this your song?" I ask, confused.

But she doesn't hear me. She's staring at him, speechless, with a huge smile spread across her face. Ella's never speechless.

Tommy moves our way, doing this ridiculous dance, dragging his fingers all seductively down his body. He grabs her hands and pulls her up from the couch. They stay face-to-face, dancing with each other, belting out the words.

Beck's arms scoop under me. He scoots my bum across the leather so I'm against him.

"Is this another Taylor Swift song I don't know?" he asks.

I snort a laugh—Mia would have rolled her eyes so hard she'd have fallen over.

"This is *not* Taylor, my love."

Carmen screams excitedly. I jump up and jerk my head to an incoming line of waitresses waving sparklers. Two of them are holding massive bottles of tequila over their heads. Another two are holding a lit-up marquee sign reading, *Model Squad.*

Tommy crouches down and throws his arm around the back of Ella's legs. She sucks in a breath as he stands up. Sat up on his shoulder, level with the sparklers and the bottles, she's absolutely beaming.

"My word!" I say, bringing my hand over my mouth. Then I'm screaming, because my feet have left the ground. Beck hoists me up next to her. I grab Ella's hand, embarrassed as all get out as we're half a body higher than everyone in the club, and the whole damn place is staring at us. But she pumps our hands in the air, absolutely loving it.

CHAPTER 37
PADDOCK INSIDER

SOPHIE

WE AGREED—MOST OF US—ON a hard stop of two a.m. It's wheels up at ten for the boys, and our flight to St. Barth's leaves at...eleven, is it? We wanted to be asleep before the sun rose, so we obeyed the hard stop—*plus one hour*. If it were up to Ollie, we'd still be at the club with the birds chirping.

I drag myself down the hall and give a warning knock, even though this technically is my room. After the way Tommy and Ella were last night? I'm not trying to walk in on a Melbourne situation again. Just as I put the key to the reader, Ella swings the door open.

"Hello, darling!" she sings, eyes half open.

I step in and take note of her ensemble—a huge T-shirt, *three guesses on whose*, and probably nothing under it.

"Everyone alive in here?" I ask.

The adjoining door between the rooms is wide open. Ollie groans, face down on the bed with a pillow over his head.

"Hardly," Carmen chokes, texting with one eye open, holding her phone over her face. "*Fuck!*" she yells, accidentally dropping it smack onto her nose.

I try to hide my snort, but she giggles too.

"Where's Tommy?" I ask, noticing the empty bed.

"He went for coffee," Ella yawns, standing at the bathroom door. "I'm going to grab a shower."

She slides the bathroom door closed. I throw Beck's room key on the desk, and I lower myself to the floor. I shove a few things into my RIMI case and zip it shut. *My word*. I'm still a bit drunk. Ella most certainly is. She's singing louder than the shower stream.

Is that what the itinerary said? Flight at eleven? I left my phone in Beck's room, so I slide my laptop out from my tote pocket. *Dead*. And guess who remembered to bring their charger? *Not this one*. I look around to see if Ella's charger's plugged in, and spot the edge of her laptop sticking out from under the bed. I crawl across the carpet on my hands and knees and grab it. I stand up and instantly regret it, so I climb onto the bed and lie on my stomach. I flip the lid open and punch in her passcode. The *Lights Out Ladies* page greets me. *Not today, Satan*. She's got her usual thirty tabs open. I drag across the trackpad to the corner of the page to open another, then do a double take. The username. The one sitting there in the upper corner of the page. *Paddock_Insider*.

My spine tingles, my mouth goes a bit dry. I glance up at the bathroom, then click the username. The page refreshes to a feed of user activity, and my heart starts to rapid-fire. I scroll past several submitted comments on posts pertaining to her and Tommy. I swallow and read a few comments the profile has left on posts about me, ones I've not even seen. I scroll a bit further, and the photo appears. It's the original submitted photo of the pregnancy test I'd ordered.

I gasp. Carmen sits up in bed.

"What the hell is this?" I ask no one in particular.

I push up off my stomach, bringing my legs up under me and the computer into my lap.

"What's wrong?" Carmen shouts.

I keep scrolling. I can't stop. My chest is pumping like mad.

She throws back the covers and rushes through the door, pulling it closed behind her.

"Sophie?" she asks nervously.

I blink a lot, then finally pull my eyes off the screen.

"Ella is *Paddock_Insider*?"

She lifts a brow, flops down next to me and takes over the trackpad. She scrolls up, and the picture comes back, centered on the screen. She rubs her eyes. I'm not seeing things—it's still there, submitted from this account, by one Paddock_Insider.

"She's the one who took this picture?" she asks, startled. "And posted it?!"

I point to the username in the upper left-hand corner. She squints at it for a moment, and her jaw drops.

I might be sick. I push off the bed and dart out the front door. Carmen's yelling after me, but I don't stop. I storm on, hyperventilating, back down the hall to Beck's room. *Fucking hell!* I forgot the bloody key! I spin around, then spin back around because I can't go back in there. I frantically pound on his door with both fists. He flings it open, and I dash inside, hysterical, crashing straight into his chest.

"It was her!" I scream, grabbing fistfuls of fabric on his shirt.

His arms come around me, he tries to pull me from under his chin, but I've gone limp. He's holding the entirety of my weight upright.

"What was her? What are you saying?" he asks, rushed and concerned.

"Ella!" I scream. "It was her!"

"Calm down," he says, grabbing hold of my shoulders. He peels me off his chest and ducks down, finding my eyes.

I angrily swipe away the tears streaming down my cheeks, my head pounding and chest heaving.

"*Breathe*, baby," he says, searching my face. "Now what happened?"

I try to swallow, but the lump in my throat's too big, and I choke. "She took the photo of my pregnancy test! She posted it on that gossip site!"

"Ella?" His brow furrows, he blinks several times. "But—why... why would she do that?"

I squeeze my eyes shut, because someone needs to fucking tell *me* why on God's green earth she would post that picture.

"Last year—your address, your old job—was that her too?"

And I'm hit again, an aftershock that's just as destructive as the first, only I'm already dizzy and weakened when it hits. My tears fall faster than he can catch them. *Has it been her all along?*

"There must be some explanation," Beck says, pulling me back against his chest. "Did you ask her?"

"She's in the shower," I choke. "I got out of there as fast as I could! I can't go on that trip!"

He strokes my hair, holding me against him. My cheeks, my eyeballs, my throat—they all may as well be on fire. And my heart may as well be a mirror shattered on the sidewalk. She's my best friend. Our lives are ingrained in one another's, my whole world is intertwined with someone that betrayed me? *Like this?* The roots of our friendship—no, *sisterhood*—are so intricately tangled together I'm not sure they could be untangled without severing vital limbs. My chest goes tight. It's not just hurt. I'm proper scared. I never thought Ella was capable of doing something like this to me.

I shake my head and pull back.

"I could out her, you know!" I sniff. "Tell the world she's Paddock_Insider! Tell everyone she and Tommy are fake!"

He takes a deep breath, looks at the mess of my tear-stained shirt, then finds my eyes again. "You could—but you won't." He rubs my shoulders. "It's alright, Sophie."

"No, it's not alright!" I yell, throwing his hands off me. I turn away from him, then turn back, and start pacing. "My mum is gone! My best friend—was possibly never my friend at all! Dad's the only safety net I've got left, and I'm losing him too!"

Everything's going a bit dim, despite my eyes being open. This hasn't happened in years. I used to get them often, and they all started like this. I put my hand out and reach for the wall. Soon, the darkness of the very hole I'm falling into will consume me. And any remaining light will get farther and farther away.

Beck grabs me and cradles my face in his hands. "You've got me, Sophie. I'm not going anywhere." I hear it, but his voice is a bit echoey at this depth in the hole. "I can be your safety net."

He searches my face. I stare into his eyes, into the brightest light I can see at the minute. *My safety net.* But there's a knock, and his head jerks toward the door.

"Don't let her in!" I shout.

"Stay here," he says calmly. He slowly lets go of me, steps to the door, and peers out the peephole.

"It's Carmen," he says, swatting the door handle letting her inside.

"Sophie!" she gasps, rushing inside. She throws her arms around me, squeezes me like she always does. "I don't know what's gotten into her."

My tears spill into her hair. "I'm not going to St. Barth's."

She pulls back, and her face falls. She grabs my hand. "Sophie, you've got to come!"

"I am *not* going," I state firmly.

She folds her lips in and takes a moment, running her thumb over the top of my hand. "Do you want me to call the Fylter reps?"

"No." I shake my head and wipe my eyes. "I'll let them know I can't make it."

She swallows and nods. "It won't be the same without you," she says all sad, then throws her arms around me again.

"I love you," she whispers.

"I love you too," I manage, but barely.

Carmen turns for the door.

"All my things are still in the room," I sniffle.

"I'll come get her bags in a moment," Beck says.

Carmen nods. When the door shuts, his arms come back around me. Very safety net-like.

"We'll get it sorted," he says, kissing the top of my head. "For now, you come with me—I'll take you *camping*."

CHAPTER 38

LEFT ON READ

I FLIP OFF THE shower handle and step out into the steam room I've created. Rather genius, if I do say so myself. I need to sweat out all I can. I kick Tommy's T-shirt out of the way. I only wore it to sleep in because it's quite comfortable, not because we hooked up or anything. I swear it! We only giggled for a minute before we both passed out. I wrap a towel around myself and crack the door. "Girls! Come have a sit in my steam room!"

Crickets.

"Oi!" I shout, swinging the door open.

Carmen's leaning over the desk, my computer open in front of her.

"Ella," she says, turning to me. "What the hell were you thinking?"

I freeze.

"Sophie needed your computer—" Her eyes flip back to the screen, and my heart stops.

"How could you do that to her?"

"Where is she? Where's Sophie?" I ask frantically, my heart beating like mad.

"She left!" Carmen yells. She crosses her arms. "Tell me then! Why would you do this?"

Carmen's never yelled at me. Something's stinging my eyes. I search for my words, choke on my stutters and finally manage, "Because I'm fucked in the head, Carmen!"

"What were you thinking!" she yells again. "Give me one good reason!"

I rush to the adjoining door, pull it all the way closed, then slowly turn to face her.

"What if I told you I did it...because I felt threatened."

"Threatened by *Sophie*?"

I nod.

"I'd say you're absolutely mad!" she says, moving her hands to her hips.

There's a knock on the door. I rush over and peer into the hall. *Beck's outside*. I take a deep breath, shakily exhale and fling the door open.

His face is blank, his eyes bore into me. "I've come to collect Sophie's things," he says calmly.

I step aside to let him in. Blood pulses in my ears like a damn drum, deafening everything around me.

"Is she..." I stop, not sure what I was intending to ask. I blink quickly.

"She's coming with me," he says, cutting me off. "She'll reach out to Fylter and apologize."

He searches the room, picking through things on the floor and grabbing things he recognizes.

"You can't be serious," I huff, panicked. "She's backing out of the trip?"

"She's upset, Ella..." he says without looking at me.

"Can I talk to her?" I ask weakly.

He pauses, grits his teeth, then exhales. "Maybe some time apart will help."

I lose my breath, like I've been punched in the gut, and someone's ripped out my esophagus.

He comes before me, reaches out and touches my arm. "You two are like sisters. It will all get sorted."

Will it? I just need to talk to her! A chance to explain. He grabs a few more of her things, then extends the handle of her bag. I watch because I can't bloody well move at the moment.

"Let me help you!" Carmen says, jumping up. She grabs Sophie's backpack and slings her tote over her shoulder. They head for the door, and the card reader chirps. Tommy pushes inside, holding a tray of coffees.

"What's up, fam?" he asks, looking proper confused.

He throws his arm on the door, holding it for them while balancing the coffee caddy in the other.

"Ask Ella," Carmen huffs, following Beck into the hall.

His eyes dart from them to me. He watches them leave. I tighten the towel around me, bring the tip of my fingernail between my teeth. There's no escaping this hell I've created. Unless I plan on jumping off the balcony, which would surely deliver me to another realm of hell.

"Baby girl!" Tommy says. "What's going on?"

He's standing there, looking at me like I should have all the answers. I roll my eyes, stride toward him and grab his wrist. I pull him into the room and slam the lid of my laptop closed. He sets the coffee tray on the desk next to it, watching me carefully.

"Got you a red eye," he says, shimmying one of the cups free.

I grab the coffee from him and set it back down. "I did something horrible."

"Oh-kay?" He waits for more.

How do I even say this? My head is absolutely spinning. When I don't provide any follow-up, he narrows his eyes and smirks. "Did you cheat on me?"

I smack his chest, and not in the playful way I usually smack him. "I'm being serious, Tommy!"

"What is it then?"

I hesitate. He loves Sophie. And what I did to her? It's bad. He might never look at me the same. And for some reason, I've come to care about the way he looks at me.

"We're friends, Ella," he says, stepping closer. "You can tell me anything."

I quickly step back, shake my head. "Well, I'm a shit friend you probably want to be rid of!"

He closes the distance between us and sets his hand on my shoulder so I can't step away again. I avoid his eyes, stare at the wheel marks left in the carpet from Sophie's bag, and start chewing on my nail again.

Tommy reaches for my hand and pulls my finger from my mouth. "Ella, just tell me."

I exhale, keep my eyes on the carpet. "You remember that picture that came out—the pregnancy test with Sophie's name on it?"

He nods. He waits.

I blink.

"What about it?"

My gaze flicks up to his golden eyes, trails down his face, across his chest and over to the door.

"I took the picture. I posted it on that gossip site."

He blinks quickly, nods his head a few times.

"Alright—" he says. "Were you at odds or something?"

I shake my head. "No, not at all. I was just—I was spiraling."

"What were you thinking, Ella?" he says calmly.

"I wasn't thinking! Obviously!" I yell. I take a breath, try to form a coherent explanation—something, anything that gives some form of insight. As if anything would be a good reason to have done what I did. The real reason, of course, has lived in my head all this time. It's safe there. I can think it. It can live in the confines of my brain where no one knows I'm thinking it, and I never have to admit I'm thinking it. I was never supposed to have to say it out loud. But now it's my only option.

"I'm not used to sharing the spotlight with anyone. There was this photo taken of us in Melbourne—just her and me. *'Sophie Collins with friend.'* And that caption, it sort of burned itself into my brain and started this whole thing."

"You got jealous?"

"She blew up!" I say, dragging a hand down my face. "It didn't bother me until..."

"Until it did?"

I look up at him and nod.

"So, I acted out—and the collateral damage happens to be my best friend in the entire world."

He continues with the measured nods, but doesn't say anything. My heart sinks further. I try to blink away the sting in my eyes.

"It's not even about her. It's about me—feeling threatened, losing my edge. I got really in my head with the Fylter deal being undecided, and Sophie—she was the name on everyone's lips, the magazine, the posts—"

"It's only human."

I stare up at him, confused.

"Ella—if anyone knows how you're feeling, it's me. You know how hard it is watching Beck have such a run? When I haven't had my moment? Racing's in my family. It's expected of me. It wasn't expected of him."

My eyes are proper welling up now. I clear my throat. "How do you handle it so well?"

"I don't." He shrugs. "I get jealous too, but you've got to control it."

A smile creeps up on his face. "I know it sounds wanky, but comparison truly is the thief of joy."

A foreign tear spills over the rim of my eye. I quickly swat it away.

"I've got you," he says, bringing his arms around me.

I rest there, against his chest. And the crazy part is, I actually believe him. He's got me, and he gets it. Maybe not what I did, but why. He's not letting me go. I focus on his heartbeat as more tears stream down my cheek. Each hit his shirt and form dark, saturated blots.

For several moments, we stand like this, until he pulls back and looks down at me.

"You still have my key?"

I quickly wipe my eyes, embarrassed. "Yes. Sorry, I forgot to take it off my ring."

"Hold on to it. If you need somewhere to go, you can always stay at mine."

I sniff. "You don't think I'm a wicked witch?"

"No," he says, trying to stifle a smile, "you're not all bad."

"You think she'll ever forgive me?" I ask, nervous.

He's smiling now; his toffee eyes do a baby twinkle. "I think we'll get it all figured out."

Sophie, please can we talk?

Soph:

Don't.

Please don't bail

I need a chance to explain

My message goes from delivered to read. And read is where she leaves me.

CHAPTER 39
MIRROR, MIRROR

SOPHIE

I EXTEND MY ARM out of the passenger window as Coop's retro Defender bounces along the dirt road. *Texas.* It's hot and dry and incredibly sunny. He's got the country music blaring, something about beer never breaking your heart? My safety net is on the bench seat in the back. I know what you're thinking. Absurdly unprofessional to bail last minute on a brand trip. I already heard it from Stuart. But can you imagine? We three were to share a room, and it's Ella and me who always share a bed. Was I supposed to be sat there, acting like a bomb hadn't been dropped on me? A bomb dropped from none other than the hands of my best friend.

Coop takes a right before a scraggly, twisted tree and pulls the car around the backside of a massive dirt hill. *My word.* Luca lowers a rifle off his shoulder. He's wearing jeans...I've never seen Luca in jeans. Charlie's in a cowboy hat.

Coop turns off the ignition, all excited. "Welcome to Texas!"

I wait a second for the dust to settle outside the car, then open the door. I drop down onto the cracked dirt littered with half buried brass. I shuffle along, brushing some of the shell casings loose. Coop fitted me with a pair of his daughter's *Hunter* rain boots. They're a bit big but better than my sandals or trainers.

"Mighty surprise!" Charlie says. Beside him, a dozen other guns are spread across a table.

Beck comes up behind me and puts his chin on top of my head. "Had a stowaway."

I keep my sunglasses down over my swollen eyes. "Sorry to wreck the boy's outing," I say nervously.

"Nonsense!" Coop yells. "Pippa's been out here plenty!"

Luca smiles. "She'll be jealous."

Beck wraps his arms around me, the same way he did for the four hours I went to pieces in his arms on the jet, when I was meant to be on a plane heading in a completely different direction.

"Have you ever shot a gun before?" Luca asks.

I shake my head. *Absolutely not.*

Dirt is piled into high walls, surrounding us on three sides. Downrange, an array of targets is lined up.

Coop lifts one of the big guns off the table and shoves a magazine into it.

He holds it out for me. "This is an HK416."

I blink at it, stare up at him.

"This one's nice and smooth," he adds. "No crazy recoil."

I lean away a tad, putting my hand on my chest. "I—I don't think I want to."

"Just try it," Beck says encouragingly.

"You've shot this one before?"

He nods. "A bit over-gassed but it's suppressed, *very* quiet." He takes it from Coop and nods his chin downrange. "Come on, love."

I reluctantly follow him.

No pressure or anything, with Luca and Charlie watching behind me. Beck sets the gun up in my arms, and Coop assists, moving my hands into the correct position. The bloody thing is half my size and looks like a weapon you'd take to war.

Beck starts to let go, but I simply cannot hold it up. "It's too heavy!"

"Here, get down on your knee," Coop instructs. "That's how my daughter does it."

I look down at the dirt, then back at him. *When in Rome.*

Coop drags a barrel over; I lower to one knee behind it. Beck props the gun on top of it and adjusts it on my shoulder.

"Lean your cheek here and look down the sights. You see the red dot?"

I move around, disoriented by the magnification, then spot it.

"I see it!"

"Alright, now put the dot on that big target in the middle."

I turn the gun slightly, aligning the dot with the center of the target.

"You ready?"

"I'm scared!" I squeal.

"You've got it! I'm going to flip the safety off now." He flips a lever on the side of the gun and leaves my side.

"Take a deep breath, and when you exhale, pull the trigger."

I move my finger against the trigger, staring at the red dot on the steel fifty yards downrange. I'm shaky; the red dot shimmies. I swallow, take a deep breath, exhale and pull.

Ping!

"Holy shit! Nice shot!" Coop shouts.

Woah.

A smile spreads across my face. I pull my head back from the stock and look over my shoulder.

Beck tosses me a wink.

"Five more in there, Soph!" Coop says. "Unload her!"

I peer back down the sights, steady my hands and pull the trigger again. *Ping!*

"Go for the star!" Charlie yells.

I move the gun slightly to the left, aiming for the red target at the top of a five-pointed star. *Ping!* The arms of the star start to spin. *That's just mental.* I move back to the big steel target but miss. *Damn.* I blink a lot, take a breath, realign and nail the final two shots.

Charlie slow-claps.

"Watch out, Beck!" Luca teases.

Coop laughs, comes over my shoulder and flips the safety switch, then helps me lower the gun onto its side. He grabs my hands and pulls me up off the dirt.

"She'll do, Beck!"

"I shot a gun!" I say, dusting off my knee. I spin around and launch into Beck's arms.

He presses his lips to my temple. "That might have been the sexiest thing I've ever seen," he whispers.

My spirits are up after Coop's. Perhaps they shouldn't be after unloading a magazine, but I would guess it counts as a form of therapy around here? Plus, I got to FaceTime with Pippa and the baby. Baby Luca's a bit nocturnal, still feeding all through the night.

And as a cherry on top, Beck's just pulled his hat on backward. I follow him between massive RVs parked up in a private lot—many housing other drivers and team personnel.

"This is us!" Beck says, nodding to a shiny black RV. Four identical ones are stacked in beside it, all with Furio flags secured on the roof. *My word, we are truly camping.*

He stops at the base of the steps, eyes smiling as much as his lips, and don't get me started with the way his eyes look in a backward hat. He unlatches the door and holds his hand out. I ditch my bag and ascend the three steps up into the motorhome.

It's quaint, but open. There's built-in bunk beds, a full kitchen, and a sitting area with a massive telly. Beck lifts the suitcases inside.

"You like it?" he asks, watching me intently.

"It's quite—fancy!"

It's not the *Four Seasons* downtown, which I did research earlier when Beck wasn't looking. You know, in case of an emergency.

I start down the tight hall toward the "bedroom." There's a fully equipped bathroom with a toilet, shower and small sink with a tiny circular mirror above it. *This totally counts as camping.* I push the bedroom door open a bit more. A queen-size bed fills most of the space. I turn around and walk back to the kitchen, which takes exactly half a second.

"There's not a proper mirror in here, is there?" I ask, looking around.

He starts opening cabinets.

I grab the handle of my RIMI case and pull it back into the bedroom, alongside the bed.

"Oh! Here's a mirror!" I exclaim.

Beck walks in, and I meet him at the foot of the bed. On the back of the door, a full-length mirror hangs.

"Well, well," he says, stepping behind me.

I still have that worn out look on my face you get when you've cried so much the skin around your eyes remains sensitive.

He sets his hands at my waist and brings his head against mine. I watch his gaze fall from our reflection to the reflection of the bed in the mirror.

"Are you tired?" he asks, kissing my hair. "You want to relax?"

A nap will have me thinking. I want to forget. I slowly shake my head side to side.

His hand slips under my top, runs over my stomach. "How is it that the most beautiful girl in the world is mine?"

His lips graze behind my ear, move down my neck and make my knees go a bit weak. I watch his hand move under my shirt until his fingertips find my nipple and tease it through my bralette.

I try to turn around, but he stops me. He guides my chin back straight to the mirror until I'm staring at the reflection of his fiery eyes staring at me.

"I want you to watch yourself."

What exactly did the designer of this motorhome have in mind when putting a mirror at the foot of the bed? The placement is peculiar, no? You're telling me it was put there so you can give yourself a wave before you nod off? So you can watch yourself wake up? *No.* It was put there so you can watch yourself come. The way I'm watching myself now—he's sat on the edge of the bed and I'm reverse astride his lap. Feels rather dark and forbidden seeing myself in such a compromising position. But at the same time, *my word*, it's sexy.

My cheeks are flushed. His arm is across me, covering one of my breasts with the grip of his needy hand.

"Slow down," he says, his other fingers digging into my hip. "Take your time."

I adjust my pace, moving my hips a bit slower, which, *my God,* might even feel better.

He pulls at my nipple as his hand releases my breast, and it migrates down my stomach, between my legs. He runs his middle finger against my clit.

"You can't do that," I spit out, all panicky.

"Why's that now?" he says, moving two fingers against me, even more tortuously.

Every nerve ending at my center is firing like mad. He's watching me, eyes glued on me in the mirror.

"It feels too good," I exhale, breathless.

"Keep your eyes open," he instructs.

My rhythm goes all over the place as I struggle to keep moving on him. The pressure of his fingers, the fullness of him, everything starts to go cloudy.

"You're close," he says, pleased.

He can sense it—he knows my body, the way it trembles. I try to watch, but the crown of my head tingles, and my eyes flip shut. I cry out as I fold over, my orgasm crashing over me. He catches my chest, holds me upright and slows his fingers. "*Fuckkk,* baby," he groans.

I've soaked his lap, my muscles still throbbing around him. I've hardly opened my eyes, but we're moving. He slips out of me, and *I'm a goner.* I instantly come again because everything remains oversensitive. He's shifted me off his lap onto the bed. He climbs over me, drapes my leg over his arm and pushes back into me. His breath is heavy in my ear. My eyes flutter open, and I stare up at the ceiling. Why haven't they put a mirror up there? I think I'd like to watch his body move on top of mine. *My safety net.* I think I'd never shut my eyes—even though they're itching to roll back. I think I might come again. I always do when he's got my leg up like this. *My word*—I think I like camping.

You're at COTA??

Yes…

Long story.

Ren marked Ella as Tommy's plus one?

Emma is coming…

No drama, right?

I'm sure everyone will be on their best behavior?

:/

Miss you.

6 weeks <3

Freaking out!!!

CHAPTER 40
SCARY ISLAND

ELLA

I STEP OUT ONTO the balcony and slide the door closed. Carmen's finishing her hair. I'm scared to listen to it—I've been tagged so many times. I turn my phone volume down and play the *In the Know* podcast clip:

"We love following some influencer drama, but not when it involves our faves!" Maggie cries. *"Girlies—are we good? People are speculating that our favorite British dream WAG duo had a falling out! They posted together only a week ago, packing for a trip to our part of the world. But post Miami Swim, it seems the last leg of the trip imploded. People started noticing Sophie hasn't been in any of the stories or content coming from the Fylter Beauty brand trip going on in St. Barth's."*

"I had my doubts because we've obviously met these girls, however, Sophie has just posted a story from Austin, Texas. So, something's up—that's our confirmation she's definitely not on the brand trip and is instead with Beck at the US Grand Prix..." Julia says.

Maggie steps back in. *"From what I've seen, neither of the girls have responded to any questions about it, which makes me nervous. I'm not sure why they wouldn't address it if nothing was going on, but stay tuned!"*

The clip ends and gives me an option to replay it. *No, thank you.* I light a cigarette. Fuck the comment section—I can't entertain that right now. I take a seat in the fancy wicker-basket chair hanging from the ceiling.

Envy—it's one of the seven deadly sins, you know? *Deadly.* I can only pray it hasn't completely killed my dearest friendship. The angel on my shoulder has had her arms folded, nose in the air with an *I told you so* look on her face since Tuesday.

Thank fuck for Ollie. He always delivers. He slipped me three of something before we left. Said it would calm me down. It did bring me closer to my baseline. But now the magic pills are gone, and I'm fully coping with the shitstorm I spun up. Hence, the ashtray is overflowing, and I'm in rare form.

Carmen's still furious with me, *deservedly.* She was forced to talk to me early on thanks to our near-death experience getting here from St. Maarten. Short runway, small plane, fucking mad crosswind. I'm talking prop plane, eight seats, maybe? We were only in the air for twenty minutes—not a second of it was enjoyable. And it wasn't just Carmen screaming. The other passengers were bracing for dear life. Carmen actually thought we were going down. I honestly did too, but I was in peak hour of magic pill, mellowed out and semi at peace with our fate knowing there was absolutely nothing I could do.

We landed, *violently*, and she literally ran off the plane. A light pink MOKE and driver were waiting for us. Us, as in three of us. Took a few minutes for the driver to get it through his head *we* were no longer a roomie trio, only duo. I slipped him a stack of cash and asked if he'd be so kind as to stop at a corner store before dropping us off. No use hiding my new habit from Carmen. She ripped one out of the pack, rang Ollie and proceeded to smoke the entire thing while telling him about the death trap we flew in. She threatened him too. Said if he ever wanted to see her again, he better find us a way off this island that doesn't include experimental aircraft and a runway for ants. She can be a bit dramatic at times. I'm sure the pilot had a blood alcohol level well within the legal limit.

Despite the magic pill, it was a bit of a gut punch walking into our beachside villa. Three jumbo baskets were sat on the beds, each with our names woven into the straw. *Sophie* and *Ella* on one bed, because we always sleep together, and *Carmen* on the other.

Carmen snatched Sophie's basket and moved it to her bedside table, as far away from me as possible. I pretended like I didn't see it, like it didn't nearly knock the wind out of me. I sorted through the contents of mine—a Turkish towel, PJs with our names embroidered on the pocket, the new lineup of Fylter sun-care products, a million little treats and a blue glass bottle with a message rolled up inside. An itinerary—a packed one, including a dozen meals, seaside yoga, working brunches, a morning hike to a different beach, shopping and a boozy boat day onboard a catamaran. Creative content hours for upcoming drops sprinkled throughout. Let's be real, when you're on these brand trips, every hour is a content hour.

The rest of the group arrived Monday, so when we rolled in on Tuesday, they already knew we were the crème de la crème due to the fact that we were busy with a wee thing called Miami Swim Week. That, however, didn't stop the interrogation. Got hounded immediately with the *"Where's Sophie?" "What happened to Sophie?"* questions. I strategically dodged all inquiries by picking up the closest drink and waiting for Carmen to explain how, unfortunately, Sophie simply couldn't make it.

American girls are proper annoying with their hand sanitizer and stupid pronunciations. Not saying I'm fluent in French, they just sound ten times dumber than I do when they attempt even the most basic word. Did I mention they ask a million questions?

"Do you live by the Eiffel Tower?" No, we live in the sixth. *"Is that where Emily lived in Emily in Paris?"* No, that's the fifth. *"Is your life like Emily in Paris?"* No, it's better, present moment excluded. I fidget around every time Tommy's name gets brought up. My nails will be a wreck by the time I get home. If things weren't how they are, I would FaceTime him, give these girls a proper look at those toffee eyes and tattoos. Instead, I chew on my nails, attempt to smile, and try to be nice (not really). Somehow, the conversation that first night flowed to Anna Wintour stepping down at *Vogue.* That's when I took a break from guzzling my drink. I couldn't miss the opportunity to remind the table that whomever they bring in, British *Vogue* will always reign superior to American *Vogue,* and if they don't understand that—that's a them problem not a me problem. That's also when Carmen pinched my leg under the table and made us turn in for the night.

Today, we hiked to Colombier Beach. Sophie would have loved it. One of the Americans threw up—like come on now, it wasn't that hard. It's impossible for one to be miserable in such a gorgeous place, no? *False.* Sophie's all I could think about. She should be here, and I ruined this for her. The only thing that kept me from flinging myself off the cliffs we hiked along was knowing she's in the one place I know she'd prefer over this. Her favorite place in the world—Beck's arms.

We're leaving for dinner soon, *Bagatelle* tonight. The Americans are all giddy because apparently this is the place where the *Real Housewives* of somewhere or another went. I'm sure they'll have questions after the ITK episode clips. I click on Sophie's story from my real account because she knows my finsta. She posted a sunset photo at the track, with a geotag and a caption:

Deep in the heart of Texas without any cowboy boots!

I'm wearing one of the AquaDuo dresses we got at the store event—the white one—because I've resorted to self-inflicting pain. Sophie bought the same one in silver. We packed them together, planned to wear them together. I put out my cigarette and go back inside.

"Alright?" Carmen asks, adjusting her top.

I do a microscopic nod. "You think she'll forgive me?"

She exhales. "I think she loves you, and you love her, and you're a Leo—it's in your nature to be a touch ruthless."

Ruthless. That's a colorful word.

"I want to talk to her in person."

"How are you going to do that?"

I swallow. "*We live with her?*" I say obviously, but then slightly panic. Is she implying Sophie's going to move out?

"She'll come home, won't she?"

"Don't know." She shrugs, rolls her eyes. She reaches under her top, rips off her strapless bra and throws it onto the bed.

"Will you help me talk to her?" I ask.

"Of course I will, but that doesn't mean I'm on your side," she says honestly.

"There are no sides," I tell her. "There's right and there's wrong, and I'm way past wrong."

Carmen turns back to the mirror to look at her top sans bra.

"I can see your nipples now, but they look rather good."

She huffs, "How is it that no one in the world has invented a wearable strapless bra!"

I almost smile. My phone pings. I check the preview, and my heart does a little flip.

Tommy:

All good?

Never wanted off an island this bad

Has she said anything?

No. She did say she's not coming to Mexico City.

She wants to get back...

That's a good sign

:'(

Going to miss your pep talks this weekend, Humphrey.

That one catches my heart in my throat. Then another comes through:

& id kill to see those legs in cowboy boots

Am I missing pretty stars out there in Texas?

Ella Blair

they're magical

And yours?

I asked a little bird

We're leaving, one way or another, on Saturday. I could realistically fly to Texas. I swallow, squashing away the smile that was creeping up reading his texts because if he wanted me there, he would have said as much.

Alright, Bagatelle was *lit*. I had a drink or eight. One of the girls had to be carried out—I'll let you guess her nationality. We'll see if she shows up for the catamaran. And the content I shot at that dinner? Well, Fylter can make the call if anything needs to be taken down. I checked, but it was one of those intoxicated, one-eye-open checks for any nip slips before uploading.

I kick out of my sandals and walk down to the water's edge, staring off into the blackness. Little by little my feet sink into the sand. Maybe if I stay here long enough, the sand will swallow me up whole. I check my phone, it's just after one a.m. Maybe Mum's feet are in the sand too. She's gotten rather chummy with this new client she's repping and has been in

Dubai more than she's been in Paris. She's either been so busy she hasn't noticed or hasn't had the opportunity to ask about Sophie's whereabouts. I ring her. I know she walks early. This time of year you've got to, or you'll simply burst into flames.

"Darling, what is it?" she answers, concerned.

"I fucked up." I declare.

"Are you alright!?" she yells, panicked. "Is everything okay?"

"Yes! *Fuck*, sorry—I'm completely fine," I huff. "Do you have a minute to chat?"

"Of course, I'm just finishing my walk."

Knew it.

"I wondered if maybe you ever did something really bad, like wicked witch *really bad* to Evelyn?"

"Nooo..." she says, drawing out the word, waiting.

I blink. *Fuck.* "Well, I did something bad—to Sophie."

"Okay—do I get to hear what it was?"

I take a breath, sinking deeper into the sand. It's up past my ankles now. I'm becoming one with the beach. "I started commenting on these gossip posts, under a fake username, ones where people were comparing us to one another. I felt threatened and started swinging."

"*Okay—*"

"But then I completely lost control—I posted that picture of the pregnancy test she ordered."

She gasps. "Ella, that was you?"

Her tone. Tears spring to my eyes. "Yes."

She doesn't say anything.

I bite my lip. I lost sight of what really matters, I realize that now. "She found out and completely bailed on the Fylter trip."

There's a long exhale on the other end of the line.

"What have I become?" I sniff. "I'm worse than those girls last year who picked her apart."

"Are you crying?" she asks, shocked.

I sniff again and wipe my eyes. "Maybe I am."

"Dear, you haven't become anything. You made a mistake, and you need to talk to her. You realizing it's wrong proves you aren't like those other girls."

"What do I do?"

"Be professional, finish your trip with Fylter—you've worked so hard to get that deal—then go home and make up with her."

"What if it's too late?" I sniffle.

"I know Sophie," Mum says reassuringly. "I know how much she loves you. That doesn't go away overnight."

I start to lose my balance, but my feet are stuck. I crash sideways onto the sand, nearly dropping my phone.

"Are you alright?"

"I fell. My feet are stuck in the sand." I form my fingers into a little shovel and start digging my feet loose.

"I don't love you being drunk and alone on the beach at night, Ella."

I giggle for the first time in days. What's the worst that could happen? Some billionaire takes me prisoner on his boat?

"Are you ever coming home?"

"I've got to. It's getting unbearably hot!"

I smile and continue the sand excavation around my feet.

"I did hear back from the charter I was telling you about. They are willing to get you a great rate."

"Really?" I stop digging—my nails are about to snap off.

"Mm-hmm. I took care of it. Happy early birthday, darling."

My stomach turns. My excitement fades instantly.

"I don't know that I'll have any friends to fill a yacht with by then."

"Don't think like that. You will get it sorted."

Will I?

"And if not, I'll go with you!" Mum says excitedly.

I sniff a laugh. I miss her.

"And what if I have to move out? Can I move in with you?"

"Of course, darling, but don't think like that. You girls will come out stronger from this."

CHAPTER 41
NO NEW FRIENDS

SOPHIE

"ITK was speaking about you two," Hannah says, scooping up the last spoonful of Patrizio's lemon gelato in her dish. She gives me a weary smile. "You don't have to talk about it."

"You listen to *In the Know*?" I ask, avoiding Coop's daughter's question.

"Everyone does!"

Hannah's a junior at the University of Texas. Coop forbade her from coming to practice Friday because, according to him, she'd partied too hard the prior semester and is retaking a class. She joined us yesterday for quali and has been stuck to my side ever since. This morning, she came into the suite with ten bags of colorful saltwater taffy from some famous petrol station I swear looked about the size of Selfridges. Beck had at least five of the taffies for breakfast before Charlie cut him off.

"I lost my best friend last year," she says, pushing the gelato dish away.

"Why's that?"

"I had to stay in one night to study, and while I was pulling an all-nighter, my best friend made out with my boyfriend."

"My word!" I gasp.

She raps her fingernails against the table. "Lost my boyfriend *and* best friend in the same night."

Feel a bit thankful that's not my case. No wonder she had a rough term.

"You never made up with her?" I ask.

She shakes her head. "I had to find a new best friend." Hannah pushes back from the table and stands up.

I swallow and follow suit. This isn't that simple. Ella and I have so much history. And while she did not share a night with Beck, *thank God*, she did betray my trust.

Hannah links her arm with mine. "You can take me back to Europe! I'll be your new best friend!"

I smile. "Finish uni—then come to Europe! Join the traveling circus—your dad would love that!"

We depart hospitality, step outside and head for the garage. I saw several clips from *In the Know*. I've been avoiding their inquiries in my DMs. I don't want a new best friend. *Ella still wants to be my friend, no?*

"I cannot get over those boots!" Hannah squeals, looking down at my feet for the thousandth time. "And your dress for quali? *Chefs. Kiss.*"

I posted one story on Instagram—that's all it took. By Friday afternoon I was kitted out with outfits. I saved the embellished denim vest and skirt set for today. Paired it with the black cowboy hat and black Lucchese boots that showed up. How thoughtful! We grabbed a photo earlier, her and I, so I could post my western wear OOTD, tag and thank the brand once more.

"Take the boots! After the race! Though they might be a bit small…"

Hannah stops dead in her tracks in the midst of the hustle and bustle in the paddock, her face all lit up.

"I will gladly squeeze my feet into those!"

Her eyes flick behind me. "I'll meet you in the garage!"

I turn, and Beck winks, walking toward me while on the phone. His racing suit is unzipped, hanging around his waist, eyes sparkling in the sun. He pulls the phone from his ear and hangs up.

I hold my hat to my head and look up at him. "Who was that?"

"Your dad," he says, matter-of-factly.

"Oh! Did I miss his call?"

"No." He smiles and pokes my chest. "Said to tell you hi."

Okay? I lift a brow. I rang him days ago to let him know my whereabouts. Didn't go into detail about what transpired, but he was worried sick. "He just called you up for a chat?"

He smirks like he's holding some little secret, leans in and finds my lips.

I pull my hat off and cover our kiss because there are bloody cameras everywhere, and isn't this what they do in films?

Beck pulls back, licks his lips and guides my hat back on. "You look so fucking cute in that thing."

"Will you two stop necking all the time?" Tommy teases, coming up beside us.

Beck fist-bumps him, then nods his chin at the garage.

"Coming!" I say, although I don't move my feet.

He walks backward a few steps, watching me, then spins around. I look up at Tommy.

"Still going home tonight, no?" Tommy asks.

I nod.

"Good." He smiles. "I know Ella wants to talk."

I swallow.

"Don't take this the wrong way, but I do understand..." He pauses. "Let me back up. I don't understand why Ella went to the lengths she did, but I do understand the feelings behind what made her act out."

I blink a few times. "*W-what* do you mean? What feelings?"

"She got jealous, Sophie."

"Jealous?" I choke, flabbergasted. "Jealous of *me*?"

He nods.

"And she confided in—*in you*?!"

He smiles and may even be blushing a bit? "Hear her out."

I turn the corner in the garage and grab my headset off the display. *What is going on between them?* I don't know if I'm more confused that Ella confided in Tommy or that her actions supposedly are the result of her being jealous? *Jealous of what?!* And when did Ella confide in anyone about her feelings? *She's never had feelings!*

I run into Luca and give him a quick hug before he returns to the grid. He's starting sixth behind Ren. Beck's starting fourth.

I take my place next to Hannah at the back of the garage. She unzips her Bottega Jodie and nudges me. "In case we get hungry!"

I peek inside. She's got a dozen of those colorful taffies on standby.

"Don't let Beck see those!" I chuckle.

She zips her purse back shut. "Dad thinks he has a shot at the title this year," she says. "You think he can do it?"

I search for him in the chaos happening beyond the pitlane fence. He pulls on his helmet and climbs into the car, disappearing from view.

"*I think he can do anything.*"

"The grid is set for the formation lap! And off they go! Our pole sitter Elijah Kaplan, leads the pack up the

hill to turn one! Holt completes the front row after Ian Matisse delivered his best ever qualifying result. Both Leo and Beck were caught out in Q3, each with a lap deleted for exceeding track limits at turn nineteen. Leo was only able to provide one clean lap, he starts third, alongside Beck starting fourth. Beck said in interviews the goal this week is retaking the lead in the championship."

The cars zigzag down the main straight, pulling back into their grid positions.

"Final check, Beck," Coop says.

"Copy."

"Let's go racing!"

Hannah bounces nervously. Five red lights above the start line illuminate one by one, then flash off.

"It's lights out and away we go for the United States Grand Prix!"

The cars take off, darting up the hill toward the massive American flag rippling in the wind. At the crest, a left-hand hairpin awaits.

Hannah grabs my arm, and the mechanics jump to their feet.

"Beck goes late on brakes! He takes the lunge at turn one! Passes Leo for third position!"

Beck rips the car through turns two, three and four at a nauseating speed.

"Maybe it was the taffy for breakfast!" I whisper to Charlie. He smiles, shaking his head.

Ten laps in, Beck's still holding third, but only just. Leo's closed the gap. Beck throws the car through turn eleven, the nose pointing down the massive backstraight. Leo tried the overtake last lap. He was within a second, but not as close. Leo's rear wing opens, he veers left, flies wheel to wheel with Beck down the straight and makes the overtake.

"And ten laps in, Leo retakes third position! But Beck's not giving up! He takes the outside into turn twelve!"

My word.

"And deep they go! Off the road! And Ren Enatsu says thank you very much! It's a double overtake! Massive move by Ren Enatsu in the Makellos!"

Beck and Leo fall to fourth and fifth, rejoining the track.

Coop comes over the radio. "Let him have his moment. We'll get him again."

"No!" Beck objects. "I'm taking every chance I get."

"Let's keep it clean. Fewer points are better than damage and a DNF," Coop replies.

The thing about Beck—he's not violent, that's for certain—but he is awfully aggressive. He's not going to back down from a fight, and this battle with Leo is far from over.

CHAPTER 42
NEW FLATMATE(S)

SOPHIE

THREW MY TRAVEL PLANS out the door at the last minute and changed my flight from Paris to London. And I didn't feel even a smidge pretentious flying first class—I survived five nights of camping! I wasn't ready to see Ella. I needed more time to think. I went back and read every comment I could find from *Paddock_Insider*. It hurt just as much as the first time I read them. But this time, after what Tommy said, I read the comments through a new lens.

It's been a minute since I've been under London's sheet of clouds. It's been a minute since I've spent time with Dad. It's never been that I've gone this long without talking to Ella.

I crashed at Beck's when I got in and woke up this morning on a mission: get to the flat where fluffy puppy cuddles await. Perhaps if these clouds start spitting a bit of rain, it could all be puppies and rainbows?

I use my old key to let myself in, finding it odd that Dad's left the lights on. Then Little Bear trots out into the living room—*he left the dog out?*

"My word!" I drop to the ground, getting on Little Bear's level. "Are you free-range already?" He slinks over with his big black eyes and tail slightly wiggling. I scratch behind his ears; he flops down onto his bottom.

"Darling?" a woman's voice calls.

I freeze.

And out of my old bedroom walks Evelyn.

"Oh!" she gasps, jumping when she spots me, hand on her chest. "Sophie!"

She's in a pajama set—top and pants—and reading glasses.

"I'm so sorry! I didn't know anyone was here! I should have called—my dad."

"No! No!" she waves her hands. "We just weren't expecting you! What a surprise!"

It is, isn't it? I stand up, and she kisses my cheeks.

"I thought I'd take Little Bear to the park. I figured he'd be in his crate going mad."

"He doesn't like the crate much—" She hesitates. "He likes me to stay with him when your dad goes in."

Dad said he got a new flatmate, *singular*—the one with four legs whose belly I'm scratching—not two flatmates. She feels awkward, I can tell, opening her lips to speak, then pressing them back together.

"Did your place sell?" I ask.

"It did." She nods.

I swallow. "That's great!"

She looks over and smiles. "You want company?"

I make a mental note to never use this key unannounced again. I would never recover from walking in on—*Gah!* Could you imagine? Evelyn comes back to the living room in proper walking clothes and trainers.

It's three blocks to the park, and we were stopped no less than three times from people dying to pet Little Bear. He's got the shyest, sweetest temperament, this one. Definitely didn't take after Scout.

"He's quite good on a lead!" I praise.

"We've been practicing every night!" Evelyn says proudly. "And you at the Beurre show! Remember how scared you were before the show last fall?"

"I had a mild panic backstage," I admit. "Did Dad have a heart attack watching the livestream?"

"Just about." She presses her lips together, hiding a smile. "I can't believe how close the championship's got. I'm sure Beck was glad to have you with him."

Closer than close. It's down to a one-point spread. *One!* Neither Beck nor Leo made the podium at COTA. They were going at it the whole race. After penalties for forcing each other off track got handed out, Beck got fourth and Leo, fifth. Mexico City is the last leg of the tripleheader—should be interesting with the tension between them running so high.

"It wasn't exactly the original plan...but he likes when I'm there..."

"Your dad said you and Ella had an issue? You parted ways with the girls after the show?"

"Yeah," I sigh. "I didn't really tell him the details."

Evelyn looks over, face all serious. "Alice called."

I stop at the side of the footpath. Little Bear trots into the grass and lies down. I watch Evelyn, waiting for her to say more.

"She'd just spoken with Ella, who was alone, drunk and crying on the beach."

"Ella? *Crying?*" I lift an eyebrow.

"Said she didn't remember the last time she heard her daughter cry."

My mouth twists. Must have been fake tears. Ella doesn't cry.

"Did you ever have a fight with Alice?"

"Little things." She shrugs. "Only one big one that I can remember."

A smile spreads over her face. "Alice started seriously dating someone, and I told her I didn't like him. I told her I thought marrying him would be a mistake."

My jaw drops, and she nods, lips pressed together.

"We had it out, didn't speak for a bit. But thank heavens she didn't listen to me because Emmett and Ella wouldn't be here."

My jaw drops even more. "It was Alston?"

"It was," she says, bobbing her head.

Little Bear stands up, pink tongue panting like mad.

"Does Ella know that?" I ask, still shocked at this revelation.

"I don't know that she does."

I almost smile thinking of her. *Almost.* "She'd like that story."

Evelyn laughs. "You should tell her about it!"

I frown and shoot her a look.

She lifts her hand to my shoulder. "I know what she did was awful. But you'll find your way back together," she says, her tone full of hope. "You know she loves you, Sophie."

I swallow. "If she loved me, I don't think she would've done what she did."

Evelyn nods, clasps her hands behind her back, and we continue on. "Sometimes we hurt the ones we love most because we know they'll be there no matter what."

"I suppose I can believe that, but it feels like there's a world between us at the minute."

"I think Ella's got some things to work through. Hurt people *hurt people,*" she says.

"I can't think of anything I've done to hurt her!" I say, on the defensive.

"You probably didn't. I think she's had issues with acting out since her dad left." Her eyes meet mine. "I think it affects her more than she's let on."

I think on that for a moment, but Tommy's face keeps popping up in my mind.

"Do you think that's why she's never had a proper boyfriend?"

"I'd say it's a good guess," she says, nodding. "Even with Tommy, Alice said she's just hanging around to help him through a breakup?"

"Well—that was the idea..." I shake my head. "But it's a bit weird seeing them together. Sometimes I wonder if she truly fancies him—*for real*."

Evelyn smiles. "Even if she did, I'm not sure she'd admit it. Feel like Alice has taught her to fully write men off!"

My word, I think Evelyn could be exactly right.

The lead goes tight. Little Bear's about done. He's dragging a bit, walking behind us now. We pause, and he immediately flops down in the middle of the footpath.

"We'd better turn back," she laughs. "He's quite heavy to carry!"

With much encouragement and promise of treats, puppy dearest made it back to the flat. He's a puddle on the floor now, all gooey puppy mode as I flip him onto his back. "You'll just love the garden when the house is finished," I tell him, scratching his tummy. "But there'll be no treats or kisses for digging in my mother's flowers!"

I straighten up and put my hands in my lap. "I think I'll go wash up, then come back for dinner."

Evelyn smiles. "Your dad would love that."

I stare down at the puppy puddle on the floor, then back up at her. "Thank you for walking with me. It really helped."

We had dinner. And dinner again the next three nights. Each night I've canceled my train and pushed it out another day. Little Bear's getting his steps in. Yesterday, Evelyn and I hit GAIL's, then the shops, *did some damage* as Dad would say. May have bought Little Bear that Goyard travel-bowl case because have you seen how cute it looks folded up as a little trunk? We went to the club last night for drinks—lovely and delightfully uneventful, with no Fredrick. Carmen's hounding me to come home, Alice is back from Dubai and apparently Ella's been staying at her mum's. Beck checks in twice a day. "*Maybe tomorrow*" is the response I keep giving the both of them.

Tonight before dinner, I took Evelyn to the studio across the street for yoga—the studio Ella and I used to frequent almost every day. It was weird not having Ella on the mat beside me. It's weird being in the flat without my, Ella and Carmen's things lying around. Evelyn's fully moved in. It's now all of her things mixed in with Dad's. It's weird having a puppy scampering around, weird seeing a proper table where Carmen's bed used to reside in the dining room. What's most weird, is not being able to text Ella about how weird all of it is.

We're in the dining room now. Dad's made his famous breakfast for dinner, full English with extras. Little Bear's under the table, waiting for handouts. Of the two of them, I wonder who's the weakest link. I have a gut feeling about who the softy is—the man who never wanted a dog happens to be the favorite lap to lie in for said dog. After, we'll tune into the broadcast of first practice in Mexico City.

"George, you must try a class with me!" Evelyn says, still raving about the yoga session. "It was lovely!"

I snort a laugh. Dad will be at yoga when hell freezes over. Although I may have also said that about him having a pet?

"I think I'll pass, dear." He winks at her.

I stab a slice of French toast and move it to my plate. "Can I go to the house? See the progress?"

They exchange glances.

"It's not a good time right now," Dad says, shutting down the idea. "I got a little carried away, let them rip into the other floors."

"Dad!"

He smiles, pleased with his decision. "It will be *splendid*—but it's a proper mess at the moment."

I watch them trade flirty little glances back and forth. *Is this what Beck and I look like?*

I clear my throat, interrupting the flirt fest. "My room—" I ask a bit nervous. "Can it still be my room?"

"Of course, darling. When we get closer to finishing, I'll let you take the reins in there."

"What do you think of Beck's new place?" Evelyn asks.

I press my lips shut, trying not to blush. You mean the Monaco dream house he says he bought for *us*? "It's brilliant, *dreamy*—really. He's going to move in over break."

Evelyn smiles.

"Elizabeth's ready to take a day and go out to a Homesense," I add.

"Now that's a trip I'll want to be in on!" she says.

Dad reaches for her hand. "We'll have to get over to Monaco and see it!" he says excitedly. "You know, Sophie, I've decided to hang up the hat."

"Pardon?" I nearly choke.

Dad smiles.

"You mean retire?" I blink. "*You? George Collins?*"

He shrugs. "I think forty years is a good run, no?"

"What about Jo? What will she do without you?"

"She's hanging up the hat too!"

"We're thinking about having a celebration when we get back from Silverstone," Evelyn pipes in.

"A party?" I ask, enthusiastically.

Dad waves his hand. "Something small at the club."

Evelyn tosses me a look and mouths, "*Not small.*"

"*Huge!*" I mouth back.

Like I've done every night this week at the table, I open my train ticket app. If I go home tomorrow, I can be back in time to watch qualifying with Carmen. I swipe out of the ticket—perhaps I'll keep this reservation.

I think I'll go home tomorrow...

Beck:

Whatever you need to do, love

Or maybe I'll fly to Mexico?

I miss you.

Not as much as I miss you.

I miss our motorhome

Camping Sophie was the best.

You were a trooper.

We get another for Silverstone!

Oh dear, I forgot about that. I was sort of joking about missing that thing.

CHAPTER 43
TO WHAT END?

Carmen demanded to lug my RIMI case upstairs herself. She's a ball of energy at the minute—was bouncing alongside Pierre behind his desk when I walked into the lobby. She promised that Ella isn't here, but I'm still a bit nervous walking through our door. I quickly take inventory and lower my tote and backpack to the floor. All's quiet. Carmen gives my case a push, it rolls across the herringbone and stops at the wall. She skips over to the counter.

"I brought this back for you!" she spins around, basket in her arms.

My name's embroidered across the front. It's sort of lopsided. I'll guess it didn't originally look like that, but after its trek across the ocean, it's a bit rough. I run my finger over the stitching. I suppose I came back feeling a wee bit lopsided myself.

"I must admit, I ate almost all the snacks that were in here," Carmen admits.

"That's alright." I smile.

She turns back to the counter and sets it down.

"Was it amazing then?" I ask.

"It was absolutely beautiful, loads of fun, but awful at the same time," she chuckles. "Rather exhausting, really," she sighs, finding my eyes. "That and Ella was a mess. She was smoking the whole time!"

"Smoking?!" I frown.

"Smoking, drinking—an absolute basket case."

I shake my head. "I knew something was off—I'm worried about her."

Then I hear the keys. Carmen's eyes flick to the door. *Her keys.* My heart sprints.

"Don't be angry with me," she says nervously. "Beck gave me permission to lie."

Beck's in on this?

The front door swings open, and there Ella is, standing in the entryway, white as a sheet. I stare at her, my best friend in the entire world, and as mad as I am at her, I'm relieved to see her. I want to hug her, ask her what I did to deserve what she did, but I hold my ground.

"Can we talk?" she asks, quiet as a mouse.

I swallow. "Are you going to explain yourself?"

"I'm going to try." She closes the door, sets her keys on the counter and leaves her hand resting on the marble.

I cross my arms. It's awkward—*it's never awkward with us.*

She's staring at her hand, running her fingernail on the counter. "I created that account when we got back from Melbourne. It was sort of an outlet, I guess." She takes a breath and looks up at me. "When Tommy and I started up, I kept it going for if and when I needed to control the narrative."

"Right." I nod. "Making sure you looked good? You couldn't do that without making me look like shit?"

Her eyes fall. She swallows heavily and starts again.

"Before this year, my status was never in question. I had the followers, I got all the deals, I felt *needed*. But now—you're you." She pauses, looking up at me. "With the Fylter deal up for grabs, I felt threatened. Why would they pick me when they could have you?"

"They'll pick you because you're the most beautiful girl I know," I say clearly. "Because you work harder than anyone I know. They'll pick you because you deserve it."

Her eyes fill up—with proper tears. She looks back down at her fingers, blinking quickly.

"Tommy told me you did it because you were jealous. Is this truly about jealousy? It's not a competition, Ella."

"You're right, it's not!" she raises her voice, all panicky. "The wins just get handed to you. You don't even try! It's all so easy for you!"

I blink, and my eyes fly wide open. "Easy for me?" I shout back. "You think last year was *easy* for me?"

Carmen gulps, she looks between us, a bit scared.

"Having my firing outed? My address posted...or was that you *too*?" I yell.

"You know that wasn't me, Sophie," she says quietly.

"Do I now?" I fire back, even though I know it wasn't. "Just the picture of the test then? And all those nasty comments?"

She nods, then huffs, might have even rolled her eyes. "You got caught up in that gossip site last year—you've got to understand!"

"Caught up *reading* it, Ella! Not *adding* to the shitstorm!" I shake my head. "Why didn't you tell me you were feeling this way?"

"I was ashamed." She shrugs. "I've never been threatened or jealous, but you blew up! You have Beck, you and Ana are so close now—you don't need me anymore."

I swallow, a bit sad. "Is that really how you feel?"

Her teary eyes come back to me.

"It breaks my heart that you feel that way." I uncross my arms, take a step toward her. "I can't lose you, Ella. I'm already losing my dad and…" I pause—a long pause, hoping to clear the lump in my throat. "I love Beck with all of my heart," I start again. "And I pray it's a forever thing, but you and me…I've never questioned whether our friendship would last. We've always been a guarantee, a constant."

The first Ella tear I've ever witnessed spills over the rim of her eye. She squeezes her eyes shut, which spills out three more.

"I'm so sorry, Sophie," she says shakily.

I can't do it any longer. I close the distance between us and wrap my arms around her.

"Ella, you're more than my best friend—you're my soulmate, my sister." I pull back and look her in the eye. "My world isn't okay when we aren't okay." I wipe a slow-moving tear from her cheek. "I'll never not need you."

Carmen throws her arms around the both of us. "I'm not crying," she half chokes, half giggles, even though she's most definitely crying.

We stand there a moment, the roomie trio, wrapped in each other's arms, crying, laughing a bit, sighing a lot.

"Ella, you know I would delete my Instagram in a second if it meant we would be okay."

She huffs a tiny laugh and wipes her eyes.

"And you certainly don't have to worry about me getting the Fylter deal now that I no-showed on their trip!"

She covers her eyes with her fingers and shakes her head.

We've broken down a wall, a wall I didn't know was penetrable. I want to ask her. I can see it on her. I've been seeing it on her for a while—this isn't everything.

"What about Tommy?" I ask.

She shrugs. "What about him?"

"Do you fancy him?"

"Of course not!" She scoffs. "I told you I could make it believable."

I bob my head and keep watching her. I glance at Carmen, who's doing the same. "But the way you act together—is it really all an act?"

"We're friends, and he's a flirt," she says, patting her cheeks dry. "He's using me, and I'm using him. That's all this is."

"To what end?"

She shrugs again. "We haven't discussed how it ends." She starts picking at her nails. Something's still stewing.

"But you can't just fake date him forever," Carmen adds.

"No. I can't," she sniffs. "But that's the other part of this whole thing—this was never about shutting my dad up. I don't give a shit what Alston thinks." She stops torturing her nails, and her eyes go to the floor. "I only jumped at the chance to date Tommy for the benefits, for the attention."

Carmen's mouth twists.

"Does he know that?" I ask.

"No." She swallows, and her eyes come up off the floor, all worried. "Please don't tell Beck. I don't want Tommy to think any worse of me. I respect him enough to tell him myself."

"I won't say anything."

She blinks and rolls her eyes. "If we're being honest here," she huffs, "I slept with him again."

"You're sleeping with him again?!" Carmen shrieks before I can.

"In Miami?!" I guess.

She shakes her head. "Not sleeping! *Slept.* One time. In Monaco, at his."

"You had another itch?" Carmen smirks.

Ella half smiles and does a little shrug. "We were both down bad, and it just—*happened.*"

I have my doubts, but we've already broken down one wall today, so I shouldn't expect to bust through another so easily.

"I'm guessing you saw the ITK clips?" I ask her.

She blows out a breath. "How could I not? They were blowing up my DMs. Didn't respond to any yet."

"Nor I."

"Well, can we post a photo together? Shut all of it up?" she asks, wiping her eyes again.

I poke her shoulder. "You wore our AquaDuo dress without me."

"I'm sorry! I only did it because I missed you."

I smile. "I say we have a drink, watch quali and have a proper night out."

Ella's face lights up.

Carmen skips to the fridge and flings open the freezer door. "I was hoping you'd say that!" She whips out a frosty bottle of tequila. "Bought it earlier in case of"—she shrugs—"either outcome, really!"

She sets it on the counter and opens the cabinet. "And we've got to tell you how we nearly died getting to that godforsaken island! It's a bloody miracle we're even alive at all!"

CHAPTER 44

STAND BY YOUR MAN?

ELLA

Everything copasetic?

Happily ever after

<3

I OPEN THE CAMERA and send him a picture of the tequila bottle.

On brand for quali!

Take one for me!

In your honor.

I've got business in Paris Tuesday

You around?

Business?

A shoot. I was going to head home after.

Unless you're around, I could come to yours

See my girl

My heart flutters. Stupid flutters because this is fake.

I suppose I'll be around

Bring me back a trophy from Mexico!

Ella…

A big one!

"Is it possible we see a mid-season shakeup at Furio? I don't see how they couldn't be floating the idea when your second seat is substantially outperforming your lead driver. There has to be some form of intervention. There hasn't been any chatter about swapping in the reserve driver yet, but with such a difference between both sides of the garage, surely they're scratching their heads. Beck has lost his championship lead, but only trails Leo by a single point. However, Valor is winning by a huge margin in the team title. At this point, Luca is holding Furio back from a chance at a constructor's title fight."

My gaze flicks over to Sophie, but she's busy taking another shot. I snort a laugh at the sour face she makes and turn back at the broadcast. Luca's out of the car in the garage reviewing the data on his final flier—the flying lap that wasn't enough to make it into Q3. The broadcast flips to Tommy pulling out of the garage in his number six marked car.

"Post COTA, MACH has dropped a position in the constructor's championship. They now sit in fifth place behind a midfield team after Holt provided a brilliant performance in Austin. Tommy Young's shown that team so much loyalty, but they've failed to deliver a race-winning car. If a seat were to open at Furio, could Tommy's eye be wandering in that direction?"

"Are you hearing this?" I ask.

I crane my neck and look over toward the kitchen. Sophie's deep in conversation with Carmen—not deep as far as subject matter goes, but everyone gets a bit entranced when they're that deep in a bottle.

"It *'doesn't count as camping,'*" Sophie air quotes. "We were sleeping in the wilderness!"

"Weren't you in a car park?" Carmen asks.

"Yes! But the car park was *outside.*"

Carmen tilts her head, confused.

Fucking hell, these two.

"*That's* camping!" Sophie gushes. "And let me tell you, that motorhome saw some things."

My ears perk up. How many shots behind am I?

Sophie cocks an eyebrow. "You want to know how many times he made me come?"

Oh dear, she's more sloshed than I realized. Carmen nods overenthusiastically.

Sophie holds up her fist and proceeds to flash three fingers.

"In one day?" Carmen says, slapping her hand against her thigh.

"No! That was only in one go at it!"

Carmen's jaw drops. "Beckham Wright dishing out triple orgasms?!"

Sophie grabs Carmen's wrist and pulls her close. "Did I tell you I shot a gun?"

"What?!" Carmen drunkenly throws her head back.

"A huge one!" she yells. "And I hit the target on the first try!"

"Please tell me there are photos of you holding a gun!"

"Was my face on the target?" I ask.

Soph waves her finger between us. "No, no. No faces. And no pictures either! I'm not trying to get canceled!"

She's wearing the silver AquaDuo dress. I'm in the matching white one. And yes, I did just wear this to Bagatelle, but I'll do anything to make Sophie smile, and anything includes outfit repeating.

***

Sophie's phone is vibrating on her nightstand. I open my eyes, blinking a bunch. We went quite hard after quali, making up for lost time, perhaps? Crawled out of Sophie's bed yesterday as dried out as a raisin. Does crying dehydrate you? Last night started very similarly to the previous. Sophie shockingly agreed to tequila again because, well, Mexico? We did not, however, make it out two nights in a row. We watched the race, finished the bottle and passed out. And for the second morning in a row, I've woken up in Sophie's bed. Back where I belong. The angel on my shoulder's been doing cartwheels for thirty-six hours straight. The vibrating stops. I pull the covers under my chin and close my eyes again. Tommy won't be bringing a trophy home from Mexico. He finished sixth. Unfortunately, Leo's lead grew. His third-place finish has him four points ahead after Beck came in fourth. Ren won his first race of the season. Her phone begins vibrating again. Sophie peeps an eye open and smiles at me but doesn't budge. The vibrating stops, and she recloses her eyes. I'm a good witch that has wicked witch moments, sure, but Sophie? She's a good witch, like *pink sparkly dress and a star on the tip of her wand* good—not a wee bit of wickedness in her. Five seconds later, the vibrating starts back up.

"Fucking hell!" she groans, flipping over.

She snatches the phone and puts it to her ear.

"You alright?" she says, voice all scratchy.

She shifts and sits up quickly.

I stare up at her. It's a girl's voice.

"Who is that?" I whisper.

Sophie mouths, "Ana."

Ana sure is yapping away awfully loud. I close my eyes and listen, say a prayer that we can go back to sleep.

"I haven't spoken to him today...yet," Sophie says.

I watch her grit her teeth, her face becoming worried.

"I will!" she says. "Ana? Don't spiral. Let's get the facts."

She pulls the phone from her ear and quickly hangs up.

"What's wrong?" I ask. "She sounded hysterical."

"*Apparently,* a wild night in Mexico City was had."

"Ren won! Good for him for celebrating!" I say, nestling back into her pillows.

"Celebrating, I'm all for—but this was something along the lines of a club with topless women?"

Both of my eyes fly open this time. "Was Tommy there?!" I ask, more frenzied than I meant to.

"Of course he was there!" she snaps. "It was probably his idea!"

"Beck was there?"

"Supposedly, yes," she huffs, furiously typing on her phone. "I just pray to God Luca wasn't."

I push myself up so my back's against the pillows.

"Carmen!" I yell at the top of my lungs.

"What?" she angrily calls back, walls away.

"Get in here!"

She groans like a bear.

"*My word,*" Sophie says. She turns her screen to me.

I swallow at the sight of the *Lights Out Ladies* page header. I rub my eyes—slept in my bloody contacts again. And read the post headline.

Stand by your men?

Oof. Now my teeth are gritted. In the first photo, Ren's got a girl in his lap—her top's gone missing. I swipe to the next, where Beck's got girls hanging all over him. I swipe past it and through several others. It seems a lot of them went out. I swipe again and swallow. It's a different girl in Tommy's lap, and his hand's a wee bit higher on her thigh than I'd prefer it to be. But that hand's not really mine, is it? He's not actually mine. I've got no reason to feel sick about it, but I do.

CHAPTER 45
SPEAK LATER

SOPHIE

I TAKE MY PHONE back from Ella. The photos were posted only an hour ago. Not sure of Beck's travel schedule today, but I ring him anyway. What do I know? He might answer from the club! Some girl might even answer! The trill of the ringer is criminal after two nights of tequila. It cuts off.

"Luuuuhve," he says, finally answering.

"Don't call me that," I snap.

Ella's mouth forms an O. She scoots closer to the phone.

"*Sophie*—" he says my name a bit patronizingly, as if I'm the one in trouble. It's quite obvious he's drunk, but wherever he is, it's quiet.

"What happened last night?" I ask, then shake my head. "I mean, tonight? Are you even home yet?"

"We went out. It was the end of a triple, for fuck's sake."

Ella hands me her phone, she's got the post pulled up. I scroll through the carousel of picture evidence of this night out.

"You went out—" he offers.

"Went out! Didn't have half-naked men hanging all over us!" I shout. "These photos—what will Shannon think about these?"

"Photos?" he asks, confused. "I haven't seen shit."

"Well, my word, there's a trove!"

He groans. "Tommy wanted to show Ren a good time before—"

"Before his *wedding*?" I interrupt him. "Tommy thought he'd get some random girl's knockers in Ren's face before he marries one of my best friends?"

Beck goes silent.

"Did these girls come back with you, then? To the hotel?"

"What?" He scoffs. "Of course not."

My thumb flies through the photos.

"Oh? Just the ones in the lift with Amir and Sanjay? Oh, and there's another one with Gordon, walking through the lobby!"

"Well, good for them—*we left*," he says, annoyed. "I'm about to crash, baby."

"And Ren? He left with you?" I ask, wanting to get confirmation back to Ana.

"Sophie, that's not our business," he says.

And a fire ignites in my chest.

"It is my business when Ana calls me hysterical, and I'm uninformed!" I yell.

Ella's eyes go wide.

"Why isn't Ren answering his phone?" I ask a bit softer, but not by much.

"He didn't leave with us! I don't know! He was wasted, though. He's probably just passed out!"

Ella pokes me. "*Ask about Tommy*," she mouths.

"And what about Tommy? Did he hook up with this girl that's sat there with her legs draped over him?"

"No."

I blink, waiting for him to say more, but he doesn't.

"Alright, then!" I say with finality.

"I love you, Sophie," my safety net replies.

"Mm-hmm," I mumble. "Speak later." I pull the phone from my ear and hang up.

Ella's blue eyes are blinking at me, her lips pressed together.

"Am I being unreasonable?" I ask, truly after an honest answer.

She blows out a breath, rubs her forehead. "I believe him. Nothing overly nefarious happened...with our boys, at least."

I watch her start picking at her nails.

Did she say *our boys*?

CHAPTER 46
SEMANTICS

ELLA

Tommy:

Okay to come to yours at 7?

I suppose.

Guess you've got some groveling to do

Oh?

Your whereabouts Sunday night?

Sophie was reeling. The betrothed is livid.

Couldn't let Ren tie the knot without some (.)(.) before

So it WAS a strip club!!!!!

(@_@)

…No?

Fuck.

I CHANGED INTO MY favorite LoveShackFancy tiered mini skirt before Tommy arrived—not for him, I just haven't worn it in a minute. A little baby tank, too, because it's quite warm today.

Tommy steps into my room and swallows. I watch him take in the disorder and try not to smile. He moves around, shifting the bits and bobs I've got on my dresser and desk. *Does he have to touch everything?* He moves on to my hat rack on the wall. Probably thirty or so hats haphazardly piled onto the hooks, stacked in no particular order. He starts taking hats off, trying them on, then holding them under his arm while he attempts to organize them better.

"Where's Carmen?" he asks, turning to me, wearing my furry white ushanka. *Man-child.*

"London." I smile, though I was trying not to. "She's got all her Wimbledon gigs. She and Ollie left this morning."

He puts the ushanka back and throws on a cranberry beret. I wonder how annoying he was in that Mexico City jewelry shop. I got a kick out of *that* bystander's picture. Tommy, cupping his hands around his eyes was peering into the closed shop's window, while Beck was holding his phone to his ear with one hand and rubbing the back of his neck with the other. *Damage control?* That was the caption.

The beret's off and Tommy's four layers deep on one hook when he stops and tilts his head.

"No! Is this?" He turns around holding an orange bucket hat. "This is the hat from last summer, no?"

"Held onto it." I shrug. "In case I ever get to go fishing."

His face pinches. "You've *never* been fishing?" he asks, staring at me like I've got three heads.

I shake the one head I've got.

"I'll take you fishing!" he says, hanging the bucket hat back on the hook.

He turns around and rubs his palms together, all nervous at the clutter.

"If you think this is bad, don't open the bathroom cabinets," I warn.

He grimaces and shakes his head a bit.

"You want to see the most exclusive lounge in Paris?"

He cocks an eyebrow.

I lift the lower half of my window, noise from the street floods into my room. I swing my leg up over the windowsill, duck and climb out. I hold onto the base of the window from the outside and peek back inside at him.

"This way!" I encourage.

He leans down and sticks his head out. I peer at the drop-off behind me.

"Oi!" he shouts. "Don't fall!"

"I won't!" I snap. "Follow me."

I crawl up the steep part of the roof and look back. He's made it out, on his hands and knees crawling after me. I turn onto my backside and scoot along to my usual spot.

He leans back on his hands next to me. "Bet there's wicked stars up here!"

"Sometimes, when it gets dark enough."

I reach up to the brick on the dormer, hesitate for a second, then continue my pursuit—I have needs. I have to tell him, and I only brought him out here because it's not exactly easy to escape. I pull the brick out and grab the lighter and pack of cigarettes.

"Do you mind?" I ask.

"I didn't know you smoked."

I sniff a laugh. "I don't." But I haven't had my head properly screwed on lately, have I?

He lies back against the slanted roof.

I fold back the top of the carton. *How fitting.* There's only one left. I lie back next to him. And take that last first drag—I'm not buying more. I already made that promise to myself. He tilts his head in my direction and brings his hand to his brow to shield his eyes.

"You look sexy when you smoke," he says, squinting in the sun. "But you look sexy doing anything."

"Is this your groveling?" I ask, then take another drag.

"Were you upset?"

"That you were at a strip club?"

"It wasn't a strip club, it was a club with—"

"Strippers?" I supply.

"Dancers?" he offers.

"Half-naked dancers?" I flick my hand at him. "Semantics," I giggle.

He shifts, turning onto his side to face me.

"For serious—were you upset?" he inquires.

"Your hand was quite high on her thigh, no?" I peek at him, then look back at the sky. "But we're not actually together, why would I be upset?"

He blinks.

"I was—worried." I shrug. "I mean, worried about our image."

"I know, I know—got an earful from Holly." He sighs and turns over onto his back again. "Sorry, bad slip-up."

"Bad slip-up *in public*," I exhale, cough a bit. "Keep doing whatever you want elsewhere."

He turns onto his side again, and his face goes funny. "I'm not talking to anyone else, Ella."

Only me? I swallow. Only me in our fake world, anyway. But also—when exactly would he have the time?

"Not even red?" I smirk.

"Red?"

"That reporter that always has her hands on you."

"Rebecca?"

I shrug. "She's never bothered to introduce herself to me."

He lets out a cocky laugh.

"She wants to bang you."

"*Christ!*" He continues laughing. "She's just a flirt; I wouldn't touch that."

That makes me feel better. I don't tell him that, though. I suppose I believe him; he really only goes for blondes. That girl in his lap was a blonde. *Rude.*

"Was Sophie truly angry with Beck?"

"Yes, but I think I calmed her down a bit."

"Maybe the diamonds will get her the rest of the way," he says, moving his hands behind his head.

"Diamonds?" I glance over at him. His eyes are closed, his tattoos are out on full display.

"Beck dropped a load of cash before we left. Made us leave early for the airport so he could get to a jeweler. Owner had to open the shop early for us."

"So you *did* get in?"

He looks at me, confused.

"There was a photo of you two—outside." I smile.

"*Fuck*—" He shakes his head. "Can't do anything without the peanut gallery."

"Was Beck that nervous?"

"No, but he'll do anything that'll get him back in her pants quicker. She's like fucking crack to him."

I chuckle at the metaphor, but only for a second because that awful feeling creeps back into my stomach. I take a drag. I don't know that anyone's ever described what I do to them like that. I tip my head up and blow out before rolling onto my side. I'm not doing the jealous thing anymore.

"Was Beck ever like this with Sabrina?"

"Nah. He was chill."

"Was he ever like you?"

Tommy peeps one eye open and winks. "No one's like me."

I roll my eyes.

"He had his fair share of hooking up, but then Sophie happened, and now he's proper locked down."

I nod my chin at him. "You've had quite a few girlfriends."

"I like a relationship." He shrugs. "Also enjoy being a fuckboy, though. You've never wanted to be exclusive with any of those boys you keep on your bench?"

"I'm not a relationship type of girl." I flick my cigarette. Not that I know I'm not, never tried it, never been someone's someone. "Weird, I guess, since both of my best friends are madly in love, but I just don't really think that's in the cards for me."

"Why not?" he asks, both eyes on me.

"I don't *not believe* in love. It happens, obviously, but I think it's rare." I stare over at the pigeons on the roofline across the street. "Didn't have the best example growing up—"

I look back at him and shrug. "Suppose that's why I've never been fishing. My dad never really cared about being a dad to me at all, especially after he left."

"His loss, Ella," he says, grabbing my wrist. "I'm taking you fishing. You don't need him."

I smile, take a final drag and put out my cigarette against the brick. Curiously I didn't enjoy it much at all. Tommy moves his hand onto his chest, and I lie back down next to him and stare up at the golden sky.

"I'm glad you got it sorted with the girls," he says a few moments later.

This is it. I take a deep breath, let it sit there in my lungs before I let it out. "Same. Now I've only got to sort things out with you."

"What have you done now?" he says jokingly.

I keep my eyes on the sky, on those wispy clouds that look like a paint smear. "I wasn't completely honest about why I was so eager to start our arrangement."

He rolls back onto his side, facing me. A line of birds flies between my line of sight and my paint-smear cloud.

"I know I told you I wanted to please my dad, but it was never about that. I don't give a shit what he thinks."

"Why'd you want to then?"

I blink, clear my throat. "I wanted the attention. I did it for the clout," I spit out.

He nods. "And how's that working out for you?"

"Quite well, actually," I admit honestly, because why not? "I'm nearly at two million followers."

"Baby girl's a star." He smiles. "But you already were. You didn't need me."

My chest has that funny tight feeling. It's uncomfortable, so I shift onto my side to face him, propping my head up on my arm.

"So you don't seek your dad's approval, but you do seek out the approval of a million strangers online. You think you look for it there because you never got it from your dad?"

I stare at him a moment, thinking over the conclusions from the psychoanalysis he's just run on me. No one has ever laid it out that simply. *Is that the reason I obsess over this job the way I do?*

"I—I suppose you're right," I stumble over my words. "He doesn't take it seriously. Influencing. He thinks it's all a joke."

"Well, he can fuck right off. You probably make double what half of the people our age make—current company excluded." He smirks.

He grabs my wrist and holds on this time. "Come on, you've got confidence like I've never seen."

"Maybe on the outside," I say, staring at his hand around my wrist. I smile, trying to lighten the convo. "Haven't been desperate enough to start selling pictures of my feet online yet, though!"

I wiggle my bare toes, and his eyes are immediately drawn to them.

"I'd be first in line for those." He reaches down, tries to grab my foot, but I curl my legs up.

"You could have told me that was your reason from the start," he says. "We're friends...you can tell me anything."

That's the second time he's said that to me. You think you know someone—but he's got a heart, this one. A rather big one.

I nudge his hand. "Let's hear it then. What's your childhood trauma?"

"Hmm…" he says, looking up at the sky. "How does being raised with the pressure of being a prodigy sound?"

I narrow my eyes, bobble my head, thinking.

"Or," he tries again. "How about getting shipped off to boarding school in another hemisphere?"

Roof chat concluded, Tommy ducks back through the window first, then turns around and holds his hands out for me. I crouch down and latch onto his shoulders. He finds my hips and helps me back inside.

Both of my feet are firmly planted on the ground, and yet his hands remain perched on my hips. I'm not sure why he's staring at me, but his eyes are looking quite toffee-like in this light. Not that they ever don't, I've just been making a concerted effort to not find myself getting lost in them. In this moment, however, I'm failing, and those golden eyes are penetrating me like twin lasers. I blink and look away, shocked to find my own hands still resting on his shoulders. I swallow and slowly drag them down, but not away. I could pull them back, but they've got a mind of their own at the minute.

My fingertips drag down the length of his chest and torso until the material of his shirt runs out. I flick my eyes up, but only for a second, enough to see his lips part. I watch my fingers dip under his shirt, running underneath it against the skin on his fit stomach. His grip on my hips tightens. I've got self-control—*sometimes*. Right now, though? Not so much. I trail back to the hem of his shirt and start to lift it. His hands leave my hips as he takes his shirt off over his head. He drops it to the floor and steps forward. He pushes my hair behind my shoulders, and in unison, slides the straps of my crochet baby tank off my shoulders. It falls and gathers above my waist, further exposing my chest that's pumping like mad. He traces his thumbs along the outside of my bare breasts.

I look up, voice shaky. "Is this happening again?"

His eyes meet mine. "Don't know about you, but I didn't quite get it out of my system last time."

I nod. "Once more will surely do the trick."

He huffs a laugh and shifts my body, guiding me down onto my bed. I lift my arms as he removes my baby tank, then reach out, slip my index finger into the waistband of his briefs and pull him closer. I unfasten the button on his trousers and tug them down far enough so he can step out of them.

I start to stand up, but he puts his hand on top of my shoulder. "Lie down." He nods behind me.

I scoot back on my bed and lower down onto my back. He drops to his knees and hooks his fingers into the top of my tiered mini skirt. He finds my knickers on the descent and takes those down with it. My cheeks flush. I'm fully exposed and *stone. Cold. Sober.*

"So fucking sexy," he says, lifting my ankles and resting my heels on his muscular shoulders.

I thought my chest was beating like mad a minute ago, but then he lifts my left foot, turns his head and grazes his lips against my instep. Have you ever had a tongue run up the inside of your ankle? There must be some nerve leading from it directly to—*Fuck!* I gasp as he slides a finger down my clit.

I bring the back of my hand over my mouth and bite into it. His mouth continues up my leg, now nearing my inner thigh. I latch onto a handful of duvet as he runs out of leg and reaches my center. His fingers creep up my stomach and find my nipple as his tongue starts sliding against me. He locks his other arm around my thigh and pulls in closer, lightly sucking my clit. *Sucking.* And *fuck* if it's not the best feeling in the whole world. I whimper into the back of my hand—this didn't happen in Monaco. That was rushed and rough. That was *fucking*. Fucking because we felt like it, and it felt good. But this? This is pure worship—I'm not one for theatrics, but this is nothing short of a religious experience.

He pauses that heavenly thing he's doing with his mouth, and his head tilts up. He reaches for the hand I'm using to cover my mouth and guides it away.

"I want to hear you," he says, bringing my hand down between my legs. He pushes my fingers against my wetness. "Keep going."

His eyes don't leave my body as he rises from the floor and removes his briefs. All while I give him what he wants, but my own fingers don't feel as good as his or his mouth. When he crawls over me, his palm meets the back of my hand. And with my fingers under the direction of his, he takes control over the pressure and pace.

His lips move across my chest, leave a trail of warmth up my neck, until he finds my mouth, and I taste myself on his tongue. My body rocks against our fingers, I release the fistful of duvet and exchange it for a fistful of his hair. When he pushes my fingers away, down his go, sliding into me. He's got the experience; he knows the angles. He pulls his mouth from mine and brings his lips against my ear. His breath is as ragged as mine as his fingers work faster inside of me. *Fuck!* I claw at the back of his neck. *He can hear me now.* Pierre can probably hear me in the lobby, and, *fucking hell*, innocent Parisians can probably hear me on the high street—I left the bloody window open.

"Come for me, baby girl," he whispers into the shell of my ear.

And holy fuck, if I allow myself to come at his command—*but I do*. I cry out as my orgasm ricochets through me, my muscles pulsing like mad around his fingers as he continues working tiny circles inside me.

His body shifts so he's on top of me now, his fingers slip out of me, but they're immediately replaced as he pushes into me. I wrap my leg around him, pull all of his weight down against me so his chest meets mine. And let me tell you, the way my name rolls off his tongue and onto my lips, the way our bodies move together—*it's biblical.*

I don't do cuddling with boys. And yet Tommy's arm is draped over my waist, his body smack-up against my backside. And how have I just slept the entire night without stirring? *This is unacceptable.* I turn over under his arm, his candy eyes are already open.

"Good morning, Ella."

I blink at him. "Did I say you could sleep in here?"

A grin touches his lips. "You didn't say I *couldn't* sleep in here."

I let him sleep in here? When he had the audacity to put me on that pullout couch at his those first nights in Monaco! His hand slides down my body and finds my ass. He's warm, and his bare chest and biceps are making my mouth water a bit. *This can't happen again.* I quickly turn back over and climb out of bed. I grab my glasses from the nightstand. I need water—my chest's feeling a bit funny at the minute and perhaps my mouth is watering only due to the fact I need a spot of something to drink.

I make it to the kitchen and chug a glass of water. My bedroom door creaks. He's coming. I start moving random things around on the counter. He walks around the island, sans shirt, and I pick up a honeydew melon. When I glance back at him, those fucking toffee eyes catch me, and I forget what I was intending to do with said melon. What the fuck is this random melon doing in here anyway? I turn to the counter—mistake. He comes behind me, pulls my hips back so my ass sits right at his crotch and our bodies press together. His hands move on my silk *La Perla* slip.

His mouth comes over my shoulder to press against my ear. "Why don't you quit pretending to be busy and come back to bed?"

"Pretending?" I set down the melon and turn to face him. "I'll have you know that I do the cooking around here—when we cook…"

I slip out sideways and step to the refrigerator.

"I didn't grow up with staff like my counterparts," I say, swinging open the door. I blink at the Prosecco, the pad of butter, and God only knows what's in that take away box.

Tommy tilts his head. "Yeah! Real chef's fridge you got there, baby girl."

I slam the door and panic. I've got to get us out of here, or *it* will happen again. I turn on my heel and smile. "I thought instead we could go get breakfast. There's a lovely spot down the street."

He moves toward me, looks down and runs his fingers along my hip bones.

"Only if you wear those glasses."

We ate. We laughed. Laughed like nothing happened, and we're the best of friends grabbing a bite. Loads of people stared. Maybe because of who he is—*probably that*—but maybe because we look rather good together? And yes, I wore my glasses. Not because he wanted me to, though, but because I didn't feel like putting my contacts in. He had to leave shortly after because he was already going to be late for his workout. And when he left, I stared at the back of the door, and for some reason, I counted the days until I'll see him next.

CHAPTER 47

ENDGAME

SOPHIE

Dad exits the M4.

"Bring your friends. It's a party for everyone! We've got the whole ballroom and terrace at the club."

Evelyn got her way—but the option of a small party was never truly on the table. Dad deserves over-the-top, and the details I've seen are George Collins's retirement party worthy.

"Do you need a DJ?" I ask, half joking but half serious. "Carmen and Ollie are here for Wimbledon!"

Dad snorts a laugh. "I think Evelyn's got the music covered."

"Alright, alright—you did rather enjoy his set in Amsterdam."

"Such a fun weekend." He smiles. "But Evelyn might leave me if she saw me acting like that."

"Like a rowdy boy at university?"

"Me? Never!" He chuckles. "You should have Ren and Ana come too, if you'd like."

I press my lips together. "Ren's in a bit of trouble—like a lot a bit."

Dad nods, attempting to suppress a smile. "You'll bring Beck, no? It might just be a party for him too."

I shoot him a look. He knows Beck's on my shit list at the minute. Dad promised he was on my side, and yet he's been defending Beck every chance he gets. I sort of hate-love it?

"Boys will be boys, darling."

"I know," I exhale.

"Doesn't mean you can't make him squirm a bit." Dad winks. He keeps one hand on the wheel and rests his other on his golf trousers. "You know, I've loved watching you fall in love with Beck. It's been my favorite thing."

I almost smile, turning to the window and running my index finger over my lips, ready to interfere if one creeps up. I should return the compliment, but watching Dad fall in love with Evelyn has been quite hard. That's a me problem, though, as Ella would say. Two things can be true at once: It is hard, but I also love seeing him so content, so happy, with the happiness not revolving around me or work for once. That, and Evelyn is simply lovely and head-over-heels for him.

"Are you and Evelyn liking the flat?" I ask.

"We love it. Little Bear enjoys the park."

"When the house is finished, what will you do with it?"

Dad shrugs. "I'll hold on to it. If I get stir-crazy bored, I could always start up something of my own and use it as an office." He looks to me and cocks an eyebrow. "You looking to get back in the game?"

I narrow my eyes. "Team up?"

He shrugs again. "Would be a load of fun, no?"

"Hmm…" I tap my chin. "I could maybe consider something like that."

I watch him and swallow, ready to ask the real question I've been needing answered. I sort of already know the answer—I'm not brainless or blind—but here goes.

"When the house is finished, is Evelyn going to move in?"

His hand moves off his thigh and back to the two-o'clock position. He adjusts his grip on the steering wheel. "Would that be okay with you?"

I look back toward the window and give myself a moment. I had a proper nanny for a minute—right after Mum died. She'd walk me home from school, make me snacks, watch me until Dad got home, but something about it completely freaked me out. It was nothing against her, she was lovely, but seeing another woman in our house—*my Mum's house, her kitchen*—so soon after her death, it did something to me. One day at school, I decided I didn't want to go home and be with the nanny. I wanted to be with Dad. I made a plan, dodged her outside at pickup and walked to the station. I took the circle line to Cannon Street and showed up out of the blue at Dad's office. Jo escorted me in. Her eyes were as wide as his.

I'd never been in that much trouble. Though I wasn't actually in trouble; it just felt like I was in trouble. Dad was pacing around, going through every terrifying possible outcome that *could* have come from a ten-year-old on the tube alone, a ten-year-old walking in the station, *walking in the city*. But no matter what he said, none of it scared me more than seeing a woman who wasn't my mother in our house. The poor nanny was in shambles, thinking someone had kidnapped me right before her eyes. When I explained to Dad why I did it, he cried. He tried to hide it, but he did. I told him it scared me, seeing a girl that isn't Mum in our house, and could I please come to his office after school instead? Because I only want to be with him anyway! He was hysterical.

After that *stunt*, he arranged for a car to pick me up from school and drive me to his office each day. I'd sit in those big chairs across from him at his desk and pretend I was some finance wizard like he was. He kept the nanny employed, but as more of a house manager. She'd cook, keep our kitchen stocked, the laundry kept up, and she'd leave when Dad and I returned from the office. It went on like that for years. I suppose I've always had an aversion to other women in our house. It's not *our house* anymore, though. It's his. I wasn't old enough then, but I'm old enough now, it's time to let it go.

I turn away from the window, back to him, and smile. "I think you two would be very happy there."

Dad drove me to the Wright's yesterday. He and James played a round at Wentworth. Dad left after, but I stayed. So, I'm here, car-less, basically giving Beck no other option but to come out here and get me. Brat move? *Yes.* But I needed a level playing field, and it's too easy to get carried away at his place. I'd be on my back in short order because, mad at him or not, I can't be without his hands on me. I'd probably forget why I was even mad at him in the first place.

I'm sat at the kitchen counter with Mia, plates of Eton mess in front of us. Elizabeth made one yesterday, adding cherries for me because she's quite simply the best, but Dad and James ate the whole thing after golf, so this morning, we made another. Well, Elizabeth made another while Mia and I sat there and provided commentary. Elizabeth has been picking little fights with James. I'm mad at her son, so she wants to be mad at her husband to share in my madness. Did I mention she's the best? Louie has already finished his plate. I suppose he picked up wolfing down desserts from Beck. He's now back on the floor with his Nintendo Switch. Outside, Scout starts barking like mad. Elizabeth's and Mia's eyes come at me. The barking travels around the house, headed up front. Pirelli's bark is more sporadic—he hasn't learned the full guard-dog ways yet.

"Stay in here!" Mia says, hopping down from the stool.

She runs through the kitchen and disappears into the foyer.

"It's him!" she yells from the front door.

Elizabeth rolls her eyes. "You don't have to stay in here."

I smile. "I sort of like her plan."

"Come on, Louie!" Elizabeth pulls him up off the floor.

I stay at the counter, moving the tip of my fork through a heap of whipped cream. The front door opens, and a car door slams. Now's about when Louie will be running down the front steps to be the first to greet Beck. A few moments later, I hear his voice, then cheek kisses. *Then Mia.*

"You're in the doghouse!" Mia scolds.

I stifle a laugh.

"Sophie's in the kitchen," Elizabeth says in a hushed voice. "And there's a treat on the counter."

"She's not the treat?" Beck asks, cocky as ever.

"And I have some words for you as well," Elizabeth adds.

Beck huffs a laugh. "Okay, Mum."

Elizabeth ushers Mia and Louie upstairs, and as the stampede of footsteps up to the first floor fade, I hear his. As much as I want to spin around and jump into his arms, I also want to pie him with this whipped cream. I scoot my plate away and keep my eyes forward. His hands come around me, and cold metal meets my chest. I peer down at the string of dainty diamonds draped over me. His fingers fasten the clasp at the back of my neck, then he spins my stool around to face him. I keep my eyes low, run my fingers over the stones. *Must have cost a bloody fortune.* Hoodie, sweatpants—it's damn near impossible not to throw my arms around him, but I refrain. I slowly look up and meet his smiling eyes—they're all crinkly at the corners.

"Are you sorry for something?" I ask.

He swallows. "I'm sorry for being there. I didn't mean to worry you."

I watch him and try not to look at his lips, by biting mine instead. He runs his hands up my arms.

"You want to know what Fredrick said to me that day in the paddock?"

He goes still, his jaw clenches.

"He said I was mad for thinking an athlete wouldn't cheat on me."

"Look at me," he says, bringing his hand against my cheek. His face is serious, eyes focused. "We don't lie to each other, Sophie. You know I would never cheat on you."

"You're a superstar, though. What if you decide you don't like me anymore?"

He shakes his head. "Doesn't matter what I am." The tip of his nose meets mine. "I don't think you understand..."

I blink.

"I'm afraid you're my *endgame*."

I squash my smile because I'm quite proud at his use of the word. Mia should have heard that. "You won't fall out of love with me?"

"I reckon it's impossible to fall out of love with you." He pulls back and stands up straight. "I mean, look at Fredrick, the poor bastard."

"He loved me—and yet he still left," I say softly.

"I'm not going anywhere." He runs his thumb along my collarbone. "And if I do, I'm afraid you're coming with."

My cheeks go warm. I'd go anywhere with him; a girl can't be without her safety net.

"Well," I sigh. "I'd be lying if I said I'm not still cross with you."

"Good." He lights up, licking his lips. "I want you to be mad. It's fun to fight with you."

He lifts my wrist and kisses the inside of it, keeping it against his lips so I can feel his breath on my skin. The warmth I want to feel when he drags his mouth across other parts of my body. A chill runs down my leg. Those big brown eyes burn into me. He knows what he's doing. *But I'm mad and need to hold my ground, remember?* I pull my hand back and run my fingers over the diamonds around my neck.

I briefly peer down at the necklace before meeting his gaze once more. "Maybe fighting's not so bad."

His eyes twinkle, his dimple appears. "There she is," he says before taking my face in his hands and smothering my mouth with his.

I grab onto his wrists and pull him closer. He sucks on my bottom lip as he pulls away. He tilts his head and nods at my plate. "Now, are you gonna give me a bite of that or not?"

I spin around and scoop up a massive forkful, overflowing with whipped cream. I spin back and bring the fork to his mouth. He gets most of it in a single bite, but I smear the remaining whipped cream onto his nose and lips. He snorts a laugh, acting like the whipped cream isn't all over his face.

"Very good," he says, eyes pinched. "Did you make that?"

"Don't think you'd be saying *very good* if I did," I giggle.

He swallows his bite, then lunges at me with those sticky lips and whipped-cream nose.

"Beck!" I squeal, wiggling around, trying to push him off. *No use.* What he didn't transfer to my own nose and lips, he's trailing down the side of my neck. I run my fingers through his hair, pull him closer and now he's got me wondering what car he drove.

Alright?

Ana Wong:

Superb!

Been sleeping like a baby.

<3

Beck should ask Ren how he's sleeping.

He's been banished to the guest room.

(*o*)

CHAPTER 48
EVERYBODY LIKES STARS

ELLA

I STAYED THE NIGHT with Carmen and Ollie. They've got a hotel in SOHO for another week or so of matches. I convinced Carmen to come do nails with me, Tommy just left HQ and is on his way to pick me up. I didn't get them done in Paris because the nail lady I gatekeep there is quite judgy and would most definitely have given me eyes. But *why* does MACH's team color have to be orange? *Ugh.* Carmen's doing tennis ball green, which looks rather good with her olive skin, and will photograph lovely with the matching green gingham set she's wearing at Centre Court tomorrow. I'm a ball of nervous energy for reasons unknown and cannot for the life of me make a decision lately. Carmen's fingers are nearly done, and I'm still looking at this bloody sample book. I shake my head, flipping through the color samples. "I can't commit to full orange."

"Do a pearl color with some orange flowers!" Carmen says.

"Hmm." I ponder—not quite sold on flowers. I look up at the manicurist, who's growing more annoyed by the second with my indecisiveness.

I swallow. "What about stars?"

Her head bobs.

"That would be cute!" Carmen agrees.

"Let's do it," I say, closing the book, setting it aside. *"Everybody likes stars,"* I whisper to myself. Tommy, for one, absolutely loves them.

I've been in a weird headspace for the last week, ever since he left our place. I've sort of been jumping every time my phone buzzes, thinking it's him, but it never is. It's only Carmen blowing up the group chat. I resisted every urge to text him and ask what he was doing because one—I know he's busy at HQ, and two—why would I care what he's doing? *But I do?* Don't worry, I never texted him. Instead, I took everything out of my wardrobe, attempting to piece together perfect outfits for Silverstone. I even went to Mum's and raided her closet. Between both of our wardrobes, nothing felt even remotely adequate! Mum agreed, so off we went, swiping in the Golden Triangle. We were out for hours. I tried everything on at least twice and got not only her opinion but the approval of every shopping assistant I could find. Since when am I incapable of pulling together an outfit? I mean, it is *Silverstone*—everyone and their mother will be there. Tommy's going to kill me—my bags might as well be carrying bricks.

My pinkie nail is coated with the pretty pearl white before my hand is transferred under the UV light.

I've got my own room this week at the track. And when I say at the track, I mean literally on the track above the main straight, a lovely benefit of MACH having a hotel sponsor. Sophie's *camping* again with Beck, though she did say to expect her crashing at some point—when she's over the wilderness and doesn't care about hurting Beck's feelings. Tommy will be in a motorhome with Sam. I check the time on my phone. The boy from Britain and his belle should be arriving at the track soon, *by helicopter.*

A magnifying glass is put over my dry hand, and an orange bottle of nail polish moves into the arena.

"You bringing Tommy to the party?" Carmen asks.

I adjust in my seat at the mere mention of his name. "I suppose I'll ask him to come!" I shrug.

"Retirement party or not, I'm excited. Ollie will be gagging for a party by then."

"Stuffy crowd, I'm sure, but the open bar and caviar?" I flick my eyebrows at her.

I lean forward and check the progress of my nails.

Carmen cranes her neck. "That's perfect!"

And I'm smiling stupidly because a galaxy of tiny orange stars is being painted across my fingernails, and it might look stupid, but Tommy has this way about him that makes me want to do stupid things.

The nail technician flips up my hand, proud of her work. "You like it?"

I fold my lips and nod because the stars are stupid cute, and I can't wait to see the stupid grin on Tommy's face when he notices.

***

I drag my bags out of the lift, and Tommy's standing there talking to one of the porters, signing something for him. The porter's gaze flicks my way, and Tommy turns around. I've never been known to be clumsy, but I nearly trip catching those golden eyes. He gives the porter a quick fist-bump.

"Let me get your bags, ma'am!" the porter says, rushing over.

Tommy puts his hand out. "She's mine. I've got it," he says all cool. The combination of the words *she's* and *mine* has me melting like a fool. He walks over, eyeing my bags like I suspected he would.

He runs his tongue across his bottom lip and nods at me. "You pack enough?"

I shake my head.

One hand takes over the handle of my RIMOWA and his other reaches for my fingers. A few heads turn in our direction as we roll through the lobby. That's a lie—every head turns.

"I was hit with a sudden onset of indecision which resulted in the packing of ten possible outfit options," I say, somehow feeling the need to defend myself.

"Bust out the straightjacket dress again!"

I scoff, then make some other unintelligible noise because he can't be serious.

"What? That dress was sick!"

"Tommy, I cannot simply repeat an outfit like that! In the paddock of all places! It would be sinful!"

He shakes his head as if I'm being ridiculous.

The lobby doors are opened for us, and I feel a bit like royalty walking out with him. Sam hops out of a waiting SUV with its flashers on.

"Sam, I hope you're not planning on repeating any outfits in the paddock this week," Tommy says.

"Never!" Sam says, then tosses me a wink. *Good man.*

I open the back-seat door.

"Where'd you think you're going?" Tommy says. He nods his head beyond the door. "We're taking that."

I push the door closed and walk to the front of the SUV. *Holy shit.* A shiny orange McLaren Senna sits in front of it—with gorgeous carbon fiber details and a massive rear wing. My eyes flip from the freakin' race-car Batmobile to the SUV and back.

"I thought ahead. I know how you pack," he says, reaching down and lifting the butterfly door. "Not even half of your shit would fit in here."

The cockpit of the Senna is tight and claustrophobic. I did not prepare for or expect a ride with only the two of us. Sam is a buffer, but the buffer just got in the driver's seat of the SUV. My mouth goes a bit dry. Tommy climbs in and fires up the engine with a button on the ceiling. People are filming us on the footpath. We're sitting awfully close, no?

He looks over. "Ready?"

I nod, and he starts to look away but does a double take. My heart rapid-fires as he reaches over and lifts my hand. I completely forgot—my manicure.

"Little stars?" he murmurs, inspecting my nails. "MACH orange baby stars!" The smile that's taken over his entire face makes my brain go to absolute mush. *It's sickening.* He leans toward the door and slips his phone out of his pocket. I can't speak, most likely due to my heart being in my throat. He moves my hand onto his thigh but keeps hold of it. He opens Instagram and swipes to the story camera.

"Amelia's going to love these," he says, snapping a picture of my star-adorned fingers in his permanently star-adorned hand. *Our hands.* When he lets go, I immediately bring a nail between my teeth because my heart's bloody jumping around.

"Wait until you see our race suits this week." He sets his phone between his legs and shifts the car into drive. My phone pings with the tag notification: *tommyoung6 has tagged you in a story.*

"You've never been out to Silverstone?" he asks, pulling away from the curb.

"I haven't," I squeak, glad to have found my voice again. "My brother used to go every season. I usually do the Wimbledon thing this time of year with Carmen."

"I suspected you had a brother."

"Why's that?"

"Just the way you are," he says, nodding over at me. "You've got that cool way about you—you've got to have a brother."

The way I am? It's not the first time he's called me cool. I suppose one has to be some level of cool, having been raised with normal older brother bullying, a tough-love Mum and a fucked-off paternal figure.

"Now, Sophie—she's textbook only child."

Says the only child...

"Definitely not the shipped off to boarding school type of only child," he adds, as if he can read my damn mind.

"Brother's older, no?"

I nod. "Emmett."

"Ella and Emmett. *I like that,*" he says, flipping his indicator. "I want to meet him."

"No, you don't."

The tires squeal as he turns onto the high street with some power. It's a short-lived little thrill though as we come to a complete stop. Traffic's awful. I'm trying not to look at his fingers that are lightly tapping against the paddle shifters on the steering wheel, but all I can think about is how deep those fingers were buried inside of me. I pull in a breath and pretend I'm interested in the bit of road I can see out the window on the lower part of my door. I'll get my cardio today just sitting here with my heart rate through the roof. *This is getting out of hand.*

I peek over at him. He's got one hand on the wheel now, elbow propped on the door. I glance over my shoulder at Sam directly behind us in the SUV.

"You good?"

"Mm-hmm!" I squeak and straighten back in my seat, eyes forward. "I forgot to say thank you—the other day," I say nervously.

He looks over. "For what?"

I keep my eyes forward, focused on the car in front of us. "For being there for me in Miami that morning—thank you."

"Of course."

I swallow. "And for still being my friend after—well, everything."

The light changes, and the engine roars. SOHO whizzes by.

"I may have thought about what you did a bit differently than most."

"Differently how?" I ask as the car slows to another complete stop.

"There are some people who see things other people have or accomplish and say, *well of course they have this or that. They have all this money.* Or they make up some excuse as to why they can't have or achieve that same thing. But some people see the same thing and get inspired—it sets something off in them, you know?"

I nod. The car pulls forward.

"Those people don't make excuses; they go after it. You're one of those people."

He changes lanes, I look in the side-view mirror and watch Sam do the same.

"Now, I won't say you went about it in the right way, and you know that. But I can still appreciate aspects of your reaction."

"*Oh*—alright..." I mutter, surprised.

He slows for the next light and looks over. "I think it's good to try to see the best in things—the best in people—when you can."

My eyes flick away from the windscreen and directly into his toffee eyes. Eyes that can witness something so ugly and still search for a bit of good.

"You've got a beautiful mind." The words fall out of my mouth before I can do anything about it. I shake my head and yank my gaze away from him, grasping for something witty to follow up with. "Have you been seeing a shrink since the day you got shipped off then?"

He sniffs a laugh. "No shrinks."

The engine purrs, and we're off again. *Fuck.* I need to change the subject.

"The commentators were saying some things about you on the broadcast from Mexico. Have you thought about what you're going to do next year?"

"Spent hours in the sim at headquarters the last few days with the new upgrades. It felt worlds better."

"That's exciting!" I say far too enthusiastically. *Get a grip, Ella.*

He clicks his tongue. "Fingers crossed! We'll see how it feels in the car. If it's more of the same, I've got some thinking to do."

"If all goes well, and you're up for it, I've got a party Monday and need a date."

"Is this party at the most exclusive club in Paris?" He looks over and quirks an eyebrow. "I quite liked it there."

I blush. "No, it's here."

"Tell me more."

"Sophie's dad is retiring. It will be a boring as hell crowd, but I know Evelyn, and I know George's budget—they'll do it big."

"Evelyn's besties with your mum, no?"

"Yes," I say, then gulp. *Oh fuck*. Mum's not going back to Dubai for another week—she didn't mention whether she would be in attendance...

CHAPTER 49
BURBERRY ONESIE

SOPHIE

THE HELICOPTER BANKS LEFT, giving us a stellar view of Silverstone circuit and its lush green surroundings.

"There it is," Beck says, staring out the window. "I've dreamt of winning this race my entire life."

The pilot's voice comes through the headset. "Prepare for landing, sir."

Beck grabs the mic on his. "Copy."

He gives my hand a squeeze, and with the other, he spins my race bracelet around my wrist. Helicopters are surprisingly smooth, not at all what I expected. Not that I expected any of this. Beck dropped at the last minute that instead of driving up to Silverstone, the team would be sending him via helicopter. I only screamed for a second or two when the thing lifted straight off the pad on the Thames, and my stomach dropped like a cannonball.

We hover now, slowly descending into a field adjacent to the motorhomes we'll be *camping* in.

The helicopter eases down onto the grass and settles. Beck removes his headset and pulls on a red Furio hat. *Backward, of course.* The copilot hops out and opens the passenger door. Beck unbuckles his harness with ease but has to help me escape out of mine. He jumps down onto the grass and shakes both pilots' hands before turning around and lifting me out. He keeps hold of my hand, and I duck alongside him as the blades whir overhead.

Coop's waiting in a golf cart. We pile in, and the helicopter hovers above the grass before taking flight once more.

Beck throws his arm around the back of my shoulders, and the golf cart lurches forward as Coop steers us away from the noisy blades.

"How was the lift?"

"Soph only screamed once!" Beck says with a cheeky grin.

"Only at the start!" I say, defending myself. "And only for a second!"

"Gotta get me one of those for the ranch!"

Our motorhome sits directly on the grass and directly beside Charlie's and Luca's. It's different from the vessel we had in Texas but equally savvy. I'll have to find where Ren and Ana are parked up—she texted earlier. She's still coming, despite the ongoing near-silent treatment she's giving him.

I push the bedroom door open and peek behind it. "No mirror."

Beck licks away a smile. "I can send for one."

I blush and return to my mission. There's a knock outside.

"Might be the luggage," Beck says, turning to go answer the door.

I set my backpack on the desk and look around for a place to hide everything I brought for him. *Nothing naughty—get your head out of the gutter.*

"Babe!" he calls from the other room.

I rezip my backpack and push it under the bed.

Beck's holding the door open, smiling down at the visitor outside.

"Look who came to see you!" he says.

My hands fly over my mouth. *Pippa and Baby Luca.* I rush down the steps and kiss her cheeks. Beck helps her up the stairs.

"That's an outfit you got him, no?"

It is—down to the tiny check socks. *My word*, he's plump. His little belly fills out the Burberry onesie.

"We brought nearly everything you got him! Had to bring the Brit vibes!"

Pippa sits down next to me on the couch. "Heard you were pretty good with the rifles!"

"Lethal," Beck corrects.

"I was alright." I shrug. Pippa transfers Luca into my arms without asking. I happily receive him; he's a little brick now! She's probably ready for a break. I bounce him a bit in my arms as his eyes wander about the motorhome. "Did he do well on the jet then?"

"He did great!"

"Brilliant! He can come for the rest of the season!" Beck says, then nods at me. "You've got yourself a built-in babysitter with this one."

"We'll have to see!" She smiles.

Beck checks his phone and rubs his forehead. "Alright—we've got a rowdy bunch incoming. My family's at the gate."

Pippa waves her hand. "He's used to it!"

Beck blinks. "If you say so! I'll go collect them."

He latches the door of the motorhome when he departs. It's just her and me now, alone with this sweet angel in my arms.

"Is your dad coming for the race?"

"He and Evelyn will be here starting Saturday—the garage will be packed."

I stare down into Luca's captivatingly dark eyes. "Are you excited to see your daddy race?" His mouth opens, emitting little squeals that absolutely melt my heart—can you imagine how many girls will be chasing this one when he's older?

Pippa wipes away the drool pooling down his chin.

"Where is Luca?" I ask.

She swallows rather heavily. "He's meeting with management."

I glance up at her, nervous.

"After COTA, they were wanting him top five every race until break."

I rewind the tape in my head. Luca didn't even make the points in Mexico City; he picked up body damage after Sanjay turned in on him mid-scrap. He finished *eleventh*.

"But they're not counting Mexico, right? That wasn't his fault."

"No, it wasn't," she mutters. "But it still counts."

"W-what happens if he doesn't make top five?"

"He hasn't been this low in the points since his rookie season," she says, adjusting Luca's sock. "They're discussing the possibility of activating the performance clause in his contract."

The threat of tears stings in the corners of my eyes.

"I'm sorry, I don't want to rain on Beck's parade—"

"You're not at all!" I interrupt her. "What's Luca saying?"

"He's been pretty levelheaded about it. He says if they take action and release him, he's had a good run, but there's also always the possibility of him getting a seat on another team. There'll be lots of moving seats at the end of the season."

"I won't have it! Luca *is Furio*."

"For the last ten years, he's given this team everything," she says, her eyes going teary.

"You're here this week! Luca's here. He's going to do great!"

She smiles and runs her fingers over Luca's dark wispy hair. We both jump as hands smack down the outside of the motorhome.

"Open up!" Louie yells.

Beck unlatches the door and swings it open, looking between Pippa and me, eyes wide. "Final warning."

Pippa sniffs and waves them in. Louie bolts up the steps but puts on the brakes when he spots the baby in my arms.

Mia pushes him to the side, hand on her hip. "You let him out of the doghouse?"

Behind her, Beck pulls her ponytail. "I was never in the doghouse! Speaking of doghouses," he says, turning to his entering parents. "You should have brought Pirelli!"

"Already had two animals in the backseat, didn't need another," James gripes, looking like he could use a pint with Dad and *stat*.

Mia cocks her eyebrow. "Animals? I'm a girl!"

"Is that so?" James fires back.

Louie grabs Luca's hand and looks up at me. "You rode in a helicopter?"

"Louie, give him space! Be gentle," Elizabeth says, kissing Pippa's cheeks. "Heavens! He is gorgeous, darling!"

Louie backs up a hair but keeps hold of Luca's hand.

"We did ride in a helicopter!"

"Where is it?" he asks, confused.

"It dropped us off in the field, it's gone now."

His face falls, and his hands drop to his side.

Beck pats him on the back. "I'll take you in a helicopter, bud."

Louie glances from Luca to me. "Are you going to have a baby?"

Mia gasps before slapping both hands over her mouth. Pippa and James burst out laughing.

"Louie!" Elizabeth snaps. She grabs the back of his shirt and pulls him against her. She gives me an apologetic look on her son's behalf.

I duck my head because I'm blushing something awful.

"*A baby?*" Beck answers. "We're having ten!"

"Ten!" Louie yells. "That's more than Gemma had!"

Elizabeth whispers something in Louie's ear. He presses his lips together and straightens up.

Beck tosses me a wink, then turns to Pippa. "Can he watch in the garage?"

"We'll see how he does! We have mini ear protection for him."

My word! His own little headset!

Beck squeezes in next to me and waves his hands. "Alright, you, it's my turn."

CHAPTER 50
OUTFIT CHECK

IT'S THE PADDOCK ENTRANCE of all paddock entrances, and I'm arm in arm with Sophie. I sort of love that? Forget the boys, we have each other. Beck brought her to my room this morning. I think slowly moving into mine is her plan, as she left all her getting-ready things in my bathroom.

Sophie drapes her paddock pass over her head to rest against the navy pinstripe set she's wearing.

"You sure I look okay?" I ask again as we walk to the swipe gates.

Sophie eyes me suspiciously. "My answer is the same as it was five minutes ago."

"Oh, right," I mumble, looking down at my white A-line poplin dress from Balmain. "What was your answer again?"

Sophie lifts her badge to the scanner. "The dress is adorable, and I will be borrowing it!"

I agree it's quite stunning, but I'm still on this kick of needing outside opinions. Anticipating the cameras, I move the beach waves I forced upon my hair behind my shoulders and scan my pass.

Beep!

Did I repost Tommy's story in the car of our hands there in one another? *Duh.* Got a million messages about it. And will I be hunting down the photos currently being taken of my best friend and me this fine morning? *Absolutely.*

Sophie's name is called out. Ana's tucked back in between the Makellos and Valor suites. Black sunglasses, black trouser shorts, black cropped cardigan—interesting color choice for a soon-to-be bride. We steer in her direction, and she moves her sunglasses to her head.

"Alright?" Sophie asks, bringing her in for a hug.

"I slept in the bunk bed," Ana grumbles.

"Ana!" Sophie scolds. "And on the jet?"

"I sat on the other side." She shrugs. "Pretended to be busy."

"Did you walk in with him this morning?" I ask.

"Yes—but I didn't hold his hand," she says, crossing her arms. Her diamond sparkles.

Oh dear. At least she's still wearing her engagement ring?

Sophie frowns.

"What! I'm going mad planning our wedding, and he's getting drunk and having tits bounced in his face! You should see what's being said online."

"Stay off the blogs!" Sophie huffs. "They don't know shit!"

"Those blogs know what I ate for dinner last week!"

A stifle a smile. She's a funny one. "If the close quarters of the motorhome become unbearable, move in with us!" I tell her. "Well, Sophie's not fully moved in yet, but I've got a room on the main straight. You quite literally could watch the race from my balcony!"

Ana swallows. "I might take you up on that offer."

"Girls!"

Ana jumps.

David's appeared behind us, bucket hat and all. "Lovely to see you, Ana! Did you and Ren celebrate his win last week?"

Ana forces the fakest smile I've ever seen. "Of course we did."

David grins and turns to me. "I've got an ask for you—totally stealing this bit from the fashion magazines—would you be up for a 'what's in my bag?' paddock edition?"

"That could be fun!" Sophie says, looking to Ana.

"Oh, what a shame, I don't have my bag!" Ana says, backing up. "I've got to run anyway," she waves a quick farewell before she dips.

"She's gone shy again?" David asks.

Sophie and I exchange a look. "We're up for it!" I squeak, moving the heat off Ana.

"Brilliant!" David waves his cameraman over. "Let's set up out here at one of these high-tops."

I'm obsessed with the way this man caters to a certain demographic of female fans. He appreciates the fashion himself, though, and I know he loves getting bits of tea.

"Alright, fans! We're here at media day ahead of the British Grand Prix, and I've wrangled two British WAGs for my first ever *what's in my bag?* segment. Sophie, would you like to go first?"

Sophie nods, amused, like she's holding a wee secret. She lowers her mum's vintage red Chanel off her shoulder. The one she got loads of grief for last year after wearing it to every race.

She smacks it down in the center of the table in front of us. "Today I'm carrying my *claim to fame* outfit-repeater bag!"

David chuckles and points to the camera. "Trolls, disengage!"

She opens the top flap and giggles, snatching a bag of Jelly Babies on top. "These are actually not mine. If you're unaware, Beck has a mega sweet tooth, so I always carry something around for him."

The Jelly Babies are set on the table, and she pulls out the Chanel wallet she was gifted last year. I glance up, immediately catching eyes with Emma, who's walking in on Imre's arm. I blink away, back toward the table. I haven't seen Emma in a minute, and it stirs up a strange feeling. I understand her a bit more now, why she kept coming back to Tommy. I reckon he'd be hard to shake for good.

"And last," Sophie says, holding up a keychain. "The key to the motorhome we're camping in, and yes, I do count it as camping."

David laughs.

She gathers up the La Mer lip balm, RIMI portable charger, the hair scrunchie and dumps the bits back into her bag.

"Alright, Ella, you're up!"

I slide my bag off my arm, and set it front and center.

David whistles.

"This is the Jackie bag from Gucci in a gorgeous pastel yellow ostrich leather," I say proudly.

Wasn't meaning for this to be a Fylter ad at all, but I proceed to pull out their shimmer sunscreen, Honey Gloss, and pressed powder.

"I'm a contacts girly, so I always have a spot of eyedrops. AirPods, in case Tommy's annoying me. And last..."

"What is that thing?!"

I wave it in the air. "This, David, is a double-sided Octobuddy!"

He squints at it.

"Watch here, you press these cups against the back of your phone, then smash the other cups onto any surface, and you've got no need for a selfie stick, tripod or anything!"

I strut over to the side of the Valor suite and push my phone against the navy metal and let go.

"No way!" David says, amazed.

"I've got a dozen of them." I shrug. "I'll bring you one tomorrow!"

"Your turn then!" I say, peeling my phone off the metal. "What's in that camera bag of yours?"

David shakes his head.

"Fair is fair!" Sophie sasses.

"Oh, alright!" David retrieves his camera bag off the ground and sets it up on the table.

Holly's walking up behind the cameraman. She stops a few steps away and watches.

David starts unloading his bag. "Sunscreen—not as fancy as your brand there, half-eaten sleeve of peanuts, Chapstick, emergency rain gear—we are at Silverstone after all," he says, looking to the camera. "And finally, lens cleaner and extra memory cards!"

Holly smiles as David finishes the segment with a cheeky outro. He's a proper content creator, this one!

When the camera comes down, Holly moves in.

"Hello, Ella," she says politely.

"Holly." I nod because I still suspect she's not my biggest fan. I scoop my crap back into my bag.

"The boys are debuting special race suits this week, and I want to do something fun for our page."

"Lovely—"

"I was thinking about having them do an outfit check. It would be on brand for Tommy, and I think it could be quite funny."

A smile touches my lips.

"You want to come along? They might need some direction, and we're in a bit of a time crunch."

I try to hide my excitement. *"I'd love to."*

Holly's ahead of me on the stairs that lead up to the second floor of the MACH hospitality suite.

"Alright, boys. I brought in a professional to observe!"

She steps aside at the top of the stairs, and Tommy turns around in a stark white racing suit that makes his golden eyes pop like the contents of a treasure chest.

"Oh, great!" he says sarcastically. He eyes me up and down as he steps toward me. His hand wraps around my hip. I suck in a breath as his lips meet my temple.

"We've only got twenty minutes!" Holly says. "Let's get this finished!"

Alek groans. Tommy steps in front of a mirror and runs his fingers through his hair. I set my bag down and peek at my manicure—the pearl base color, the orange baby stars—*it's a perfect match.*

Alek stands up and shakes his head, confused. "What are we to say?"

Holly's gaze shifts in my direction.

"You're telling me Viktoria has never made you do this?" I ask him.

"Fuck no!" he says abruptly.

"Language!" Holly calls, bringing her hand over her face.

I flick my hand, ignoring him. "We've got so much to work with here—first, the all-white is quite striking." I take a lap around Alek. "The orange stripes and silver details, love the racing numbers," I finish my circle and look up at him.

He blinks at me, unamused.

"And look at this gorgeous embroidery on the flags!" I point down Alek's sleeves at the array of logos. "And of course you've got to throw a bone to the sponsors!"

I turn back to Holly. Tommy's next to her, a smile splitting his face. I blush something mad.

"Don't forget an intro *and outro*!" I add.

I grab Tommy's arm and trade spots with him so I'm back next to Holly.

An argument breaks out over who will be forced to do the intro.

"Boys!" Holly huffs. "We don't have time for this!"

"Rock, paper, scissors!" Tommy shouts.

Alek rolls his eyes. Sassy, this one.

They each hold out a hand, shake their fists and both proceed to flash *paper*.

Alek panics. "Again!"

This time Alek goes scissors and Tommy takes no time to crush Alek's scissor fingers with his rock fist.

"Fuck!" Alek yells.

"Oh, calm down!" I swat my hand through the air. "That's the easier job anyway!"

Alek covers his face, like it's the end of the world.

"So dramatic," I mutter under my breath.

"Like children, these two," Holly says under hers.

Tommy nods at me. "Any last advice?"

My eyes shift to the outfit-check novice. "Don't be awkward!"

Alek's face pinches.

"Be chill, be loose and have fun with it!" I add with a smile.

He blows out a bit of air.

This should be a trip.

After adjusting their positions, the cameraman flicks the boys a thumbs up.

Alek points at the camera. "Outfit check for Silverstone." He turns to his counterpart. "What are we wearing, Tommy?"

Holly grabs my wrist, all excited.

Tommy's smile doubles in size. "Special suits this week for MACH's home race." He runs his hands down his chest. "We've got a full white suit, orange racing stripes down the sleeves and leg, a touch of silver sparkle cause we've got sick chrome details on the car this week as well."

I suppress a giggle.

Tommy grabs Alek's shoulders, spins him around and points to the number eleven on his back. "Big orange racing numbers." He turns Alek back, facing forward. "All of our brilliant sponsors' logos add some color on the front, then, of course"—he wiggles his fingers at the camera—"can we get a close-up on this embroidery? Got the Union Jack for the team, Russian flag for Alek. And the Aussie flag over here," he says, slapping his hand over his heart.

Alek nods and points back to the camera, all cool. "Let's go racing!"

Tommy tosses me a golden wink, and I nearly faint.

"And cut!" The cameraman straightens up. "I think we've got it!"

And I think I've got a problem. A big one that makes my heart beat something mad.

CHAPTER 51
COMING CLEAN

ELLA

My headset comes to life.

"That's a good lap, Tommy!" his engineer reports. "P3!"

"We're back, boys!" Tommy says with a swagger that runs a chill down my spine. I can't see his face, but I can picture the wicked grin those words came out of.

"MACH took their time but has shown up in Silverstone! Mega laps from both drivers! That effort from Tommy Young moves him to the second row in P3!"

Sam swipes his hands together, the mechanics are rowdy. The angel on my shoulder is matching their energy, punching pom-poms in the air. Where on earth has she gotten those from?

1 KAP

2 WRI

3 YOU

4 KHO

5 VAN

6 ENA

7 LOM

"It's provisional pole for Elijah Kaplan! He's denied Beckham Wright pole position at his home race. Can Leo put together an even mightier lap? It's looking that way, a purple middle sector for him!"

"And Luca bails out! It's a good save, but well over track limits at Copse. That will keep him in seventh position."

Amelia spins around in her seat at the pit wall, where all the bosses and anyone with the last name Drake are sat. She claps as the chrome accents on Tommy's car flash by. He's jacked up and backed into the garage. I wave back at her, while she wildly waves both hands at me. Leo's name shoots up the standings.

"And he's done it! By one hundredth of a second, Leo VanBelle secures pole and knocks Beckham Wright to the second row!"

Fuck.

Tommy and Alek fall to fourth and fifth. Lost position aside, the MACH upgrades have proven brilliant, with strong results in each practice and quali session. Tommy's starting higher on the grid than he has all season, Alek too.

He lifts himself out of the car and pulls off his helmet. I move my headset down in an attempt to listen. Tommy looks at the standings and his shoulders slump. There's a sudden tug on my newly discovered heartstrings. His engineer points at a blip in the data on the screen, and his head drops. He pulls off his gloves, sets them on the bench and then turns around, eyes as gold as ever. This white racing suit will be the death of me. Where can I sign the petition to make these suits permanent?

At the back of the garage, Sam hands him a Lucozade. He pops the top and squirts some into his mouth.

"Fucking Valor!" Tommy groans, his hand finding my lower back. I walk beside him down the hall. "Final sector was rubbish. I should have waited, gotten a better tow—"

I rerack my headset. My fake boyfriend was only two-hundredths of a second slower than Beck. His lips continue to move, puffy and pouty.

"I wanted top three. *Fuck!* I know I could have—"

His waffling comes to an abrupt end thanks to my thumb and index finger. I hold his lips closed, and those toffee eyes widen. Warm, melty, sticky toffee that sticks in your teeth, sticks to your fingers and can even stick to and make a mess of my stone-cold heart. Have I lost the plot, you ask? *Completely.*

"You just had the best qualifying you've had all year," I mutter.

He attempts to reply, so I press a little harder.

"And *tomorrow*—you're going to make the podium."

I slowly let go, and his lips part, a smile creeping up at the corners of his mouth.

"Hell fucking yes!" Alek says, walking up behind me.

Tommy's eyes shift away to receive the incoming fist-bump.

I suppose you can't get everything you wish for. *Rebecca*, or whatever her dumb name is, has in fact *not been fired*. She's back in the post-quali media pen, and her little advances have kicked up a notch. I'm telling you, it's this fucking white race suit. She throws her head back, giggling like a fool at something Tommy's said, and reaches out and touches his hand. I clench my jaw, my nostrils flaring a bit.

"Alright?" Sophie asks, standing beside me.

I exhale and give her a quick nod.

"You look a little bothered," she says, watching me.

I choose not to respond, partly because I am quite bothered, and partly because I'm stuck in a bit of a trance at the moment.

"Tommy looks handsome in white," she adds.

He also looks handsome with his shirt off, with his face between my legs, his hands in my hair—

Sophie nudges me.

"Hmm?" I mumble, eyes still glued to my fake boyfriend.

"Tommy," she repeats. "I fancy him in white. Really makes his eyes pop. Proper caramel color, aren't they?"

"More like toffee. *Warm toffee.*" Is my brain in the room with us? I think not. I jerk my head around, snapping out of it. Instantly want to smack myself in the face. Have I, the witch, allowed a fucking spell to be cast over me?

Sophie's turned in on me now, staring, eyes wide and wild.

"You caught me, alright?" I whisper, going against every fiber of my being.

"What?"

"I like him, okay?" I say a bit louder.

"*I KNEW IT!*" she screams.

I rush to cover her mouth and look her dead in the eyes. "People are staring!" I whisper through gritted teeth.

She murmurs against my palm and nods. I slowly pull my hand back. Her lips are smashed together with so much force it looks like she could combust. She grabs my wrist, all excited. "He fancies you," she shrieks. "I know he does!"

I wave my finger in her face. "No, no—no, he doesn't."

"Does too!" she wails.

I give her stern eyes; she's getting loud again.

"*No.*" I say firmly. "He likes to fuck me—there's a difference."

Her eyes grow even bigger. "Did you fu—*sleep* with him again?"

I swallow. "I will neither confirm nor deny."

She jumps up and down, happy as a fucking clown.

"What the fuck am I doing?" I pinch the bridge of my nose. "How did I fall for the fuckboy?"

"You *love* him!" she squeals.

"I hate him!" I press my fingers into my eye sockets. "Is this what it feels like? He hurts, and it makes me hurt? He's smiling, and it makes me bloody smile? I've never taken on someone's emotions like this!"

"Since when!"

I blink. *Fuck me.* "If I'm being honest? It's been for a minute or two..."

"Ella! You need to tell him!"

"Absolutely not!"

"But why? You could end this fake dating thing and actually, *truly* be together!"

"He doesn't want to be with me! Not for real! The whole point of him doing this is to get revenge on Emma."

Her eyes roll a bit, amused. "He's *way* past Emma!"

"If you don't care about someone, you wouldn't care about getting revenge—he's obviously still bothered by it."

She shakes her head, all confident. "He's only pretending it's revenge—he wants *you*."

"After the devil-cunt things I've done of late? There's not a snowball's chance in hell!"

"He knows the real you, Ella, and I see the way he looks at you! Look at him!" She waves her hand. "He's staring at you right now!"

I glance over, and my heart shoots up my throat. His eyes are pointed at me. Probably only due to the fact Sophie's making such a bloody ruckus.

"Have you told your mum?"

"Abso-*fucking*-lutely not!" I say, taking the time to enunciate every syllable.

"Tell her, Ella! She would be over-the-moon happy for you!"

"No, she'd tell me I've lost my damn mind."

Sophie frowns. "Well, I'm afraid your little arrangement with Tommy has to end."

I look back in his direction, microphone in hand, rubbing his eye. "But I don't want it to end..."

"Then you *must* tell him. And if he doesn't want the same, you have to end it, or you'll end up hurting yourself more!"

I blink a lot, take a breath. "When?"

Her eyes light up. "Tonight!"

"Before the race?! Are you mental?"

"Alright, fine." She giggles. "After the race."

No fucking way! Tomorrow is too soon! "Can't I wait until after the wedding?"

"No!" she scolds. "Before. At least go into the wedding knowing what his feelings are."

"Why? So I can be miserable after I confess, and he stands there scratching his head?"

She looks over at him, thinking. "What's the worst thing he can say? 'Let's keep it friends?'"

I squeeze my eyes shut. I would simply die. I don't want to be his *friend.* But I don't think I can keep pretending either. I was bloody brilliant at pretending at the start, then I had to go and lose my mind.

"At least then you can go knowing as much and protect yourself!" She crosses her arms. "I'm not letting you drag your heart along any longer than you have to."

It's eating me up, the not knowing if he gets the same funny feeling in his stomach that I get—that I've been getting for a minute. It's time to come clean.

"Fine," I agree. "Before the wedding then."

"The sooner the better." She smiles before her face turns proper serious. "But I swear, if he hurts you, I will kill him!"

Are you coming in for the party Evelyn's throwing for George?

Alice Humphrey:

Yes! Monday morning.

Emmett and Anabelle are coming down too!

CHAPTER 52
GOD SAVE THE KING

SOPHIE

FREDRICK'S HERE TODAY. I saw him this morning in the lobby where Ella's staying. He smiled and gave me a little nod but didn't approach me. I knew him well enough at one time to know that the nod was sort of an acknowledgment that he gets it now. Beck and I are in deep; there's no going back for me.

You should have seen Ella this morning, running around all flustered. There's this whole new part of my best friend coming out, and it's equal parts bizarre and beautiful to witness. A crush looks good on her—everything looks good on her.

It's a shame the boys are on different teams, and we're separated by multiple garages. I'd love to watch her *watch him*. Louie belts out the last words of *God Save the King* as the Red Arrows rip through the overcast sky, streaking red, white and blue smoke beneath the clouds.

Beck was upset with his qualifying position, but woke up this morning confident as ever. Luca's spirits are high, higher than I've seen all year. I love having Pippa back in the garage, and baby Luca? He's been featured on the broadcast twice already in his wee headset. After being passed around between Beck's parents, Dad and Evelyn, he's completely passed out in his wrap against Pippa's chest. I hope he can last a few laps. It's probably a pipe dream to last all fifty-two!

The navy Valor's pull through the final chicane, followed by Beck and Tommy, all zigzagging down the main straight to the start line. I pull in the deepest breath I've probably ever taken in my entire life and exhale it slowly. This race means everything to him.

Dad gives me a reassuring nod and my hand a squeeze.

"It's a Valor lockout on the front row, while best mates share the second! Will it be another win at Silverstone for Leo VanBelle?"

"Final car pulling in, Beck," Coop says.

I wait for his voice to fill my headset.

"Lovely day for a hunt," Beck says in a threatening tone.

One by one, the five lights glow red above the start line, then flip off.

"It's lights out and away we go for the British Grand Prix!"

My word.

"And a dream launch off the line for Beckham Wright! He lunges forward. Elijah struggled to get that car moving, and they go side by side into the right-hander of turn three!"

My whole body tenses up.

"That's tight there! But Beck makes the overtake on Elijah Kaplan through turn four!"

The garage goes bonkers.

"He carries the momentum through turn five and sends it down the Wellington straight!"

Hunting's hard when the prize is a three-time world champion. Elijah's been left in the dust. A DRS train is holding up any action behind. Lap after lap, Beck rips the car through Maggots and Becketts, chasing after Leo.

"Mistakes out of Leo are few and far between, but he's got to crack at some point. Beck's applied seventeen laps of unrelenting pressure, and he's not letting up!"

Baby Luca's awake, starting to kick his legs a bit, bored with the DRS train his daddy's stuck in. A collective gasp fills the garage.

"And there's the first mistake! A moment for Leo in Chapel! He opens the door, and Beck answers! Right on his gearbox down the Hangar straight!"

Dad and James grip onto one another.

"And it's the two title contenders neck and neck into Stowe corner...

...and the boy from Britain takes the lead of the British Grand Prix!"

My word. I can't be crying already! I take several quick breaths, blinking away the tears, eyes glued to the broadcast.

"He said during Thursday's press conference that, championship aside, winning this race would mean the world to him. He's confident he has the car to do it, and his entire family, his partner and her family—they're all piled into the Furio garage!"

Louie jumps up and down. The pitlane starts to see some action.

"Finally out of the dirty air. Beck's running these laps like he's qualifying! And Leo pits!

...he's going for the undercut! His tyres are cooked after that stint."

"The wind's picked up out here," Beck reports from the lead.

"Copy," Coop says. "We've got light to moderate rain on the radar in three laps' time."

"My tyres are toast."

"If you can hold on to it, we'll box for inters."

It wouldn't be an English summer without a pop-up rain shower. *And God bless it*, Leo pitted for slicks and had to come back in to swap for inters five laps later. But he's a master in the wet, that one, making up for Valor's flawed tyre strategy with multiple overtakes. Somehow baby Luca is content as can be, happy with the rain shakeup. A proper racing fan already!

As the rain ends, Beck hounds Coop to get him back on slicks after the first glimpse of a dry racing line appears. Luca's back on slicks too, holding sixth position. One position lower than the team demands, but he's looking racy down the main straight.

"And Luca's absolutely flying! He's brought the tyres in, and Alek's unable to match the tyre mastery of Luca Lombardo! Luca passes the MACH through Luffield corner! Up to fifth position!"

Pippa's ecstatic; she ducks her face into baby Luca's head. I clap his little feet together.

"Elijah won't be able to hold position against an angry Leo! And it's the move Beck pulled on him earlier

through Stowe! Leo Vanbelle retakes second place after steamrolling back through the ranks!"

1 WRI

2 VAN

3 KAP

4 YOU

5 LOM

6 KHO

7 ENA

8 NOW

9 HAH

10 WHI

My hands are sweating. Leo's putting up the fastest lap again and again, inching closer to Beck's lead.

"Alek couldn't hold fifth, but look at Tommy Young in the lead MACH! He's loving the performance he's found from the upgrades! He's threatening the Valor now!"

My word, I wish I could see Ella! *You can do it, Tommy!*

"And Tommy goes late on the brakes! He overtakes Elijah Kaplan through the Vale chicane!

Can Elijah answer? Into Club they go, but Tommy holds onto it! Down the main straight! And the MACH garage is going mad at the moment!”

Holy shit! Tommy's up to third! Ella must be on the floor!

There are only two laps to go. Pippa squeezes my hand and nods to the hall—she knows how loud this garage is about to get.

She kisses my cheek before departing. "Congratulations!"

My lips quiver. James and Dad are teary-eyed.

"Beckham Wright front-loaded the season with massive points, and little by little, Leo chipped away at his lead.

...After losing the lead in Montreal, these two scrapped lap after lap at COTA. Beck tried to make up ground in Mexico and failed to do so, but today he will retake the lead in the Championship!”

Chills cover my every extremity. James lifts Charlie up into the air. Mia and Louie are bouncing off the walls. Evelyn's consoling a sobbing Elizabeth.

"And the grandstands are roaring! The Italian team with the British driver will win the British Grand Prix!

MACH promised upgrades, and they've delivered! Tommy Young will bring home the first MACH podium of the season!"

"It's yours, Beck!" Coop shouts through the headset.

Beck flings the car through the final corner. Dad's arms squeeze around me, and my tears roll like mad.

"Beckham Wright wins the British Grand Prix!"

CHAPTER 53

KNIGHT IN WHITE

I DIDN'T WALK—I FLOATED down the pitlane on Amelia's arm along with the flurry of bodies that poured out of the MACH garage. Tommy did it. *He actually fucking did it.* I grasp onto the top of the waist-level fence in front of me.

Leo's car parks up. The nose of Tommy's car smacks into the third-place flag.

"If you don't kiss him, I will!" Amelia shrieks at my side.

Beck stands up in his brilliant red Furio and thrusts his fist in the air. He jumps down and drops to one knee, putting his hand against the sidepod and resting his helmet against the halo. He's overcome with emotion, the Furio bunch is roaring, the grandstands are going bonkers.

He pushes up and takes off for the sea of red that waits for him behind the fence.

Tommy pulls himself up out of the cockpit and flips his visor open. And suddenly it feels like someone's turned on every light in the world. I could never relate when Sophie would say she felt out of control—but I do now. I've lost control of my body, my thoughts, my mind and my heart, for that matter. All of it is out of my hands.

Tommy speeds for the fence in his white-knight in armor racing suit and throws his arms around his engineers. He moves down the fence until his arms scoop around Amelia and me. She's screeching something to him, but I'm without words, unable to really breathe at the minute.

He pulls back, his glove cups my cheek and his eyes find mine. "*Got you a trophy, Ella Blair.*"

And into a puddle the swooning angel on my shoulder melts. Thomas Edward Young trots off, taking all the air in my lungs with him. And my heart floats away, following him like a balloon tied at his wrist.

He finds Beck, and their chests collide in an emotional, heartfelt embrace. The cameras surround them as they hold on to one another, smacking each other's helmets.

Leo congratulates them both with a handshake, then Beck lifts Sophie beyond the fence, holding her up in the air under her armpits like some ridiculous film scene. She's a sobbing mess. That's when my balloon heart tied on Tommy's wrist is popped by a pinprick because what if that's never us? *We're pretend.* And I could very well be the only party that wants to turn our fiction into fact. Sophie's right, I've got to tell him. No matter what, it's going to hurt. I don't wear my heart on my sleeve; I wear it in a cold cell tucked away where not even a chest X-ray could find it. Admitting I've fallen, speaking into words my true feelings, goes against every rule in my ego's book.

Tommy's smile hasn't stopped for a single moment. For the second time today, *God Save the King* stands the hair at the nape of my neck on end. It's the smallest trophy on the podium, but he looks at it like he's holding the world in his hands. Confetti cannons burst, and the boys lunge for the champagne. Sophie finds me in the crowd as Tommy and Beck douse each other with the bubbly.

"Can you believe it?!" she screams, holding my face, bringing our foreheads together.

"I'm going to tell him." I swallow. "Tomorrow."

CHAPTER 54
A SATURN RETURN

SOPHIE

"Mighty sparkly," Beck says from behind me, clasping my diamond necklace.

I run my fingers down the red silk gown I picked for Dad's party. It wasn't the gown I'd originally planned on wearing—it's a bit loud—but given the circumstances, color me Furio red.

I've never worn all three pieces at once—the bracelet, the necklace, the earrings. I spin away from the mirror to face him.

"Is it too much?"

His eyes fall down my body. He balls up his fist and bites it. He likes the dress, but he'll like it even better pooled on the floor when he pulls it off me later.

I playfully flick my finger toward the door, dismissing him. "Out with you!"

He lets out a husky sigh and turns to rejoin Ollie, Tommy and the PlayStation in the living room. I couldn't craft a more epic weekend—the race, watching him climb to the highest step on the podium? Truly stuff out of dreams. And lest we not forget, my best friend coming to the groundbreaking realization she's capable of falling for a man. And not just any man, but a man I adore and a man I have an inkling suspicion feels the same way about her. The "Ella Effect," that's what Instagram was saying about Alek and Tommy's hilarious race suit outfit check. I trust you saw it. Twelve million people saw it, last I checked. Ella was tagged as the director. Even with Pippa's help, I'm not sure we could ever get Beck and Luca to do one of those. Luca finished fifth, so everything's got to be fine and dandy with the team. I'm not letting myself think anything otherwise. He's a brilliant man and was absolutely over the moon for Beck.

After endless media, Beck and I bid farewell to the motorhome, *thank God*. Remember when I was all excited about getting to camp? Can't imagine the *real* version of camping, though he swears he's making me try it. Like tent on the actual ground version. We were back at Battersea late, his trophy sat strapped into its own seat on the helicopter. And now the dreamy weekend continues, rolling into Monday evening.

I step back into Beck's bedroom that the girls and I have completely taken over. Dress options, five spare sets of heels, multiple vanity cases and handbags litter the bed and floor.

"Is this his thing?" Carmen asks. "Every time he cocks up, he drapes you in diamonds?"

I give her eyes.

"You should let him fuck up more!" She shrugs, then goes back to her eyeshadow.

"That's not true!" I huff. "The earrings were my birthday gift, and the bracelet was a just because."

"Only thing left now's a ring." She winks.

Ella pushes up from the bed, flustered. Normal *ice in her veins Ella* has left the chat. She's now a quiet, nervous, jittery thing, though I'm sure the volume in her head rivals a screamo concert mid-set. If she doesn't open her mouth or start insulting people, Carmen's going to know something's up.

She walks into the bathroom, scoops her hair up and turns in the mirror from side to side. I stay in the doorway. Blonde curls, metallic silver dress, an absolute starlet. Her eyes keep shifting to the door when expletives fly from the boys.

"Should I have done my hair up?" she asks restlessly.

"I fancy it down."

She drops her bouncing curls with a sigh and strides past me back into Beck's room. She picks up a hung black dress from the bed and holds it out in front of her. Her head tilts side to side, then she exchanges the black dress for a summery green jacquard gown.

"Should I wear this one?" she asks.

Like she's been doing all weekend with her paddock outfits, my friend, who usually dresses me, is now questioning her every choice.

"The silver you've got on is lovely."

I come up beside her, take the dress and lay it back on the bed. "Don't be nervous," I whisper.

"I'm freaking out," she whispers back before turning and laughing it off. "My head's a proper mess! I've been struck with such indecision lately!"

"It could be the dawn of your Saturn return!" Carmen says, excitedly spinning away from her pop-up vanity mirror.

I blink. Ella blinks.

"Carmen," Ella says, still blinking, "what in the actual fuck does that mean?"

"It's a good thing, it is! It's supposed to be uncomfortable!"

Carmen turns back to her mirror. "Maybe a bit early, but it's the time in your life just before true adulthood when you have a marked reevaluation of yourself!"

Ella's eyes dart in my direction like daggers.

I hold up my hands and slowly back up into the bathroom. "I didn't say anything," I mouth.

"Well, I'm sorry to your beliefs," Ella huffs a laugh. "But I'm not returning to Saturn. I just have the unfortunate dilemma of looking equally lovely in each of these gowns, which is making it impossible to choose!"

Carmen tips the end of her brush. "Pretty girl problems—that could also be it!"

It's the truth. I haven't told Carmen or anyone else—besides well…Beck. He knew something was up, and let me tell you, he was *gobsmacked*. This secret Ella and Tommy have been pedaling produced an outcome neither of us expected or even thought possible.

I check my hair a final time, then flip the bathroom light off. "You ready?"

Carmen tosses a brush into her vanity case and picks up her clutch.

"Almost," Ella mutters.

I pick up my beaded bag from the bed, give her wrist a squeeze and whisper, "There's liquid courage waiting on the counter."

Carmen follows me out to the living room. We've got to be going soon.

"Oliver Goddard! You look awfully handsome!" I praise.

"And you, babe!" He leans down close to the gold and bronze trophies sat on the counter and checks his reflection in their sheen.

"Doesn't he?" Carmen says, adjusting his bowtie. "With his Wimbledon tan!"

Ella's heels click on the floor as she walks out, and *PGA Tour* on the PlayStation gets paused.

"Baby girl." Tommy whistles.

Ella tries to hide her smile.

He pushes off the couch, eyeing her up and down. "Feel like I'm back at school going to a ball! Should I have got you a flower?"

"A shot will do!" She says, brushing a nonexistent bit off his lapel. She's playing cool, but if you watch closely, you can see her hand shaking.

Tommy spins to the counter, pulls the cork out of an uncracked bottle of tequila. Beck joins us at the bar, his hands finding the silk around my waist.

"Did you clean up after yourself, Ella?" Tommy asks, pouring tequila for each of us. He pauses and points the tip of the bottle at her. "Destroys bathrooms, this one."

"And this one's got the most annoying mix of anal and OCD," she fires back.

"I was finding remnants of glitter and that powder shit for days!" he returns.

"Destroy away." Beck smiles. "Movin' out soon anyway."

Ollie nods his chin at Ella. "I hear we're taking a yacht out for your birthday?"

"What?!" Tommy scoffs, insulted at being out of the know.

"After the wedding," Ella says, nose in the air. "You'll get an invite if you can recite my birthday."

"Let's hear it, Tommy!" Ollie challenges him. "When's her birthday?"

Tommy smirks, narrows his eyes. "Augustttt—fif—*second*."

Carmen claps.

"See, I remember?" He nudges Ella's arm.

Beck squeezes my hand.

Ollie nods at me now. "Alright, how badly can I behave at this party? From one to ten."

I lift a brow. "Ten being swinging from the chandelier, Ollie?"

He nods.

"Five?" I say.

His eyes roll to the back of his head. He takes his shot, not waiting for anyone else. Carmen smacks his arm. He flicks his finger, asking for a refill.

"Everyone will be double or triple our age!" I say, attempting to add clarity to my chosen level.

"Exactly!" Ollie says. "Gotta show 'em how it's done!"

Beck passes out the shots. "Tommy makes the toast."

He clears his throat and grins, all honored, and raises his shot. "A toast to this lot of trophies before us!" He sets his hand on the top of his bronze cup and continues, "But even they don't hold a candle to these beauty queens that bless us with their presence."

"Tommy!" Carmen coos. Ella goes red in the face.

My word.

I clink my glass against the group's and throw it back quickly, trying not to gag too loud.

The glasses clatter back down to the counter, and Tommy starts to refill. "Am I the only one who's not met Ella's mum then?" he asks.

I catch eyes with Ella.

He nudges her arm. "She as hot as you?"

CHAPTER 55
EXIT STRATEGY

ELLA

THANK GOD HE'S NOT in white. I chew on my fingernails to try to keep my fingers at bay when all they want to do is run down the silk lapels on his jacket. His hands? They seem to enjoy the silver foil jersey fabric that's tight against my body.

We're at Storey House, George's favorite. Not sure why he bothers being a member anywhere else—because he *is* a member *everywhere* else. While most others ate their way through school on TESCO meal deals, Soph and I were the ladies that lunched, tea-ed, drank and dined at the best private clubs in the city. Storey House isn't one I'm overly familiar with—it's old money, quiet wealth, very George Collins-esque. A bit boring, to be honest—probably the club where you'd be least likely to find people racking up in the toilets if we were to judge on that data point.

We make our way to the second floor. Evelyn's hired out the entire ballroom and terrace. At the top of the stairs, Sophie points to the largest champagne tower I've ever seen, as if any of us could miss it.

"That was my idea!" she cheers. She rushes off into the crowd to find her dad, pulling Beck behind her.

Loads of people fill the low-lit space, anchored by the bubbly tower. There's a gathering in the corner around a pianist, who's riffing at a gleaming grand Steinway. Heavy velvet drapery frames the windows. Miss Amelia would very much approve of this party.

"That's her!" Tommy says, nodding his chin. "It's got to be."

Fucking hell. Mum's already here. Is it that obvious? Blonde hair, shoulder height, SIMKHAI gown. I know because I've tried it on, if that tells you anything about her figure. What the hell was I thinking asking him here? Granted, I extended the invite before I knew she'd be in country.

"Meet us at the bar?" Ollie says, more as a statement than a question.

"Mm-hmm," I mumble.

Tommy goes for my hand, but I slide past him. "Come on, then!"

Mum knows this is fake, so this should be easy, no? I take a series of quick, short breaths, then push my shoulders back and layer on my poker face.

"*Darling!*" Mum says, reaching for me. Her hands land on my stomach so she can fidget with the fabric at my waist like she always does. "You look exquisite!" she says, moving my hair over my shoulder.

"And you!" I say, side-stepping with a quarter turn. "I'd like you to meet Tommy."

Her eyebrows shoot up. "Oh my!"

"You must be Ella's sister?" Tommy says, taking Mum's hand in both of his.

She blushes, speechless at the compliment. *Fuck.*

"C-Congratulations are in order!" she says, finding her words. "Stellar job yesterday!"

"Thank you, ma'am."

"Alice, darling," she corrects, patting his hand.

Those toffee eyes come my direction, falling down my body. I suck in a breath. "Where are Emmett and Annabelle?"

"Running a bit behind but on their way!"

He lifts his hand against my back; I flinch but try to hide it with a smile. Mum can read me like a book. Does *he* remember she knows this is fake? And he's doing it anyway?

"Shall we get a drink?" I flash him a desperate look.

"*Let's*," he says, eyes on my lips before they jerk to Mum. "Can I get you something, Alice?"

"Hendricks, darling." She bats her eyes. "On the rocks."

I grab Tommy's arm and make fucking haste to the bar. Halfway there, he's stopped by a group wanting to shake his hand. I continue on without him.

"There you are!" Carmen says, sipping a lychee martini.

I grab it from her and down a massive gulp before handing it back. Beck's got a whole entourage around him too. That's when Tommy's fingertips arrive at my right hip. "What are you drinking, baby girl?"

"Whatever you're having!" I say quickly, voice far too high.

He looks at me suspiciously, orders two tequila sodas and Mum's gin.

Sophie dances over. "Have you shown Tommy the terrace? It's lovely!"

I give her a wide-eyed warning, hoping that will shut her trap because I'm not nearly ready.

Beck escapes his fan club. He joins us at the bar and immediately pulls Sophie against him and whispers into her hair. Must be something dirty because her cheeks go pink, and she bucks around in his arms.

Tommy pushes a drink in front of me, double-fisting his and Mum's. "Am I to deliver this on my own?"

I look up at him through my lashes. "I trust you can handle that."

He licks away a smile, and I wait half a second before turning over my shoulder and watching him saunter off.

"My word!" Sophie gasps. "It's dad's assistant, Jo! I'll be right back."

I watch Beck watch her drift off. He clicks his teeth together, then rubs his jaw. This is behaving for him—usually, he'd have her back against a wall already.

"You're struggling," I say, sucking down two gulps of the tingly tequila-soda mixture.

He smiles but still hasn't taken his eyes off her. "Why's she got to wear a dress like that?" He swipes his palms together like he's a fucking addict who just had his drugs stolen right out of his hands.

His eyes finally come my way. "I'm glad you found your way back together. You had me worried there for a minute."

I slurp the last sip. "You forgive me?"

"You made it right," he says honestly. A cheeky grin spreads across his face. "You going to chat with Tommy tonight, no?"

I freeze, blinking at him.

"Don't be mad." His smile grows. "Had to pry it out of her."

And I want to die. Bury me in the ballroom. A glass of champagne is set in front of him.

I nod at the glass. "Didn't get enough champagne on the podium?"

"Do you know how much it hurts to get champagne sprayed into your eyeballs? It's also the best feeling in the world."

"You got each other pretty good up there."

He nods his chin, not giving up. "Tonight though?"

I turn over my shoulder. Carmen and Ollie are occupied being all smoochy behind us. Tommy's still with Mum, drink delivered, entrapped by a group of biddies petting at him. A him problem that's most defi-nitely become a me problem because I don't fancy watching anyone pet him.

"Maybe after a few more," I say and set my empty glass on the bar.

Beck slides me the champagne and nods at the bartender for another. "I've never seen you this nervous, Ella."

"It's fucking stupid is what it is." I pick up the glass and tip it back.

"Telling him your feelings doesn't make you weak," he says encour-agingly. "In fact, it's quite the opposite."

"What if I'm scared?"

His replacement champagne is delivered. "Of course you're scared, but no risk, no reward, right?" He clinks his glass against the rim of mine.

I take a sip and absentmindedly begin tapping my fingernails against the bar. His eyes dart downward. I quickly curl my fingers into a fist, but he's bloody quick, this one. He grabs my hand, inspecting my *Tommy x MACH* inspired manicure. Crinkles form at the corners of his eyes, and he looks up at me, all smiley. Sophie's always going on about how his eyes twinkle. They do. They're not golden like Tommy's, not dark like Sophie's either, but a blend of the two.

He pats the top of my hand. "I think you go for it."

I take a deep breath, pull my hand back and pinch the bridge of my nose. "And what if he says '*no thank you*'?"

"Then he's a fucking idiot." He shrugs.

"Beck!" I gripe, "not helping!"

He nods, amused by my anguish. "He told me he missed you in Mex-ico."

"Is that so?" I give him a flutter and smack the bar top. "That's why he had that girl sat in his lap!"

Beck huffs and rolls his eyes—walked himself straight into that one. He catches the barkeep, orders four shots and turns back to me. "He said he likes having you around."

"*Around?* Around to make Emma jealous or having me around regardless because I'm a fucking delight?"

He shakes his head, proper confused, and runs a hand down his face.

Four shots are set in front of us. He pushes two down to Carmen and Ollie. We are most definitely the only lot shooting tequila at this uppity thing.

He throws the shot back, I tip mine back slowly, watching him try but fail to suppress a grin.

"Alright, out with it!" I say impatiently.

He inhales rather sharply and sets the empty down. "He also said you hooked up when you stayed at his."

"*And?*" I scoff. "You can't say that and not give me a full rundown!"

"Said he was gagging for it, having you flit around his house all weekend and finally said fuck it."

I narrow my eyes. "Right."

"What are you two doing!" Sophie interrupts. She slides in and slides her hands up under his jacket.

"Giving this one a pep talk." He stares down at her and runs his index finger down her nose.

And there goes Beck's focus.

"You missed a shot!" I graciously inform her. "Let's have another, then!"

She spins around, and Beck pulls her back against his chest.

"Enough procrastinating!" she complains. "Take him out onto the terrace!"

"Oh, that'd be cutesy," Beck pipes in from over her shoulder.

I roll my eyes, then peek for the hundredth time at Tommy. "He looks a bit preoccupied, I'm afraid!"

"He needs rescued!" She flicks her eyebrows and grabs my hand. "Come on, then!"

She wiggles free from Beck's grasp, and his drugs are taken away for a second time.

Sophie pulls me through the crowd. I need to do it, get it sorted, get it over with. At this rate, if I wait any longer, I'll be inebriated, but perhaps that's a better course of action?

Tommy's eyes lift from the ladies surrounding him and come at me, full-force toffee.

"My girls!" my mother says, bringing her palms against mine and Sophie's cheeks.

"Come find Evelyn with me?" Sophie asks, taking her arm, pulling Mum away.

I avoid his eyes, brushing my fingertips against his lapel, going after a bit of nothing. "Can we step out for a chat?"

His smile quirks up, and I can't help but look. "Outside?"

I nod over at the balcony doors. "Just there."

With every step, my thoughts flip-flop from wondering if I'll be walking back into this party a changed woman and if I should grab one last taste of liquid courage. Beside the door, a cocobolo humidor is sat on the table next to a rack of red velvet smoking jackets. Has me craving a cigarette for half a second, but I remind myself I'm over my smoking bit. He holds the door open, and much to my delight, the terrace is empty. No one is partaking in the cigars just yet. Unsurprisingly, his head is tipped back, searching for any star he can find. The clouds are broken, but the only twinkles I'm seeing are the ones that land or take off from Heathrow.

I step up to the railing and peer down at the tip of Berkely Square.

"I like your mum," he says, joining me.

"And what were you two banging on about?"

"This and that." His head wobbles, not giving anything away.

I blow out a breath and draw a complete blank on how I'd planned to begin the discussion—*confession?* Then he sets his hand on top of mine atop the railing, and I panic.

"I thought it might be time to chat about our situation's exit strategy," I blurt out.

"You want out?" he asks, appearing quite taken aback.

"I mean—have you even thought about how we would end things?"

"No," he states frankly, then shrugs. "I haven't."

Right. *What was I to say next?*

He pokes my shoulder. "Are the boys on the bench begging for your return?"

I swallow. I haven't had so much as a single thought about a single one of them for months. I glance at him, but I'm unable to soften my eyes or even flutter them so they dart around like a scared, caged animal. I look back down at the square, shocked to learn my usual tricks are unusable when I'm this jittery.

"I just thought we've both gotten what we wanted out of this, no? Your heart's on the mend. You got your revenge."

"Right." He nods, looking down at the street. "It's been fun."

Fuck. This isn't at all what I had planned and rehearsed *repeatedly,* but here I am dancing around what I actually mean to tell him.

I go to open my mouth, but his is already open. "After Austria, it'll be summer break. I suppose break would be the most natural timing?"

I blink, trying to hide my devastation—my time is running out.

"I mean, you'll still come to the wedding with me, no?"

My heart flutters at the possible sign of disappointment in his voice. "Of course." I nod, trying to keep my own voice calm.

He pushes off the railing and turns. "Probably a good idea." He winks. "Before either of us catches feelings."

I huff a laugh and follow him back toward the door. My breath is shaky, I'm feeling rather faint. Have I completely misread the signals he's been giving? The way he's been acting toward me? Sophie too? She was bloody sure he wanted me for real, for keeps. Only the smallest bit of sand is left in the top of my hourglass timer. The angel on my shoulder is on her knees, pounding her fists against the ground. It's now or never.

He reaches for the door handle, and I reach for his arm.

"Tommy—" I squeak, my voice wavering.

He lets go of the brass and turns to face me.

I swallow, pushing down my heart that's made its way up into my throat. "Would it be the worst thing in the world if I have caught feelings?"

Playlist

The songs of Young with Benefits:

Acknowledgements

Don't hate me. I completely understand if you do, but I swear, the end of the story is coming! As always, thank you for reading this book. Whether you are a seasoned F1 fan or newly introduced, I hope you enjoyed this wild ride. Formula 1 has a special way of capturing people's hearts, don't be surprised if you quickly go from watching races to attending races.

A huge thank you to my brilliant editors at EJL Editing. I truly appreciate your continued patience, enthusiasm and feedback during the editing process. And finally, thank you to my proofreader Brandee Paschall Books LLC.

In the meantime, if you are bored and craving more of this world, check out Formula Love—Beck and Sophie's origin story.

Find me online:

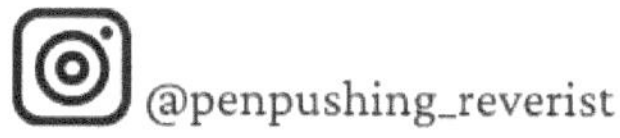 @penpushing_reverist